SHAILENDRA PANDEY/*TEHELKA*

TARUN J. TEJPAL is a journalist, publisher, novelist, and founder of India's leading news magazine, *Tehelka*. He has been named one of India's most influential people by *The Guardian*, *Businessweek*, and *Asiaweek*. He is a celebrated novelist as well as a journalist, and his fiction has been awarded France's Prix Mille Pages and was a finalist for the Man Asian Literary Prize. His debut novel, *The Alchemy of Desire*, was hailed by V. S. Naipaul as "a new and brilliantly original novel from India." His next novel, *The Valley of Masks*, will be published by Melville House in February 2014. Tejpal is married, with two daughters, and lives in New Delhi.

See the back of this book for a reading group guide for Tarun J. Tejpal's *The Story of My Assassins*.

PRAISE FOR
THE STORY OF MY ASSASSINS

"Clever and inventive. In the profoundest way, Tarun Tejpal writes for India."

—V. S. NAIPAUL

"[A] complex, dark, exhilarating novel … [Tejpal] avoids cliches to render the tragedy, comedy, colour and violence of modern India better than anything else I have read in my three years as correspondent here."

—JASON BURKE, *THE GUARDIAN*

"Tejpal writes with splendid élan: His novel is a stylish, erudite potboiler that reads like a mix of Alexandre Dumas and India's ancient national epic, the Mahabharata … Exhilarating."

—SAM SACKS, *THE WALL STREET JOURNAL*

"Tarun J. Tejpal is brilliant. A master storyteller, he writes with graphic detail so stunning in spots as to make the reader pause for breath."

—*NEW YORK JOURNAL OF BOOKS*

"Tejpal's masterful U.S. debut is an epic tale of modern-day India."

—*PUBLISHERS WEEKLY* (STARRED REVIEW)

"A gripping exploration of the country's underworld … Leaves us mulling over the gnarled and vibrant tapestry of modern-day India."

—*MOTHER JONES*

"*The Story of My Assassins* is a dark, brutal, and yet often funny narration by a journalist of an attempt on his life … The result is a meditation, a commentary, on the convoluted venality of modern India."

—*NEWSWEEK*

"Overlooked in the general rush to adore *The White Tiger* and *Slumdog Millionaire* … With a much richer understanding of the politics of poverty … [*The Story of My Assassins*] deserves wider attention."

—HARI KUNZRU, AUTHOR OF *GODS WITHOUT MEN*, IN *THE GUARDIAN'S* BOOKS OF THE YEAR

"Intrepidly conceived and ingeniously executed, *The Story of My Assassins* casts an intimate, often humorous, but always unflinching, eye at the squalor of modernizing India. Combining a fierce political imagination with a tender solicitude for the losers of history, it sets a new and formidably high standard in Indian writing in English." —PANKAJ MISHRA, AUTHOR OF *AN END TO SUFFERING*

"One of the most attractive Indian writers in English of his generation." —*THE TIMES LITERARY SUPPLEMENT*

"Aims to break from the old ways of thinking about India in the hope of portraying its society in all its vastness, complexities and contradictions." —*NEW STATESMAN*

"*The Story of My Assassins*, as ethical as it is entertaining, reminds us how humane, how necessary, realist fiction can be." —*THE JAPAN TIMES*

"*The Story of My Assassins* is a quality read and the conclusion is both unexpected and emotionally satisfying." —*NEW INTERNATIONALIST*

"Set aside some time for reading Tarun J. Tejpal's *The Story of My Assassins* … You will read about an India in great flux, in great turmoil, but also one of extraordinary humanity." —*COUNTERPUNCH*

"Takes us into the unexplored depths of Indian life … Brilliantly evoked." —*THE INDEPENDENT*

"These days it seems almost impossible to be an Indian novelist without simultaneously aspiring to be the Indian novelist and, with this book, Tejpal lays serious claim to the title." —*THE LITERARY REVIEW*

"Mystery, mayhem and fast-paced humor set against India's sprawling slouch towards modernization." —*THE DENVER POST*

"Rich, empathetic . . . It's the most satisfyingly dense, Dickensian read." —*SEATTLE WEEKLY*

"The novel consistently grasps the reader's attention, and even touches on greatness." —*FINANCIAL TIMES*

"A devastating tale about political power and its malignity ... A lesson in geography that takes in its sweep huge swathes of the underbelly of India ... It's not a pretty India story ... [With his] ferocious new book ... with his ... compelling writing, Tejpal ensures, hopefully, that Indian exotica will never sell." —*THE FINANCIAL EXPRESS*

"This book is a must-read ... Extraordinary for its portrayal of modern society ... Shatters any illusions we may harbour of being tolerant and just ... Weaves an extremely powerful plot and tells it skillfully."

—*BUSINESSWORLD*

"A complex page-turning plot ... A commentary on power, sex, corruption and poverty." —*VERVE MAGAZINE* (MUMBAI)

"Make way, Messrs Vikas Swaroop and Aravinda Adiga, for the definitive story of the Indian underbelly." —*THE INDIAN EXPRESS*

"A story masterly told ... *The Story of My Assassins* is an argument with power ... Tejpal is not picnicking in the proverbial Other India ... [He] rewrites the idea of victimhood in an India where the subterranean deceptions of power know no bounds." —*INDIA TODAY*

"An instant classic ... Far, far better than anything I've ever read by an Indian author." —ALTAF TYREWALA, AUTHOR OF *NO GOD IN SIGHT*

"For the awesome story it tells and the stunning impact of its prose, this is, quite simply, the best Indian novel in English I have ever read."

—NAYANTARA SAHGAL, AUTHOR OF *RICH LIKE US*

"Without doubt the best Indian book written in English. Driven in turn by stunning prose and a deep empathy with struggling India, this novel makes Aravinda Adiga's Booker-winning novel look dipped in treacle. This magnificent tome will be the India testament for many, many years."

—BINOO JOHN, AUTHOR OF *THE LAST SONG OF SAVIO DE SOUZA*

THE STORY OF MY ASSASSINS

TARUN J. TEJPAL

THE STORY OF MY ASSASSINS

First published in India by HarperCollins Publishers, India

First Melville House printing of the paperback edition: July 2013

Melville House Publishing
145 Plymouth Street
Brooklyn, NY 11201

and

8 Blackstock Mews
Islington
London N4 2BT

mhpbooks.com facebook.com/mhpbooks @melvillehouse

ISBN: 978-1-61219-261-1

Manufactured in the United States of America
1 3 5 7 9 10 8 6 4 2

Library of Congress Control Number: 2012532878

For

NEENA,

artist of generosity, my oldest friend

1

NEWS OF A KILLING

The morning I heard I'd been shot I was sitting in my office on the second floor looking out the big glass window at the yellow ringlets of a laburnum tree that had gone in a few days from blindingly golden to faded cream, as if washed in rough detergent. Beyond the balding tree, losing its ringlets prematurely in mid-May, the sky was blamelessly blue. In minutes it would begin to bleach and the sun would paint such a glare on it, it would be impossible to look up, even briefly, to catch the full bellies of groaning aircraft swooping down to land.

It was not yet seven in the morning.

I had slipped away early from my darkened bedroom with barely a glance at the sleeping splash of my wife, lying spreadeagled on her stomach, arms and legs akimbo, as if quashed by a giant foot. Brushing my teeth in the dining-room sink I had glanced at the weekend newspapers, full of the excitements of food and cinema, and eschewing the tea Felicia had set to brew, quietly let myself out.

The lane lay in Sunday morning stupor, not a leaf stirring in the row of gulmohurs or the lone peepul. Rambir, our night watchman, had abandoned his post and was probably sleeping in his bed-sized room or doing the stuff one has to in the morning. The only thing moving was the mongrel of the lane, foraging for discarded food in the heaped refuse in the corner. Cast in many shades of brown with a rodent's long face, one bad eye and one bad leg, he had been christened Jeevan after the nasal, sneering Hindi film villain of the 1960s, by the cloying old uncle of C-1. The old man, Sharmaji, who cracked silly jokes with the colony children and stroked their arms slowly, would stand outside his gate and call out to the children, and if the dog was around, he'd adopt a nasal sneer. The children, eyes averted, mostly sprinted past his house.

Before Jeevan could limp up to me, tail wagging, I rushed to the car and slammed the door shut. For four years I had successfully managed to keep from opening up a relationship with him. That was one thing I could do without.

More relationships.

At the office, the parking lot was pleasingly empty but for a plump green Bajaj scooter, battered and old—head cocked, eyes cracked—resting on its stand. Its owner was sprawled just inside the front door, on the armless sofa in the reception. When I walked in he scrambled to his feet, swaying, making a grab for his unbuttoned trousers.

I said, 'Motherfucker Sippy, you've again been hitting the bottle all night!'

He said, 'No sir yes sir no sir.'

Sippy looked like he had been masturbating himself to death for the last fifty years. He had the wasted air of stereotype—hollowed eyes and cheeks, thin strands of hair on a pigmented scalp, arms and legs of stick and the wheedling manner of someone looking for just one more rush. He was struggling to align the buttons on his trousers and find the keys to my room at the same time. I slapped his fumbling hand away from the open drawer, and reaching into the jumble of brass and steel inside, picked up my set of four long slim keys anchored to a miniature high-heeled, knee-length brown leather boot. Someone's mad European fantasy from a foreign catalogue or film? Who, in all of India, thought up such key chains?

When I bounded up the stairs, Sippy was still rummaging purposefully in the drawer. It would be a few minutes before he realized this sequence was over. He was like that, with some kind of delayed-response metabolism. Changing a light bulb, he'd continue to stroke it long after it had come alive. Often, while making repairs in the jungle of wires and fuses in the main junction box under the stairs he would touch a naked wire and get a jolt; we'd all see the wires spark angrily, then, several seconds later Sippy would leap up, clutch his hand and scream, 'Oh, my mother's dead! My mother's dead!' The office boys called him Uncle Tooblite and everyone shouted their instructions at him twice, thrice, four times. If he was ever offended, he didn't show it. He always met you with a serious expression and a willingness to do whatever he was told.

When I pushed open the door of my office on the second floor, the phone was already trilling. It was Sippy asking if I'd like some tea. I had barely turned on the lights and pulled open the plastic blinds when the phone trilled again. Sippy. Wanting to know if he should get me a bun-omelette too. The computer had just finished booting when Sippy was back on the line. One omelette or two? I said, 'Motherfucker, one hundred! And they should all be round like testicles and pulled out of a hen's ass!' After the customary delay, he said, 'Okay sir.'

I waited as the icons lined themselves up at the top and bottom of the screen, like two teams of football players before the start of a match. After the great era of literacy the world was going back to the pre-literate age. For centuries there had been the hunt to find a word for every image, every sensation, every feeling; now we were working at finding an image for every word, every sensation, every feeling. Advertising, television, cinema, photography, computers, mobiles, graphics, animatronics—everything was geared to turn the squiggle of the word into the splendour of image. Across the globe, Photoshop Picassos crouched at their machines marrying unlike images to produce such unlikely images as no word could hope to withstand. The imagination no longer needed the word to negotiate its darkest recesses. The imagination was having its most fantastical meanderings served up in prefabricated images, for all to share. Our Mordor was the same. Our Frankenstein was the same. Our Tinker

Bell was the same. We didn't have to imagine Davy Jones—a graphics company in Silicon Valley was manufacturing him for us. We all picked our visuals from the universal pool. The individual monster was dead. Private passion was dead. Personal grief was dead. Anger was an icon. Love an image. Sex an organ. The future a matrix. If you could imagine it or feel it, it would be shown to you—in any colour, from every angle—without the exertions of the word. Even god would, finally, be shrunk to size. No larger than the screen. No denser than a pixel.

I had not yet put an icon into play when the phone rang again. An unknown voice, in Hindi, asked to speak to me. Sippy must have put the switchboard line on direct before he went out. I said today was Sunday and I would not be in office. The voice said could it speak to anyone else, or could it be given my home number. I said there was no one here on Sunday morning except me, the cleaner, and I was not authorized to give out phone numbers. The voice said it was critically important, critically. I said so is sahib's Sunday. The voice said, 'You are a chutiya and you deserve to be a sweeper all your life!'

The players were ready and the screen was still, but there was nothing to do, really. I was just escaping the house. Even surfing the Net was not an option; the server downstairs was shut on Sundays.

I looked out the big window in front of me at the laburnum flowers, bleached and dying young, that littered the balcony floor—like a low-wit parable on transient beauty. Laburnum. How melodious the name sounded. How sweetly the Malayali girl had said it before she wet my palm. I had barely noticed the tree until then, but she said its name with more ardour than she did mine, and I was forced to pay attention, feigning curiosity so she wouldn't stop to move. A botany lesson punctuated with slow deep gasps. A few weeks later, when it was over between us, the only memories that remained with me were the names of some trees and how she'd insist I rub my cheek against hers. I didn't mind that. I like dark skin, even though my mother had launched a hunt for the fairest girl in north India when she'd wanted me married off. The Punjabi girl she had finally picked hurt the eyes with her whiteness and had tiny bumps on her skin when naked.

My mobile phone began to buzz on the table's glass top like a trapped insect. Mother calling; probably to ask if we were going to visit her today. I put a folded hanky under the phone to dull the noise. Some seconds after the vibrations had ceased, they started up again. Still Mother. I leaned back in my chair and looked at the mobile's small screen pulsing light. It died; and came alive once more. Not Mother this time but a number I didn't recognize. The number vanished and was replaced by another one I didn't recognize. Now Mother was on the line again; now another number I didn't recognize; now Pramod, the office accountant; now a number that looked like one of the earlier unknown ones; now the home number; now Mother again; now my wife. The jittering mobile moved the hanky slowly across the table. Mother, I knew. What was wrong with the rest of this demented city? On a Sunday morning?

Then the land line trilled. I picked it up to deal with Sippy. A vaguely familiar voice in Hindi said, 'Give me sahib's mobile number, it's urgent.' I said I was not authorized to do so. The voice said, 'Chutiya, you don't even deserve to be a sweeper!'

My silver and black Nokia had juddered itself and the hanky to the edge of the table. I waited and, as they plunged, caught both deftly in my left hand like a sharp slip fielder and replaced them on the glass top. The small screen was pulsing light without pause. My sister from Bombay; my wife; Mother; an unknown number; another unknown number; the circulation manager; the space-selling boy who had joined two months ago; Mother. Probably some new bullshit in the papers. The switchboard line rang again.

I picked it up. 'Sippy?'

Sippy said, 'Sirji, they are saying you are dead.'

I said, 'Motherfucker, *you* are if I don't get my tea now!'

The sun had now climbed past the tree and hit the window. You could see the drip stains on the glass. Fifteen minutes more and the vertical blinds would have to be half closed. The room would then become striped in sunlit lines. It was the backdrop photographers who came to take my picture favoured. Yes please, move back please, just a little, good, very good, eyes in dark, mouth in light, chest in dark, belly in light, groin in dark, thighs in light. Smile please.

Sippy came in, weaving slowly, a plastic tray in hand. He wore tattered leather shoes with ragged laces. His leathery skin was grey with unshaven bristles, his eyes swimming in a soup of yellow and red. The first thing he said was, 'Sorry sir.'

I said, 'Who called, motherfucker?'

Sippy said, 'I picked up the phone and the man said, Bloody chutiya! So I said to him, You are a chutiya, your father's a chutiya, and your son's a chutiya! He said, Your sahib's dead, and so should you be! Now give me his mobile number! I said, Why? You want to phone him in heaven?'

The tea already had a skin on it. I peeled it off with the tip of my forefinger and stuck it to the side of the tray.

Sippy said, 'Sirji, should I get you another one?'

I looked at him.

He said, 'Sorry sirji.'

The mobile had been trembling all the while, making its way across the table. Sippy looked at it intently for some time, then said, 'Sirji, phone.'

I looked at him, stopping mid-bite into my bun-omelette.

He said, 'Sorry sirji.'

The land line trilled. Kept trilling. When I finally picked it up, Sippy asked, 'Do you want me to pick it up?'

I said, in Hindi, 'Hello, Sub-inspector Shinde speaking from Kiskiskilee police station.'

Mother screeched into the phone, 'How bad is it? How bad is

it? Why is no one picking your mobile phone? Why must you talk such nonsense even at this time?'

I said, 'Madam, it is a criminal offence to speak to the Indian police like this.'

Mother screamed, 'You fool, turn on the TV! Turn on the TV immediately!'

I picked up the remote, swivelled in my chair and detonated the TV. With a soft pop a chorus line of singers exploded into the room, throwing their legs and breasts about. I said, 'Mother, it's from *Kismet*—the hero is about to enter the don's den.'

Sippy giggled. 'Kiskiskilee police station. Kis kis ki lee!'

I looked at him.

He said, 'Sorry sirji.'

I flipped channels. An amazing smorgasbord of mythological costumes, American cafes, ornate quiz shows, thrashing crocodiles, goggled cricketers, striding golfers, bare-chested godmen, film stars talking, film stars dancing, film stars acting, all kinds of old and new films flitted past in several languages before I hit a news channel. There was a still of me, with my mouth open. Perhaps from some press conference, caught mid-sentence. The words 'Breaking News!' emblazoned in red ran across my chest. I read the ticker below: Attempt on journalist foiled. Five hitmen arrested.

I flipped some more. Another news channel. A different picture—from before I had shaved off my moustache. Again, Breaking News! The ticker said: Scribe survives murder attempt. Delhi police foils bid. I turned up the volume. In a grave voice the pretty girl said that I had been saved in the nick of time. The police had been acting on intelligence tip-offs. Sophisticated weapons such as AK-47s and automatic pistols had been recovered. No information had been released yet on the motives, but inside sources hinted these were contract killers.

Now Sippy said, 'Sirji, that is you?'

I put the receiver to my ear. 'Mother, they are saying I survived.'

Mother screeched, 'It is the glory of Shiva! It is the mercy of god! It is the power of my prayers!'

I said, 'Mother, they are saying it is the power of Delhi police.'

There was a moment's silence. Then she screeched, 'My son! My son*nnn*!'

I threw the receiver over to Sippy. He put it to his ear and said, 'Hello good morning, Eagle Media Company speaking.'

Dancing on my hanky the mobile had reached the far end of the table again. I leaned across and picked it up. An unknown number glowed angrily. I pressed it to life. A girl's urgent voice said, 'Please hold the line—I am putting you through live to the studio.'

The studio voice that came on belonged to a young girl too, but it sounded grave and important. The voice said they had me on the line—live—before anyone else in the country. Fast and furious.

The studio girl said, 'Thank you for coming on our channel exclusively! How are you feeling now?'

I said, 'Okay.'

'Are you badly shaken by the events?'

'Yes.'

'Have you been receiving any threats lately?'

'No.'

'Do you have any idea who the killers are?'

'No.'

'Have you felt any sense of danger in the last few weeks?'

'No.'

'The police are saying they are contract killers. Do you believe them?'

'I cannot say.'

'Do you think the government has any hand in all this?'

'I cannot say.'

'Is your family worried? Scared?'

'I cannot say.'

'Are you scared? Worried?'

'Not yet.'

'What do you plan to do now?'

Eat the egg pulled out of the hen's ass.

'I haven't thought of it yet.'

'Did you have no inkling at all?'

'No.'

'What did you do when you got to know?'

'Nothing.'

'Who informed you?'

'Sub-inspector Shinde of Kiskiskilee police station.'

'Who?'

'Sub-inspector Shinde of Kiskiskilee police station.'

There was a moment's silence at the other end. Much too long for live television to stomach. Then the voice said, even more urgently, 'Thank you for coming exclusively on our channel and giving us the first exclusive insights into your murder!' Then, before I could kill it, the line went dead.

Sippy had put the receiver back on the cradle. He said, 'That was your mother, sirji. She shouted at me for spoiling your life. She thought I was some friend of yours. I told her I am Sippy from the office, electrician-cum-chowkidar. She said I don't care whether you are a sippy or a hippy, just leave my son alone before you have him killed. She said she's coming over just now and if she found me here she would pull all my hair out.'

The land line was trilling without a pause and my mobile was beating out an unending string of known and unknown numbers. I got up, popped the TV shut with the remote, slipped the vibrating phone into the pocket of my trousers and told Sippy to lock up the office. I took the stairs down two at a time.

When I came out the front door onto the veranda of the shopping complex where our office was, I saw my wife getting out of her small yellow car. She was in light blue jeans and a white tee shirt, her short straight hair pulled back into a tiny tail. Her eyes were hidden behind the fake silver-rimmed Guccis I had bought her from Singapore. She saw me and stopped, in the midst of turning the key in the car door.

Uncertainly, she said, 'Is everything okay?'

I said, 'Do I look dead?'

She said, 'You weren't picking your phone. And everybody was calling the house, and everybody said you weren't picking your phone.'

I said, 'I was busy.'

She said, 'I got very worried. The TV channels were saying all kinds of things. I thought I'd come and check if you were okay.'

'So what do you think now?'

She said, 'Don't be angry. I was really worried. I barely brushed my teeth—I just rushed here.'

I said, 'Well, go back and brush them now.'

By now I had reached my car and opened the door. She was still standing by hers, turning the key. Behind us, Sippy was hanging on to the steel shutter of the office, his stick-like arms and legs flailing, struggling to pull it down in slow noisy jerks.

She said, 'Are you coming home?'

I said, 'Eventually.'

She said, 'Where are you going now?'

I said, 'Why? You want to inform the TV channels?'

I couldn't see her eyes, but I could read her face. She didn't move. Sippy was on his knees now, trying to push home the rusty latch at the bottom of the shutter and lock it. I got into my car, slammed the door and pulled out of the parking lot. In my rearview mirror I could see her getting into her car, and Sippy swimming steadily on the veranda floor.

She opened the door at the first chime of her singsong bell, glistening with some lotion she had hurriedly slopped on. I brushed my cheek against hers in a half-hug and went straight into her bedroom, cool with the rattling air-conditioner, and lay on her bed. The only light in the room came from a weak yellow table lamp. The window was blocked with heavy blue drapes, tucked around to frame the plastic-grille air-conditioner. The brand name stuck on the cream-coloured grille said 'Napoleon', which meant it had been knocked together in some backyard shop in the city. Napoleon air-conditioners, high-heeled leather boot key chains—this country was in imaginative heat.

She said, 'You want some tea?'

I nodded, and began to take off my clothes. The back of the study-table chair had a large flowery towel drying on it. I picked up a corner and sniffed: it was musty. I slid it off, kicked it into a corner, and draped my jeans, shirt and boxers there instead. When she came back with two mugs of tea I was sitting propped up on her side of the double-bed—crumpled and warm from the night—one leg pulled back to conceal what was happening to me. I had pushed her reading pile of papers—NGO reports, magazines, books on development economics, and an anthology of Hunter Thompson's I had given her that she was making heavy weather of—I had pushed the whole heap to the far corner of the unused bed and thrown a pillow over it to still the fluttering. She gave me my mug and sat down on the edge of the bed, not touching me. In the lamplight I could see the fine down on her upper lip. The sun had roasted her slim arms a darker shade of chocolate. When she lifted her mug to take a sip, the cross-hatch in her armpit was dense.

She said, 'How come you've been let out on a Sunday morning?'

I said nothing, looking her in the eye, demanding to change the register of the moment.

She said, 'What? The same old same old? Well, sorry, it's Sunday, this crèche is closed.'

I put my hand deep into her thighs and she held it tight, her flesh full and smooth. I waited, feeling the heat radiate. Then I saw the moment catch in her eye and come over her. Her muscles relaxed a fraction, letting me in. She was ready. I danced my fingertips slowly, setting up an overture. She gave a start, then grew still, not a muscle moving, holding on to her tea mug, challenging me with her eyes. Time to play. I responded with the length of a finger. She pulled in a short breath and her eyes dilated, but she didn't move. I pulled my hand out and touched her upper lip with the tips of my shining fingers. She looked back at me, unmoving, in full activist mode. Desire rocketed in me. I straightened my leg and, putting my hand on the side of her head, pushed her down. She fought, stiffening her neck. I pushed harder.

I said, 'Look what you've done to me.'

She said, 'Anyone can do that to you.'

Her head was halfway down now, but she was still holding on to her tea. I put my left hand on the side of her head, and reached out with my right. I said, 'Give it to me, you whore!'

She looked at me, challenging, demanding.

I said, 'Saali randi!'

She took a long draught of the tea and released her grip on the mug. By the time I set the mug down on the bedside table, I was swimming in a tea-warm mouth. I slumped back, my hand moving slowly in her frizzy hair. Then I began to abuse her, relentlessly, in Hindi, in English, recalling words and phrases I had learnt in school, street words, cheap porno phrases, stringing them out absurdly like overheated boys do. And with each crude volley—especially the Hindi—she became beautifully uncontrollable, giving and taking, giving and taking, in the simplest and most complicated transaction of all.

Later, while Napoleon Bonaparte cooled the sweat off us and we drank some more tea, dipping chalk-dry Marie biscuits in it, I looked dispassionately at her naked body as she lay opposite me at the foot of the bed. She had two beautiful halves that belonged to different bodies. Above the waist, from her fine nose to her frail shoulders, to her breasts made for pleasure not lactation, she was narrow and fragile. Below she was full, with the hips and thighs of a woman made for bearing children. Not for the photograph, as she was above, but for real-life excitements. Two trademark moles stamped her body as being a single unit: a gaudy beauty on her right collarbone, and its mysterious twin marking the start of the dense hairline at the top of her right thigh. She had found a solution to her two unmatched halves, dressing in long flared peasant skirts and close-fitting sleeveless cotton blouses: concealing the excess, flaunting the fragility.

Now, head propped on her left palm, she was talking. It was what she did best. She was talking politics, sociology, anthropology, history, economics, ecology, all in a magnificent jumble that exhausted and fascinated me. She was dismembering the new liberal economics that was opening up India to the world, cursing the scourge of globalization, abusing patriarchal politics, demanding lower-caste mobilization, declaring the death of the idea of India at the hands of a surging Hindu right. In five years, by 2005, this would be a fascist state. She and I, and those like us, would be in hiding. Everything—every freedom—we took for granted would be gone. It would be worse than the colonial past, because this time we would have done it to ourselves. I think she saw the smile in my eyes for she broke into a rage. She jumped up, rummaged through her bookshelves and brought out an Oxford anthology of English poetry.

'Listen to this!' she barked, opening a flagged page:

About suffering they were never wrong,
The Old Masters: how well they understood
Its human position; how it takes place
While someone else is eating or opening a window or just
walking dully along...

She read the poem aloud with a hard anger, with the voice and rhythms of a protestor, not a lover of poetry. She finished and looked at me balefully. 'You know what Wystan Hugh Auden is saying?'

I shook my head.

She said, 'Wystan's telling us that fascism is creeping up all around us, and we don't even know! He's telling us that we suffer from the Illusion of Normalcy. He's telling us that the worst horrors take place around us while we go happily about our everyday lives. Just because the newspapers keep coming, the televisions keep humming, the planes keep taking off, the trains keep running—just because our daily crap goes on doesn't mean all is well. My dear phallo-foolish friend, Icarus has plunged into the ocean and is drowning while we are chattering away merrily on the sailing ship!'

I watched mesmerized. She was walking up and down the room, her two different bodies moving differently. The pleasure legs in rolling motion; the photo arms waving angrily. In her, sexual satiety brought on not the customary torpor, but a great intellectual and moral anxiety. It was the stuff of research. I thought of the wild Hindi profanities she had been urging me to heap on her just minutes back.

'You,' she said, rounding on me. 'You!'

I said, 'What have I done now?'

'Nothing! That's just it. Nothing. You know who Wystan Hugh was writing for? For people like you—who are worse than people like them! They don't have a voice so they can't speak. You have one and you barely whisper. Surely you don't think your little exposé and stories are all they are cut out to be? You know they are basically ego massages. And that preening, posing partner of yours! Him and you, and your little boys getting their rocks off! Being given a bloody cannon and using it to shoot peas!'

Boy. The postcoital social contract. I was drowsy and no longer interested. The crazy bitch needed a dose of the Vedanta to cleanse her head. Hindi abuse for the body; Hindu philosophy for the soul.

Her problem was too little Hinduism, too much occidental crap. I was thinking about what the television channels were saying. I had been shot. By whom? My phone already showed more than forty missed calls, and the count was going up by the minute. I closed my eyes and her words became a fading noise.

When I came to, minutes later, she was no longer talking, just pacing up and down, her photo arms folded across her breasts, looking at me with contempt. I washed myself at the sink, draping my smelly hanging flesh over the enamel rim, pumping soap from the Dettol dispenser, splashing water from the tap with a cupped palm. In the frameless mirror it looked like a third-rate postmodern painting.

She pushed open the bathroom door and hollered, 'Stop pissing in my sink you stupid clunk!'

It was all so third-rate.

Back in the parking lot I turned on the engine and the air-conditioner, leaned my seat back as far as it would go and closed my eyes. In the end it was always exhausting. It took no time for every damn relationship to spill out of the functional. Suddenly even the prospect of home seemed like a relief. At least I wouldn't have to talk, or listen to anything. And if things got insufferable I could shut myself in my tiny study and stew—and bugger you Wystan Hugh—and not see anything either.

The sun had obliterated every nuance from the world by now, and was pouring down white heat. No dazzle was permitted in this enclave of the nondescript, of boxy colourless buildings and endless Maruti cars. The trees in the parking lot looked as if they'd had all the green syringed out of them, leaving them coated with settled dust. Most of them seemed stunted, throttled by a tourniquet of concrete. Every now and then an excitable-irritable family—mother, father, couple of sated, snotty kids going to fat—tumbled out of dark holes in the boxy buildings flaunting their Sunday best, scrambled into a car, slammed doors, and left.

I had directed all the air vents at myself but was still patchy with sweat. The synthetic grip on the steering wheel was burning, barely touchable. The phone was a trapped insect and had not ceased buzzing for a moment. I began to swiftly parse my missed calls and messages. Everyone I knew had called or messaged. Even as I scrolled the calls the phone kept buzzing and letting new ones in. I was about to pull out of the parking lot when her name began to appear insistently on my phone. When it wouldn't go away, I said, 'Yes?'

She said, 'Moron, why didn't you tell me?'

She must have turned on the television after I left.

I said, 'There was nothing to tell.'

I sensed the activity even before I turned the car into our lane. There were several unfamiliar vehicles parked at the corner, and men hanging about under the shade of the massive peepul, at least two of them in uniform. I took the turn slowly. Under the overhang of the tiny porch of my house a small crowd milled. The iron gate was wide open, and a police Gypsy was parked right in front of it. Jeevan was checking out its radials with his good eye, wagging his tail and spurting piss.

I walked into the tumult to a chaos of greetings, questions and blessings. I could see family, friends, colleagues, neighbours, cops, and media men with eyes growing out of their shoulders—a mad democracy's ever-open third eye, marrying us all in a grand collective of sorrow and celebration, lament and lust, brands and stars. The masterly sleight: conformity through freedom. What Mao and Stalin could not pull off through violence and coercion.

Mother leapt on me like Tom on Jerry and clung to my midriff, mewling, even as I staggered about shaking hands and making incoherent noises. Everyone held a glass with clinking ice; nimbupani was doing the rounds. Everyone had the same questions. What happened, how did it happen, who were they, what did you do, where have you been, are you okay, can I do anything.

Yes please, turn around and get the fuck out.

My wife was leaning on the door jamb, slim, tall, fair, expressionless—as ever, uncertain of what to do around me, all beauty flattened by joylessness. Her fat mother, eyes red-rimmed with forced tears, was holding her daughter's right forearm and stroking it. Her balding father sat in the living-room, shrunk into the chair, timidly awaiting his moment. A clerk for all occasions.

A portly, round-faced man in a cream-coloured bush shirt, with close cropped hair and a bushy moustache, whom I had never seen before stood to a side, arms crossed on his chest, benignly witnessing the circus. Beneath his loose trousers he was hoofed in pointed black leather shoes. Beside him stood a tall fair young man, almost a boy, with hairless cheeks and a coiled air about him. The loop of a nylon lanyard was visible just under the right edge of his grey safari suit. I shuffled up to them—Mother still draped around my midriff—and gave the portly man my hand.

He said, with an understanding smile, in a low flat voice, 'Shall we sit inside?'

When I had ushered him into my chokingly small study, I stood outside the closed door, peeled my mother away from my body and told her to bugger off. My pretty wife and her ugly mother were hanging by too. I told them both to bugger off as well and to encourage every idiot present to do the same. The party was over. My mother opened her mouth to let out a monster wail but I clamped my hand down hard on her mouth and looked at her with such venom that all three of them quietly melted away.

I took the plate of orange-cream biscuits Felicia had brought for us and latching the door behind me sat down on the frayed sofa. He was sitting on one of the two wooden chairs in the room—the one in front of the small work table I sometimes used. He had taken a book from my shelf and was looking at its cover. *The Naked Lunch.* I set the plate down next to him.

He put the book down on the table, took a biscuit in his left hand and gave me a limp right hand. He said, in his low flat voice, 'We all admire you—you are doing very good service to the nation.'

I said, 'We all do what we have to do.'

He said, 'No, we do what we are told. You are doing something different, something great, something for the country.'

I said, 'You do very important work.'

He picked up *The Naked Lunch* again and started to caress it. Between slow biscuit bites he said, 'We do what those above us in the department tell us to do. And they do what those above them tell them to do. And what they tell us is not always right. But it's not our job to ask why. If we all began to ask why, there would be only a mountain of whys, and no department. When I joined the force our instructor told us every day to always remember that in our line of work nine right and one wrong is wrong, but all ten wrong is right. And so we do what we are told and we are always right even though we are often wrong.'

He said all this in his low flat tone, without a single inflection. His name was Hathi Ram—his father had served as a soldier in the British Indian army in Burma and developed a fascination for elephants. His father had told him to be like a hathi, gentle but strong, obedient but incapable of being pushed around. He said his father was a fool, a simple army man, from another world and time. In the force these days you had to be a bahurupiya, a quick-change artiste, a master of impersonation, capable of putting on a face for every occasion. A mouse in front of seniors, an elephant in front of juniors, a wolf with suspects, a tiger before convicts, a lamb around politicians, a fox with men of money. So he was not always Hathi Ram—sometimes he was Chooha Ram or Lomdi Ram or Sher Ram or Bakri

Ram. In the force these days who you were depended on who was sitting in front of you.

I said, 'So who are you now?'

A full smile cracked his face. His close cropped hair was more grey than black, though his bushy moustache was dark with dye. Thick salt and pepper tendrils spilled out from his open shirt collar. He riffled the pages of *The Naked Lunch* like a pack of cards, and said, 'Now I am Dost Ram. I am here as a friend. We have to look after you. We don't want any harm to come to you.' Through his avuncular pudginess, his eyes were still and hard.

I said, 'What's happening? Who's trying to get me?'

He said, 'We don't know too much. We are still trying to find out.'

I said, 'But surely...'

He said, 'I told you, sahib, those above us order us and we do. Our job is not to ask why—otherwise there will be a mountain of whys, and no job.'

I said, 'How many were they?'

He said, 'I think five, but I only know from what I heard on TV.'

I said, 'Hathi Ramji, if you know nothing, then why are you here? Surely not to find out from me?'

He said, 'Sahib, I did not become a sub-inspector by going to big colleges and answering three-hour examinations. The force is full of lovely boys whose teeth are still milky white and pubic hair still boot-polish black, and I am sure they know things of which I know nothing. I became an SI by dragging my khaki ass through the alleys and byways of this benighted city for thirty years, and one of the things I learnt, wearing out my soles, is that nothing in this city is what it seems. But I also learnt that one of the best ways to deal with things is to keep them simple. Small men like me can go deranged trying to figure out the motives and the means of big men. There are people in the force who spend all their time trying to find out these things. They take news to big men, and they bring back instructions. I don't. I just do what my officers tell me. I am not washed in milk and I am no angel. But I am a bahurupiya out of necessity, and no more. Sometimes I do right and sometimes I do wrong. But I do it in the line of duty, and it is not for me to judge. I simply follow the Gita. Do what you have to do. Do you think it was right for Arjuna to kill the great Bhishma by shooting from behind Sikhandin? Do you think it was right for the noble Yudhishthira to speak a lie so that the great Dronacharya could be killed? Lord Krishna made them do these things. The Lord alone knows what is right and wrong. Men can only do their duty.'

Not one inflection, just that low flat tone, and a continual riffling of *The Naked Lunch*. When he finished he picked up an orange-cream biscuit, opened its two halves and put into his mouth first the less creamy one and seconds later, the other.

I said, 'And what is your duty today?'

He said, 'To make sure you are safe, and you stay safe.'

2

REIGN OF THE SHADOWS

I did not see SI Hathi Ram again for several weeks, but the fair boy with the hairless face and the telltale loop of the lanyard became a daily fixture in my life. His name was Vijyant, and he was shy, wide-eyed and young enough to take his job seriously. He sat outside each door I was inside—office, home, restaurant—and leapt to action the moment I appeared, looking right, left, all around, and beating down with his eyes anyone who glanced our way. In the car he rode in the back while I drove and was always out of his door and covering me before I had killed the engine. He kept his big, black, slightly worn-looking, 9mm pistol tucked into the front waistband of his pants, the business end of it presumably nestling cold and deep in his crotch. Sometimes when I pulled aside the bamboo chik to look out of my study window I would see him sitting in the tiny porch, the 9mm in his lap, caressing it gently with his fingertips and humming the Mukesh number, Chal akela chal akela chal akela, tera mela peechhe chhuta rahi, chal akela.

Hathi Ram alias Dost Ram had said, 'Golden boy! He's my golden boy! He's a jaanbaaz—would punt his life in a moment. When we got him I told the inspector, Where is the kiln this one was baked in? I need some more like him. The inspector said, Give him a year, then we'll talk! But the inspector was wrong—even we have failed to corrupt the boy. He could be with ministers, MPs, VVIPs, but no, I want him to be with you, because for me your life is more important than theirs.'

All this had been said within earshot of the boy. When he'd finished he'd looked at him, standing slim and coiled in his safari suit, and said, 'Why? Have I said anything wrong?'

Vijyant had smiled shyly and patted his iron crotch. 'It is my duty.'

The boy was as educated as I was—a BA, a Bachelor of Arts—and had graduated in the same subjects, political science and history. It was quite possible he had scored better in his college exams than I had. The difference was that he'd have studied in Hindi, in Hapur, and when he finished his father would have urged him to try for a government job. After all, the government, the sarkar, was maibaap—father, protector, keeper.

Once you became part of maibaap, you were invincible. Cyclical storms of joblessness could not touch you; germ and disease would find their match in government hospitals; soaring real estate prices would tiptoe past maibaap's houses; sarkari schools would ring with the happy cries of your children; and when your hair fell out and your limbs grew infirm, maibaap would let you go home but keep sending you a cheque every month for your old age. Once you entered the embrace of maibaap you were taken care of till your very last day, till it was time to be thrown onto bamboo sticks and be carted off to the cremation ground. And by then, if you were truly blessed, your children would already be in the secure lap of maibaap, steeled against the depredations that blighted other ordinary lives.

From the tiny eyehole of Hapur—with its forsaken streets, sludge gutters, dimly lit shops, coagulated traffic, and the thick rough blanket of dust on everything—from remote Hapur the world would have looked dangerously non-negotiable: much too large, much too complex, much too malevolent, and much too full of very smart, very rich, very powerful people. Hapur was too small for a smart boy; the world too big for a small boy.

His father would have been terrified of sending him out of Hapur with scarcely a weapon for survival; most likely Vijyant himself would have been terrified of venturing out too. Government, sarkar, maibaap: father, protector, keeper: that was their only hope. In the grand monument of maibaap you did not need to command a bedroom or an office—even scuttling rats had a space and were secure.

A search would have commenced; a journey. First, for someone—a relative, a friend—who knew someone in Delhi. Ideally in government, a broker or a fixer. Yes, the boy was good and might make it on his own, but did you want to take a chance? Never!

They would then have been handed down a chain—in which each man laughed and said, 'Hapur! Hapur ke papud!'—till they were finally facing the man who would spell out the deal.

This man would be an artist, well aware of his place in the universe, the keeper of the doorways. He would have styled himself—gestures, tone, the movement of his head—on a film star—Dev Anand, Dilip Kumar, Raj Kapoor—of his youth. By turns he would be voluble, phlegmatic, withdrawn, haranguing, dismissive, comforting, and philosophical. Always philosophical. Jugglers of morality, dribblers of ethics, need philosophy more than priests and professors. He would leave no doubt that he was the enabler, the altruist; the corruption and greed all belonged to the men who had come to his door.

Many bargains, pleadings, assurances, counter-assurances later, the father would have returned to Hapur to rustle up the pay-off.

Because the boy was a simpleton, likely to raise an innocent question, he would be kept out of the process, told to just prepare for the physical examination. Push-ups; sit-ups; litres of bubbling milk.

Because his father did everything right, because the artist of the doorways exercised his munificence, Vijyant would be embraced by maibaap, given the rank of a constable, his lifelong cares taken over by the sarkar, fully secure to scuttle in maibaap's mansion for the rest of his days.

Now all he had to do was guard me. Against I did not know what.

Nor was he the only one. He was the first to show up on that Sunday morning with SI Hathi Ram, but then over the next few days two more were assigned to look after me. Both of them were much older than Vijyant—crusty veteran thullas, with bellies and phlegm—but for some reason I always assumed that the young boy was in charge. The three of them were supposed to rotate work in eight-hour shifts, but had hammered out some complicated timetable among themselves that would see them on duty for anything between twelve and twenty-four hours. I never knew when they would change shifts and who would be coming on next. Nor did I care.

In the beginning there was the novelty and the unease, like suddenly having a beautiful woman on your arm. Everywhere you went you were aware of this presence by your side, and every moment you felt all eyes were on you. Then swiftly, as with beauty, the novelty and the unease faded, and I soon ceased to be aware of them. In a few weeks they had become nothing but shadows—they went where I went, moved when I moved, vanished once I went indoors; dying in the dark, materializing in the light.

Because they were never in uniform, a loosely hanging shirt being the only constant, it was even easier to forget their presence. In any case, I ensured they remained true shadows, never speaking unless spoken to, managing their meals and ablutions in the inadvertent gaps my life afforded them, actively discouraged from asking questions about my schedules and plans.

After the initial curiosity about Vijyant, I decided I didn't want any intimacies with any of them. It was best if they remained faceless, nameless, storyless. I didn't want to know about the villages they came from, the schools they went to, their family problems, their struggling parents, their working woes, their caste, their religion, their dialect, their opinions on politics, nationhood, the economy, Gandhi, Nehru, corruption, crime, cricket, Hindu, Muslim. Nothing.

There was just too much opinion in this country, too many sob stories. Nobody wanted to put a lid on anything; everyone wanted to say it all, about everything. If you as much as said hello to someone on a train or a plane, you were in for the unexpurgated memoirs.

Nehru in 1947 had declared us a nation finding utterance—but in fifty years the utterance had become a mad clamour, a crazed babble, an unending howl. We were a nation of Scheherzades, afraid we'd die if, for a moment, we shut up. For myself, I'd mastered a face of steel, and an inscrutable nod. It did not always shut everyone up, but it did to some extent dam the ghastly flow.

The irony was matters were being constantly worsened by those in my business. Desperate bleeding hearts, agents of hype and frenzy, they thrived on the purple phrase, the overblown image, the apocalyptic analysis. They helped create a public mood of weep and lament and chest-beating. A great great noise. It was grotesque, the continual emotion-letting, the rona-dhona, in private, in public. It was as if no one knew a thing about the Hindu mind that was their inheritance.

When Gudakesha, the great Arjuna, scorcher of foes, archer beyond compare, first among equals, stranded between the arrayed armies of the Pandavas and Kauravas, grief-stricken in his moment of emotion-letting, told Krishna, 'I will not fight', then Hrishikesha, Govinda, Krishna, the all-knowing, the Lord, smiled and said, 'You speak as if you are wise, but you are grieving for those that one should not sorrow for. The wise don't sorrow for those who are dead or those who are alive. It is not that I, or you, or these kings, did not exist before this. Nor is it that we won't exist in the future. The soul passes through childhood, youth and age in this body, and likewise, attains another body. The wise don't get bewildered by this. O son of Kunti, because of contact between senses and objects, feelings of warmth and cold, pleasure and pain result. But these are temporary and are created and disappear. O descendant of Bharata, therefore, tolerate these! O best among men, the wise person who is not affected by these, and who looks upon happiness and unhappiness equally, attains the right to immortality.'

But we had become a people who could neither question with the humility of Gudakesha, nor hear the wise words of

Hrishikesha. We just wanted to let it all hang out, as in the confessionals in teen magazines, as too, increasingly, in the breathless pages of high-sounding newspapers. *Cosmo* meets Bollywood meets MTV on the hallowed plains of Kurukshetra for the great battle of the Mahaphuddus!

I became so indifferent to the two new shadows—belly and phlegm—that I didn't even register their names. Not that they were the sort who cared. Both of them came and went with barely a nod, no doubt disappointed at being made PSOs, personal security officers, to a lightweight like me. Often enough they'd let me know the names of the high-wattage politicians they had been attached to—men who commandeered the fates of millions, outside whose doors the rich and the influential bowed and scraped, who could transfer officials with a nod, grant licences with a squiggle, make and break careers and fortunes between the taking of toast and tea.

One shadow was forever talking about a former minister for communications who lavished his staff with foreign whiskies and non-vegetarian banquets. Sitting slumped in the backseat while I drove, hands on his belly, he would say, 'Never have I seen such plump chickens, never—god knows where he got them from! We were not guarding him, we were attending an unending wedding feast! Never have I swallowed so many digestive pills! What a good man he was!'

Wristwatches, wall clocks, clothes, mobile phones, boxes of mithai and dry fruit, pens, kitchenware, crockery, cutlery, calendars, music cassettes, movie tickets, cricket bats, framed photographs, even fresh vegetables and sacks of grain—these offerings, it seems, would continually fill the front room of his Lutyens' bungalow, and from there flow to the staff. The shadow may not have been exaggerating. The minister, charming and eloquent—a modern, techno-savvy man, three mobiles in hand, data crunchers working computers in his backroom around the clock—had a reputation for making his millions but also for his generosity.

The minister had built a makeshift air-conditioned gym on the grounds of his sprawling government house, and was sometimes seen on TV giving panting sound bytes from an angled treadmill. Generously, the staff too was allowed to embrace the Nautilus, and when the minister went to five-star hotels and did his business—of money and pleasure—his entourage ate at glittering coffee shops where the opulence of the marble humbled the mind, the names of the dishes twisted the tongue, and the desserts were works of art to be admired. In contrast, there was the tiny overhang of the porch at my house, a splintering cane chair, a folding bed propped against the wall, and tea and glucose biscuits three times a day.

Unlike Vijyant, belly and phlegm felt no awe for moral lustre. Like Hathi Ram they had been cops long enough to acquire the skills of a bahurupiya, to wear the face the man in front demanded. With me they were simply Billi Rams, cool cats, neither aggressive nor deferential, just aloof and uninterested. Any curiosity they may have had about me, from following the news, was quickly exhausted seeing my small house, battered car, mean life, and desultory office.

Basically, they were fools. Complete idiots. Of the strain that had made us vassals for hundreds of years—vassals of dumb royals and ruthless white men. More than fifty years of freedom and democracy had changed nothing. Anyone with a loud voice and sharp clothes could have these mahaphuddus on their knees—the vassal gene was instantly triggered by the vaguest hint of power or money. Those were the two great attributes that awed them. And to a lesser, and lessening, extent, language—if you had some English you could potentially wreak terror.

In school in the early seventies I had seen my football coach, Rashidmian, give the perfect demonstration of this on a train to Gorakhpur. When the ticket checker, a bird-like man in a frayed black coat, came by to check the tickets of which we were three short, Rashidmian, tall, fair, with faded brown hair, launched into the English alphabet at such rattling speed that the clacking of the passenger train was drowned out. *Abcdefghijklmno*...he went without breaking for breath, and then repeated it swiftly three times in different rhythms and intonations, singsong, staccato, guttural. The iron wheels clacked, the train shook, the boys gawped, and the dazzled checker left without tallying the count.

Mahaphuddus, that's what we were.

So I treated them as such. Giving them no explanations of my life or plans, not letting them know how long I would be in any place, when I would be leaving, when coming back. At any time of day or night I would walk out and they had to be there ready and waiting to move. When they asked me for permission to go off to eat, I just nodded, and let them interpret it any way they wished. A couple of times I emerged from a meeting to find my shadow missing—and just left. Later, belly and phlegm fretted about how foolish it was to have left alone, unprotected, and how I was putting their jobs on the line. I gave them my face of steel. It was their job to watch out for me, not mine for them. They could try to hold in their piss and hunger for eight hours.

Several people told me to be careful: that the shadows had actually been planted not for my protection but to spy on me. Information of my life and movements was being funnelled straight back to the Intelligence Bureau, and from there to the highest echelons of government. In thick-walled rooms, under pools of yellow lamplight, grim men in grey suits were decoding the significance of my eating a burger all alone at McDonald's.

At the office, Jai, my partner, a bearded bleeding heart—who saw a conspiracy in every step of the state, and spent his evenings in some expensive living-room slitting his wrists over some banal people's issue—my partner Jai said, 'They are just preparing a big dossier on you before they plant something on you to fix you.'

I said, 'What?' The American McBurger.

He plucked at his thick black beard and said, 'Let's not be naïve. These guys are capable of anything—could be heroin, cocaine, fuck knows what. You visit a place three times—one, two, three; the fourth time you come out and under your car seat, a pouch of white powder. They stop you at a naka, put their hands under three seats, one, two, three, and then under the fourth, and there it is! Ponds talcum powder! Straight up your nose!'

He was enjoying himself.

He said, 'And now, from being mister investigative you are mister drug dealer—or at best, mister drug user. On every channel, in every newspaper, in every office. Now go hoarse trying to say you know nothing! Try brushing off every fleck of the talcum! Of course you will, eventually, but by then ten years of your life would be over, and the whole circus would have moved on a long time back, with no interest whatsoever in your innocence! They kill by the sword anyone who dares live by the sword!'

We were sitting in his room, right next to mine. The gold on the laburnum was now totally gone, the trees branches scraggly, with no hint at all of their dazzling potential. The sky was low and painted in heavy colours of grey and was leaking rain in stop-and-start dribbles. It was a peculiar monsoon, refusing to open up, hovering overhead, teasing with thin fleeting showers, sudden charcoal darkenings and occasional overtures of light thunder. Looking up, Sippy would say, 'His balls have swollen up—He can't piss properly and He's complaining.'

From inside the room, through the clear glass window, after the hammering white heat of so many weeks, the day seemed cool and dark, full of poetic allure. But outside, without the air-conditioning, it was muggy and clammy, a wretched waiting.

Jai was now intense and angry—a convincing performance, it had served us well in many a sticky situation. He said, 'Okay, tell me, do you know why they are guarding you? Who is it who wanted to kill you? Why does anyone want to kill you? You only know what they are telling you. Why have you suddenly become so believing of them? So far all we've done is to trade charges and accusations with them! Accused them of lies, perjury, unconstitutional conduct, vendetta. And they've repaid the compliment. How come they are suddenly so concerned with your well-being?'

I said, 'The talcum powder.'

He said, 'Fuck off, maaderchod!'

I put my arm around him and gave him a full smile and a half-hug.

It's true that the shadows had a thick fold-over log book, a sort of police diary with a maroon cloth cover and stitched sheets. And it's true I had often caught them, at all hours of the day, making painstaking entries in it. And it's also true that they hurriedly shut it and jumped up each time I appeared. But unless they were really working their imagination, there was nothing to write.

Office, home, sports club, lawyers, restaurants, movie hall, Sara. That was the universe. Nothing to report back on; not the best of places to credibly sprinkle the talcum. The only spot in the universe that had bothered me initially was Sara's flat. I tried to give them the dodge the first few times I went to her place but that got them quite agitated, and I didn't want them alerting the police control room to track me down, sirens singing, to the boxy colourless building where I lay naked and fevered, in a paroxysm of Hindi abuse, in front of the humming Napoleon.

So I would take them along and let them rot under the sucked brown trees, imagining whatever they could. Sara stood on her toes to peep at them from the tiny window high in her bathroom, and said, 'They don't look as if they can protect you against anything. That one looks like the fat lala of my old college canteen!'

I looked at her unequal body, the promise of her fullness, and said, 'The Indian police wages war by deception. This man is nothing short of a real cool killer.'

I stood behind her, her fullness soft against my thighs, her frizzy hair smelling of some fruity shampoo under my chin, her photo shoulders in my hands, and followed her gaze. The real cool killer sat at the edge of the parking lot under a dusty papri tree in leather chappals, his bush shirt buttons open till the waist, fanning himself with a magazine in his right hand, the forefinger of his left stuck deep in his ear.

She said, moving her fullness against my thighs, 'Meditating?'

I said, 'The methods of the Indian police are deadly and inscrutable.'

Well, the inscrutable part was true. Weeks went by and no one came to tell me what was really happening, what it was all about. The shadows claimed to know nothing, and even if they did, it was unlikely to be anything beyond their basic duties. SI Hathi Ram had not shown up again after the first two visits. I refrained from calling him, though he had left his mobile number with me, or from making any other inquiries. I felt, instinctively, that this was some kind of game. To show the anxiety of Jai and the others would be to concede it. We were still in the preliminaries, the warm-up stage, limbering up, circling each other, watching the moves, trying to read apprehension and uncertainty in the other. The intensity of the real bout would depend on how well we sized up each other's attitudes and ability.

In my life I had learnt a few things about power. I knew, for one, that it fed off fear. Grand power is about control; but petty power is only about fear. At the village I had always seen my uncles thrash underlings, and the one with the most cringe got it extra. There was one, Ghoda, a low-caste, a big enough fellow who would start shrinking into a small fist the moment one of my uncles began to move in on him, and well before the first blow landed he'd let out a piercing whine. 'Hai they've killed my mother! Hai they're going to murder me today! Hai somebody save a poor man! Hai cruel lord why was I ever born!'

So loud, so piercing, were his wails that everyone working the spreading fields would know the show was about to begin. Ghoda screamed hysterically through his beatings, begging for mercy, begging forgiveness, summoning mother, god, justice, fate. No pain could have created such lament: it sprang from abject fear. And everyone enjoyed thrashing him, even my fifteen-year-old uncle, and most times the bashing only stopped when their arms were spent.

It was not unusual for them, sitting around on their charpoys under the shisham tree in the front yard, getting bored, to suddenly say, to entertain themselves, or a visitor, 'Want to see the circus? Ghode da gana? The horse who sings!' The low-caste would start to shriek from the moment he was summoned. The terror in his eyes would excite everyone. One of my uncles would look at the visitor—at us—and say, 'Ever heard such wonderful singing in the city? On your Bush radio? Now listen to the fantastic tunes our local Radio Ghoda produces!' And with fist and foot, stick and stump, they would fall upon him.

The cops, I knew from my years at work, were pretty much the same, all purveyors of petty power. They needed their daily diet of fear. They woke every morning deflated dolls, and as the day wore on, filled themselves to fullness and more by drinking in dread. There was no cop I had known who felt more complete than in the presence of the helpless. At such a moment, most of them became whole and complete to the point of being cinematic, speaking with a sense of drama, intuitively aware that an unequal relationship creates a stage that demands theatre.

I knew if anyone—from the lowly shadows to the dizzy heights of the great state—if anyone detected fear in my eyes they would become ravenous. For, through the centuries, we had not only been mahaphuddus when vassals, but also had a track record for being barbaric mahaphuddus when in control.

So I asked nothing and was told nothing, and the weeks rolled by, and the shadows came and went, with an occasional face changing and transiting through my life namelessly.

I was hard at work performing my fortnightly duty when Felicia knocked on the door. The room was dark, the lights off, the thick curtains drawn. I preferred it that way, it made it less difficult for me. But before I could move, Dolly—that's what her family called her though on our wedding card she was Sangeeta—Dolly held my shoulders, and stopped me from getting up.

It was Saturday morning and Dolly's school was closed and she had reached for me as I slept, unknotting my pajama, cuddling up against me. Now her long blue nightie, with tiny flying golden cherubs, was pulled up around her breasts and my pajama was around my knees and I was labouring. She had her slim athletic legs wrapped tight around my middle, keeping me in place as I floundered in her swamp of wanting, struggling to be man enough to stay there. My face was buried in her neck, under her short straight hair where it was bristly as a boy's, and turned away as far from her mouth as possible. She was panting and moaning, occasionally calling my name. I had my eyes shut tight—and Sara on her knees—as I tried hard to not die in the swamp before Dolly was delivered. I was already losing the battle, wilting, despite Sara's pungent ripeness, when Felicia knocked. I reached for the opportunity, but Dolly held me back in desperation, flexing her wrapped limbs frantically. Her seeking need made it worse. I tried to imagine the hard wet grasp of Sara's reluctance, her maddening mix of hauteur and desire. And then Felicia knocked again, and that was it. I stopped trying and Dolly too went still.

We were both coated in sweat.

Without rolling off her, I shouted, 'Yes?'

In her diffident tribal accent Felicia said, 'One Huthyam has come to see you.'

I patted Dolly's damp forehead and got up, knotting my fallen pajama. When I switched on the bedside lamp she turned over on her side, her cherub nightie still around her dipping waist, her fair slim legs curled up, the dark line of her ass sharp and straight, the yellow light catching the wet shine on it. I threw the sheet over her, straightened my kurta, patted my hair in place, and opened the door.

Coal-dark Felicia, rancid with the sweat pouring out of her body, was waiting right outside. She scuttled away, trailing a broom in her hand. She was terrified of me. We had never exchanged a full sentence.

Huthyam was sitting in the study, in his pointed black shoes and loose bush shirt, caressing *The Naked Lunch*. He had been to the barber recently, for the grey hair was spiky like a mowed lawn and the bushy moustache gleaming black with dye. The pudgy avuncular face was smiling; the eyes hard and still.

He gave me a limp hand and said, in his low voice, 'Saturday is for the wife and the family and I am sorry to bother you, but you know for the police there is no Saturday or Sunday, no holi or diwali, no winter or summer, no day or night, no wrong or right, no mother or father, no wife or girlfriend.'

I said, 'Hathi Ramji, you all do great service to the nation.'

He said, 'Please sir, please don't mock us! We all know how much water there is in this milk. In fact, the whole world knows. No one trusts the police, no one likes the police. And it is true, were we not such eunuchs the very look of this country would change. But we have to just do what we are told to do. We are meant to serve the people, but those above us decide how we have to serve them. Sometimes when we are working over a misguided boy in the thana and he is screaming too much, we tell him, "Maaderchod, keep quiet, just remember we are serving you, be grateful." We do what we are told. We cannot ask why. If we start asking why, there will be a mountain of whys and no police. And that would be worse. Some milk in the water is better than none. At least there is the illusion of it. In our poor houses they put two spoons of milk in a glass of water and the child drinks it as milk and is happy. We are a poor country, and we have to feed ourselves illusions when there is no milk. Don't be harsh on us. We are only one of our great country's many illusions. Arre sir, if you look around you'll see that all of us are basically just merchants of fantasies. Khyali pulao, sut-sut ke khao.'

He said all this without a single inflection, in his low even voice, slapping the two halves of the orange-cream biscuit together like a pair of cymbals, providing accompaniment. Such equanimity could come only from a long and intimate association with violence and injustice. I had seen it only in veteran cops, perhaps doctors and dictators have it too. A meditative calm about the nature of the world, far removed from the exhorting moralities of textbooks and art and media and religion. A zone of functionality not inclined to agitate over the death of the body, not inclined to exalt the body's sacredness. Men died, evil was done, wrong was often—fairly or unfairly—right, and there was nothing to breast-beat about. You could spend your life thinking about it, or deal with it. In fact, even as one spoke, there was more death and chaos storming in through the door. Flood, earthquake, rape, murder, arson, bomb blasts, calamity, germ, terror. So you set aside the ululations, and simply did your job and went home, and sometimes if you had to work on Saturday, you just got out and did it, banging biscuit halves like cymbals and caressing *The Naked Lunch*.

Huthyam said, 'You are very safe.'

I nodded.

He said, 'People like you are very important for the country. It is our job to make sure not a hair on your body is harmed. You are very safe.'

I nodded and waited.

He said, 'We are going to make you even safer.'

I said, 'What's happened?'

He said, 'All is well, no problems. But we are just increasing your security to the next level.'

I said, 'Hathi Ramji, don't treat me like a chutiya. I too am a man of the world. Tell me what's happening.'

He said, in the same flat tone, 'There is nothing, sir, that I am hiding from you. All is well. Just that we've received orders to up your cover.'

I said, 'But I thought the boys had been caught.'

He said, 'Yes, they are with us. We are taking care of them, giving them a good time.'

I said, 'So who are they? You still haven't told me anything.'

He said, 'We are talking to them. Gently, patiently. You know how reluctant guests behave? Always slow to open up, taking their time to feel at home, to start speaking freely and happily? We are giving them a good time, settling them in. Soon they will want to share their whole lives with us.'

I said, 'So there is nothing at all that you can tell me?'

He said, 'Nothing. Nothing that I know. Except that you are safe. My job is to keep you safe. The investigation is someone else's work. They will not tell me anything either. I am a very small nut-bolt in a very big machine. The big machine tells me what to do, I cannot ask it why. For if every nut-bolt like me begins to ask why, there will be a big mountain of whys and no machine.'

I just looked at him—so quiet, so unamused, so apparently sincere—as he delicately stuck the two halves of the biscuit together and placed it deep inside his mouth.

Before the weekend was out I had begun to feel like a drug lord, or more aptly like a political villain in a Hindi film. The category to which I had been upped sounded ominously important. Z. The one man thrilled by it was Vijyant. He said to me, 'Who knows, they might soon make it Z+!' For him the pomp of my new situation was unbearably giddy.

Well, from having one plainclothes cop with a 9mm pistol as a shadow I had now acquired a virtual platoon:

Three uniformed bodyguards, cradling mean, perforated carbines.

One middle-aged leader of the pack, black 9mm stuffed into crotch.

One white Ambassador car with a civilian driver.

A small heap of sandbags outside my house.

Another small heap of sandbags outside the office.

Two stationary policemen in uniform behind each, with heavy self-loading rifles.

A spotlight that shone bright on the house gate all night, while leaving the sandbagged policemen in the dark.

A large khaki-olive tent—its mouth always half-open as if in dismay—at the end of the back lane, to which the platoon retired by turns.

Next to it—a sackcloth shower cubicle, that began at a height of one foot and ended at four, held up by four bamboo staves, with a floor of flat, loose bricks, supplied water by a rubber pipe pulled from our backyard and slung around the neem tree.

A big police truck that appeared every few hours and with a great clanging of its tailgate dispensed tea and food to the garrison.

And a few sets of walkie-talkies that crackled gibberish at all hours.

The pack leader and two of the carbine boys travelled in the white Ambassador, tailing me ferociously, as if tied to my fender. The third carbine boy travelled with me in my car, sitting next to me as I drove, the black carbine cradled across his chest, its short barrel, riddled with little holes, pointing out the windscreen.

At the back, mulling his place in the new scheme of things, sat one of the original shadows. If it was Vijyant, it was with a puffed chest and a new sense of importance; if it was belly or phlegm, with a mousy air and a sense of great diminishment.

Jai said, stroking his beard, 'They are setting you up! Setting you up! Much too clever. The maaderchods are much too clever! They still haven't told you a thing about who, what, why—in the meantime they are doing all the right things. Making all the appropriate moves. So when the crap hits the ceiling, they'll shrug their shoulders and say, Look we did everything to take care of him, to protect him, but if he wants the powder up his nose what can we possibly do!'

My in-laws behaved like Vijyant, luxuriating more in my suddenly acquired stature than worrying about an assassin's bullet. Sangeeta/Dolly/folly, in her fair-foolish way had no opinion on any of it (except to keep repeating in that horribly solemn tone—Please be careful), but her ugly mother would monitor the platoon as if she were a recruiting agent. Where are they? Are they outside? Have they had tea? Biscuits? Shall we send them something to eat? One of them seems to have changed? What happened to that tall Jat? You have a Bengali among them now! That fellow, that Musalman, he doesn't look trustworthy—ask for him to be replaced. In the DDA block in which she lived she would inform her neighbours when I was visiting and encourage them to peer out their windows to gawk at the army. A buzz would go around the moment our cars stopped and the shadows jumped out, flashing their hardware. Sometimes she would have some fool from next door in for tea, some middling government officer or company executive who would try and give me his stupid thesis on the state of India and ask me searching questions about things—politics, religion, stock markets, bureaucracy—which made my acid rise. As the man in the iron mask, I'd give differing nods and they would, anxiously and gratefully, supply the answers themselves.

My mother, of course, only wailed. She would look at me, trailed by guns and uniforms, and start loudly lamenting her fate, my fate, the fate of her forefathers; start begging forgiveness for her misdeeds, my misdeeds, her forefathers' misdeeds; pledge atonement in this life, the next, and the next. 'My lord let no harm come to my son—take my life instead.' If I was not looking she would fall upon the platoon: 'Even if you have to give up your lives, nothing must happen to him. Promise me! All of you promise me! Promise me now!' She was insufferable.

My father watched it all, her and me and the ululations, in near silence and with averted eyes. Scared to speak to me; scared to speak to her. He stuck quietly to his dietary regime—no oils, no sugar—and to his morning-evening walks and focused simply on the central concern of his life, his unending struggle with paper. The reading of newspapers and the filing of bank statements and tax returns and insurance papers and postal deposits and telephone bills and water bills and cable TV bills and property papers and loan repayments and recurring deposits and share certificates. A full life of hiding behind papers thrown at him; shuffling them all day like a cardsharp waiting for the tables to fill and the big game to begin. Watching him sitting there, in his beige golf cap, which he'd bought in Nainital from a roadside vendor, reading every line of his two newspapers, he filled me with pity and contempt: the cardsharp whose tables would never fill, whose game would never begin. Once, the shuffled papers had been examination-sheets, job applications, account opening forms, passport applications, bank loan applications, housing applications, leave applications, medical applications, departmental memorandums, governmental communiqués, officers' instructions, transfer requests, promotion requests, school reports.

A life devoted to the management of paper. Like my father-in-law, a clerk for all occasions. The reality of the shadows—the carbines, the walkie-talkies, the pistols—was not something he could easily comprehend. Had the security detail come as a three-page memo, with a formal number to it, some gibberish code of alphabets and numerals, he would have instantly absorbed it and asked me a few questions.

My relatives, of course, thought I'd become the prime minister. They crawled out of every sad hole to phone us, visit us, invite us—people I had not heard from in years, some whose names barely rang a bell, cousins from my father's side, mother's side, uncles, aunts, old friends of the family, from parts of Delhi I had never visited, some from places which I had never even heard of. Typically the phone would ring when I was in the middle of a meeting and an energetic unknown voice would exclaim, 'Oye, we saw you on TV last night! You were looking django! What fun it was! We told everyone! So tell us when are you coming over for dinner? And where's masiji?' Worse still were the older lot, who launched into a litany of concern and blessings: 'You must take care. Don't go out in the night. Don't trust anyone. You can't trust anyone these days. These are very dangerous people. They can do anything. But remember god is with you. Guru Nanak said those the lord picks to protect, nothing in the world can kill. I am going to go to our Santji and get a protective ring for you. Once you start wearing it you won't need any guard-shards. And when did you grow a moustache?'

When did I grow a moustache? In the thirty years you haven't seen me.

Soon enough, I had to corner each of the three women individually—mother, mother-in-law and Dolly/folly—and terrorize them into not accepting any invites or inviting anyone home. I did not want to see anyone, or talk to anyone, even on the phone. They were free to go and meet whom they pleased. Dolly/folly looked chastened and compliant, the mother-in-law sullen and swollen, and

Mother let loose a blood-curdling wail. I wanted to bang her head against the wall.

All her life Mother had chanted the Bhagavad Gita every morning, loud and long, not understanding a word of it. Sitting in her gaudy puja corner, surrounded by gods in brass and silver and cheap framed prints in lurid colours, she'd let rip early every morning, after a bath, before a single defiling sip of water had travelled down her gullet. Sitting cross-legged on her prayer mat, her head covered with a dupatta, she'd rock back and forth chanting raucously, the Gita Press hardbound edition from Gorakhpur lying open on a walnut-wood stand in front of her, the cotton wick dipped in thick mustard oil burning strong, and vapours of sharply sweet incense curling about, completing the hokum aspect. When she was done—hitting a crescendo of shouted-out exclamations to the gods—she'd mark her page with an old peacock feather and devoutly wrap the book in a red satin cloth. Eighteen days into the cycle, when she got to chapter 18, the end—Om Tat Sat!—she'd start over. Again and again. Month on month. Year on year. And never understanding a word of it: 'To protect the righteous and to destroy the sinners and to establish dharma, I manifest myself from yuga to yuga. O Arjuna! He who thus knows the nature of my divine birth and action, he is not born again when he dies, but attains me. Many, purified through the meditation of knowledge, have immersed themselves in me and sought refuge in me, discarding attachment, fear and anger.'

In all her decades of chanting, Mother had managed to discard nothing but her sanity. And all that she had acquired was the wail, which she deployed recklessly. I often wondered how my father had been surviving her. If he had ever come out of his paper tomb he would have surely strangled her, if only to cut out the noise.

Sara reacted like Jai, with the informed world view of the urban sophisticate. Looking immediately for the story behind the story. Unlike him, she didn't look for white powder conspiracies. Typically, she peered through the opposite end of the telescope. She was not interested in how power wanted to fix me—through lead or talcum—but how power manipulated the disempowered to do its bidding. From the moment the first shadows had shown up, she had slit her wrists, fretting more about their situation than mine.

Each time I'd walk through her door she'd start the inquiries: 'Who's there? Belly? Phlegm? Vijyant?' Then she'd stand on her toes, peer through the high bathroom window while I held her unequal body from behind, and harangue me about my indifference. 'I hope, when the moment comes, they show as little concern for you as you've shown for them!' From there she'd rapidly spiral into a rage, 'Why should they be risking their lives for you? What's so valuable about you, mr peashooter? I can bet you their lives are more worthy, more deserving of protection! Each of them probably takes care of a desperately struggling family—toiling wife, ailing parents, children in unaffordable schools! While you, mr peaman and your lovely ms white lead the good fraudulent life, hating each other and your idiotic parentage, and pretending to save the nation.'

After she'd gone on for a bit, walking up and down the room, photo arms waving, I'd say, 'Bloody whore!' through clenched teeth, and her breath would catch. Her babble of baiting would grow louder, more disjointed. 'The state uses these poor buggers for their own damn end! They are cops. They should be protecting the ordinary folk who need protection and have none, who are harassed by anyone with a bit of money and muscle! They should be in the bloody villages and the slums, working for the wretched, not spending their days escorting an elitist bastard, while he wanders about looking for his weekly screw!' I'd watch her impassively and when the moment was right, spit, 'Saali randi!' From there to backing her against the wall was mere minutes of trading abuse—in English and Hindi, juvenile, repetitive, mostly the absurd naming of genitalia. Just as I'd nail her to the wall, her ideological tirade would turn into a taunting sexual challenge, now purely in Hindi. 'Arre take your little luli away somewhere else! I've seen scores like you! Longer than you, thicker than you! Take your little matchstick away and light a fire in dollyfolly! What's needed here is a flaming torch!'

She was made to be taken standing, and when I was in her, her photo shoulders braced against the wall, her toes stretched, her body curved like a bow, when I was deep in her, holding up her fullness with my hands, her tone would begin to change. As I kissed her cigarette-mouth, it would became increasingly tender, soft, full of endearments, gratitude; all Hindi would now vanish, only sweet English phrases would bloom. Yes please, my god you are lovely, how good you feel, love how you move, I miss you so much, don't stop, why can't you see me every day, god you are amazing, love what you are doing, love what you are doing, love what you are doing.

Later, naked in front of Bonaparte, flat on her back, she would begin to slit her wrists again. Now in a gentler way, teasing out speculation about the cops and the killers.

Slowly, over the weeks, she had become convinced that the whole thing was a frame-up. But, after the peculiar way her mind worked, it wasn't me she was worried about. She thought I was more than capable of taking care of myself. 'Fully bloody enlisted member of India's most elite caste, the only true brahmins of modern India—the upper middle-class Anglo! Right school, right language, right friends! Patronized by the system, understands the system, can work the system inside out, and outside in! In fact, pretty much invented the system! The one fucking caste that the Brits created, to ruthlessly dominate old Dr Manu's four!'

I made a note to gift her a copy of the *Manusmriti*. But I knew what she was tilting at. She was basically concerned about the poor sods the system was using in the frame-up. Those who were supposed to guard me; and those who were supposed to have shot me. In her words, India's true low-castes, with neither money nor influence—ruthlessly deployed against each other to fulfil the agenda of the master class. Whose fully bloody paid-up member I was.

In the beginning it was just about her wanting information from me, about both shadows and shooters, and I failing to provide any, which led to her rants. 'How can you not want to know? How can you be so indifferent?' And so on, till the nailing on the wall. Then it became a growing suspicion of a sinister plot. In this story I was just a decoy, my fate unimportant; and the cops were minor victims, collaterally damaged for having to fuss over me. The actual victims were the assassins. These were innocent men the system wanted to fix—for reasons of business, politics, religion or terror, this we did not know yet.

Yes, Jai's talcum had been sprinkled.

I was the talcum.

The killers—the killers were the real victims.

3

MR LINCOLN MEETS FROCK RAJA

That year the rains meandered on right into September in a kind of epileptic way, with sudden fits of rain, a sharp cascade of large luscious drops that would stream suddenly, bringing back memories of childhood monsoons when a daily soaking was inevitable. And even as the fit uncurled its full force, before the first hour was out, the drains overflowed, the roads flooded, and the traffic snarled at every intersection, every underpass, the mouth of every colony. Sara's master class would suffer stalled cars; her low-castes would slip down uncovered manholes. At such a time it was difficult to believe this was a modern city—seemingly so organized, so ornamental under clear skies and bright sun, its roads wide, its trees lush, its flyovers leaping up to the heavens.

The canker seemed to be concrete.

In an excess of sprucing up, the city had been choked. Delhiites, seeking ever new ways of displaying their affluence, had bought up every kind of new tile and stone hitting the market and laid it out where they could. Marble—green, pink, Bhutanese, Nepalese. Stone—Jaisalmer gold, Kota grey, Agra red, Jaipur pink. Granite—black, brown, speckled. Tiles—Italian, Moroccan, Spanish. Sidewalks, backyards, gardens, driveways, open areas, walkways—everything was being paved and cemented. Every pore blocked, every breath stemmed: the earth was given a hard, impregnable gloss. The fat drops simply bounced off it.

And then, as if in reparation, days would go by without a falling drop, and the power supply would fluctuate and the feeble inverters die and the thrum of generators and the stench of diesel fumes would stain the air, and the swelter would get under skins and fray the nerves, and the city would curse and scan the festering skies.

And Sippy, in his odd moment of lucidity would say, 'Sirji, it is a curse of the times—just as there is very little milk left in milk, there is very little rain left in the rain.'

There was time for idle bullshit like the weather because we had nothing else to do. Jai's friends had by now completely lost their stomach for the enterprise. They had been slowly turning off the taps for months; the magazine had steadily dwindled from a hundred and twelve pages to ninety-six to seventy-two to forty-eight. At each stage Jai had addressed the staff as if he were Abraham Lincoln delivering the Gettysburg Address, assuring them that immortality and the turnaround would both be theirs, in fact were just days away. All each of us had to do was to resolutely stand by our posts and keep firing. At what, he didn't say. The fucker was so eloquent, with his burning eyes and waving arms, that even I fell for his talk. Each time, when the trance broke, I thought: through millennia men like him have led thousands to their untimely graves.

Now we were down to forty pages—the magazine was as spineless as a pamphlet—and nearly one month's salaries in arrears. The investors, Jai's school friends, three of them, christened Chutiya-Nandan-Pandey by us, had stopped taking our calls, and even their executive assistants, though unfailingly polite—'we'll certainly pass on the message'—had frost in their voice. Unusually, the accounts man Santoshbhai, an old-timer with a Hitler moustache and six strands of hair glued across his bald pate, was still very warm each time we called him pleading for a transfer of funds. But, of course, he was helpless. 'Arre bhai, I only count the money, not earn it. If I could give it, you wouldn't have to ask twice. Just get me one nod from the chhote sahib' was all he would say. But chhote sahib, Nandan of Chutiya-Nandan-Pandey, was busy imbibing Scotch and slapping flesh and was nowhere to be reached.

In desperation, not knowing what to do but needing to do something, we'd keep calling Santoshbhai in the crazed hope that one day, suddenly, miraculously, he would be reckless enough to send us the money and explain it to chhote sahib later. Like the old good-hearted family retainer in Hindi films who finally earns the ear of the young Turk.

I have to say I was not surprised things had gone badly. I had always been sceptical of the trio, and I don't think they liked me either. In his blindly enthusiastic way Jai had been profuse in spelling out their virtues when we first set out. 'Good guys, have made their millions, not really chasing money any more, want to do social stuff, things for the soul, I've seen them since they were in their chuddies, always been decent chaps not rich brats, anyway there'll never be the perfect investor for what we want to do, these guys are about as good as it'll ever get, at least they talk our language, at least we'll be able to hear each other, think of the guy we went to in CP, who wanted our asset sheets—we didn't even know what he was talking about, think of the buggers we've worked for, surely nothing can be worse than them!'

Actually these guys were worse. They were complete fools. Not smart enough to just focus on making the money; stupid enough to have bought this magazine thing from Jai in the middle of a wrist-slitting festival one posh evening.

The very first time Jai took me to meet them, at a hotel bar, I concluded they were chutiyas. Chutiya-Nandan-Pandeys. They were dressed sharply in crisp fresh clothes, with manicured hands and hair, and were awash in cologne. Very briefly, in the beginning, they had American accents—two of them had done university abroad. In between struggling to ask serious questions they had cracked dumb jokes and guffawed loudly, randomly slapping each other's backs, hands, thighs; they were still in their school dorm getting giggly about the geography teacher's bra-strap.

They were all garment exporters and had earned countless millions working sweat factories that supplied dirt-cheap apparel for the big stores of the West. Bondhu Ram fashioning Calvin Klein—that sort of thing. Two of them did undergarments and were called Kuchha King and Kuchha Singh (he was a shorn sardar). The third was called Frock Raja, after his special act. Coming from the same posh school as Jai, incapable of much else, they had been set up by their fathers at a time of great export incentives. Before economic playing fields were levelled, they had made enough for five generations. The chasm between Bondhu Ram and Calvin Klein—between Jaunpur and Fifth Ave—was big enough to accommodate vast wealth and all its excesses.

The bar was all burnished wood and glass with windows the size of walls through which I watched a white-skinned mamma working the length of the heaven-blue pool on the other side. She wore a yellow bikini and opened her mouth in a big O each time she broke a stroke. She should have worn an orange burqa and kept her mouth closed. The water in the pool sparkled as if each drop had been diligently polished before being flowed in by the super servile waiters who whispered by our side. Most of India would have gladly drunk it, like sherbet.

Remembering Guruji, I had quickly become the man in the iron mask, dug into the bowl of salted peanuts and settled back to watch the proceedings. Jai had striven to humour his pals with weak smiles and fey ripostes. He had an amazing ability to shrink himself down to the dumbest fuck. Mr Lincoln Goes to the People.

By the time the third round of whiskies had arrived, they were already talking about the first anniversary party—the venue, the music and the starlets they'd like to invite. They had given up trying to involve me and were in the swim of their own happy lake. I had, meantime, fed my entire bowl of peanuts to the iron mask and was now burrowing deep into Jai's, setting in motion the engines of great flatulence.

The parting was demonstrative, with effusive hugs and loud wisecracks. Mr Lincoln was flung from embrace to embrace. On the granite-floored lobby of the hotel there was much of this, very similar, noisy happiness reverberating all around. The fastest growing national affliction: opulence euphoria.

I had pumped hands, sick with the peanuts.

When they had been driven off in their Mercedeses and Pajeros, and we were waiting for our small cars in the foyer, Jai said, 'So what do you think?' I said, 'Chutiya-Nandan-Pandeys.'

Jai had laughed and said, 'Who else would back crazies like us?'

The next time, we were invited to meet them at Frock Raja's farmhouse. It was five acres of la-la land, just behind the boxy Vasant Kunj flats where Sara lived. There were water-spurting Scandinavian marble mermaids with large Indian breasts, a topiary of dinosaurs, a swimming pool shaped like a flounced skirt—with a submerged bar at the waistband—bulb-lit Halloween masks on pruned branches, undulating manicured lawns with colourful steel birds poised for takeoff, lines of mast trees trimmed to precisely the same height flanking every pathway, piped Clayderman tinkles at every corner of the garden, a Yeats pond with the fifty-nine swans of Coole, a dining-room in a mock stable with two handsome horses tethered in a corner for atmospherics, so you could chew to the music of shuffling flanks and scuffing hooves.

Inside was an equal riot of the imagination. A mad medley of statuary, paintings, carpets, fabrics, lamps, furniture, antiques, waterfalls—far eastern Buddhas, Greek Aphrodites, Wild West saddles and sombreros, old flintlocks, Japanese silk screens, Amazonian machetes, African masks, a massive ebony rhinoceros, Persian rugs. You negotiated your way through the decorative traffic, bending and braking. Mr Lincoln made slippery sounds of appreciation as Frock Raja guided the tour with practised aplomb. I had jumped into the iron mask at the sight of the first big-breasted mermaid in the driveway.

After we had been led through many sitting-rooms, many dining-rooms, many bars, many enclosed verandas, we repaired to The Stable—the bar-cum-dining hall where the horses shuffled. The two large handsome chestnuts were tethered beyond a low glass and wood partition, slightly lower than the planked floor we sat on. I suppose so you could—if that was your thing—look deep into their sad eyes. Their skin shone, the tart smell of horse flesh was contained to a minimum; they had probably been hoovered for the party. Mr Lincoln asked searching questions about their breed and speed. Mr Lincoln Goes to the Races.

I fed my mouth fistfuls of roasted cashew-nuts. Iron Mask Inaugurates the Flatulence Factory.

Kuchha King, Kuchha Singh, and Frock Raja guffawed and slapped each other wherever they could. Messrs Chutiya-Nandan-Pandey Discuss Bra Strap of Geography Teacher.

At one point, Frock Raja used a remote to turn off all the lights. Suddenly above us shone thousands of faux stars and galaxies. Given the snorting horses, we could have been out in the Wild West, under the open sky, preparing for a gunfight at OK Corral. It was quite something. Mr Lincoln broke into appreciative mewling noises. Frock Raja spoke of the peace of the universe, and gave many loud sighs of satisfaction.

Then the lights came back on and everyone fell again to slapping flesh and to debating the virtues of different single malt whiskies. Highland, lowland, speyside, backside, bog, peat, nose, palate, amber, gold, glen, fen, dour, sour, bouquet, shouquet. And Michael Jackson! That befuddled me, till I realized it was another man and not the dancing alien. Throughout, Mr Lincoln dazzled—all waving arms and burning eyes. Fully worthy of the bloodshed of unsuspecting investors.

The happy exchange of loud claims and famous names only shifted when Jai tentatively brought up the specifics of the deal, the money needed for the project, the equity split. In the next hour all the expansiveness of big-breasted mermaids and thigh-slapping jokes and star-spangled firmaments and glen-fen dour-sour faded as the three of them systematically disembowelled Jai.

Mr Lincoln was reduced to a gawky, gangly, uncertain Abraham to the sound of shuffling horse flanks, and while the man in the iron mask ruthlessly destroyed every cashew-nut in sight, a deal was concluded that gave us barely a third of what we had been hoping for. We all leaned forward and shook hands to mark the partnership. Then the three fell once again to slapping flesh and guffawing. By now Abraham was in short-pants, all eloquence a faded memory.

Outside, on the driveway of mock stone, Abraham was flung from embrace to embrace, while the mermaid ran clear water from her mouth. Trailing them all, I grabbed a quick feel of a faux Venus de Milo's alabaster breast. It fit in my palm and felt quite good.

When we were safely out of the big iron gates and nearing the concrete boxes of Vasant Kunj, a recovering Mr Lincoln, climbing back into full pants, said, 'Sad bastards! Sweatshop merchants! Bloody chutiyas! Anyway we got what we wanted!'

I looked at him, and sick with the salted nuts, rumbled my stomach in response.

I didn't tell anyone any of this. My parents I hadn't spoken to about anything substantial since I started earning my first rupee. Dolly/folly was simply too dumb to ask anything or to be told anything. And the narrow world of in-laws, recurring deposits and school reports that my sister inhabited had no room for anything but our annual transaction of the rakhi. This time I left even Sara, my usual confidante, out of it. I knew she would break into an uncontainable rant if she heard about the horse dining-room and the marble mermaids. And this time it wouldn't be foreplay for the nailing on the wall, but genuine disgust. I could intuit where the line on these things lay with her and the three bozos were way beyond the boundary.

All I told her was that the investors were friends of Jai, and I had christened them Chutiya-Nandan-Pandey. That pleased her a great deal. She said, 'Good! Abuse is the revenge of the proletariat.'

I didn't tell anyone—bar Guruji, that is. Over time I had learnt to keep nothing from him, not even Sara. He had a way of divining all that was happening in my life; and this time I desperately needed his guidance. Before we signed the shareholders' agreement, I jumped into the car one evening and hit the Grand Trunk Road. By eight o'clock I had turned off the Markanda bridge, skirted Shahabad to my right, and in the luminous dark found the old banyan that marked the dirt track to his ashram. With the many lengths of flapping red cloth—some new, most fraying—tied to its branches it appeared alive and moving. Guruji's followers were growing, their wishes draping the ancient tree.

I drove slowly, in second gear, the car heaving like a boat on choppy waters. The rains and the tractors and the bullock carts—with their harrows and trolleys—had gouged holes and gullies in the track, and you had to be careful where the wheels went. Each time you got the alignment wrong and hit troughs on both sides, you heard the sickening sound of the undercarriage dragging the ground. The headlights dipped and skewed in a sea of black. Dust rose in small explosions, drenching the car. A few times I had to stop dead for it to settle, so I could see the way ahead. When I stopped I could hear, distantly behind me, on the main road, the screech and roar of tearing trucks.

Soon the lights of Guruji's dera were visible. Four of them: one, strong, on the roof; and three, diffuse, catching the extremities of the boundary walls. There was a sentry at the iron gates, and I had to lower my window so he could recognize me. He was an old man with a flowing white beard and a blue turban loosely wound around his head. He carried an old double-barrel with two triggers, its strap made of thick green canvas. A bandolier of red cartridges was slung across his chest.

Guruji said the covenant of spiritual power was unchanging and clear: he could protect others but not himself; he could enrich others but not himself; he could heal others but not himself. He alone could take care of the multitudes; but the multitudes, collectively, needed to take care of him.

It was the answer I would have given to the cynicisms of Sara and Jai, if I could be bothered about them. The vanities—and limitations—of reason.

The dera was rudimentary. Just naked bricks pressed together untidily with grey cement. I parked the car by a makeshift shed of six slim pillars capped by corrugated iron sheets. A part of the open shed was taken up by Guruji's white Sumo—gifted to him by a grateful flour-mill owner from Yamunanagar, whose truant daughter's marriage he had salvaged—and the rest was stacked with charpoys that had been stood on their sides. During the day these charpoys were dragged out and clustered around the large neem, each one laden with many a peasant body.

At this hour the dera was muted. Guruji withdrew from the throng at six every evening to meditate in the inner sanctum and then was only available to some, selectively, after eight, once he had emerged, bathed with cold water and eaten his dinner.

All around, green fields washed right up against the brick walls of the dera. The fields were in ankle-deep water now—to grow paddy—and the pulsing moonlight bounced off them tantalizingly. Now and then one heard the guttural query of a bull-frog, picked up and loudly repeated. Sometimes this was followed by a tiny splash as one of them decided to take a swim. The hum of cicadas underlay it all. The main road was not visible from here, but occasional screams of traffic wafted through.

Someone called out to me from the roof, leaning out over the low cement railing. The straight, steep flight of stairs, without a protective balustrade, was around the back. When I walked around the main hall, where Guruji received his disciples, I could smell the acrid dung cakes being burnt in the open kitchens. There were enough chullahs here to prepare a repast for more than a thousand people—an event which happened twice a year, on Guruji's birthday and on the samadhi day of his Baba, 31 December.

Last year, from her little eyehole of Anglo activism, Sara had attacked me. 'You are as dumb a dick as the guys who prance around at idiotic parties shouting Happy New Year! You want to get your rocks off doing some pseudo mystical shit with pirs and babas! You may as well go and jerk around at Djinns! Get a proper mix of pseudo modernity and pseudo mysticism!' She was angry. She wanted us to usher in the new year sitting in bed watching Costa-Gavras's *Z*. Followed, presumably, by an invective carnival. And at the stroke of midnight I would scream, Saali randi!

Instead, at the midnight hour, I had chosen to witness a greater frenzy at Guruji's. As his devotees jammed the dera in their hundreds—wrapped in coarse blankets, faces hooded against the biting cold, children asleep in their arms, sitting, standing, huddled everywhere—as they chanted in a growing fervour, in his small inner room Guruji had begun to sway like a palm tree in high wind.

He was seated on the old maroon satin cushion with gold tassels that had once belonged to Babaji and was his to sit upon only one night in the year. On the wall behind him were framed pictures of

Hindu gods and goddesses, of Buddha, Mahavira, Jesus Christ, and in Persian calligraphy, the praise of Allah, all lit up with special garlands of tiny twinkling lights.

Guruji was naked but for his dark red dhoti, his body splendid in its spareness, the ribs etched clean, the sinews taut wires. His long thick hair streaked with silver was loose, and in flowing motion, as Guruji rotated with gathering speed from the waist. His legs were crossed—the ankles clear over the thighs—and still as stone. His torso was rubber.

He sat on a wooden dais. There was no one near him but his old mother, a tiny insect of a woman with delicate features and radiant eyes, her snow-white head covered with a white dupatta. A gold stud shone on her nose but her arms were bereft of bangles. She held on to Guruji's left ankle with one bony hand. She was there to hold on to him; to keep him, when the moment came, from ascending into unreturnable regions.

Just six inches below him, off the dais, the room was packed with his most loyal and intimate devotees, some cross-legged, some on their haunches, and some on their knees. Hundreds of incense sticks created a slow swirling mist, drowning out the smell of sweat and blankets.

I was fighting to retain my position at the open door, which was jammed with people wedged in sideways. My right hand was clamped to the wooden frame above to anchor my place. The small open window opposite was crammed with a dozen wide-eyed faces. Behind us, all the way through the narrow corridor, out into the open courtyard, packed bodies oscillated gently, pushing forward for ingress, being pushed back, their movement keeping time to the chant: Bhole, bhole, bam bhole! Bhole, bhole, bam bhole! Old-fashioned, open-mouthed loudspeakers made of tin were lashed to the pillars and trees, and someone was at the microphone, pacing the believers.

As the minutes ticked to the stroke of midnight, the chant went into allegro and Guruji—in a meditative trance—began to rotate faster and faster at the waist. His old mother held true to his ankle, her eyes washed with the same wonderment that was reflected in every eye in the room. All fidgeting, every distraction, had died. The room was barely breathing. Suddenly, inexplicably, Guruji's wiry body began to lose speed, every rotation a little slower than the last. The mother looked at her son, concern filling her face. Then she turned her head and motioned with her eyes to one of the loyal minders, Bhura, a middle-aged Majhbi Sikh with a polio leg, who lived at the dera and served Guruji at all hours. Bhura scanned the window, the door, the room. At the far corner was a group of six-seven women, of all ages, very old to young, huddled close together under brown blankets, faces covered to their eyebrows.

Trailing his bad leg, Bhura picked his way with his right foot, planting it by nudging aside the bodies. Every eye tracked him. Reaching the corner he bent low to the ear of a fat bibi with the face of a bulldog and rolls of flesh hanging off her arms. She heard him with a cupped left hand, and then began to whisper to her caboodle with a cupped right. There was a hushed exchange. Now the fat bibi had caught hold of the ear of a pretty young girl and was twisting it. The girl grimaced, pulled her face away, rose, and averting her eyes, minced her way through the crowd and out the door, squeezing past us with some difficulty. Even great pirs were daunted by the blood of a woman.

The old mother's face relaxed and she nodded at Bhura, who was now back at his station near the door. The lame retainer took up the chant with a loud roar. Guruji's gyrations again picked up pace. His torso moved in full circles, his hair flew. The chanting intensified. Now his head began to rotate to a different rhythm, the neck supple rubber. In no time he became a blur, gyrating separately and swiftly at the waist and the neck. His lower limbs remained still as stone, grounded by his mother's bony claw.

Suddenly he whooped—a kind of strange preternatural sound

emerging from the depths of his belly. The room froze in anticipation. Guruji's neck swivelled like a top and his thick long hair whipped about his face at blinding speed, obscuring his face. An occasional glimpse revealed his eyes were closed tight and his features twisted. Many in the room clasped their hands in obeisance and in prayer. Guruji's old mother bowed her head low to escape being lashed by his flying locks.

There was another deep whoop, a rumble from some unknown place. In clenched excitement, the man next to me began to shake and mumble: 'He's coming! He's coming! He's coming!' Many of the devotees were now trembling. One young man passed out with a quavering moan and was carried out—parcelled from hand to hand—without a fuss. I looked at my watch. Less than a minute left. In Delhi, Jai would be dancing in a strobe-shot room with his arms in the air and a conical hat on his head to some frantic Hindi-English-Punjabi medley, bumping his body joyously against Chutiya-Nandan-Pandey and their ilk. Sara would be in bed, in front of the TV, stoking her rage as the anti-war demonstrators of Gavras got beaten up. Someone would have to pay for it. Could well be me.

Guruji was all flying hair now, moving to some celestial melody, tethered to earth only by his mother's claw. There was a loud echoing rumble—much louder than the earlier whoops—like approaching thunder, like the roar of a tiger in a forest. It drowned out the chanting, smothered every breath; and when it had faded, Guruji was still, and every sound was dead. Guruji's hair hung damp around his gaunt face as if drenched in water, and his face and torso shone with sweat. His eyes were still closed. But he wasn't panting. From where I stood—no more than eight feet away—it didn't even seem like he was breathing. Everyone waited, motionless.

It was my first time, but there were people there who had seen it before. That didn't diminish the awe; if anything, it seemed to heighten it.

Moments later, when Guruji opened his eyes, they were not his eyes. His old mother immediately fell prostrate and touched her forehead on the floor before him. Then lifting her head, she said in a clear ringing voice, 'Babaji di jai ho!' Instantly Bhura shouted, 'Babaji has come! Babaji di jai ho!' And in one roar the devotees from every corner of the dera shouted, 'Babaji di jai ho!'

So did I. It was mind-bending.

Babaji, the great Pir of Machela, who had once diverted Nadir Shah's invading army away from the villages under his patronage by opening up, overnight, a protective ravine in the marauder's path; whose very touch could drain carbuncles, dry abscesses, mend bones, ease pain and heal disease; who could tell the future and the past, and alter the present; who did not distinguish between Hindu and Muslim, and belonged to neither; whose blessings made the most barren of cattle and women fertile; whose munificence brought a bloom to the efforts of the married and the mercantile; who could summon rain when the land cracked and the sun when it drowned; who lived for a hundred years and did not die but entered his samadhi. This was the Babaji—the great Pir of Machela—who three hundred years later had chosen Guruji as his anointed disciple, and bestowed on him his transcendent powers. At no time were these powers more potent than on the night of the samadhi, every thirty-first of December, when Babaji entered the very body of Guruji and literally became him.

Now through this magical night, every problem of carbuncle, cattle, commerce and career, of pain, passion, property and progeny, everything that had vexed his followers all year, defying solution, would be addressed by the great Pir himself.

The very first supplicant at his feet was the old lady, Guruji's mother. She leaned forward, posed her problem, was answered, and then blessed. Next came Guruji's father, tall and wizened, once a lowly contract tiller, working the plough all day to partake of another's land, his inconsequential life transmuted by his fathering of the holy man. Then the dark low-caste, Bhura, Guruji's most beloved disciple, maimed of leg and soaring of heart. Then Guruji's wife, son, daughter. Each prostrating, asking, receiving blessings, and retreating—prostrating not to their father, not to their spouse, not to their son, but to the spiritual one, the ascended one, the most powerful one, who was now in their midst. It took nearly two hours for the room to clear, as each intimate got his annual moment.

All the while Guruji-Babaji did not budge below the waist. He remained firmly seated on the maroon cushion, his feet over his thighs. As each supplicant brought forward his roster of woes, he cocked his gaunt head, listened patiently, asked, answered, asked, answered; and when it was done, took a coin from a huge glass jar by his side full of old ten-paisa and twenty-five-paisa coins, new fifty-paisa and one-rupee and two-rupee ones, and occasionally even a five-rupee one—and touching it to his forehead, concentrated for a moment, and then bestowed it on the seeker.

The coin was talismanic. Protector, intuiter, connector.

Bhura always said, with a grave laugh: 'This is Guruji's mobile phone system. Through it he can keep in touch with all his beloved.'

The coin was meant to sit in a bowl of clean tap water in front of the house deity—whoever it was—through the day and put under one's pillow at night. When one travelled and no holy image was available it was to be kept at the base of any tree or plant, even an indoor one as there was no difference between the energy of the gods and that of the natural world. One could always substitute for the other.

It was past two o'clock by the time I fell at Guruji–Babaji's feet. His old mother had left her white dupatta tied to his ankle, as a harness on his surging power. When it was all over, and Babaji had withdrawn, it would be untied and reclaimed by her. At the moment, the blood-red dhoti and the snow-white chiffon dupatta, flowing from the right side of Guruji's waist where his left ankle rested, were like the beautiful plumes of some exotic bird of paradise. Guruji's laughing eyes were today replaced by Babaji's sombre ones. There was none of the special play with which he normally greeted me, calling me 'Shehri sher'. A city lion.

Even with the windows and door open, the room was clammy and heavy with body heat and body smells. Occasionally the thick perfume of the incense sticks caught the nose and drowned out the body odour. On the wall behind Guruji some of the tiny lights festooning the images had fused, leaving black holes in the garlands. The rest were twinkling away. Glowing oysters in their yellow, red, green, blue shells of rough and cracked plastic.

I said, 'Babaji–Guruji, am I doing the right thing?'

He said, in a voice that was not his, 'Be unafraid, son, you will know when you are not.'

I said, 'Will there be success in what I am planning to do?'

He said, 'Success is an illusion, my child. You know that. But, yes, you will get such success as you are seeking, and such as you deserve.'

I said, 'Can I trust those I am going to be doing this with? I have not yet met them, but Jai says they are good people.'

He said, in the other voice that was not his, 'Be watchful. Always be watchful. The very rich and the very poor always deceive with their appearance—one flaunts how much he has, the other flaunts how little. You are dealing with people who only think about themselves. They have no concern for you. They have money but no morals. They will suck you dry and spit you out, like the stone of a mango. You must use them before they use you. Don't be the mango; be the mouth that sucks. The mango is tasty, but never forget it is the mouth that feels the taste.'

I said, still touching his motionless knees, 'And Jai, my partner? Will it be okay with him?'

Eyes half closed, Guruji–Babaji said, 'Be watchful of him too. He also has no concern for you. When you brought him here once, I saw how he looked at me. With disrespect, with suspicion, with arrogance. Many men like him in the big cities think the truth can be found by working in big offices and by reading fat books. But the truth only comes to him who accepts a guru, who accepts one greater; and who in turn accepts another greater. Even the guru needs a guru. Even the very lords of the universe, Brahma–Vishnu–Mahesh, bow to each other in prayer when they confront a riddle whose answer they cannot find. Each day men must remove the apparel of pride if they wish to bathe in the waters of truth. Your friend wears too much pride, too much vanity—no truth can touch his skin. In fact, he was even afraid you were in my protection. You must use him too before he uses you. Suck him before he sucks you. Be the mouth; make him the mango.'

It was one of the great merits of Guruji. The practical heart pumping away in the body of spirituality. He understood that the two had to work as one coordinated entity to mean anything. I had seen him offer advice on how to outwit avaricious neighbours through subterfuge, how to sell a head of cattle before its deformities showed up, how to ensure your mother-in-law returned to her own house posthaste; how to bring recalcitrant children to heel through coercion and deceit. How to woo your boss into giving you a promotion; and how to seduce the bank into giving you the loan.

As I leaned forward and spoke with my head bowed, the room behind me was becoming increasingly chaotic. For every disciple who took Guruji's blessings and left, two others were trying to squeeze their way in. With the tension of the metamorphosis over, the crowd had ceased to be silent. There was a steady buzz of disciples whispering, inquiring, urging the one in front to get a move on. Bhura was using a slim, freshly skinned tree switch to chastise the more unruly. There was order only in the exact space in front of Guruji.

I said, 'Guruji–Babaji, is there anything in particular I need to do?'

In the voice of the great Pir, he said, 'Stitch your lips up. Find the strongest twine and use it to stitch your lips together. Talk can confuse the enemy but silence confuses even more. Let the enemy flaunt the abundance of his arrows; and let him keep guessing whether your quiver is empty or overfull.' He closed his eyes, dipped his left hand into the glass jar and felt around among the coins. Then he took one out, placed it on his forehead while mouthing his benedictions, and put it in my palm. A heavy five-rupee coin. He placed his hand on my head and was done. I had to wrestle my way out of the heaving room.

Guruji–Babaji would not move till five o'clock next evening, till every single disciple of his had been heard, advised and blessed with coin and hand. Then there were the rituals of return. The old mother would untie the white dupatta; Guruji would descend from Babaji's maroon gaddi; his children would bathe him in a bucket of stored Gangajal; his long hair would be knotted once again, a saffron safa wound around it; and he would break his thirty-six-hour fast with a hot glass of milk, even as Bhura massaged his limbs.

At the time I had still not met Chutiya-Nandan-Pandey, only heard about them from Jai.

When I went back many weeks later—but before the signing of the shareholders' agreement—and climbed up the straight stairs at the back to the roof, the acrid smoke of dung-cakes in my nostrils, Guruji was sitting cross-legged on a charpoy. Squatting on a rush mat on the floor, cocooned in dark blankets, were a few villagers. It was the second week of February and frost-cold out in the open, but Guruji was clad in only his thin white dhoti with a coarse brown shawl draped over his shoulders, his wiry torso naked and visible in the light of the hurricane lamp. He had wound his saffron safa on his head and he was bubbling his big hookah. The first thing he said to me was, 'Haan, Sher Dilliwalla, have you had your dinner or not? Go and eat before you speak.'

Twenty minutes later I was back on the roof, the gobhi-dal-roti warm in my belly. The blanketed figures were gone, only Bhura was with Guruji, pressing his calves.

He said, 'Have you done it?'

I said, 'No. No. Not yet. Would I, without your blessing?' Then I explained the deal to him, my meetings with the investor trio. At one point when I was describing Frock Raja's farmhouse, he guffawed and said, 'That's why they say—to those the gods wish to make into fools they give wealth in excess!'

I finished, saying, 'They are giving us much less than we had expected.'

He was quiet. I could hear the occasional cry of a night bird, sometimes right overhead. I was cold even in my thick quilted jacket, and had pushed its hood up around my ears.

Guruji said, 'You are wrong.'

I waited. Looking up, trying to spot the faint splash of the Milky Way. A shooting star singed a path. The dome of the sky was so large—so studded with stars—that only god could fill it.

He said, finally, 'What do we have? Nothing. Can we do what we want to do with nothing? No, we can't. If our work flourishes do we gain? Yes, we do. If it fails, do we lose? No, we don't. The wise traveller uses any horse to get to his destination. He doesn't agonize about who owns the animal. He only thinks about the pleasure of riding it, about getting it to take him where he wishes to go.

'We have goals, but no horse. We need a horse—even if it wears a woman's frock. Let us ride the beast waiting outside our door. Later, if we find a better one, we can change it. Let us not be the fool who sits in his garden arguing about the journey; let us be the adventurer who embarks on it. When pestilence and pitfalls have to claim you, they will do so as readily in the house as on the road. Better, then, to meet them bravely in the open than cowering fearfully in your room.'

I thought of Frock Raja and his leaking mermaids. Only Guruji could have construed something so elevating out of such poor material.

As I left, Guruji told me to give two kilos of flour and two of rice to the poor every Monday outside a temple, and to float a burning diya on flowing water on the first day of every month. He said I should not eat meat or drink alcohol on Tuesdays, and if I could give them up all together the great Pir of Machela would be overjoyed.

He also said I should sign the shareholders' agreement between five-thirty and six-thirty in the evening, when the hour was neither dark nor light, neither day nor night, on the hour when the army of djinns who moved at his command were at their most powerful and would hover by my side, protecting my every interest. It is what I did, insisting on the time—without offering any explanation—letting them know that I would go as far as to step out of the deal if they did not comply.

My set face kept Jai from launching into a counter harangue.

We did it by the frock-shaped pool, with Kuchha King's Mont Blanc pen, with the light dying delicately across the manicured trees, with Clayderman tinkling in the grass, and followed it up with a great deal of flesh slapping. A big green bottle of champagne was fired and frothed and I had to struggle with the sour taste. Then Mr Lincoln delivered a speech that made the hair stand and grown men weep.

4

PENGUINS AND KILLERS

There was a moment—when I first saw them—that I experienced a fleeting rush of curiosity and distaste, but it was quickly gone, submerged in a profound indifference. All I wanted to do was to get out of that place as quickly as possible.

The huge high-ceilinged room was packed. There was a continuous eddy of movement as bodies pushed in and out, talking to one another in whispers. The emotional registers all around were high: every face appeared marked by anxiety, fear, aggression, resentment, despondency. The only calm ones seemed to be the black coats dotting the landscape, penguins in their element, skating smoothly through the heartless glacier of organized justice.

Within five minutes of entering the stately iron gates of the Patiala House courts I'd become aware that I was entering a zone of experience that would forever change the way I looked at the wonder that was India. Before the day was out I would know that no middle-class Indian, from any old st mary-john-mark school with trilling nuns and caning fathers, who twittered in the queen's English and held forth on freedom and democracy, had any real idea of this country if he had not wandered through the frozen glaciers of its legal system. If he had not befriended a frisky penguin and been shown some chilling X-rays of the grand body of Indian law and order and justice.

Outside the gates of the courts ran the wide stately roads of Lutyens' Delhi, curving with an imperial assurance around the imposing edifices of the National Stadium, the National Gallery of Modern Art and the India Gate, then taking the high road to Raisina Hill where the monoliths of North and South Block continued to be metaphors for the imperiousness and inscrutability of the state, before finishing up inside the excessive sprawl of the presidential palace, an appropriate metaphor of shallow decorativeness. Patrolled by police jeeps, these were ceremonial roads, cocooning a space where the state could continually convince itself of its power and purpose. Any dwarf wearing the ensemble of the state could bring the tallest citizen of the country to his knees.

But inside the high gates of the courts, the splendour of the state was in disarray. From the moment you entered the grounds you battled your way though parked scooters and bikes and cars, weaving through thick clusters of petitioners, penguins, policemen—weirdly, holding hands with their criminal wards as lovers would, since the Supreme Court had banned the handcuffing of small-time offenders. Everywhere was dirt and offal and loud voices, and random chain-link fences you had to hop over. The hum all around was of transactions. A brisk bazaar, where you could strike any deal you wanted as long as your attitude was unburdened and your wallet thick. Going around to the back of the building to meet my lawyer, I saw advocates' kiosks that looked more like they dealt in minor merchandise—cigarettes, paan, biscuits, candy—than in the sombre questions of law.

Inside the once opulent building built during the Raj to serve as the Delhi outpost of the royal house of Patiala, the state's glory was equally in tatters. The sweeping staircases, the marble floors, the teak balustrades, the carved windows, the fluted ceilings, all were in distress. Everything was soiled, dirty, peeling. Every corner had a chiaroscuro of blood-red paan stains. Despite their grand scale, the corridors were dark and musty and poorly lit, with the illumination from the windows and ventilators truncated by dirt and furniture. The windows were further obscured by human bodies—sitting, standing, trying to wedge their way through. Many of these were clearly peasants, their faces unshaven and gaunt, their thick blankets and bodies giving off the rank odour of animals and sweat. I had to put out my hands and literally push people aside to make way for us. My shadows did the same, their elbows jutting out. At one point, just when I was beginning to enjoy shoving the idiots around, Sara poked me in my ass, warning me angrily to take it easy. When I went to take a leak in the makeshift urinal under the staircase, I had to pay a rupee for the privilege and survive such a stench of fresh piss as could have deterred the stoutest litigant.

The fear of the law clearly unloosed the bladder.

In this hellhole, we were led by my penguin into a high-ceilinged room that was no less nondescript and soiled. It was bursting with a silent clamour, as routine mayhem tried to rein itself in, in deference to the setting. The milling bodies moved around the ugly wooden cupboards littered all over, in random array, filled to oozing with dusty files. These were all tied in strings of different colours, and had dirty ears of paper peeping out. Each time an attendant opened a cupboard the files began to topple out, and had to be desperately held in check with one hand even as the right one was located and extracted. As at the dera on the night of the metamorphosis, there was only one point of calm in this melee: the elevated platform at the end of the room where, behind a wide wooden desk, sat a clerky-looking man in black-rimmed spectacles.

The guruji of this equally surreal realm.

Unlike my guruji, this one needed help with his appearance. He was young, with a weak pasty face and a collapsed jaw. He didn't look like he could adjudicate a spat between his own children. Someone should have given him a curly white wig and fastened a false beard to his chin. A couple of real clerks sat around him taking notes, one punching away into a grimy cream-coloured computer, and a wastrel at his side rudely shouted out case numbers and names as another, even lower down the food chain, near the door, immediately took up the call. On the three rows of ramshackle wooden chairs in front of the pasty boy sat an assortment of penguins and litigants.

Arguments were being made and heard in conspiratorial consultations. Not orated, not declaimed, not stated. A number and name would be barked out and one clutch of penguins—trailed by their glassy-eyed clients—would wriggle through the throng and present themselves right under the high chair. Some sort of urgent whispering would ensue to and fro, left and right, strung out on a chorus of milords and yoronours. Then, absurdly quickly, a consensus would be arrived at—simply, the next date of hearing—and yoronour, guruji of the high chair, would say something to the computer man on his right, close the file, pick it and fling it at the other clerk. Instantly the wastrel—busy all the while cutting side deals with penguins who sidled up to him; speaking to them through the corner of his mouth with his eyes on the high chair—instantly the wastrel would bark a name and a number, junior wastrel would echo it, and the throng would begin to undulate, pushing forward the next clutch of players. It was barely noon, but going by the shouted number, yoronour was cleaning up society lickety-split and had already delivered justice in twenty-eight cases.

Curiously, all the penguins seemed to be friends, even if their clients were trying to kill each other. Before they showed up under the chair of yoronour, they appeared to be jointly working out their opposing strategies. My penguin, Sethiji, was fat and middle-aged, with the jocular, can-do manner of a middleman. He was some distant relative of Jai's, and in his smooth ability to work people, a sort of cruder, more down-market version of him. In our passage through the sweeping staircases and jammed corridors everyone seemed to know him. When I had emerged from the pissoir, barely breathing, he was upset that I had paid, asserting that the attendant should have known who I was with. He wanted to go right back in to retrieve the rupee.

In the high-ceilinged room, the clerks half raised their hands to salaam him, while the wastrel gave a full salute. He said, with a happy smile, 'I pay them to do this each time there's a new client.

It boosts the confidence of the client. I am telling you this because you are family.'

The happy smile never left Sethiji's face, and he shook a hand after every sentence. Hustling, everywhere in Delhi, is a desperately tactile affair: slapping flesh, pressing flesh, rubbing flesh. In disgust I put my hands in my pockets, and so he began to grab one of the shadows. He called Sara 'bhabhiji', assuming she was my wife, and bowed to her courteously every few minutes, making her glower. In the room, he had a chair cleared for her but she declined to sit.

Sethiji's belly was so spectacular he needed suspenders to keep his pants up. The black coat and trousers were worn to a shine, the white shirt's collar was frayed, the leather shoes battered. He said, 'Lady Justice, you know, is blindfold. Only weight on her balance matters. More weight better chances.' His thumbs were hooked into his suspenders; they came out fleetingly after every sentence to reach for someone.

He had three very young penguins with him, a son and two nephews, who circled him watchfully, awaiting orders. Sethiji was a true king penguin, a master of his game. He never spoke loudly or rudely, just whispered his instructions with that bemused smile; a look of comic wonderment. The boys—in sharp black attire, with gym muscles, shining skin and gelled hair—darted off to comply. At one point he shepherded us out to a cordoned-off corner of the corridor and his boys served up hot tea, cold lassi, and crisp samosas. The shadows attacked everything; I downed the lassi; Sara said, 'What a bloody racketeer!'; Sethiji said, with his smile, 'You can survive the law, but you cannot survive hunger,' and reached for the hand of a shadow.

The corner had a huge window—built for princely eyes—but it was grimy and closed. It looked out over lush green trees, and Sara stood there gazing out, an arty charcoal sketch, her unequal body a sudden invitation. I knew she was simmering, raging at all the kind of stuff she liked to rage at. This place was a rager's paradise. By bringing her here I had already given her fuel for weeks of ranting. And we were not done yet. Poverty, justice, class, democracy. Some spectacular nailing on the wall was in the offing.

Sethiji was, of course, stoking the embers continually. At one point his mobile rang. Leaving his left thumb in the striped elastic, he pulled out his clunky phone with his right hand and placed it two inches from his ear. 'Hello, my dear,' he said, slowly with his wide bemused smile. 'No madam, I need no loan. Not for home, or marriage, or car, or carriage. I would marry again, but my wife eats two spoons of Chyawanprash every day and does not look like she'll die for another hundred years. Education? Madam, it is better to burn the money than spend it on my sons' studies. Their principal says, Sethiji take them home and you will better serve the cause of education. Madam, that's why I am thinking I will make them both lawyers. Only the rejected can understand the pain of the dejected! My car, madam, is a Maruti, a red one. Do you really think I should buy another? And just stop the medical treatment of my father? He's dying of cancer you know. Of the bowels. You know, the bowels? Of course you do, everyone knows the bowels! But he's old, no problem if he dies now. Maybe I can take him to the cremation ground in the new big car. That would please him! No, no madam, don't go yet! Wait I have something to tell you too! Is there anyone in your family who has been raped or murdered or has committed suicide? Madam, my law firm specializes in handling cases of rape and murder. No, no madam, you cannot just go now—you called me, you must listen to me now. Okay, okay, not your family, any of your friends who have been raped or murdered? No? No. Very lucky you are, madam! But in future if anyone you know is raped or murdered you know whom to call! You have the number—you just called it! Advocate Sethi and Sons—one son actually and two nephews—specialists in rape and murder. Hello? Hello! Madam! Madam? You called me, madam, you must listen to me!'

With the phone still inches away from his ear, he swivelled around slowly and gave us all his smile of bemused wonderment. Son and nephews were grinning, and so were the shadows. I was too, but I had turned away from Sara. She was thunderous. I could sense the fury radiating from her clenched body. For a moment I was anxious she'd say something needlessly unpleasant to the fat lawyer and I'd be forced to step in; and it would lead to weeks of simmering rancour between us. He was just a fat man making light of his sad life. There was no need to throw *The Female Eunuch* and the Constitution at him.

She peeled away from the window and stalked off, back into the high-ceilinged room.

Sethiji said with his bemused smile, 'Bhabhiji's not feeling well? Or is she upset with our phuddugiri?' I smiled and he said, 'I don't blame her. We are just such crude scum of the earth. Not fit to be in the presence of any woman! Leave alone a high-class one. The problem is we know nothing about women. Only two women have I known in my life. First there was my mother, who beat me and loved me. Then there is my wife, whom I beat and I love. Men like me don't know what to do with a woman if we can't love her or beat her. We are full phuddus from an outdated factory. I keep telling these young boys, don't end up like us. Don't just keep combing your hair, also clean your tongues. When you meet a woman and open your mouth, flowers should fall out, not drool!'

The three boys grinned as he gave them each a clip on the ears. 'But they are determined to be full phuddus! Not their fault. Just third-rate genes.'

The next time we went in I saw them right away.

Sara, leaning against a wooden cupboard, was looking at them intently. They were standing at the far corner under the platform, five of them, in a row, at an angle, facing yoronour. Flanking them were two policemen in uniform, holding on to the wrists of the ones next to them. Behind them stood five more policemen with clunky Enfield rifles—the infamous threenoughtthrees—slung on their shoulders. This was hardware from the Second World War, standard issue for the Indian police in most states, seconded by the Indian army, and so heavy and unwieldy that it was reckoned a fleeing man could run clean out of Delhi before it could be taken off the shoulder, loaded and fired. The 303's only virtues were its range and power—so if your aim was true, you'd get your man even if he'd crossed over the border into the next state.

In that swirling room, the five of them stood out because they were handcuffed, and loosely roped together. One—just one—on the extreme right, had his ankles shackled in iron. The shoes under the iron were trendy red Nikes. His body was fleshy, filling out the blue jeans and mauve shirt, and where the policeman held him the arm was thick and full of muscle. He looked young, not thirty perhaps, and was unusually fair. He had the moustaches of a brigand, the ends twisted to a rapier's tip, standing clean away from his cheeks. Every few minutes he reached for them—taking along handcuffs, policeman's hand, everything—and gave them a slow hard twirl. He stood legs apart, on powerful sprinter's thighs, his big shoulders squared. Nothing in his eyes or stance suggested fear or contrition. When he spotted me, he displayed a flicker of recognition before unblinking contempt filled his eyes once more.

The others were fairly nondescript. Short, thin, almost weedy, unlikely to stand out in any crowd. One of them was dark as burnt coal; and one very fair, with north-eastern, Nepali features—Sippy would have referred to him as a Chingfunglee. They didn't look like they could kill a gutter rat between the four of them. The fair brigand, on the other hand, looked as if he could kill all four before breakfast and then be ready for a day's work. Even with the rope stringing them together the four pressed close to each other and clear of the boy. Their eyes were averted and they were talking to each other in hushed voices. The young brigand paid them no attention, and after showing me his contempt turned away to stare at yoronour conducting his business in conspiratorial whispers. The policeman holding his arm was big built too, by far the biggest in the detachment of six.

I could sense that in that swirling mad room, every eye had slowly come to rest on him. I saw even yoronour in all his pasty majesty sneak a look or two.

Sethiji said, 'They say he is the future king of western UP. His name is Hathoda Tyagi. Before he was nineteen he'd killed his first five men by caving their skulls in with a hammer. Full brain curry. Now, of course, he shoots people—through their ears, in their mouths, up their assholes. Today he kills you, tomorrow your enemy. Like Sethiji gets up and comes to Patiala House courts every morning, he goes out every day and dispatches a few sorry souls to Yamraj directly. He works only for the big mafia dons now. When they want a big job done, they send for Hathoda Tyagi. You should be proud. Not just Sethiji, even the mafia thinks you are a big man!'

Sara said, 'They are being framed.'

I looked at her.

She said, 'Can't you see they are being framed!'

I said, 'How can you tell?'

She said, in a hard whisper, 'Oh don't give me those lofty peashooter ones! Even a blind man can tell they've just been set up! Look at those four poor guys—seems like they've been dragged off the road to settle someone else's agenda. They wouldn't know how to kill a chicken for dinner!'

And what about him, I said with my eyes. He looks like he, in one joyous spree, could hammer in the brains of the entire courtroom. Mass brain curry. Served steaming fresh, at the altar of truth and justice.

She said, in an even harder whisper, 'Oh don't always get taken in by looks mr peashooter! Just because he has some muscles doesn't mean he goes around killing people!'

Yoronour caught her hard tones and looked our way, frowning sharply. The clerks and wastrel instantly broke into shushing sounds. Sethiji, his smile still beatific, immediately said, 'I am sorry milord.' Then swivelled left and right and loudly admonished everyone, 'Silence! Please learn to maintain silence in the courtroom.' For a moment I thought Sara was going to say something, but before that could happen, Sethiji had caught my hand and put it on her photo arm and whispered, 'Take Bhabhiji out, I'll call you when our number comes.'

We had barely exited the room—the shadows in hot pursuit—that she turned on me. Wriggling her arm free, she said, 'You are not going to allow the bastards to use you to frame them! Can't you see you are being used?'

We were in the middle of the corridor, a river of people flowing around us. Using their elbows and hips, the shadows had fenced off a tiny island for us. I said, 'I know nothing about this. Nothing! All I know is what that Hathi Ram has told me. And he claims he knows nothing. I've told you what they've told me or not told me. I know nothing more and am not interested in finding out either!'

Many people had stopped by the cordon and were listening in. One young man with a gaunt face and handsome nostril hair had literally stuck his head into our space and cocked his right ear towards us. I said to him, 'What are you listening to, tiger sandoz—the sermon of Bhagwan Ram?' He looked at me foolishly with his mouth half open. One of the shadows caught him by his bird neck, twisted it around, and slowly pulling out the black pistol from his crotch, showed it to him. 'Shall I put this in your ear, hero? Want to hear it? The bugle of Bhagwan Nine MM.'

Moving like a striking snake, Sara grabbed the shadow's wrist, and shouted, 'Stop it! What do you think you are doing?' The shadow immediately let go of the bird neck, his face filling up with bewilderment and shame. Bird neck, his mouth still half open and his eyes dazed, quickly backed off and melted into the crowd. All the other onlookers leapt into the surging river and flowed away.

The shadow—a new replacement, middle-aged, balding, but full of energy—stood there struggling with his sudden diminishment, working on a weak smile, his entire vocation called into question.

I looked at Sara, and saw she realized she had gone too far. The shadows were clearly out of bounds. Ignoring them was one thing; active intervention in their work, another. They were on dispatch from the state, doing their duty, and any interference in it was basically unacceptable. Ostensibly the man lived to save your life; you could not piss on his so brazenly.

Then I made the mistake of not letting remorse do its work. I forgot Guruji's cardinal lesson that you can wound and destroy more effectively with silence than with words. I decided to pluck a quick feather for my cap. I said, coldly, with a sneer, 'It's time even you learnt where to draw the line.' And before I had finished saying it I knew I had thrown away all advantage. Regret vanished from her face like a midsummer mirage. Her eyes hardened with contempt; she folded her photo arms across her chest like armour. 'And where, mr peashooter, in your opinion should the great line lie? In sticking a gun into a poor bystander's ear? In helping the state frame innocent men on charges of murder? Or in asking desperate women who call you up to sell some harmless things if they'd care to be raped? And how amusing you find all of it! So tell me, mr peashooter, where do you draw the line? Wherever your day's selfishness finds it convenient?'

I knew I had tipped her onto a track that did not lead to a nailing on the wall. This one led to badly bruising places, to prolonged trench warfare that I had no inclination for. In the past my instinct had been to exit such a situation quickly and completely. The last one—the Malayali girl who gave me tree names and wet palms—had ended on sulk number three, in week number nine.

The truth is I had no time to argue with others; I had too many arguments going on with myself. I was happier recalling her lustrous dark skin, the watermelon red slash at its lovely core, than entering a spiral of you didn't call, why didn't you call, where are you, with who are you, do you feel, what do you feel, you don't care, why can't you come, why can't we go, why can't you say something, what are you saying, you only want that, you don't want anything, where is this going, this is going nowhere, I thought you were strong, I know you are strong, you are making me weak, I am not weak, you don't want to change, you've changed, you make me sick, you are sick, you don't really love me, I really love you, how can anyone love you, actually you hate me, actually you hate yourself, actually I hate you.

I had discovered, over time, that the workable cycle was about sixteen weeks. Two weeks of wooing; four weeks of passion; and ten slow and painful weeks of disengagement. By the time it ended there was poison everywhere, with every fine feeling in tatters. When the last lingering tendon was finally snipped, with one of us saying something barbaric that could have easily gone unsaid, there was a euphoria not dissimilar to that of the weeks of passion.

Sometimes the process was less corrosive, when she too understood, like cops and doctors do, that the world is what it is, ephemeral, uneven, to be squarely dealt with, and not to be conjured out of weak romantic novels. But few seemed to possess the gift of leaving the room while the laughter was still in the air and the spirits high. For the most, everyone seemed to be committed to creating a heap of debris before walking away from it.

With Sara it had turned out different. She had surprised me, derailed me. The sixteen weeks had turned to sixty, and I was still wandering around inside the room, refusing even to look at the exit door. At times it angered me. I had even attempted a few times to disconnect completely, wash her out of my system as I had so many others in the past; then, within days, irresistibly drawn by her maddening mix of rebellion and surrender, by the beauty and lust of her unmatched halves, I had rushed back to the boxy building and thrown myself in front of Napoleon Bonaparte to be showered with her abuse and love.

Not since I was ten and beginning to flee the domination of my mother had I felt so helpless in a relationship. What made it worse was Sara seemed to not know the hold she exercised on me. That, at least, would have involved a game—tactics, strategy, wit, play—something I could train myself to excel at. But she was not a player. She was an original, a force of nature, declaring herself in any way that seized her, and it was up to you to tackle it as best as you could. She was like Jai in her rage and articulation but without the calculation. She spoke such nonsense sometimes that I wanted to tear the Gita page on page and stuff it down her throat. But, even less than with Jai, there was no point going down that road with her. Looking back, my only victories, in more than a year, seemed to be the fleeting ones against the wall.

Now, in the grand squalor of Patiala House she was declaring war again, opening a new front. I was trying to give her my inscrutable, half-smiling expression—reserved for my clueless moments—when Sethiji's junior penguins saved the moment by rushing out and demanding our presence in the courtroom.

Sethiji, the public prosecutor, and the lawyers for the five men, were all in a convivial huddle at the foot of yoronour's desk. There was much flesh pressing going on between them after each whispered exchange as they all smiled happily at each other. It must have been a terrifying sight for the accused. Was their freedom being negotiated, or their lives being thrown away? Was this flock of waddling penguins just going through the motions with little concern for the outcome on their lives?

The public prosecutor—a balding clerkish-looking man like my father, but with the alert eyes of a shopkeeper—said to me, 'Do you know these men?'

I looked at them. Four of them lowered their eyes. The brain-curry man looked at me as if I was the accused. 'No, I don't.'

The swirl in the courtroom seemed to have stilled a bit.

'Do you know that there has been an attempt to kill you?'

'Yes, I do.'

'Do you live under twenty-four-hour police protection?'

'Yes, I do.'

'Do you know who would want to have you killed?'

'No, I don't.'

'But do you agree you may have enemies, people you have offended or harmed by your work, who may want to get rid of you?'

'Yes, sure, it's possible.'

'You have no reason to believe that these men may not be the contracted killers?'

'No, I don't.'

Yoronour gave me a grave, pasty look as if I had said something of profound importance. Someone really should have stuck a beard on his chin.

The lawyer for the defence, more a little sparrow than a penguin, in an oversized shabby black coat and an old-fashioned pencil moustache, said, waving his arm in a cultivated flourish, 'Look at them very carefully. Do you know any of them?'

'No sir, I don't.'

'I repeat—look at them again. Very carefully. Have you ever seen these men?'

I actually did what he asked, scanning their faces slowly. The policeman holding the wrist of the one on the extreme left yanked his face up—prominent cheekbones, a big nose, black stubble—and the other three put up theirs in instant reflex. They looked like each other. Everymen. The roads, bazaars, offices of India were full of men like them. Nameless men who did faceless jobs and perished unmarked in train accidents, fires, floods, epidemics, terrorist blasts, riots. At best, statistical fodder. But I also knew this was how criminals really looked, not like the stylized stars that the movies everywhere in the world loved to essay. More criminals fashioned themselves on film stereotypes than the other way around. Of the five, only brain-curry man was a serious student of cinema.

I said, 'No sir, I haven't.'

Actually I could have seen them all my life and not remembered.

The tiny lawyer said in a forcefully mannered voice, 'Tell me, were you at all aware that someone wanted you killed?'

Clearly this little semicolon of a man had also fashioned himself from cinema. Everybody in this damn country was an imitation of a Hindi film character. He stroked the lapels of his oversized coat, and worked his mouth fully, the pencil moustache mesmeric. I could see him—a wimp in school, a wimp as a son, a wimp as a husband, a wimp as a father, but in the courtroom the master of the moment.

'No, I wasn't.'

'Was there any indication of a threat at all? A phone call, a letter, some rumour, a friendly remark—from a colleague, a source?'

'No sir, not really.'

'But you were under police protection?'

'I was.'

'Since when?'

'The last few months.'

'Why?'

'I don't really know. I was not told anything.'

'You were not told anything. Of course you were not told anything. Who put you under police protection?'

'The government, the police department...the intelligence bureau...the sub-inspector arrived with his men the day the news broke, and I was just told that I needed to be under protection.'

'You were told, you were told, in the way the police tells us all kinds of things. You were told. And you didn't bother to ask why, to question what you were told? You just believed what you were told. By the same police that you keep exposing for its lies, its human rights violations, its abuses and its excesses! Such a fine journalist, yoronour! We all respect his work. Fighting against corruption, fighting the government's wrongdoing, the police's wrongdoing, standing up for society. But this time you believed the police. You believed it was telling the truth—which I am sure it was, I am sure it was. Even the police tell the truth sometimes. So you believed everything the police told you?'

Sethiji's smile was getting a little rigid. Yoronour seemed to have started some other consultations on the side with his clerk and another penguin. Sara was looking as ferocious as the brain-curry man. Together they could have dismembered me in minutes, he making a hole in my skull and she uprooting my tool.

'No. I didn't believe or disbelieve. I just let them go ahead and do their job.'

'Good. That's good. The police must be always left alone to do their job. Even by investigative journalists. So can we say you trust the police?'

'No, I wouldn't go as far as to say that.'

'So mostly you wouldn't trust them, but in this particular case you did?'

'Well, yes. As I said, I just left them alone to do their job.'

'Let us be hypothetical. Do you like hypothesis? I am told all journalists like hypothesis. Do you?'

'Sure.'

'Let us hypothetically say the police wanted to fix some innocent fellows. For whatever reasons, personal, political, pecuniary, whatever. This police that you mostly don't trust. So this police charged them with trying to kill you, gave you police protection and locked them up. Of course the police would never do something like this. We are only trying to form a hypothesis.'

Fuck, was Sara part of his defence team?

The public prosecutor with the alert shopkeeper eyes, who had been smiling and chatting with Sethiji all this time suddenly said, 'Objection yoronour, what are all these misleading questions? The honourable counsel cannot make up any hypothesis and ask the witness to comment on them. This is a courtroom, not Sheikh Chilli's adda!'

Sethiji said, 'Yes, my lord, honourable counsel must stick to the case!'

Pastyface said, 'Don't waste the court's time, Bhandariji. There will be enough time to go into all this.'

The sparrow's feathers were unruffled. He stroked the lapels of his frayed coat with deliberate slowness and said, 'Milord, we are talking about the lives of five innocent men. Sometimes there is only a hypothesis between the rope and the neck.'

'Hurry up, Bhandariji.' The magistrate had again turned away from us and was talking to the clerk in whispers. Two penguins were leaning over to be part of the confabulations. The general swirl in the room was unabated. Even where I stood answering the questions, I was being continually pushed and jostled.

Turning to me the tiny lawyer said, 'So shall we say that you mostly don't trust the police?'

'Sure.'

'Shall we say that you have never before in your life seen any of these men?'

'Sure.'

'Shall we say that at no time did you have any apprehensions that your life was in danger? No sign at all?'

'Sure.'

'Shall we say that you have no reason to assume that these men wish you any harm at all?'

I looked at Hathoda Tyagi. He seemed like he wished to harm all of mankind. Make universal brain curry.

I said, 'Sure.'

'Shall we say my little hypothesis could be true? Just as a little hypothesis, nothing more?'

'Sure.'

Before Sethiji hustled me out of the room, I took a last look at the men. Four of them were shuffling their feet, looking at us, and around us, in a glaze of unknowing. The brain-curry man was motionless, head high, his eyes, unmoving, on me.

When I reached the door I realized Sara had lingered behind. I turned to look for her and she was talking to the little sparrow, her right hand on her chin, her elbow cupped in her left palm. Her unequal body, in a long peasant skirt with a tribal motif and a slim-fit sleeveless shirt, clearly seemed to be emanating some aura, for the swirl was steering clear of her, leaving her and the defence lawyer in a clear island. How tough men fear tough women! She was listening; the sparrow was chirping, no bigger than her, his entire frame delicate as her photo torso.

I sent one of Sethiji's gelled-gymed junior penguins to nudge her along. The look she turned on the hapless boy was of Kali in the moment before commencing carnage. He hotfooted his way back, ashen faced. One more provocation and she'd have decapitated us and strung our heads in a garland around her neck. Yours truly between Sethiji's wide smile and gymed boy's gelled hair, with shopkeeper-eyes right across, just below pasty-faced yoronour.

Our complement—shadows, Sethiji, junior penguins—waited outside in the madness of the corridor, one of many small armies doing opaque battle in the once royal corridors of Patiala House. When she finally emerged she strode right past us, straight into the crush, and we had to scuttle to follow. Sethiji said, nodding his wondrous smiling face, 'Bhabhiji is not an ordinary woman. No phuddugiri with her. You have to follow her. Not like our sad wives. You cannot just beat her and love her.'

5

THE ART OF BALANCE

The next time I nailed her to the wall I realized she wasn't quite there with me. I reached deep into my school memories to excavate every obscenity I had traded with my classmates, every vulgarity I had read in the hand-stapled, one-rupee novellas of Mastram Mastana that regularly ignited onanistic mayhem in the back benches. Every boy in the Hindi belt had dirtied his hands on Mastram. His across-the-line carnivals, grubby, taboo-trashing and incestuous—joint families, master–servants, teacher–students, buses, trains, bathrooms, dead-of-night surreptitious encounters—were so direct in the language that often boys succumbed in a weak heap before the first page was done.

But even Mastram unplugged couldn't cut through to her. The ringing expletives, the hammering, nothing led her eyes to dilate, nothing altered the tone of her voice, nothing instigated abandon in her body. What made it worse was that I could see it was not deliberate. She was not trying to shut me out. She went through the paces—the challenge, the baiting, the abuse, the surrender—but in the desultory way schoolchildren go through their morning prayers at assembly. When I finished and took her off the wall, she was limp not with satiety but with disconnect.

There had been similar retreats in the past, mostly when we hit a vista that we read differently. Thanks to her years in American universities and a ceaseless itinerary of seminars, summits and other modern talkathons, she had acquired occidental eyes. A continual hysteria of rights and wrongs, a continual need to name and frame and explain and blame, a continual urge to display virtue, a continual desire to fix the world as if it were a dollhouse waiting passively.

There was an explanation for the universe, the good, the bad, the rich, the poor, the less, the more, the pain, the pleasure, the eternal, the ephemeral—but it was not be found in the manicured beauty of purdue–brown–harvard–berkeley–yale, in gleaming classrooms and shining skins, in categorizing Olympiads, in bookshops bigger than factories. It lay in the inheritance of her blood; in the millennia-old meditations of naked men with matted hair under hairy ficus trees; in the unsigned, uncopyrighted wisdoms handed down endlessly from master to pupil, from flowing mouth to soaking ear; in the eternal riddles of karma and dharma that were their own answers.

She'd bought this whole occidental bullshit about fixing the world, about the grand march of logic and reason, all the way presumably—with delicate sips of Starbucks—to Auschwitz and Birkenau. The watchtower of rationality over the gateway of progress through which ran the lines of cold iron, the straight railroad to hell. Alight from the cattle cars and breathe the sweet forgetfulness of xylon. Embrace the modern moksha of death by science.

If she'd listened to the inheritance of her blood she would have known the world does not need to be fixed, it only needs to be balanced.

And the art of balance demands you tread lightly, not leap about in a continual frenzy. The art of balance demands you know your designated role in the game of life, not start muscling in on everyone else's. The art of balance demands an absence of panic, a rippleless internal calm. The art of balance demands knowledge of timelessness, of birth and death and rebirth. The art of balance demands that you know the world cannot be fixed, it must be endured; it must, simply, be kept forever in splendid play.

Sara wanted to fix the world.

She wanted action, answers, victories. Liberty, equality, fraternity. She wanted final solutions. She wanted my killers to be declared innocent, and freed. Nothing anyone said or did was going to deter her from her course. And I was not, I soon realized, to be involved in this campaign. I was a compromised party. I was on the other side. I had set myself up to be killed.

It took a little while before I realized she was in touch with the tiny lawyer in the oversized coat; that she was lending her formidable energy to help plan the defence of my assassins.

One day, as I lay spent yet frustrated in front of Napoleon, calming my heartbeat after one more insipid nailing, I saw the file on the unused side of her bed where her books and papers always lay in an untidy heap. A dirty brown file, tied with a red string, dirty white papers peeping out of its edges. She was in the bathroom washing me off her, and I pushed aside the newspapers that lay over the file, to discover there was not one dirty brown file but several—five, six—in a thin pile. The neat ink mark of a rubber stamp at the top declared: Advocate M.S. Bhandari, Llb, Llm.

When she came out, in a blue wraparound knotted in a big bow on the right and a thin white slip, her photo nipples provocative against it, she smiled and said, 'Checking on your killer boys, mr peashooter? Go ahead. We must all know what kills us. And what doesn't.'

I shut the file that I had just nudged open, flung the newspapers back onto it, and swung myself out of the bed. 'You've lost it,' I said, pulling on my jeans.

'Found it, mr peashooter,' she said. 'Found it. And tell me when you want me to share it. I'll be happy to.'

When I told Guruji about all this, he laughed. 'She's a spirited one! Blessed are those who choose to do. But doing without thought can often be worse than non-doing. One must understand the lesson of everything. When the guru sends his disciple to empty the ocean with a mug, he is not teaching him the virtue of perseverance, but the lesson of futile action. The stupid disciple empties the ocean for the rest of his life and finds his peace; the intelligent disciple finds wisdom, throws away the mug, and moves on in search of more. The disciple must not only perform the task, he must also contemplate the task. Action is god, but so is stillness.'

Then his eyes laughing, he patted my shoulder and said, 'And you know two gods are better than one.'

I was sitting at his feet in his sanctum, in front of the wall stuck over with religious icons. The tiny fairy lights, undraped from the wall, lay rolled in a tangle of wires, heaped in a corner. The doors and windows were open and the last light was pouring in. The splash of sky through the window was shiny orange with the dying sun. The guttural cries of oxen being steered by men cutting the final plough line of the day wafted in from the fields. Bird sounds flowed past in a rush—screeching parakeets, warning crows, questioning lapwings. Guruji was clad as always in his dhoti, luminously frail, his skin, from cheek to ankle, stretched taut over bare bones. His hair was tied, a basanti safa wound around it.

I said, 'So what is the lesson in all this? Is it for her or for me?'

His eyes laughing, he said, 'That is for you to find out. The guru can give you the mug but you have to empty the ocean. The guru can show you the path but you have to walk it. Truth cannot be taught, truth must be experienced. The good disciple walks paths even the guru has not, before arriving at the same truths. And sometimes even different ones. That is the wonder of the world, of all creation, that the journey to truth is a pathless one. There are countless ways of feeding the soul, just as there are countless ways of feeding the stomach. Some foods feed us well and thrill us, just as others taste bad, wreck our digestion, and destroy our health and sense of well-being. You have to discover what fits your palate, stomach and body. It may be the same as her, and it may just not.'

His eyes were laughing. But that didn't mean he wasn't dead serious. It's how he addressed everyone's problems—except on the night when he became the great Pir of Machela. 'Remember,' he always said to the complainants at his feet, 'there's always someone with a deeper well of sorrow just around the corner.'

I said, 'So shall I say nothing? Shall I just go ahead and let her keep doing what she is doing?'

He said, 'Of course you must not keep quiet. It is about you too. Silence has to be a strategy not a refuge. A weapon, not an escape. Listen to her for a bit, go along with her. She cannot help it. She has to vent the great noise so much education has filled her up with. It is bursting her insides. When it is spent there will be space for wisdom to flow in. In any case, you must never fight a woman if you can avoid it. Bring her to your side, or go over to hers. She is the greatest ally, and the most corrosive enemy.'

Guruji. Doctor of souls. Physician of the practical.

On the other hand, Jai, who didn't know Sara, did an about-turn. He said, 'Actually I am not too sure about the talc any more. Your hammer boy doesn't sound like someone who could be set up easily. And I don't think we can credit these buggers with such fine efficiencies. The government, we know, leaks like a sieve at the best of times. After seeing these five jokers in court, I doubt these government guys would have the audacity or competence to set them up. They can barely get simple things right, leave alone an elaborate frame-up involving dozens of people. You would need home ministry guys in the loop, police guys in the loop, judicial officers in the loop—too big a sieve, impossible to plug. Bound to leak, and no one could run that risk. My friend, rejoice! I am beginning to believe you may really have genuine assassins on your ass!'

SI Hathi Ram said, banging together biscuit halves like cymbals, 'For a few rupees. In this country anyone will kill anyone for a few rupees. Sons will kill fathers, brothers will kill brothers, husbands will kill wives—what is it to kill a stranger! Anyway, the bastards are beginning to sing. First they will sing like bathroom singers, slowly, badly, out of tune—difficult to understand what they are singing. Then they will become drawing-room singers, full of melody and confidence, full of pleasing sounds, too polite to be trusted. And finally they will be like the great qawwals at Nizamuddin, swaying to the god deep within them, chanting in frenetic unison, loud and long, in a wonderful trance of truth-telling.'

I said, 'So what's the story? What have they said?'

Hathi Ram delicately smelt the pink cream on one half, then banged them together and said, 'I have no idea. I am just speculating. Making them into great singers is not my work. My job is to only make sure you are safe. Song and dance is the department of gifted policemen. I am only Hathi Ram, a lowly and simple sub-inspector. Named to be an elephant but living like a mouse.' He sounded like the director of a song-and-dance academy. The choreographer of a thousand weeping confessions.

I said, 'So do you think it's possible these men who've been arrested may not really be guilty?'

Suddenly he became even more still than he was, the cymbals frozen mid-clash. Fixing me with his expressionless eyes, he said, 'That's the biggest problem with this country—suspicion. Everyone suspects everyone. Brothers, brothers; husbands, wives; wives, sisters-in-law; sisters-in-law, mothers-in-law; sons, fathers; masters, servants; servants, servants; employers, employees; colleagues, colleagues; farmer, middlemen; middlemen, traders; traders, government; government, the people; the people, the police; the police, the people; the people, the people. We are born khabris. It is in our blood to be informers—for one thousand years we have been informers for kings and for seths and for white men. Now there are no kings and no white men, and seths we can all become, for seths have neither colour nor lineage. But suspicion has still not stopped coursing in our blood. We suspect those we love, we suspect those who love us, we suspect those we work for, we suspect those who work for us. And we suspect those who save our lives, and suspect those who guard us. Be in no doubt ever, those men were paid to kill you, and given enough weapons to kill fifteen of you.'

Dolly/folly said, her eyes dilating, 'Be careful, please.'

My fat mother-in-law said, 'Who went with you to the court? I hope that Usman fellow was not there?' She knew the names of the shadows better than I did.

My mother wailed, 'Why did you have to go to court, my son? I hope those low-caste killers didn't see you! Every curse be on them and their families! May worms eat them as they live! May their teeth rot, may their hair fall, may their skin shrivel! Tell me, did they see you, my son? Will they be able to recognize you now?'

My father said, from behind his curtain of newspapers, 'Did they make you sign any papers?'

Dolly/folly's father said, from behind his curtain of newspapers, 'Did they make you sign any papers?'

Sippy said, his fly buttons unaligned, his eyeballs swimming in a soup of yellow and red, 'Sirji, I believe you went to the court and saw the murderers. You should have taken me along. I too would have liked to see who these fannekhans are who think they can kill you. Don't these chutiyas know that Kabir has said, Jaako raakhe saiyan, maar sake na koye!'

Kabir, not Wystan Hugh, is what Sara needed.

None can bring distress to he whom the lord protects.

The next time I was lying naked in front of Napoleon, I said, 'They could actually be innocent, couldn't they?'

Sara had finished sluicing me off her body and was pacing the room, photo arms crossed across her chest. Yet again, she had gone up the wall and come off it with minimum ardour, and it was clear to me that it was time to take Guruji's advice.

Without breaking step, she said, 'Of course not, fucker, why would they be. They kill just like you shoot peas! For money and pleasure!'

I said, 'Do you think that Bhandariji will be able to get them off? He's a sharp guy, but Hathi Ram says the police have a strong case.'

She said, without looking at me, pacing away, 'Of course he won't. Men like them die every day in this fucking country. It's the peashooters who live on.'

I said, 'I think we should help him.' She said, 'With what? Selecting the right rope or the right hangman?'

The hair in her crotch was dark and lush. She never trimmed it, it was long and shiningly shampooed, gathering in an even richer black line in the middle.

I said, 'We can bank on the police screwing up. What we have to ensure is that Bhandariji does his best. Chances are he'll get bored, the case will drag on, the cops will soften him up, and these five jokers will have no one around to chase him down. We know lawyers go to sleep if the client goes to sleep.'

She said, 'So do you want to tell the cops that you want to now actually protect your murderers? And instead of protecting you from them, the police should now protect them from the police?'

No one, I thought, should ever trim their hair. American porn like American food undid all curiosity, all good taste. Everything standardized, everything cut from one mould, everything drained of subtlety. All of it served up like a smooth slab of meat.

I said, 'You are doing the right thing by getting fully involved. I obviously can't, but if they are being framed, we could save them yet.'

She said, 'Don't make me weep, mr peashooter! Your concern is twisting my heart!'

It was not just the way it looked, so full of mystery and seductive promise. It was also how it smelled, so sensually ripe. The aromas opened up slowly, as you burrowed deeper, and filled your head.

I said, 'I am sure we could even talk to some friends about raising a small fund to support the case. This Bhandariji will lose interest unless some decent money is put on the table. And except for that Tyagi guy, the rest don't seem like they could have any.'

She broke step, looked at me, and said, 'I think you should stop now, and go home. Miss Dolly might restore you to your good humour with her black-black eyes and white-white skin and little pink-pink you-know-what!'

Guruji was not the master for nothing.

The next time we met we didn't go into the bedroom but sat in her living-room, on her second-hand cane sofa, streaked black where the cane was rotting, and we talked. She was wearing a turquoise wrap patterned with plump green fish—something she'd picked up on a beach in Goa—and a white sleeveless cotton slip. She sat opposite me with her legs crossed under her, using both her hands to rub her bare feet, which were flat and knobby, with none of the grace of her torso. Maybe it was her parents. A stout, fleshy father and a slim, delicate mother—nature's cruel idea of affirmative action. And the genes had neatly claimed one half each. Mercifully, the division worked. The other way around would have been a disaster.

She was talking. Telling me what she thought, what Bhandariji thought, what might really be happening. Her tone was quiet, ruminative, the way I'd heard her one time when she'd spoken about her childhood growing up in the hills. Sara was for all purposes a full-time dragon, scorching all who crossed her path. I knew that even her colleagues who worked with her in their small gender advocacy group wore asbestos around her. Everything set her off. You could almost never say the right thing. Those who befriended her did so for the scourging she handed out. Either punishment was their thing, or they were on some self-improvement trip. I was there for the pleasure that arose from some complex mind-body alchemy in her that I had not been able to unravel.

For the rest, I thought she was full of bullshit.

I didn't care a damn what she thought of the brain-curry man and his four johnnies, and what she wished to do to save them. I just wanted to reignite the frenzy in her body. I had become addicted to her high-wire act. The music of abuse, the wantonness and denial, the electrified body, the exploding finale. I craved it with the desperation of the young wasted needle-men scavenging in the dark mouldering alleys of Chandni Chowk.

I also knew by now that I could not reignite her by labouring on her body. I had to open up the engine—her mind—and tinker with its peculiar valves and wiring.

Now she was talking. Her arms were no longer folded across her chest. We were drinking tea in her big heavy ceramic mugs—enough of it to wash your face and ass with. She drank from these mugs all day. If I had two back-to-back I could piss a hole into the ground. Maybe it was the gallons of tea that kept her so wired. At the moment I didn't care. I was relieved. I was back inside the charmed circle, the tight small circle outside of which lay the vast universe she held in contempt. As ever, I wore an intensely attentive look while barely listening to what she was saying. I admired her sharp opinions and quirky mind, but hated her ceaseless droning. Many would not agree I suppose but this too was a kind of love—to work hard at practising deceit in order to find ardour.

It had to be a kind of love.

I certainly felt it so.

So while she dragged on about all the conversations she had had with Bhandariji, I struggled to look intense. I was actually thinking about the accelerating collapse of the magazine. Three weeks ago we had dropped to thirty-two pages, and now two months' salaries were in arrears. The staff was steadily peeling away like passengers from a bus reaching its last stop. The empty rows grew more derelict by the day. Soon there would be no one, just the waiting depot, just the driver and conductor, just Mr Lincoln and me.

Kuchha King, Kuchha Singh and Frock Raja had literally

disappeared behind the high walls of their farmhouses, beyond all contact, beyond any appeals, presumably under their shining faux galaxy, by the shuffling horse hooves, reconciled to writing off their losses with a small mountain of Calvin Klein undies.

Jai had been scuttling around, working up his public school buddies, delivering orations on media, democracy and the social contract. How, after indulgence, after excess, after aggrandizement, money must start to produce the moral moment. Mr Lincoln was quite something—capable of stirring bricks and stones and worse than senseless things. But men with money are quite something too. So far he had turned up nothing but a few soft loans that were soaked up by the office like water by parched land.

A few prospectors had come visiting and had been effusively shepherded around by Jai. They had pumped hands with wide smiles and never returned. There were no cobwebs blocking the doorways yet, but the dereliction of the abandoned chairs, dead computers and unpeopled rooms was enough to strike terror in the heart of any investor. The armed policeman in the sandbagged post outside and an unbuttoned swaying Sippy inside, were enough to close out all remaining doubt.

We were contaminated by controversy and political scandal, married to commercial vagueness and a tarred balance sheet. In truth Mr Lincoln was casting for a virgin in a bordello. Money, mostly, has no interest in systems of equity, liberty, justice, democracy or any such fanciful notions. Money is only interested in systems that make more money. Jai would close the door behind him and try and talk it all up with me, in a maddening mix of rousing optimism and despondent alarm. To me, he seemed in some state of mounting delirium.

For my part, I sat in my room on my chair all day with my feet on the table and stared out the window at the dirty blue sky and the scraggly tree—whose great moment of beauty had vanished without a trace. Guruji said life was like the Brahmaputra, the grandest of grand rivers, the very son of Brahma, the creator, ever moving, surging without a pause, unequally distributing joy and distress, seeking finally to merge into a receptacle that was even greater. You had to learn to flow with it. Sometimes you saw something on the banks that you really wanted, and then you beat your arms and kicked your legs and swam for it. At other times you just floated with the current, soaking it up, revelling in it, being one with it.

Guruji had said I was not to worry, the river would take me places, offer up new things. Too much frenzy, too much thrashing about, could be a big mistake. It could leave you in the same spot, struggling but not moving, robbed of the fantastic journeys the currents were going to take you on. Did I wish to tread water or savour the rich unknown? Guruji said, float freely and without fear but keep an eye on the shore. So I was looking out the window, counting the full-bellied planes coming in to land, watching the magpie robins in their shining black and white coats, and as far as I could see there was nothing on the shores for me for miles and miles and the river was flowing too sluggishly to open up fresh vistas.

I realized she had stopped talking and was waiting for me to respond. I had hardly registered a thought, just some stray words. Patiala House, Tyagi, Bhandariji, Tihar jail, and the names of two of the killers, Chaaku and Chini. She had also mentioned the names of some other lawyers she was considering for the defence team. A couple of names were outrageously famous—men who charged lakhs of rupees for a single appearance, men whose names and pictures filled the newspapers and TV channels, men who could strike fear into prime ministers, save mass murderers, turn evidence upside down so that judges hung by their legs from ceilings and gave out verdicts that had nothing to do with the truth. I also knew with her it wasn't kite-flying: if she set herself to it she had the ability to reel them in pro bono.

My assassins could not have been safer than in my lover's hands.

I said, 'You are right. You are right about it all.'

She said, 'So should we move on it then?'

I didn't know what she was talking about. I said, looking at her intently, 'Yes, but let's sleep on it for a day or two. Maybe we can consult a few other people too.'

She put her forefinger sharp under my chin, and said in a hard voice, 'Such a weak, indecisive bastard you are! I don't know why I suffer you!'

Her nipples were stiff against the white slip.

I caught her finger and squeezed it till it hurt and she grimaced. Looking her in the eye, I said, 'Bitch!'

She said, 'I should stop seeing you. In fact, would you please leave this very moment?'

I said, 'You whore! You have someone else coming in to make you happy?'

She said, her pupils dilating, 'Yes, but why should it concern you, you limp bastard!'

I took her finger that I had caught in my hand and slowly pushed it between her thighs, parting the fat fish on her turquoise wrap. She resisted, hissing, 'Stop it! Stop it, you bastard!' Her finger was unbending in my hand and I guided it into her lushness, striking water on the surface and digging deeper. Her eyes were half-closed now. 'Stop it, you dog,' she hissed, more softly now. I said, 'Saali randi! Always so open!' She gave a loud moan and virtually squatted on my hand. I immediately unleashed a stream of Hindi invective. She spat back more. I picked her up and nailed her to the wall, and kept her there till her foul mouth had turned beautifully fruity, and she was whispering sweet love to me and beseeching me to stay buried in her for life, and beyond.

She was free to save all my killers, present and future, if that's what kept her thus.

Guruji, truly, was not the master for nothing.

6

CHAAKU

i

The Son of Dakota

In the first few years of his life, Chaaku saw so little of his father that he assumed he was his uncle. The man who was his uncle, his father's younger brother, he took to be his father. It was done in the unconsidered way that children do these things. It's not as if Chaaku began to call his uncle Pitaji; he continued to call him Chacha, and his own father—when he saw him—Pitaji, but he just assumed that Chacha meant father. In the first ten years of his life, he did not see his father for a total of more than three; Chacha was there almost every single day.

Their village in Haryana lay several kilometres off the Grand Trunk Road and was named Keekarpur after the grove of thorny keekars on the sandy mound behind the hamlet. But they didn't live in its untidy cluster of naked brick and mud houses. To reach their eight-acre plot you had to walk a full fifteen minutes through the fields and then ford an ankle-deep stream by balancing on a fallen tree trunk. When they had visitors from the town, the directions given were: Ask anyone in the village for Fauladi Fauji's homestead, and after you've walked in the given direction for ten minutes and see only spiky fields of wheat and bajra all around you, you'll spot two tall date palms crossed at the neck, as if hugging each other. That's where the stream and the fallen tree across it lie. Step across it, and you're home. The dogs bark angrily, but don't bite.

Chacha, like the date palms, was into perennial hugging. He

greeted everyone with great slapping embraces, and always there was occasion to do so. Every week someone dropped in from near or far. The ones from close by, from Karnal and Kurukshetra and Pipli, stayed for a night or two; the ones from far off, from Amritsar and Gurdaspur, and occasionally from Delhi and Meerut, stayed on for weeks. Chaaku's grandmother didn't mind, nor did his uncle. He hugged everyone and cracked jokes with them; she cooked for them uncomplainingly, the chulha being set to fire from crack of dawn to late into the night.

The moment guests showed up, extra charpoys were put out under the neem tree and glasses of tea started to circulate as family stories were told and retold, news exchanged and dissected. At some point an old pack of cards, held together with a red rubberband, was brought out and rounds of Sweep commenced. Four players, many divided supporters and much banter and abuse. Chaaku always hung close to his Chacha—reading the cards from over his shoulder—and learnt to play expertly by the time he was seven.

At the time nobody called him Chaaku. His name was Tope Singh—a tribute to his father who was in the armoured corps of the Indian army. Each time the boy did something smart, especially helped win a trick at Sweep, his Chacha would say, 'He is not just a tope, he is India's hope!' And someone else would say, 'You have to admit, the tope may be small, but the bomb it fires is big!' His prowess at Sweep gave him a place among the adults, and a grand idea of himself. He learnt early that all it took to impress big people was some quick sleight-of-hand, some dazzling moves, a disarming smile.

While his Chacha presided over the Sweep tournaments—on days watching desperately for someone to ford the stream so that a game could begin—and his grandmother kept the food fires burning, his grandfather Fauladi Fauji sat by the fodder chopper outside the hay room, bubbling his hookah. Once in a while he cast a sidelong glance at the quiet frenzy under the neem tree, but almost never sent a word in its direction. On first arriving, when visitors dove for his feet, he simply grunted, 'Is everything okay?' or, 'May you live long.' After that, he exhibited no desire to speak to them, save sometimes after dinner, when he returned from a slow walk through the fields and drinking his nightly glass of boiling milk, called out sharply to one of the visiting males, 'Come here, Sukha, and tell me how you've been wasting your life.' And Sukha, jumping to it, would say, 'Oh Fauladi Taiya, it's the only degree I've managed to get in my life! Everything else has been a zero.'

By then Sukha, forty years old, would have tried his earning hand at more than a dozen things. As a serial entrepreneur he'd have launched and closed shops selling electrical goods, household provisions, bicycle spare parts, textiles, sweetmeats, hardware, fruits and vegetables. He'd have taken a shot at dairy farming, rising before dawn to squat on his haunches and supervise the milking of his buffaloes. His foray into poultry farming would have ended in a spectacular failure that saw him and his friends eating up every single bird. There would be no bank in all of Ambala that had not extended him a loan; no self-employment scheme of the government of which he would not have availed. He would also have been a registered agent of the life insurance corporation; a link in many multilayered marketing chains, selling everything from home appliances to bits of gold. He would have played his part in many wild moneymaking schemes—lotteries, committees, jackpots—all of which would have ended in chaos and disgrace. In between, in periods of fallowness, he would have held jobs too—doing accounts at the local sugar mill, teaching in a school, supervising the truck movements for a local trader.

But a job was always the last resort. Essentially, he'd have hated working for someone, earning a salary, steering by office hours. In spirit, he was an entrepreneur, a risk taker, the dreamer of fabulous dreams. 'One doesn't have to just eat! Even Bija does that!' he would say, referring to the low-caste who worked on the farm, and now grinned, squatting near the charpoys, watching the game of Sweep. When urged to a job, he would say, 'Nah bhai, I don't want to spend my life listening to some lala's recriminations. Did you put one spoon of sugar in your tea or two? Did the foreman wash his hands twice? Does he think the soap comes for free? Sack that Sharma, he took three days of leave last week. But, lalaji, his mother is old and dying—he had to take her to the hospital. So what? Do you think ours are young and flying! And is he a doctor that he needed to stay on there?'

But Sukha, what about a government job, someone would urge. And Sukha would get up and stick out his buttocks and do a duck waddle around the charpoy. 'Have you ever seen a government officer who doesn't look like he's walking around with a thick finger up his ass? The smart ones have their own finger up their hole, the fools have someone else's. Well, I don't want to put my finger up anyone's ass, and I don't want anyone's up mine!'

Sukha's life, at forty, would be rich with experience and failure. Many of the young men who came to the farm across the stream were like him, freewheeling failed men, trying to chase and ride every new scheme and dream that caught the air. In their own way, creative men, playing the long shot, trying desperately to overturn the odds with one magical move. The thing Tope discovered about them was that they were not only the most interesting men, with the greatest fund of stories and anecdotes, but that they were also the most happy.

The ones who were dour and complaining were those who held steady jobs, drew secure salaries, and went to work on time and returned home by six every day. Their stories were always about some stupid family problems, some child's illness, some scooter or house loan to be repaid, the travails of a hatchet-tongued wife, or a boss who didn't let them off on time, some damn increment that was denied, but mostly about the impossibility of balancing the domestic monthly budget. These men either mourned ceaselessly or were sullen and bitter.

In contrast the freewheelers like Sukha always came with a hilarious tale of a recently collapsed venture and the excitement of a freshly brewing one. They were always canvassing the others present into investing in their mad plans, and though they were always broke—sometimes dangerously in hock—they seemed to be having a good time.

Once, for two weeks, Sukha came and hid out at the farm because there were creditors in Panipat looking out for him. He had taken twenty thousand rupees from two traders as an advance to secure them a gas agency. His commission of five thousand he had burnt on his friends and revelry, and passed on the remaining fifteen to the government middleman in the petroleum ministry in Delhi, who had promised to do the job. Well, the agency had gone to someone else; the middleman refused to see him any more; and the traders had sent their goons to collect. Hiding at the farm, Sukha had been a riot.

He'd told little Tope, 'Your father is a lance-naik, but I am appointing you a naik. Above him. Two stripes instead of his one. And his Vijayanta tank is nothing compared to the Neema tank I am giving you.' And he lofted Tope into the crotch of the tree, and curling the thumb and forefinger of both his hands into tiny circles he put them against his eyes, and said, 'Here, I've also given you the best binoculars in the world. Now keep an eye on the borders of our country, and if you see the enemy moving in our direction, fire a loud fart! It should strike terror into the enemy's heart, and give us enough time to bring up reinforcements!'

Then Chacha and Sukha would sit below, cross-legged on the

charpoy, and play cards and swig the pale santri. Every now and then he would look up and holler, 'I hope you haven't gone to sleep in your tank? I haven't heard a fart in a long time!' Immediately Tope would mimic one by blowing hard into the back of his hand.

Sukha was slim as a bamboo. His thick hair fell to his ears and his face always sported a light stubble. He wore pointed Patiala juttis on his feet and smart bush shirts with small stiff collars. He had friends in the university campus in Chandigarh and he told many stories about their lifestyle. While Tope manoeuvred the Neema tank and scanned the borders with his binoculars, Sukha, on the charpoy below, gave graphic accounts of the boozing, the parties, the motorcycles, and the amazing girls. He described how stunningly beautiful the girls were and how brazen the clothes they wore—the tight trousers, the red lipstick, the open collar shirts—as Chacha made sounds of disbelief. Tope's hands grew clammy on the steering of the Neema as he heard how the girls visited the rooms of the boys and willingly did things that could barely be imagined to be true. Chacha clearly too was sceptical. Like a police detective, he asked intricate questions, details of physical features, postures, what was said, done. Like the finest of investigators, he asked for everything to be described to him again and again. Sukha spared no detail. Tope went faint and feverish by turn, even taking his hands off the tank to clutch himself. Often he felt he would simply explode, taking the magnificent Neema with him. Each time Sukha finished an account, Chacha waved his thin arms and shouted, 'Behanchod, fuck off from here! You are going to make me go mad!' And Sukha, scraping his stubble with his fingers would say, 'Wait till I tell you what we did with Ruby of the big-big booby!'

Occasionally someone not immediately recognizable was spotted crossing the stream. Sukha then rushed into the small mud room at the back where the grain was stored. The room had no windows but some light seeped in from under the eaves and from the chinks in the thatch. Tope brought in a hurricane lamp and Sukha and he sat on the cool golden heap of winnowed wheat—digging out comfortable seats for themselves—and played Sweep. It was here that Sukha first showed him his flick-knife. He said it was a Rampuria. It had a handle of wood with three visible screws and a four-inch blade, bevelled in two surfaces and curved to a hard sharp point. The catch was in brass, easily worked with the tip of the thumb. Tope was allowed to hold it, open it, close it, run his fingertips along its gleaming steel. He even tested it against his skin, without breaking it. Sukha said the four-inch was better than the six-inch—that is, if you were looking for efficiency not exhibition. The short blade, with an equally matched handle, gave better leverage when you cut hard or dug.

Tope asked him if he had ever knifed anyone. Sukha smiled and said, 'What do you think?' Tope asked, how many. Sukha opened both his hands, closed them, and then opened four fingers of the right. It was late afternoon, and the light in the small mud room was a peculiar mix of a weak sun leaking in from here and there and the small pool of yellow light created by the lamp. The room was set too far back in the house for the voices of the visitor and Chacha to reach them, but there was the continual scurrying of animal feet in the thatch above. Tope looked at Sukha's face in the mixed light, and it was not smiling. He said, 'Fourteen?'

Sukha nodded.

He said, 'Killed?'

Sukha lifted the forefinger of his right hand.

Tope said, 'The rest got away?'

Sukha said, 'Oyee Tantia Tope, I am not a killer! That one was also a mistake. It was in the beginning, when I didn't know how to handle this. A knife is a beautiful thing. It is not meant to kill—for that you have the pistol. A knife is meant to strike terror, to sow the memory of fear in your victim. A knife is a goldsmith's instrument; a pistol is an ironmonger's. A bullet can never give you the finesse, the precision of a blade. With a knife you can decide the exact punishment you want to mete out—cut a five-inch-long line, dig a two-inch-deep hole, chop one half of a finger, blunt the nose at the tip, dice the tongue in half, slice out one testicle, expand the size of an asshole, chop the ears into new shapes, draw a flower on the chest, a star on the cheek. You can do all these lovely things; and if the occasion really demands it, you can excavate the entrails, carve out the heart, plant a flag in the brain. With a pistol you can only do one thing: blow a hole in flesh. Pistols are used by butchers; artists use knives.'

Little Tope was agog. He stared at Sukha's handsome face in the shifting light as he delicately ran the open blade across his stubble. How strong and calm he was.

Sukha said, 'You want to see what good artists can do?'

Tope nodded, lost for words.

Sukha picked up the hurricane lamp with his left hand and bringing it close to himself pulled his shirt up to his chin. His face vanished into the dark, and in the pool of yellow light a flower of knotted flesh appeared on Sukha's chest. The artist had drawn the flower like a child. Six petals around the heart of the flower which was Sukha's left nipple. Sukha said, 'Four of them held me down, while he drew. I screamed enough to have burst the lord's eardrums, but the artist's hand did not shake for an instant. See how beautifully he's made it. Can you ever do that with a pistol? Each time I take off my clothes, each time I have a bath, each time I run my hands over my body, I remember that artist, I remember his helpers, I remember the mad pain that made me want to die. That is the power of the artist—he is always remembered. No butcher ever is.'

Then Sukha showed Tope his other exhibits of flesh art. A thick rope climbing from the inside of his right thigh to his groin; a little pink-red motte on his left shoulder; and then, turning around, a supremely surreal second spinal cord next to his first.

Tope said, 'Did it pain a lot?'

Sukha said, 'You must never think of the pain. If you think of the pain you got, then you can never give it. If you fear getting pain, you will fear giving it. What do our elders always tell us—don't think, just do. If you think too much then you lose the ability to do. But our elders are wrong when they say, always act with a cool mind. Different situations demand different responses. Sometimes you have to carve beauty, and sometimes you have to repel ugliness. Sometimes the odds are stacked against you, and what you need in the fight is not coolness but madness. You must pump the rage up from the bottom of your stomach, it must scream through you, it must take you beyond all considerations of pain. The knife must become an extension of your arm; it must cut, slice, dig with a fury born in hell. You must become a dervish. At such a time there should be nothing calm in your head or body. I have seen a five-foot mosquito set four big men to fleeing because his fury was bigger than all of them. When you work with a knife you need both skill and courage. No weak man can put a knife into human flesh. I tell you, there are men who cannot even stick it into a live chicken! When you work with a knife you have to be both—artist and madman. And you know, actually, they are the same thing.'

Tope blanched. He knew how he himself recoiled each time his Chacha trapped a chicken between his feet and decapitated it; how he averted his eyes when the blood spurted and the chicken flopped about looking for its missing head. Even the defeathering and skinning repelled him. Only when it was washed and clean, the pink flesh succulent and soulless, would he begin to feel good about it.

By now they had sunk deep into the mound of golden grain, and Sukha was scooping the cool wheat and running it through his fingers, and pouring it over his forearms and legs, his lungi pulled up to his thighs. Tope was playing with the Rampuria, testing its spring, feeling its blade, trying to grip it in different ways, for an underhand drive, for an overhead stab, for a roundhouse slash.

Sukha said, 'Well done! You are learning.'

Tope said, 'I want to learn,' shredding the air ruthlessly.

Sukha laughed and said, 'You want to be a chaakumaar? Your father blasts bombs from a tank, and you want to be a chaakumaar! Okay, I'll teach you, but only if you run out now and get me a hot glass of tea.'

It was true. His father's wielding of the mighty Vijayanta tank, or his grandfather's exploits in the army, did nothing for him. He had heard their stories all his life. How his father won a mention-in-dispatches in the 1971 war against Pakistan for assisting in the destruction of a Patton tank; how his grandfather was recommended for the Military Cross when he helped his platoon hold off a Japanese charge in Burma towards the end of the Second World War; how his father had been the regimental middle-weight boxing champion for eight continuous years; how his grandfather could bend an iron rod on his thigh or his shoulders—hence the moniker Fauladi Fauji; how Burgess sahib told his grandfather that he was the pride of the British army; and how Major Khan told his father that he was as strong as the tank he manoeuvred. He had seen the old uniforms and ammunition boots packed in the dented black army trunk; he had seen the dull medals and the ceremonial lanyards, and the cummerbunds and the faded ribbons, and the frayed woollen socks and the moth-eaten olive cardigans, and the stiff rain cape with two gaping holes for the arms; and the assortment of jungle hats and berets and balaclavas. There were also the yellowing pictures, stuck on yellowing cardboard, with rows of crew-cut men—in stiff uniforms and floppy sports shorts and battle fatigues—all looking the same, till the old man jabbed his finger and pointed himself out as a young man. The reverence with which they handled this junk bored him; their continual talk of discipline, exercise, obedience, rules, regulations, timings, glory, honour was a pain.

Even at the age of ten he could see they were flakes, cut off from reality, living in some place and time that was mostly make-believe. His grandfather managed to stay in this unreal place by loftily removing himself from everyone else around. He almost never spoke to any of the workers on the farm, had dismissive exchanges with the villagers who chanced by, and was brutally laconic with relatives and visitors. For nearly thirty years, from the time he was pensioned from the army, he had done nothing but bubble his hookah and stare out at the fields. Twice a day, morning and evening, he took a long walk past the outer fields, carrying his military stick—of knotted bamboo—in one hand and an empty brown beer bottle in the other. Chacha said, 'You have to hand it to him. He makes even a crap look like a regimental inspection.'

Often, when the labour was working the wheel of the fodder chopper, he would, sitting close by on his charpoy, stare at the slicing leaves of grass exploding with rich green aromas, as if locating some deep meaning in it. By speaking minimally, doing nothing, and possessing a legendary past, he had come to be seen as a repository of wisdom and strength. Everyone tiptoed around him; no one crossed him; and when he gifted someone a monosyllabic moment, gratitude and awe flowed back.

The grandchild was no exception to this minimalist treatment. He too was spoken to gruffly, and expected to live in awe. In the beginning, when he had dared ask the grand man some questions, he was always dismissed; children must not be so curious. Later, after Tope had stopped trying to talk to him, the old man would often track him with hard critical eyes, as if walking through the fields without chanting left-right-left-right was a crime. His strategy was good: he conveyed disapproval but never expressed it. That left everyone on the back foot, struggling with it, trying to gauge its extent, and yet never having the opportunity to challenge or rebut it. Tope often found himself hoping his grandfather would just say something nasty to him so he could hit back. But that was not to be. You had to contend with the lofty disapproval that arose from nothing and was directed at everything, without ever being articulated.

Tope's father, Dakota Ram—Fauladi's unit had just been offloaded from such a plane when he received the news of his son's birth—Dakota Ram was doubly marred. For years he suffered his father's inarticulate pretensions, and then the army slopped on a fair share of its own. The result was a tragically two-dimensional man: one part receiving orders, instructions, rules, regulations; the other, implementing and executing them to the letter. It was quite likely that a careless impulse had never coursed through his body; an original thought never sparked in his head. He had always done what he was told—by his father, by the army—and every situation he ever faced had set responses that he knew. When he didn't know he simply asked someone who did. There was nothing about life or the world that had to be examined, analysed, questioned or understood. There were just processes and rules, just the brass and polish, just the doing.

When Dakota Ram came home on his annual two-month leave, he continued to wake before dawn, cut a close shave, exercise twice a day, eat his meals as in the battalion, at six, twelve and seven, and not indulge in small talk with his family. Like his father, he retained the army starch at all times, a clear distance from ordinary frivolities. He was a man who rode in a thousand-ton tank, who could blast holes in the horizon big as houses, who had lived the din of battle, death and destruction, whose officers spoke clippetyclop English and ate with shining cutlery and had fair-skinned wives with buns on their heads big as melons. Whose regiment had a hundred-and-twenty-year-old tradition of bravery and honour, whose grim job it was to defend the country. Sweep, idle village banter, indulgences of petty affection and love, were not for him. He was happy to give a sombre hearing to issues of village development and serious problems, but no backslapping gossip was allowed. He met everyone, including his small son, with a formal handshake. Every evening before dinner, he knocked back two large tots of dark Hercules rum with four fingers of water but he did it alone, with a sense of ceremony and ritual. In his first year in the regiment Lt Oomen had told him, 'Dakota, whatever you do, do it with the style of the white man! They shoot you as if they are giving you a medal; they shit as if they are having a conversation in the drawing-room; and they drink as if taking part in a religious ceremony. And look at us! Always down on the ground, shitting, swilling, getting shot!'

Sometimes Chacha was invited to join in, but never to have more than the prescribed two, with Dakota measuring the drinks, holding both glass and bottle up to eye-level as he poured. Chacha would then wander off and quaff his santri, and tell his mother, 'It's like giving a berry to a lion! Sher nu ber! Doesn't even wet my tongue!' To his father, Dakota gave one large and one small tot. But they sat fifteen feet apart—Fauladi near the chopper; the tank man near the neem tree—and drank in silence, while the tube wells began to rumble water and the fields cleared of the last workers and a final rash of redness bathed the skies and the birds winging home filled the air with the day's chatter. Behind them, the woodsmoke from the open chulha rose in slow waves and mixing with the aroma of bubbling dal spread through the darkening evening and the chewing of the buffaloes at the feeding trough grew steadily louder, joined by the oxen just in from their labours. The barking of dogs began to mark the scattered homesteads as night fell and a zillion stars burst through the roof of the world. Through the magical transition—which the city can never know—the two army men, father and son, gulped their rum, locked in their individual armour, incapable of giving and incapable of receiving.

The boy stayed close to his Chacha and far away from the stiff stranger under the neem tree. Fleetingly home, the tank man had nothing to say to his son, nothing to offer him. The regiment taught you nothing about this kind of fatherhood. In the regimental kind, the commanding officer was the father, and he gave you not emotion and affection but orders and a protective umbrella. His was the voice of god. Never to be questioned, in life or death. The other fathering that Dakota Ram had known, of Fauladi's, had been no different. Regular thrashings, unswerving obedience, and no display of feelings. Recruitment, training, boot camp, while a nightmare for most of his mates, had been a romp for him. With a deep sense of piety, Dakota actually approved of his father's ruthless rules of upbringing. He felt they had served him well. Made a real man out of him, indifferent to pain and privation, dauntless in the face of death. He too made it a point to thrash his son once every week while he was home on leave. That was a minimum of eight thrashings during his annual leave and two during his casual. Sometimes it troubled him to do so, but he knew any weakness on his part would ruin the boy's character.

Sometimes it was difficult to locate a reason to beat Tope. The boy tended to steer clear of his path and to keep his voice down. Then Dakota would summon him and berate him for his indifferent performance in school, and follow it up with some really tough time-and-work sums. Tope Singh would struggle with the maths, his limbs and mind already going numb at the thought of the thrashing to come. For variety's sake, Dakota Ram sometimes used his cane, sometimes his canvas belt, sometimes his army boots, and sometimes just his big hands. He never hit the boy with all his strength—that would have killed him—but with just enough to hurt him. In fact, the rage only rose in Dakota after he had begun to whack him—it was the boy's squealing that got his juices going. The first blow was always desultory, cold; the last always hard, heated.

His own father, Fauladi, watched it all impassively from his post on the charpoy by the chopper, gurgling on his hookah. And Dakota, occasionally, to earn his father's unstated approval, gave his son an extra brutal blow or two. Tope Singh's mother, Dakota's wife, was in no position to help matters. The philosophy of regular chastisement that applied to the son applied to her too. Her quota was one thrashing a week, but for the sake of decorum it was carried out indoors. Of course her screams could be heard everywhere. This was also a family tradition Dakota Ram had imbibed from his father: even now the old man gave his old lady an occasional passing blow. The women took it well—fate could have been more cruel: left them unmarried, son-less, widows—and the pain seldom persisted beyond a day unless the buckle or stick caught a bone.

After the beating Tope's grandmother would heat a stone and wrap it in a chunni and give it to Chacha, who would gently apply it to him while telling him stories from the Mahabharata. In time Tope's favourite character in the epic became Bhima. The other Pandava brothers—Yudhishthira, Arjuna, Nakul and Sahadeva—were too rule-bound and quiescent. Bhima alone raged at the injustices heaped on them, and threatened vengeance on all who gave them grief. Bhima of the boundless strength, Bhima who would in the great battle seek out and slay each of the hundred Kaurava brothers for the ignominy they had heaped on his wife Draupadi, Bhima who understood that beyond a point moral niceties were a weakness and a sin. Often, when the blows were raining on him or his mother's screams tearing at his ears, Tope would imagine himself as Bhima, the mace of havoc on his shoulder, wreaking retribution on his father and grandfather as they begged for mercy. When he walked through the fields alone he swung his arms like a warrior, smashing the stalks of wheat, shouting, Bhimsen, Bhimsen, Bhimsen!

As it turned out Tope's body lived up to neither his own name nor that of his god. He went from twelve to thirteen to fourteen to fifteen with the speed of time, but his frame remained slight, the limbs thin, the shoulders narrow, the chest small. Nor did he gain the expected height, ending up much shorter and much thinner than his father and grandfather, more and more like his Chacha, so far the runt of the family. As if, by osmosis, the uncle's love had made the boy's physicality akin to his own.

The old man's eyes became even more dismissive. He told Dakota, 'Tope Singh! Look at him! You should have named him Pistol Singh! Doesn't even look like you!' The metronomic chop-chop of the fodder being sliced filled the air. The smell of bleeding green was everywhere. The old man pulled hard on his hookah, coughed, and continued, 'And which army are you going to send him to—the dwarf and midget brigade?'

The tank man said nothing, just kept gulping from his tumbler of dark rum. After some time he rose, went in, and wordlessly thrashed his wife and son.

At fifteen, the humiliation hurt more than the blows. Tope held his tiny sobbing mother close and said to her, 'I want to kill him.' His mother, married as a small girl at thirteen, already an old woman at thirty-two, who in her life had known only two modest homesteads and many beatings, whose only warm memory was the love and care of her own mother, Tope's sobbing mother said, 'Don't say such things! But I know what you mean.'

The boy first tasted blood at sixteen.

It was so much easier than he had imagined. For nearly seven years he had played with the fantasy, sitting alone in the gloom of the grain room, and against the naked brick wall of the tube well, and in the heart of the sword-leafed sugarcane fields, and by the sluggish stream that only surged in the monsoon, and under the hugging date palms, and in the lonely walks to the village school, and under his thick quilt on chill winter nights.

As sound is created by simply turning the knob of a radio, the fantasy began with the flicking open of his knife. His thumb pressed the smooth lever and the blade sprang out, gleaming. Suddenly there was menace in his eyes, in the angle of his arm, in the sneer on his lips. He didn't feel small any more. He felt dangerous, lethal, capable of unleashing mayhem. All around him men and women—mostly faceless, but also his father and grandfather—cowered in respect and fear, averting their eyes, treading soundlessly. As he walked through the bazaar, a hushed whisper of awe filled the air. As sound is killed by turning off the radio knob, the fantasy vanished the moment the knife blade was clicked close. Only runty little Tope Singh remained.

For seven years, the boy had treasured the Rampuria like a priceless jewel. He had managed to keep it hidden from all the prying eyes at home and in the fields. The only one who knew about it was Chacha, and he was sworn to secrecy. In turn the uncle had sought a vow that Tope would not ever carry the knife outside the homestead, certainly not till he was twenty-one. In other words, never use it on man or beast.

On the other hand, Sukha, glorious Sukha, freewheeling Sukha, laughing Sukha, the gifter of the blade, the philosopher of the knife, had merely said, 'Treat it well, handle it with care. Don't use it to cut vegetables and don't use it to sharpen pencils. Don't use it to trim your nails and don't use it shave your beard. Don't use it to dig holes and don't use it to kill chickens. Remember, a Rampuria has only one purpose. It is like a sword or a dagger or a gun. It is a weapon. It's made to strike fear in the human heart. It's made to slice open human flesh. Remember, it may be only four inches, but it'll add many feet to your stature. A Rampuria makes you a man, it makes you a warrior. In a world where respect is hard to come by, it brings you respect. Both money and power—who care neither for character nor kindness—find in themselves respect for a man who sheathes a Rampuria.' Sukha had then clicked the blade shut, massaged the sleeping knife in his palm for many long moments, and handed it over to the young boy.

Instantly Tope had recognized the truth of everything Sukha said. When he turned fifteen he went to Rafat, the village tailor—an old squint-eyed Musalman, who had no gift for running a stitch-line straight—and asked him to craft him a tight inner pocket for his trousers.

Rafat's mud and brick shop was in the outermost circle of the village and a shallow open drain of slow-moving sludge ran past his door. The shop was bare but for a clattering Singer foot-pedal machine, a worn brown and yellow durrie on the uneven mud floor, and the chair on which Rafat sat. A neat stack of tailored clothes stood in one corner and an untidy heap of semi-tailored ones, arms and legs flapping about, were tossed in the other. Rafat wore a faded green measuring tape around his shoulders and a shrapnel of blue chalk in his ear, but seldom took any measurements because he already knew most of his clients' sizes. The main thrust of his work was not fresh tailoring but the refitting of hand-me-downs doing the endless carousel between fathers, sons, siblings, cousins. There were pieces that he had refitted five, six, seven times, an adult trouser finishing off as a boy's 'half-pant', a man's kurta ending as a baby's slip. For years the tailor had altered Dakota Ram's old olive trousers and shirts for both Chacha and Tope, leaving in the blank epaulettes, the flap pockets, the belt loops, the pleats. When done, they looked as they were—ragged, giveaway army clothes, without the starch, the shine, the finery. Because Rafat was such a poor craftsman, the adapted clothes were always crooked and ill-fitting. When someone made the mistake of complaining, the tailor looked scathingly at him over his glasses. 'And look at you! Off to dinner with the deputy commissioner!' Astutely, however, he made up for the bad aesthetics with excessive robustness. He ran and re-ran many wavering lines over every seam so his clothes never came apart, no matter the strain. The only way the clothes died was by being worn threadbare. It gave him a great reputation.

So Rafat gave him a slim pouch, from the inner waistband, along the line of the fly, in his father's old olive army trousers. He made the pouch from tough khaki canvas, so that an accidental triggering would not flick open the blade and slice the boy. The knife dug into his flesh, and sometimes when Tope was out for too long it made his skin sore. It was a negligible price to pay. Apart from what it was, where it nestled gave him a heightened sense of potency. Often, when he stood around or walked, he felt for it with his fingers, thick and unyielding along his inner thigh.

He practised drawing it rapidly for a fight, like a revolver from a holster. Often, at midday, he went down to the soft soil by the stream, behind the high sharp rushes, and standing with his feet apart, in one move, shot his hand into the waistband, pulled the knife out of the pouch and flicked it open, shouting 'Hahh!' Then he stabbed the swaying rushes, or slashed them shallowly as Sukha had once instructed him, just opening up the skin with the steel tip, causing great pain but not deep injury.

For some time in the beginning he tried to become a knife thrower, practising his skill against the scaly trunks of the embracing date palms across the stream. Standing about ten feet away he chucked the knife at the trunks again and again, but it virtually never stuck. It was not that his aim was bad. He invariably hit the trees but never with the leading tip so that it wedged in. Tope tried tossing it from the shaft, from the blade, underhand, with the wrist turned in, but the knife didn't seem weighted for attack by throwing. It turned poorly in the air, and never managed a clean trajectory.

After each training session, like a good warrior, he would tend to his weapon, pulling out the smooth five-kilo stone he kept in the rushes by the stream. The stone was shaped like an embryo, smoothed to satin by millennia of running water. Tope would put the embryo on its back and in the curve of its torso begin to strop his blade. He would do this sometimes for nearly an hour, squatting on his haunches, pouring palmfuls of water over the burning steel. Once in a while he brought some mustard oil in a tiny medicine vial and gave the blade a viscous coat. Then it was all rubbed down with soft soil and an old rag.

When Tope first put his knife into Bhupinder's flesh and in one swift stroke drew an artful cummerbund across his belly, a profound sense of power and ecstasy filled his being. Big Bhupi, bullying Bhupi, with his tight blue turban, his already thick beard, his loud hectoring voice, big Bhupi who had just pushed him in the chest for the second time, took a moment to react. Then blood spurted in a line like juice from a sliced mango and Bhupi screamed, 'Hai I am dead! Hai the maiovah has killed me!'

Before the sardar found the nerve to reach for the short kirpan in its brass scabbard that hung by his left side, Tope put a neat cross on his left shoulder. Like Eklavya who mastered archery by practising in front of the statue of Drona, Tope had learnt the lessons of Sukha through unflagging repetition. The cuts were shallow, sucking out the blood without severing anything critical; he himself was balanced nicely between rage and calm; and how sweet, how supremely sweet, the unleashed knife felt in his hand. He so hoped that one of the two other boys with Bhupi would make a move, allowing him to extend his sublime dance, to decorate more flesh.

But the boys were in a paralysis of terror, all the laughing bravura of a minute ago silenced by the flick-knife. Bhupi who had picked on him for months, calling him a runt, making him the butt of his schoolyard humour, Bhupi who had hustled him into the guava orchard and asked him to open his pants and show him and his gang the smallness of his penis, Bhupi now held his spurting stomach with his left forearm and the cross on his left shoulder with his right hand. There was blood everywhere, on his shirt, pants, and dripping on to the ground, into the mulch of fallen leaves. The sardar had begun to sob, big tears bubbling out of his frightened eyes: 'Hai I've been killed! Hai the maiovah has killed me! Hai someone call my father! Hai my mother I am dead!'

Tope noticed the guavas on the trees were still deep green and rock hard, thousands of them glistening in the dappled light of midafternoon. Another week and they could start plucking them. There was one strain in this orchard that had pink hearts—he loved eating those, though they never tasted as good as they looked.

Almost playfully, he took a step forward, the knife hard in his extended hand. The three boys immediately recoiled, stumbling back over the mulch. This was the dominant group of the village school, skippered by Bhupi, the biggest landlord's son. Boys like Tope had been kicked around by them all their lives. His pants had first been yanked off by them when he was eleven, and then whenever they chose. Passively, he had felt the pain and pleasure of their hands and bodies. There was nothing they had not done to him, and he had learnt early that brutality always accompanied the joys of the flesh. He could feel it now, in the way his steel tip opened up Bhupi's skin, just as the sardar's had his, so many years ago. Now all he could see in their eyes was fear. It was beautiful. The juices were surging in him. In a delirium of artistry he could have decorated all of them. Festooned them with red ribbons of flesh.

They must have seen it in his eyes. The fervour beginning to swirl the dervish. Bhupi wailed, crumpling to his knees, clutching at his leaking skin, 'Maiovah, the fauji's runt has gone bloody mad! He wants to kill all of us! Wait till my father plucks his cock out and feeds it to the mongrels!'

Moving to his own music, Tope cut a divine arc through the air and spliced the forearm of the boy nearest him as he raised it in protection. Like juice from a mango sprang the line incarnadine. Jeeta, of the elephant ears, his family tenant-tillers of Bhupi's family acres, screeched, 'Oh fuck my mother's cunt he's ripped me too!' He turned on Tope ready to storm him in anger, but then saw the abandon in his eyes, the slow rotation of the Rampuria in his right hand. Tope followed him a step and slashed the air open with a lazy swing of his arm. Backing in panic, elephant-ears Jeeta stumbled upon Bhupi and fell in a heap. The sardar was now dribbling from his nose too, and the two fallen boys were cowering behind their arms.

The third boy, Bhupi's fourteen-year-old cousin Lucky, who

had been trying to support the crumpled sardar, now tried to make a run for it. With a graceful lunge, Tope sank the tip of his Rampuria into the fleeing boy's soft left buttock. The boy fell with a thud and a screech that startled the parakeets from the guava trees. 'Hai my mother I've been killed! Hai I am dead!' Bhupi moaned. 'My father will peel the skin off your body. He will break your arse. You will regret that you were ever born.'

Tope turned slowly and with a finely calibrated jab hit the writhing heap of Bhupi right between his arse cheeks. His scream almost scared the feathers off the birds. 'Oh my mother! My mother! My mother! Fuck my mother!' Jeeta was trying to bury into the mulch, his head down, eyes averted. Lucky was lying as if dead, on his stomach, both his hands on his arse, one running red. Bhupi was heaving with sobs, but struggling to keep the noise down. The mulch was sticking to the mucus flowing from his eyes and nose.

What an embarrassment of opportunity! Which to decorate next? The sun pouring through the gnarled guava branches fell as filigree on the ground. The three boys lay in heaps, in shade and light, in a gentle choreography of moan and twitch, arms and legs contorted in an attempt to stem the new openings in their bodies.

Tope said, to no one in particular, 'Show!'

He tried to use the same tone that had been used on him five years ago, and then again and again. Just the word. 'Show.'

No one moved. The bodies just curled in on themselves even tighter.

'Show!'

When no one responded, Tope gently put the tip of the Rampuria between Bhupi's arse cheeks. With an ear-splitting wail, the sardar turned over, crumpled leaves and twigs sticking all over his face, glued in place by the mucus and the beard. His entire shirt was a sticky mud-brown.

'Show!'

The sardar's hands were so slippery and shaky that he had trouble pushing clear the fat button of his trousers, which too were soaked with the thick seeping of his red cummerbund. 'Show!' said Tope, bending low and bringing the Rampuria closer. The sardar immediately went into a panic of babbling and tugging. When Rafat's reinforced last button was yanked free, the last string pulled loose, there lay revealed nothing but purposeless hair and loose flesh.

The true measure of things. The tyrant after the court has vanished; the policeman shorn of his uniform; the man who is no longer a minister; the schoolmaster in the bazaar. The tormentor bereft of his trappings. The molester leached of his tumescence. Nothing to make the juice rise, nothing to inflate the mind and the flesh with power and passion. Just a small mess of loose flesh drowning in purposeless hair.

Tope put his right foot on the shrunken tormentor and pressed down gently. The sardar wailed like a baby through his mucus and clutched at his ankle. It was not as bad as it looked. Tope's keds were the flat rubber-soled mud-brown hand-me-down standard issues used by army men. Light, smooth, not a single groove remaining on their thin underside. The other two boys, faces averted, were looking at him from the corner of their eyes. The filigree of sunlight could not camouflage their terror. That young boy Lucky, they had been breaking him in, tutoring him to extract pleasure from terror. He had been put to practice on the migrant labourers working their fields. Behind hay ricks, inside tube wells, amid the cane, by the rushes. Now he lay there, a second small hole in his bum, burrowing into the mulch.

All it took was a knife! A Rampuria. Not size, not wealth, not numbers. Not caste, not creed, not class. Just a knife.

For the first time in years Tope felt beautiful. Strong and beautiful. Like he used to when Sukha put him on his Neema tank and entrusted him with guarding the borders with an arsenal of farts.

Suddenly Bhupi squirmed, attempting to push his foot away. In cold anger, Tope pushed his foot down hard and gave it two slow twists. The sardar's scream must have reached the village, and loosened the bowels of the other two boys.

Then, as he'd seen in one of the nine films he'd been taken to in town, Tope bent down and wiped the Rampuria on the writhing-screaming sardar's shirt—at the shoulder, where it was still unbloodied—and flicked the knife shut.

ii

The Prince of Bundpangas

There was hell to pay. For a very long time. But Tope did not pick up any of the cheques.

By the time he meandered back to the embracing palms, walking on air, the news had already reached. Chacha grabbed his arm as he hopped off the tree trunk across the stream and literally dragged him to the far south of the fields where the eucalyptus grove rose like a garrison of pale ghosts waving at the skies. In no time they were deep among the spectres, the only sounds their panting breaths and the scrunch of the crisp leaves underfoot. Chacha was not letting them walk. They moved at a steady speed. Neither boy nor man exchanged a single word. The hallmark of a robust relationship is knowing how to act in a crisis without anything being said. There would be time to talk. Now there was not enough time to run.

They emerged on the other side of the waving ghosts and stayed with the fields, running on the narrow mud bunds, both in flat brown keds, Dakota's army seconds. When the dividing mud line was too narrow they ran straddling it, in an ungainly waddle, swaying from side to side. Fortunately the fields were close to harvest and there was no water or slush to impede their movement. The late afternoon sun was heavy on their backs. They crouched as they ran, as if dodging bullets. The fact was, away from the grove, the land stretched clear for acres and acres on all sides. The ripened wheat was not too high. If your eye was good you could spot a paddy bird taking flight hundreds of metres away. Chacha took a line distant from the homesteads and tried to steer clear of the steadily balding squares where wiry migrant labour, men and women and children from eastern UP and Bihar, were on their haunches slicing the golden stalks and tying them into bundles. A few times, unavoidably, Chacha and Tope stumbled onto a patch being freshly tonsured, but the small burnt figures—heads padded with cloth, curving sickles in their hands, wearing muddy sarees and dhotis—did not question them. They merely turned their heads to look at the panting duo without expression, their eyes containing neither curiosity nor alarm.

These were people who had left their dark huts and minuscule holdings, tied their pots, pans and clothes in bundles, taken every able family member, and every child below one and above eight, and travelled hundreds of kilometres on foot, bus, truck, train in search of the feeding wage. It was a cyclical pilgrimage to where the crops grew and the rupees were paid. To reap the wheat, to plant the paddy, to cut the cane. They lived as all men had once, by the seasons. In the nights they sang haunting folk songs by their cooking fires, and at the end of season they returned to their waiting homes with money and food and clothes. And the wild hope that some miracle would make the next journey unnecessary.

You saw them everywhere with their stick limbs and burnt skins and blank eyes. Inside themselves they carried a deep well of loss and lack and sadness and exploitation and struggle and uncertainty, a well so deep that they could hardly see anything around them, anything outside of them. Death, disease, destitution, trauma could not distress them, for they were all of it. A boy and a man running through the fields—with nothing obvious chasing them—was just another passing oddity in a very odd world.

What really worried Chacha were the homesteads. Any farmer seeing them was bound to hail them; any farmer seeing them run was bound to wonder. And when Bhupi's family and retainers came asking, the flight path would lie wide open. They went through fields and farms they knew—Bant, Doabi, Lal Singh, Pramukh, Pali, Tau—steering away from the tube wells and houses, and, miraculously, did not run into anyone. Every now and then they scattered flocks of babblers and partridges out at picnic, and the occasional blinding-white egret, which insouciantly took two flaps of flight before landing and carrying on with its strut.

At every unmarked boundary line, a posse of lean dogs picked up on them, and set pace by their heels, barking and running them out of their domains. Like the birds, the dogs did not worry them. As farmers they knew the only dog to really fear was the odd one that turned rabid. These dogs were all racket and no bite, fit only to terrify the townsfolk who came visiting. They were alarm bells, not defenders. If you walked into them they would keep backing off, all the way into their own doorsteps.

From the embracing palms by the stream, the highway, the Grand Trunk Road, was over ten kilometres as the crow flies. Chacha had crossed many farms and half that distance before he allowed Tope or himself to slow down to a walk. There were a few other villages that lay between Keekarpur and the main road, but they had managed to sidestep them all. The mango trees under which they now sat were old and barren, and under the canopy of their dirty green leaves it was cool and dark. They sat on their haunches, opposite each other, backs against the rough trunks, panting like hunted animals. Outside the arc of the grove's darkness the world was shining bright, the sun glancing off the golden wheat.

When his breath had calmed, Chacha finally asked, 'How bad was it? Will they live?'

Tope said—suddenly a man, suddenly in the course of a morning, suddenly in six slashes of a knife, his Chacha's equal—Tope said, 'Not bad at all. Nothing is going to happen to them. I just nicked them here and there. But if you heard them screaming you'd think I had pulled their intestines out.'

Chacha looked at the boy. In the gloomy dark he could not read his expression, but his tone had changed. It was no longer the voice of his runty nephew who spoke little and spent his days trying to stay out of everyone's way.

Chacha said, 'Did you not know what would happen?'

Tope, the man, said, 'I did not care.'

Chacha said, 'You know what Bhupi's father can do.'

Tope said, 'But Bhupi's like a fucking eunuch. In fact, I nearly made him one.'

Chacha suddenly saw the cussed gene that was the boy's inheritance. No different from his father; no different from his grandfather. Those two had aligned it behind the Indian army and the barrels of their guns. The boy it seemed was going to do so behind the curve of his Rampuria.

Chacha said, 'Where is the knife?'

Tope stretched out his right leg, sucked in his stomach, and drew out the folded knife. He pressed the brass lever and it flicked open. When he pressed the blade between his forefinger and thumb, the steel was sticky. Slowly he palpitated its cold length, feeling his skin peel and stick. He needed to wash the blade and work it on a whetstone.

Chacha said, 'Give it to me.'

Tope did not move. 'Why?'

'We need to hide it. We should bury it here. We don't want to be found with it.'

Tope said, 'No.'

The voice of Dakota Ram. The voice of Fauladi Fauji. There was no arguing with it. All these years Chacha had thought his nephew was like him—a slice of his mother's side. Not like his father, not like his grandfather. That, like him, he was made of gentler stuff, weak in body and in temper. Chacha, who was ten years younger than his big brother Dakota and had always been treated like a boy; Chacha, who failed the army recruitment tests because he was so puny, his legs bent, his chest small, his bones weak; Chacha, whose opinion the big men never sought; Chacha, who milked the buffaloes and helped the women shop in the town; Chacha, who had failed to produce children in eight years of marriage; Chacha, who sang the lullabies that put Tope to sleep, who helped work through Tope's exercise books, who heard out the traumas of his schooldays. Chacha who had always thought Tope was his spiritual son.

In that dark cove of mango trees, as he watched his nephew feel the knife, he knew clearly whose son the boy was.

The two of them sat in silence as the glare of the sun was sucked out of the day, leaving behind a marmalade glow.

Then as night fell, bringing on a thick moon and high stars, the fields turned grey-blue. You could still see a man at fifty metres, and a man with a lantern at a hundred and more. But now the landscape was spectral: full of moving shadows; behind every waving stalk and bush, a hiding man. The true guide to the world now was the ear not the eye. Sound was the demon of the night, empowered, enhanced, travelling with a speed and strength it could never possess in daylight hours. No one could sneak up on them unless they moved on the padded feet of animals.

Inside the mango grove it had become pitch dark and the undergrowth had begun to talk up a fury. Chacha pulled steadily on his Lal Batti beedis, the burning tip the only visible sign of the two fugitives. His bundle of twenty was almost over and the grove was acrid with their stench. Tope had nodded off, the fatigue following the rush of adrenalin.

Chacha, having acted with alacrity and courage for the first time in his life, was now slowly beginning to wonder what the future held. Its contours were so terrifying, he felt the panic surge in him. Just then he heard a volley of distant noises, of dogs and of men, and when he ran to the edge of the circle of mangoes, he saw far away a swarm of lanterns bobbing through the grey-blue night like dancing fireflies.

His body turned cold with fear. On quavering legs he hobbled to the boy, pushed him awake, and they began to run. They stumbled out the other side and sprinted blindly, not caring where their feet fell. Through the standing wheat, through the cut and tied bundles, through narrow water channels, through freshly ploughed squares, through muddy feeding troughs, through knife-edged rushes, through slivers of swamp, through stands of eucalyptus, past baying dogs, past throbbing tube wells, past hailing voices. This time the boy had the lead and Chacha struggled on his infirm legs to keep pace. Each time the terrain changed, each time there was a stumble, Tope looked back to ensure his uncle was not in distress.

In the course of a day, in six slashes of a knife, the equation had changed irrevocably.

By the time they crossed the Gurari nullah, on the east of Shikarpur village and clambered up the muddy incline, they had no more wind left in them. They stretched out flat on the grassy knoll, hearts pounding like wedding drums, their clothes wet and muddied, the sky and stars swimming above them in a haze of exhaustion, ready to die where they lay. Chacha actually held Tope's forearm as he wheezed in loud cycles. 'I don't know about Bhupi,' he said, 'but I think you've certainly killed us.'

No sooner had he spoken he was struggling to his feet again. When Tope suggested they linger a while longer, Chacha folded his hands and begged him not to argue: 'O great Chaakumaar, let us just start walking. It'll keep our legs from cramping, o prince of bundpangas.'

Chaaku liked the sound of that. Asshole-scrapper. Made him feel like Sukha. Footloose and tough and irreverent.

The walking proved tough work. The panic of the mad run had been much easier. The night breeze worked their wet clothes into a chill, and the ache in their limbs oozed to the fore. They walked stiffly, soaked cloth shoes squelching, slipping as they tried to stay on the mud bunds. The fields lay luminous; the silence of deep night ripped open occasionally by the cry of a nightbird. Through the slip and scuff of their feet, the two men kept their ears trained for danger, but they didn't hear a single sound in pursuit.

As fear receded, hunger intruded and began to grow a hole in their bellies. But there was nothing to be done. There were no great familiarities this far out, and to risk the boundary of any homestead at this hour would be foolhardy. It was dangerous even to wander into the guava groves. The dogs would be unloosed and noisy and would not be calmed till the watchmen were roused. Without being asked, Chacha said, 'The great thing about hunger is it kills itself after some time.'

Tope turned around and looked at him with a surge of affection and pity. His Chacha was born to lose. Damned both by genes and environment. What he had done today was against the grain, extraordinary. A show of his love for his nephew. He put out his knife hand and squeezed his uncle's narrow shoulder. With a smile he said, 'The great thing about life, Chacha, is that it kills itself after some time.'

Without breaking step, Chacha said, 'And if you become a bund-panga champion then it does so in no time at all!'

Instinctively, they didn't take the straight line to the highway. The two bus stops that flanked the point where the dusty village road opened itself out onto the Grand Trunk Road were dangerous places to head for. One fronted a cluster of shops—puncture and motor repair, tea and biscuits, paan and cigarettes. The other was at Gharyali village, opposite the graffiti-painted back wall of the school. These were among the first places the sardar's men would head for.

Instead, they walked at an angle, heading off to the right. As the scream of traffic from the road that never sleeps began to grow, their path became increasingly angular. Soon they were walking parallel to the highway, behind lines of ghostly eucalyptus standing in swampy ditches. The sound of the hurtling trucks and buses was deafening now, and the play of their full-beam headlights mesmeric. Heads cocked, the man and boy watched and walked, in single file, so tiny against the trees, so slow against the road.

At the edge of the highway, at this hour, there was nothing that offered itself up to the stomach. Not a guava tree, not a shahtoot tree, not a ber tree. No field of tomatoes or radishes or carrots. No melons. The cane was gone, the mangoes had not come. And his Rampuria was now scraping his pubic bone steadily, working up a bad sore that would not heal for weeks.

Chacha's game plan was the oldest one in the world: to run as far as you possibly could. He had heard that these days, because of police and political interference, they broke the bones of offenders in all kinds of innovative ways. The popular method was to remove the iron handle of a water-pump, wrap it in strips of cloth, and then lay this muffled club where the occasion, or individual preference, demanded. Fibula, tibia, patella, femur, ulna, radius, humerus, carpals, tarsals, pelvis, phalanges. Broken singly or in combination, depending on whether the victim was expected to return home on his knees, his hands, or flat out on a stretcher. Later there were no telltale marks, no incriminating weapons, just the mind-bending pain that nothing could quell. Just the unmuffled screams, the crooked limbs, the abiding fear. And the weapon was replaced, screwed on to the pump, and a myriad hands worked it up and down, and the water gushed forth, so clean and cool and pure.

Minor transgressions received the standard treatments. A few incisors and molars dislodged with a screwdriver or yanked out with a pair of pliers; a spoonful of acid poured into one eye, or into both; a couple of fingers processed through the fodder chopper, mixed with the fresh greens; the rectum burnt from dirty brown to char black with the steady flame of a candle; and if the purpose was to create some theatre, then a chopped nose or ear wrapped in paper, gifted back to the victim. If the idea was to produce humiliation and pain without damage, then rape—of wife, daughter, mother; or bright red chilli powder up the ass, with finger and stick; or a firm tapping of the testicles with a hammer; or red ants under the foreskin after the knob had been dipped in sweet syrup; or simply plain old gang buggery, with the farmhands being allowed a last go.

Chacha had heard all the stories. The landlords against the tenants, the Jats against the Jats, the Sikhs against the Muslims, the high-castes against the low-castes, the low-castes against the lower-castes, the landlords against the landlords, the Jats against the Sikhs, the Muslims against the Hindus, the landlords against everyone, everyone against everyone—there was no possible combination that had not squared off against each other and wreaked vengeance. This being Haryana, the super heavyweight in this arena was the Jat landlord, with a truly superior clout and capacity for cruelty. His chief challenger, the Sikh landlord. The others worked at lying low, quietly tending to their jobs or a few acres.

Fauladi Fauji had never had trouble before, not because he was a former army man—the area was full of them—but because he owned only a few acres, and he kept to himself. An eccentric old army man, he posed no threat to anyone, and was allowed to keep his dignity. It was no different for Dakota Ram, his son, accorded his stature as the itinerant tank man. The younger stunted son, Tattu—a mule in comparison to the older who was an aeroplane—received contemptuous affection. There was space and dignity for everyone as long as you never transgressed the lines. The world had order unless you chose to break it.

Now as Tattu hobbled after his equally runty nephew, blinded every few seconds by a charging headlight, he knew his world had been ruptured forever. He was going to walk as far as he could, in the lee of the trees, and when the first light of day began to spread across the world, he would get on to the screaming road, cross over to the other side and jump on to the first vehicle—bus, tractor, truck, van—and get off only when it either stopped or the road forked nearly a hundred kilometres on between Amritsar and Chandigarh. On the outermost wedges of Chandigarh where Punjab lapped at the city's modular borders, there was a new town being born, and there was a man there who could help. He was old enough to recognize an emergency, and strong enough to face it. The man was his mother's youngest brother, and Chacha—Tattu—hoped he would also be generous enough to extend his hand.

Sardar Balbir Singh, Bhupi's burly father, personally led the army that trashed the farm by the embracing palms.

In times of crisis, like this, the various extensions of the Singh clan came together. Sardar Balbir Singh's three brothers who, over the years, had gone their separate ways to manage their large holdings—they had hundreds of acres amongst them—were at their sibling's farm, with eight of their sons and scores of farmhands, well before the sun had begun to sink. By now the slashed boys were at a private nursing home in Karnal, being stewarded by Balbir's father and wife. They were in disgrace for having given such a poor account of themselves. The police-in-charge from the chowki was ensconced in Sardar Balbir Singh's sitting-room, sipping his third cup of tea, cap on the table, legs stretched out. The FIR was to be registered only after he was given the go-ahead: it would be more fitting if the Singh clan delivered justice without police intervention.

The first thing Sardar Balbir Singh did after crossing the stream was to shoot the two baying farm dogs. They were whippy brown mongrels from the same litter. As they ran up snarling, the sardar without breaking step put his double-barrel gun into the mouth of one and squeezed a trigger. The sound was a bit muffled but the canine's brains flew out, flecking the clothes of the posse. When the other one wheeled to run, with a loud whine, the landlord pulled the second trigger and caught it by its left ear, this time with a loud bang. Its head vanished too. Without pausing, he broke the gun, pushed in two lurid red bullets that were handed to him, and snapped it shut.

The small tube well throbbed, meshing the sound of the belt and the engine. In the far left corner of the mud-and-dung washed front yard, from behind the half wall of mud, lines of smoke curled up from food fires. Under the neem tree, the charpoy lay empty.

The farmhands had all run away into the fields and beyond. They had begun to melt away hours ago, soon after news of what had happened in the guava orchard began to circulate. There was no sense in ending up as casual victims. Only Pappu, the twenty-two-year-old son of their old retainer who had died of malaria years ago, remained. He stood by the bundles of unchopped fodder, trying to stay inside the lengthening shadows. The sun was dying in a splash of violent orange. Fauji pulled on his hookah unsteadily, one bony leg tucked under him. Tope's mother and grandmother and Chacha's wife were huddled around his charpoy by the fodder chopper, their dusty dupattas pulled over their heads and eyes, the two younger women cowering behind their mother-in-law.

Sardar Balbir—with a rotund belly, and a dark beard waxed and pulled tight under a net—sat down at the foot of Fauji's charpoy, where the ropes were strung, the two barrels of his upright gun extending past his big blue turban. Between the rest, there were only two more firearms: one compact black German Mauser and an Indian ordnance single-barrel rifle. The man with the rifle had a bandolier of red bullets strung across his chest. The Mauser, worn by Balbir Singh's younger brother, was in a shiny brown, leather shoulder-holster, its flap buttoned down. The rest had swords, not strung around the waist but held inside their scabbards in their hands. Others were armed with lathis and gandasas, the curving blades at their head freshly whetted. Everyone but the landlord stood loosely ranged around the yard, looking in different directions.

In a flat voice, the sardar said, 'Where is the boy?'

Fauji gurgled his hookah, bony hands trembling.

The sardar waited. Fauji was now shrunk into himself, both his spindly legs pulled under him, the thick tendons on his scrawny neck jumping. He said in a low, slow voice, 'Boys make mistakes. Boys make mistakes. That's why they are boys.'

The sardar said, 'Where is he?' His left eye was twitching. The posse knew the sign. A slight ripple went through them. The three women, faces covered, had literally fused into one behind the patriarch. The old man could not pull on his pipe any more, his hands shook so much. He put his hands together, the brass nozzle of the hookah between them, bowed his close-cropped grey head and said, 'I promise you, sardar sahib, he is not here. He never came back, and I don't know where he is.'

In one fluid movement Sardar Balbir Singh pulled his gun into his hand, placed its two-mouthed head right under the old man's ass and detonated a barrel, blowing a hole through the ropes and into the ground. The report was deafening. The old man leapt into the air with a wild cry, holding his singed pajama. The three-in-one women set off a mad wail as if they'd been shot.

Leaving the gun head resting on the ropes, the sardar again asked, 'Where is the boy?'

The hookah pipe now lay where it had fallen on the paved mud floor, a curved dead snake, the grey-black-red embers from the cup sprayed all around. The old man's limbs were shaking like those of a puppet whose master was having a malarial fit. He had never heard a bullet strike so close, not even as a young man in the army. His rheumy eyes were watering copiously and his jaw seemed unhinged, out of control, the ill-fitting dentures rattling loosely. The three women fused even closer, squatting on the ground, all strength in their legs gone.

As Fauji failed to find his voice, the old woman spoke up, folding her palms in supplication: 'Please forgive us, sardar sahib. It is no fault of ours. You have known us for years. We quietly go about our small lives and work. We have never harmed anyone. We have always respected the glory and power of your family. The boy has done a very terrible thing. We beg forgiveness for it. We will atone for it. Please, sardar sahib, I beg you, as old as your own mother that I am. Forgive us.' The fused blob was a strange sight. One face, one voice and three pairs of outstretched arms, hands clasped in abjection. A many-armed goddess fallen on bad times.

By now the old man had lost all focus. He was looking about him sightlessly. His lower lip hung loose, running drool.

It was then that the sardar noticed the boy in the shadows by the bundles of green fodder. He gestured with his head. Pappu came forward with his eyes lowered. He was a robust boy, his shoulders and arms muscular with labour.

The landlord said, 'Where's the mongrel?'

Pappu's palms were already joined in supplication. 'I don't know, sardar sahib.'

Balbir Singh half-turned his face and said to his posse, 'Put his hand in.'

The boy began to scream for mercy even before three pairs of hands grabbed him. 'Oh bauji, I only work here! I am only a poor labourer! I know nothing about anything. Tope has run away! How can I know where! O my mother, what have I done to harm anyone!'

But he only began to struggle in complete panic when they had dragged him to the chopper. 'O bauji save me! O biji tell them I know nothing! I have served you like a slave! I have never stolen a paisa, never done anything wrong! I always told you Tope would do something horrible with that knife! I always told you to take it away from him! Save me my lord, save me!' One of the sardar's men caught him on his mouth with the blunt end of a bamboo stave. A short crisp blow that opened up his lips, spilling blood. Pappu's screaming stopped, and he began to cry like a small boy, with loud sobs, tears of pain and fear running down his cheeks.

By now the blob of women had also begun to wail and beg for mercy for the boy. They moved without disentangling and with their many arms fell at the landlord's feet, the old woman's desiccated hands on his fat knees. Their dupattas were off their faces now, so that their contrition and desperation could be seen. Without looking at the roiling animal at his feet, the sardar said, 'Vadh doh.' Hack it. And lifting the right hand that was stroking his netted beard, he raised a fat finger.

They put the index finger of the boy's left hand into the iron mouth of the chopper. The dark grey of the square mouth was stained with the green juice of life, tiny shards of grass stuck in it. When Pappu refused to cooperate, wriggling frantically, the man trying to isolate the marked finger said, 'Shall we chop them all off then?' To illustrate the point the swarthy Sikh behind him ran the three-feet curving blade of his sword screeching across the mainframe of the chopper. Immediately, all fight went out of the boy and his body slumped.

Sardar Balbir rose from the charpoy, kicking away the many-armed goddess wailing at his feet, and taking his double-barrel walked off to gaze at the fields. There was a last thin line of orange left on the horizon and the birds were moving in noisy flocks. The fields were bald and hairy in uneven patches as the reaping gathered momentum. He turned his back to the yard and its symphony of screams.

The two curving blades of the chopper, set at opposite ends inside the wheel, were moist with green juice too, the cutting inch a lighter grey than the rest. The executioner didn't push the wheel. He went around the other side to catch the wooden handle and pull it towards himself. Pappu was mewling now, his body limp, held in place by two sets of strong arms. Like the sardar landlord, the old man, Fauladi Fauji, looked out unseeing at the day dying across the fields. In fifteen minutes all the poses of a long life had been destroyed. How fragile are the constructions men make of themselves.

As at the moment of a child's birth, above and beyond the general moan and noise, one clear piercing shriek announced that the event had occurred. The Jat pulling the chopping wheel was efficient, bringing the blade down in a hard quick move. The finger—strangely so much smaller when removed from the body—was left in the steel mouth, while the boy collapsed to the floor and curled into a wildly sobbing ball. Drops of blood dripped from the chopper's jaw as from the lips of a feasting animal.

While Sardar Balbir Singh admired the lyric loveliness of the Indian countryside, the cool evening breeze, the stars beginning to switch on one by one and then in chandelier-like clusters, the clean lines of a richly milky moon, the soothing music of cicadas and tube wells and sweetly questioning lapwings, while he thought of his childhood and a life spent amid such beauty, while his brother held the shoulder of the old woman, and the old man sat drooling on his sagging charpoy with a hole shot through its heart, his men picked up the other two parts of the three-in-one goddess, and gagging their protesting mouths with their own dupattas, dragged them into the sanctity of the mud rooms.

Now that no one could see him, the sardar allowed his eyes to well with tears. How mercilessly his son had been slashed. What a poor job he had done bringing up his boy, in training him for survival. In comparison, his own father had taught him everything a man needed to know about courage and leadership. Aloofness. Action. Arrogance. The will to violence. The stomach for cruelty. He had taught him that a leader must arouse fear not love, for eventually men also come to love what they fear. But he, the great Sardar Balbir Singh, in turn, had made his son flabby. His sentimentality had destroyed the boy. He wiped his eyes with the sleeves of his kurta.

The men had begun to stagger out one by one from the dark hole of the main doorway, tightening their turbans, settling their clothes, picking up the naked swords and gandasas that they had leaned against the mud walls. Some were at the handpump, working their body parts through water. The sardar looked from the corner of his eye. The queue at the doorway hole was nearly gone. Thankfully, not everyone was into it. But then there were some who went back in again. The sooner this was over the better. They needed to get a move on, run down that fucking runt and his equally runty uncle. Slice their balls off. How had they dared? Rage spiralled in him.

Turning around, he said, 'Finish it all off. Make sure they remember god and us in the same breath for the rest of their lives.'

Now the homestead was set systematically on fire. The house with all its belongings, the reaped bundles of grain in the fields, the cattleshed, the tube well hut. No one was killed. The raped women, the amputated boy, the unhinged old couple, were all pulled clear into the front yard and dumped on the charpoys. The three women coagulated into a moaning blob again, and the boy remained a sobbing ball. The cattle were untethered and whacked with the gandasas, forcing them to canter off. As they left, the men kept setting fire to the standing crop, the ripening stalks of golden wheat. Soon the night was full of crackle and smoke and swirling soot, and the odour of kerosene, which had been splashed everywhere.

Sardar Balbir Singh had begun to walk away from it when they started, and was now near the stream where the headless mongrels lay. One by one his posse joined him as the dark lit up warmly orange all around. When the last man had arrived, the sardar moved to cross the stream. With his foot on the log bridge, he paused and asked, 'What did you do with the finger?'

A voice from the dark said, 'I left it inside the older one.'

iii

Shauki Mama and Mr Healthy

Tope Singh—alias Chaaku, alias the son of Dakota, alias the new prince of bundpangas—never went back to the farm by the embracing palms. He never again set eyes on his kind grandmother or his mother or his screwball grandfather. Even when they died over the next few years, he held back. Landlords cultivate long memories, and power does not grow out of forgiveness. As it was, Bhupi's virility and fertility remained a question mark.

Dakota Ram rushed back on casual leave but chose to give the police procedures a go by. He pretended not to know that the women had been raped, and to Pappu he gave the reassurance that he still had nine fingers left. With his old father he remained locked in the silent communion of complete knowledge and ignorance that had marked their lifelong relationship. They met as if nothing could have happened. His frail mother he held in his arms and wept like a boy.

He went to meet the landlord in his olive-green lance corporal's uniform—one white V on his left upper arm—and sat on the same chair that the policeman from the village chowki had, in the small outer sitting-room kept for village visitors and petty officials. Sardar Balbir Singh and he agreed that for the moment the score was even. In fact, his men had been anything but excessive. Only two mongrels killed! So it must never be forgotten who had provoked the mess and that the boy was not yet forgiven. The sardar said, 'I respect your uniform but I tell you the runt will have to pay. My men have taken Bhupi's slashing badly.'

Clutching his beret tight in his hands, looking down at the red oxide floor, the army man tried to say, 'But what of my wife and...'

The sardar said in a voice more menacing than their swords, 'You think a wife is more important than a son? Remember lance-naik, nothing happened. Nothing. Nothing that she can't forget in a day or two. My men didn't slash and slice. They didn't put a knife in her and open her up where she shouldn't be open. Remember lance-naik, my son is in hospital, his body ripped open. All his life the stitches will show on his skin like on Rafat's clothes. Don't ever forget, lance-naik, that I am the only aggrieved party here. Nothing has happened to you. Nothing!'

The policeman came by when night was falling, and Dakota and he sat on the charpoy under the neem tree and drank the dark Old Monk rum. Near the chopper, Fauladi Fauji, more shrivelled than ever, sipped his share. The sun was gone, its last trace a thin red line. The fields in front were burnt black, feathery ash still taking occasional wing. But not all of it was dead: the fire had licked around the farm unevenly, leaving a few squares still with grain. Today Dakota did not drink with military decorum. He drank to kill the fat bottle. The policeman said, 'You did well to let it go. You are a wise man. The mess of a police case, of courts and lawyers, would have wiped out whatever little is left here.'

The wood fires were burning behind the low charred mud wall—the last meal of the day cooking. Dakota could see his wife and sister-in-law moving about in the shadows, like fugitives, the dupattas curled around their heads and under their chins. They had not spoken about that night. They probably never would. It would only add to their mutual shame. The army man said, 'I want to kill the motherfucking dogs. Each one of them. Tie them to the barrel of my Vijayanta tank and blow holes through them.'

The policeman said, 'Motherfuckers. Bloodsuckers. The Lord will make a hard reckoning with them one day!'

The army man said, 'I don't want to leave it to Him. Why should He do our work? I am personally going to chop off their balls and feed them to the village mongrels.'

The policeman said, 'I would love to do it myself. I would do it now were it not for this fucking khaki uniform. Drag them out by their hair, one by one, and slice their pricks off and pickle them like carrots in a big glass jar for my motherfucking officers to eat.'

The army man said, 'No! I will eat all of them. Every motherfucking one of them.'

The policeman said, 'Yes, you are right. They belong to you. You should eat them. Each one of them. I will pickle them and you will eat them. The motherfucking dogs!'

The army man said, 'And then I will do the women. Each one of them. Make them scuttle and squeal like the village pigs!'

The policeman said, 'Yes. And then I will do the same.'

The army man said, 'After me.'

The policeman said, 'Only after you.'

The bottle was almost over. Dakota poured the last bit evenly between his tumbler and his guest's. From another glass lying nearby he splashed some water into the rum. His father, old Fauladi Fauji, had collapsed on his charpoy and passed out. The tube well was silent, not a throb in its burnt body. The farmhands who had run away that night had not yet returned. It didn't matter. There was nothing to be urgently salvaged. The cycle of land, plant and season would take its own time.

The army man said, 'But no killing anyone. We have to make them suffer. Each day when they pull off their underwear to piss they should look down and know that they are no longer men, and then they should remember us. Each time they piss they should remember us with fear.'

The policeman said, now half-slumped on his charpoy, 'Each

time they remember our names they should piss with fear. And they should have nothing to hold when they piss but the air.'

The army man said, 'And that Laudu Maharaj, Sardar Balbir Singh, dick of dicks, I am going to shave off his beard and all his hair till his head shines like a panda's on the ghats of Banaras.'

The policeman said, 'And I am going to shove that double-barrel up his asshole and rotate it like a top. And then blow his intestines out of his mouth.'

They were barracking loudly now, slumped on their sides, looking up at the bright stars hurtling down. Their voices floated across the scorched fields, filling the earth, challenging the gods. Huddled near the cooking fires, the women watched through their muslin dupattas.

The army man said, 'But who will pull the trigger?'

The policeman said, 'I will. I am the policeman. I have to make him pay for all the crimes he has committed on innocent people.'

The army man said, 'No, o policya, I will. It is my house and women he has raped and burnt.'

The policeman said, 'Don't fight, my friend—it's a double-barrel! You pull one trigger, and I'll pull the other.'

The army man said, 'I will pull it first.'

The policeman said, 'Behanchod fauji, then there'll be nothing left for me! What do you want me to do, hunt for little shreds of his ass to shoot at?'

The army man said, 'O phuddu policya, you create too many problems. Nothing satisfies you. Okay, we'll pull the trigger together. At the same moment. Exactly. One, two, three...fire!'

The policeman said, his head lolling over the edge of the charpoy, 'Yes, my friend, yes, you are right. At the same moment. One, two, three...phire!'

Shauki Mama was a man who had learnt early to work the world. He had never been one to waste his breath on the business of sermons, ideology, principles. If he wanted to discuss something he talked about things that could be consumed—bought, sold, eaten, felt, seen, worn, penetrated. He was interested in how things could be done, in the calculus of give and take that keeps the universe humming, not in the whys and wherefores.

He'd always thought his elder sister had married into a family of cranks. There was the father-in-law who sat grandly on his charpoy, not condescending to talk to anyone, chugging a hookah as if he were Jalal-ud-din Akbar overseeing the spread of his great empire. And all he had ever been was a dumb sepoy in the army. Worse still was the son, his great brother-in-law, Dakota Ram, who thought he was nothing less than Shah Jahan. If you saw his airs you'd imagine he wasn't driving a clunky tank but building the Taj Mahal on the border. The truth is with a few instructions Shauki's truck drivers could have done what Dakota did. He had twelve drivers like Dakota on his rolls, his very own tank squadron. But the army driver gave him attitude as if he were a grand emperor and Shauki a commoner in his court. Bloody phuddu! And he drank that awful horse rum, with tepid water. Shauki Mama only drank IMFL, Indian Made Foreign Liquor, either Aristocrat or Peter Scot. With soda and two cubes of ice, and always with something to munch—sliced cucumbers, tomatoes, radishes with a rain of salt, lemon juice and red chilli, or boiled eggs, or boiled eggs fried in a coating of besan, or richly sweating tandoori chicken succulent between the teeth. Coarse dark rum, pump water, and yards of pretension. It was, he knew, the uniform, the olive-green uniform, and it never ceased to amaze him how something so trivial could create such persistent delusion.

Now the errant pup of those cranks had become his problem. Well, there was nothing to be done. The boy was his sister's son, and he'd been brought for asylum by the only man he liked in that weird family. Runty Tattu—a warm, real man, willing to cut a hand of

Sweep any hour of the day. The problem was, for the moment, Tattu too was his problem. The uncle and son's account of their flight made it clear that neither of them could head back to Keekarpur for some time.

So they had to be sheltered and they had to be put to work. The line-up of Shauki Mama's businesses was fairly simple: trucks ferrying construction material—sand, gravel, bricks, timber, iron girders, cement bags; trucks ferrying cylinders of cooking gas; and trucks ferrying sacks of grain. There was a great deal of private work to be had, but what Shauki Mama angled for were the government contracts. Dealing with individual owners was a nightmare of bargaining and bickering. Rates, quality, quantities, delays; and then chasing payments endlessly. They always settled as if they were doing you a favour, and always after making some random deductions.

The government in contrast was an honourable enterprise. You got what you had agreed upon—sometimes more, if there was cause for you to make some claim. Nor was it so distrustful and petty as to haggle over quality, quantity, or delays. The government behaved as men ought to with each other: with an understanding that there would be failures, shortfalls, mistakes, that both men and their endeavours are fallible. And because it had compassion, because it was so generous of heart, you gave back to it freely. Shared with its staff your every stroke of fortune, let the sweets and the alcohol and the goodies flow. Often, at a moment of rejoicing on receiving a new contract, he had personally delivered gifts of colour televisions and music systems. Sometimes to help these warm wonderful men of the state—with their children's education, the marriage of their daughters, the treatment of old parents—he had forced upon them small tokens of his friendship in bundles of rupees, sometimes up to ten thousand. It was rare to find such deserving men anywhere.

He put Tattu at the adda, the yard from where the trucks were parked and dispatched. His job was to help maintain the roster of coming and goings, and the distance travelled on each sortie. These were then squared off against litres of diesel consumed. A ten per cent variance was permitted, in fact it was encouraged. Shauki Mama's philosophy was: 'Everyone needs some kind of transgression to feel whole: it's best to keep them all satisfied with small ones.' He told Tattu, 'Better to lose a few bottles of diesel every few trips than have them run off with the truck one day.'

But the major transgressions were—no surprise—finely streamlined. All the siphoning off of provisions happened at source and the spoils were shared with the drivers and helpers. The sacks of wheat, rice, gram, cement, marble chips—were neatly unsewn at the mouth and a few kilos drained from each. When the truck drove off, it left a little pile behind, like the dung heap of an animal moving on. This pile was packed into fresh sacks and moved separately into the market.

The cardinal rule here was to not be lax in the accounting just because the droppings came for free. Every kilo, every sack, every brick, every pile of sand and gravel had to be reckoned seriously. The more professional you kept it the less illicit it appeared, and the workers were less likely to treat it like a free-for-all bonanza. Getting a truck to drop dung was business, converting the dung into commercial cakes was business, and in business you counted every unit and squared every rupee; there was no scope for slack.

Tope Singh, alias Chaakumaar, alias the new Prince of Bundpangas, on the other hand, suffered a false start, trying to resume his school education. There was a private school operating out of a two-hundred-fifty-square-yard house in Mohali, where Shauki Mama sent his nephew. The school was called St Green Meadows High School, and its narrow building rose two-and-a-half storeys high, box-like room piled upon box-like room. Many were further subdivided by plywood partitions, and if the students in one grade were insufficient two classes were arbitrarily collapsed to create a single viable unit: seven children of class seven and nine of class eight to create sixteen in class seven and a half. And may every parent live in wonder.

The maximum number of children were in the primary classes. The numbers dwindled as you went up the order. Like many faux Saint schools of its kind the attrition at Meadows was high: spitting out only one child at the top for every ten it sucked in at the bottom. Only the principal's room had a window and the whole school smelled of urine, flowing down copiously from the makeshift toilets constructed on the roof. It was on this roof that Tope Singh practised mutual masturbation with the senior boys, and learnt to smoke cigarettes. For the rest of his life the smell of piss would spark in him the craving for a drag and instant arousal.

How inferior are the affectations of class to the flourishes of violence. It took two months and a few slashes of the Rampuria to overcome the handicap of being a village boy. Once the city boys had genuflected to the blade, Tope Singh came to be christened Chaaku, the knife, an honorific that would one day find its way into official documents and crisp newspapers.

Chaaku had never had so much fun. His new friends fought to be close to him and introduced him to the excitements of Chandigarh's cinema halls, restaurants and ornamental parks. Some of them had scooters and motorcycles and they would tear down the broad roads sucking in the wind, waving their arms, heady with life. Then he learnt to drink, starting with beer and graduating to whisky—and it all became even more grand. Each day, Chaaku wondered at what a reward he had reaped for having gently opened up a few skins, for possessing the constant bulge of the Rampuria in his pants. Sometimes he drank too much and then he ranted and wept about what had been done to his family by the landlord. At such time he and his friends promised each other that soon they would lead a crippling attack on the sardar and his clan and visit on them a retribution that would not be forgotten for ten generations. Chaaku would say, flicking and furling his knife, 'I will chop off the pricks of all the maaderchods—even the little children—and pickle them and sell them in jars on GT road!' After that, like a good butcher, he would elaborate on what he would do to all the body parts, male and female. At the very end he would break down and weep like a child and his friends would hold and console him.

Not being a moralist, Shauki Mama ignored the complaints about his nephew gathering at his door for a long time. Then one day he spoke to him. It was a dialogue not entirely between unequals. Like most successful men, the uncle had built his fortunes not by lecturing others but by understanding the virtues of even the most errant. The older man recognized that the boy had a gift that had led to his expulsion from his own world and quickly earned him a place in a strange new one. In turn, Chaaku reassured his uncle that he was not a fool, and he knew how to use his weapon in a way that married menace with restraint. He would slice skin, never artery; he would put in the fear of life, never take it. People wrongly assume that men are either fearless or fearful. The truth is, like most things, courage has many degrees. Chaaku did not, yet, have the nerve to kill. Even in his most inflamed slashing he was fully conscious of the damage he must not cause. Shauki sighed with relief. This was the city, and it had the media and officials and too many contesting interests. You didn't run things here on the whim of Sardar Balbir Singh's cock.

In no time at all, Chaaku became a part of his uncle's trucking business. With every month his hours at St Green Meadows dwindled, and by the time March came around and he wrote his class ten exams he was primed for failure. Since fleeing the village he had learnt a million things; not one of them in the classroom. The maths paper was a disaster, the English worse.

When the results were declared, his uncle asked, 'You want to try again?'

Chaaku said, 'No.'

At the yard he did not slide into the kind of work Chacha was doing, keeping logs and accounts. His Rampuria marked him out as different. To begin with he was put to travelling with the trucks, sitting high up in the cabin in front, understanding the rhythms of drivers and helpers, the metabolism of loadings, unloadings, tea breaks, diesel stops, sleep hours, and most importantly, dung heaps and collections. Shauki Mama instructed the boy to be both friendly and distant: his task was to learn all about the truckers who worked for them and ensure that every trucker feared him. To nudge matters along, the businessman referred to his nephew only as Chaaku in public. The nephew was also obliquely encouraged to cut open some skin at the earliest so that the legend was suitably amplified. This Chaaku soon did, and more. In time he became Shauki Mama's sword arm, the man sent to make the petty collections that were falling into dispute. The bulge of the flick-knife was always visible in his trousers, and it was mostly enough to do the trick. Sometimes it had to be unveiled in its naked glory; and rarely, very rarely, was he required to play a small game of noughts and crosses on someone's arm.

By now the first lessons of Sukha and Bhupi had matured into a full education. Chaaku learned that almost all of the world lived in colossal and constant fear. Afraid of everything—the police, officials and courts, the thugs, criminals and mafia; afraid of the establishment and the anti-establishment; afraid of failure and of criticism, of being humiliated and of being mocked, of being ugly and of being bald; afraid of cockroaches and of cats, of the seas and the skies, of lightning and of electricity; afraid of priests and physicians; afraid of dying and of living. More than hope, people's lives seemed to be defined by fear. Most hope, it seemed, was only about somehow being able to negotiate fears successfully. A tiny minority managed to cross the line of fear—of the police and courts and failure and censure and priests and cockroaches—and this tiny minority then became the shapers of the world in which the rest lived.

This fearful world, Chaaku realized, was easily terrified by the mere shadow of a knife.

Chaaku also now understood something even more important: that fear was not a line on the ground, it was only a line in the head. Inside everyone's head. And if people were pushed too far they could sometimes walk over that line in the head and become formidable themselves. The idiot Bhupi, by shoving him one time too many, had sent him—Tope—over that line and paid a big price for it.

It was then that Chaaku understood the lessons of the Gita he'd always heard bandied about: of fearlessness and action and the legitimacy of violence.

In later life, Chaaku looked back at these years as his halcyon period. He owned a Yezdi motorcycle, whose emblem he had turned upside down to read ipzeh. It was full of adornments: extra horns, rear blinkers, leather satchel, faux fur seats, red wheel hubs, and above the headlight a small many-coloured plastic fan that whirred madly and kaleidoscopically when he drove. On lean days his friends and he rode up to Shimla, roaring around the mountain curves without helmets, denim jackets flapping open, guzzling up the cool air. They drank beer from the bottle and tossed the bottles down the ravines. They raced other bikes and cars, and waved at them in triumph. Occasionally they sang Hindi film songs at the top of their voices—songs about friendship and love and the melancholy mysteries of life. In Shimla they walked up and down the old colonial mall road, admiring the pretty women, joking about the honeymooning couples, licking ice creams, eating chicken curry with hot naan and raw onions.

Shauki Mama encouraged these excursions. The last thing he wanted was a fearless knife-wielding nephew getting obsessed with his business. Shauki was not looking for an heir, just a competent bogey man. He need not have worried. Chaaku's world view was not very different from that of his father or grandfather. Simple soldiers, splendid in the narrow frame—of obeying orders, exhibiting loyalty, displaying courage.

Like a good army man, Chaaku would have soldiered on endlessly—making the dung heaps, riding the trucks, occasionally flicking the knife for collections—had the village not arrived at his doorstep one afternoon.

It was winter and he was dozing on a charpoy at the back of the yard, in the sweet spot where the sun cut past the tamarind tree and the corrugated tin awning of the shed to create an oval pool of hot light. His lunch of tandoori parathas and lassi was heavy inside him, and he had pulled a coarse brown shawl over himself for additional snugness and to keep away the flies. The stop-and-start buzzing of the mechanical lathe as Bauna—the dwarf mechanic—retooled truck parts was a reassuring background sound. A crow had been cawing on the tree since morning. A few flung stones had seen him take off and circle right back. Bauna, his short muscular arms shining with oil and grease, his child's pants a nondescript black-brown and tattered in a dozen places, had pronounced, 'We are definitely getting visitors today.' Driver Jassi, his long hair open after a bath under the handpump, had said, chewing lazily on a sugarcane stick, 'Yes, of course, your future in-laws, to size you up. I am so happy you've come dressed for the occasion!'

Chaaku was wading through a familiar dream. He was hiding in the burning fields on the farm by the embracing palms. The wheat field he was crouching in had not yet caught fire, but he could feel the growing heat as the orange line licked itself steadily towards him. The glow from the fields spread to the dark homestead where he could see armed figures moving about. He could hear his mother's screams detonating from inside the house, and see his father and grandfather lashed to the neem tree, which had once been his tank. While Dakota Ram was raging, screaming and straining at the ropes, Fauladi Fauji was as ever unperturbed, calmly bubbling the hookah whose pipe had been left in his mouth. Men were staggering out from the house and washing their fat cocks in the rich gush of the handpump. Working the handle steadily, with a high-pitched mechanical creak, was Pappu. He had no fingers, and was pumping up and down with his palms. In the foreground, double-barrel in hand, strode Sardar Balbir Singh. His eyes were dark with fury, and he seemed bigger than ever before. In fact he appeared to be growing by the minute. Suddenly two men came up—tucking in their cocks—and began to urgently whisper to him. Chaaku wished his mother would stop screaming so he could hear what they were saying. Then one of them pointed to the field in which Chaaku was hiding. The sardar, now looming big as the neem tree, levelled the gun in his direction and bellowed, 'Tope Singh!'

For some reason, Chaaku did not jump off the charpoy and respond when he heard his name being called. The sun was scalding hot above him now and the rough shawl felt uncomfortable. The voices were coming from the front of the yard, just inside the main iron gate, near the makeshift room of naked brick in which the log of truck movements was entered.

The voices were not familiar but something in their tone spelled a warning. Lifting his shawl a little, Chaaku squinted through the intervening clutter of trucks and makeshift rooms, the sun and the shadows. At this angle all he could discern were several legs and torsos, and the curve of swords in scabbards held in hands, two bamboo staves and the black steel of a double-barrel gun, pointing downwards.

It was his name that saved him. Neither Jassi nor Bauna had heard of any Tope Singh. Nor of a village called Keekarpur, nor of Dakota Ram, nor of Fauladi Fauji. A voice, clearly of the man who had directed them to the yard, said, 'They are lying. Of course the boy works here. I have seen him going in and out. He's thin and short and has a fancy Yezdi motorcycle, with a whirling fan over its headlight.' Bauna said, in his thin voice, 'But that's Chaaku!' A commanding voice said, 'Chaaku! Maiovah Chaaku! That's him! Phuddihondya Chaaku! Where's he?'

In five bounds, Chaaku had thrown off the blanket, put a foot on the water drum, and leapt on to the tin roof of the lean-to against the back wall that served as the yard toilet. Through the blood pounding in his ears, through the loud clang of the corrugated sheet, he heard voices shout, 'There's the fucking runt! Catch the bloody dog! Shoot the maaderchod!' He vaulted over the wall of the yard and landed in a tumble on the hard earth, just missing the bushes but not the offal the men threw over the walls—used tea leaves, banana and orange peels, rancid food, empty packets and containers, oil-stained rags. The fall soiled his clothes and knocked the wind out of him, but he was up and running without a pause. Instinctively, as he rolled and stood up and ran, he felt for the Rampuria in his pocket and was reassured by its hard length.

This was a suburb just being born, and most of the lots were still empty. Fertile fields—furrowed, fecund, fed by water channels—rolled away on one side, a stark reminder of modern India's urban amoeba slowly sweeping over older vocations and older ways. Farmers suddenly with thick wads in their pockets but no soil under their feet forced to confront new realities, a life less dignified. In less than a generation an ancient way of existence would be gone, the rhythm of seasons dead, the logic of sky and water and the exploding seed lost, and they would all be petty pawns working the implacable engines of cities, feeding the fantasies of men who had somehow annexed the world by crunching numbers, not growing things or shaping lands or expounding ideas.

Chaaku was pounding through the cabbage lines—like florid buttons on a sere shirt—heading for the square of sugarcane close by, which the truckers often raided. As the sparrows and mynahs scattered in front of him, he heard the sharp report of a rifle and voices shouting. Looking back without breaking his sprint, he saw several faces above the wall, standing on the tin roof of the lean-to. The barrel of a rifle was tracking him. He crouched low, breaking into a panicky zigzag. There was a second sharp report, then a loud expletive, 'Maiovah, are you trying to kill the ground or the man!' Flurries of birds had taken wing and were wheeling around.

Just as Chaaku gained the sugarcane fields, he heard a soft thud and another expletive: 'O behndiphudimari!' One of the men had jumped and landed badly, and was struggling to his feet. The sardar with the gun was waving him on angrily from the wall and screaming. As he looked back a second man took the leap.

Chaaku ran through the thicket of sugarcane as if it didn't exist, the razor leaves opening up his skin everywhere. There was a small nullah on the other side, sluggish with unclean water, and then the road. He tried to leap over the nullah, fell short, into the dirty water, and came to his knees. In a flash he was out, and in the middle of the road, scaring down a young boy on an old Bajaj scooter. By the time the pursuers emerged from the sugarcane patch, the puttering scooter had gained a few hundred metres.

This time the price was paid by his Chacha, Tattu, the mild, meek uncle who had been his protector, guardian, friend and tutor. Sardar Balbir Singh and his henchmen broke one radius, one ulna, two metatarsals, two metacarpals, one rib and one femur; they pulled out some hair from his chest and his pubes; they tested the elasticity of his sphincter with the tip of their bamboo lathis; and they squeezed his testicles by turns till his screams for mercy became high notes of pure gibberish. For his interventions, Bauna had two of his buck teeth pulled out with his own pliers. The sardar said, 'How nice he looks now! Do you think we should also lengthen his legs?' The skinny bhaiya from Bihar, Ram Bharose—who manned the gate, opening and shutting it, and cleaned the yard—was asked if he wanted some dental treatment too. When he gibbered, the sardar delivered a swinging kick between his buttocks that sent him sprawling to the floor where he lay whimpering and unmoving. Even as Chacha continued his testicular wail.

Driver Jassi played it safe, cowering silently on his haunches by the tailgate of his truck—ok tata bye bye—keeping his eyes averted from all that was going on. When he was asked if he too would care to taste some village hospitality, he wordlessly clasped his hands and looked down at the ground. Later he would say, 'Can there be bravery in committing suicide! Even Guru Gobind Singh had to take flight from Aurangzeb's much bigger army, and then recoup! Would you like to live with your testicles in your pants or in a jar?'

Shauki raged with a rare fury. But he did not go to the police. These were clan transactions, and uniforms and penal codes had no role to play in them. Something had once been done: retribution was inevitable. Chacha was sent to hospital and put in various plasters. But at least there was a definite upside for him. His account stood squared. Now he could go back to his village and the farm by the embracing palms.

But Chaaku was still in the crosshair. The yard was no longer safe for the boy, nor was the Chandigarh suburb. And the pervasive militancy in the whole area meant that the sardar could always get someone else to do the job, maybe even the cops. The state was awash with vigilantes, terrorists, criminals, compromised policemen, spooks from various central agencies. Shauki's trucks were commandeered by all sides all the time, and he had to skate the ice with great skill and trepidation to keep it from cracking. There was more illicit money and weaponry floating around in the Punjab than since the Anglo–Afghan and Anglo–Sikh wars. Anyone would break both his legs for a thousand rupees and put a bullet, or many, in him for less than ten thousand. But the boy was his nephew and the boy still had his uses.

In less than a week of the attack in the yard, Shauki had loaded Chaaku, his gaudy motorcycle and his suitcase of belongings on to one of his trucks heading for Delhi.

Five years of relentless terrorism—assassinations, bus massacres, Hindu killings, bomb explosions, cyclical extortions—had made the Punjab a fragile place to do business. Shauki had begun to hedge his bets, to transfer some resources to Delhi to try and set up a hub there. His son had been travelling by the Haryana Roadways buses, carrying cheap plastic bags in which bundles of soiled cash were buried amid clothes. This money was being funnelled into small properties: a two-bedroom second-floor flat in Punjabi Bagh and a shop in an upcoming market complex in Rohini, another wasteland suburb beginning to protrude out of Delhi.

Built on a two-hundred-square-yard plot, the flat was dark and derelict, all sun and light cut off by the houses crowding it in. It had one bathing bathroom with a leaking brass tap, and one Indian-style crap cubicle with an old-style iron cistern strapped high on the wall with a dangling chain that activated with a heart-stopping clang. Each floor, counter and finish in the house was grey mosaic. Even with all the lights on it felt like a dungeon. All the window sills and grilles were daubed with bird droppings—mostly pigeon—and the bathroom slats had nesting sprouting from them like tufts of hair from an old man's ears.

Inside, the furnishings were cut-rate and rudimentary. Clunky wooden chairs, a couple of tables, and box double-beds in the rooms, capable of having their bellies prised open and locked after they had been stuffed with crumpled currency. There were only two adornments on the walls: a poster, slightly swollen with moisture, from an

Indian girlie magazine, pasted above the mosaic line in the bathing toilet; and in the drawing-room a framed poster of a famous film actress playing the role of the goddess Santoshi Mata, with a garland of marigolds that had died weeks ago, the yellow petals dried to a dark crisp, strung around it.

The larger bedroom was mostly kept locked and was exclusive to Shauki and his son. Chaaku was told to set up residence in the other. The room already had an inmate. He was called Mr Healthy, and he had been shipped out from Amritsar.

Mr Healthy's arms and legs were so thin they could be encircled with a thumb and index finger. His face was gaunt and his nose disproportionately long. His chest was less than the span of one hand. All of it was compensated for by the size of his dick. Even flaccid it hung to mid-thigh, thick as a wrist, and when erect it made his body seem like the appendage rather than the other way around. He would sit on his side of the bed, propped against the wall, painfully thin, naked but for his loose cloth underwear, reading the daily papers, his formidable cucumber peeping out. It was hard on the nerves.

But it was not the size of his organ that brought Chaaku under his thrall. It was his razor-sharp mind. He could crunch numbers, he understood money, he understood politics, he could make all the connections, and he knew wonderful words with which he could express complex ideas. Mr Healthy talked about the murky roots of terrorism in Punjab, the impending doom of the Congress party, the Cold War convulsions between America and the Russians, the way the black money economy worked, how mosquitoes were getting the better of quinine. He knew the names of ministers, the different companies industrialists owned, how much cricketers were paid, and which film star was sleeping with whom. Chaaku was flabbergasted. This nondescript man, living like him in this crummy flat, sleeping in the bed next to him, working, like himself, for his Shauki Mama, how could he possibly know so much?

What made Mr Healthy even more daunting was that he never joked or smiled. There was no easy backslapping, no trivial loose talk that was permitted with him. When they sat in a restaurant or dhaba and there was easy banter all around, he stared at the others with steely eyes. When they emerged from a movie, while everyone around smiled and chatted or cribbed and argued, Mr Healthy set about dissecting it with quiet seriousness. Frivolous interactions were the only kind Chaaku had ever known, and he suddenly felt the sheer smallness of his life so far. All he could do was ride a motorcycle and slash with his Rampuria, and in a small gesture of genuflection he gladly put both these feeble talents at Mr Healthy's feet.

Chaaku was in awe. He was ready to be Mr Healthy's slave—to cook for him, clean for him, fetch for him, do as he ordered—even minister to his monstrosity.

In turn the savant gave him an umbrella of confidence and reassurance he had never had. He introduced him to reading the morning newspaper, taught him to think about his life, its purpose, why he was doing what he was. He directed him to posh commercial areas like Connaught Place and Khan Market and South Extension where he pointed out opulent stores and brilliantly turned out men and women alighting from cars and jauntily making packets of purchases. He made him drive them through Lutyens' Delhi pointing out lane upon lane of sprawling Raj bungalows with famous nameplates and grand old trees and guards with guns and white official Ambassador cars sweeping in and out.

Money and power, he told him. Only two things drove the world. And neither of them had any. But he would change all that. Chaaku must not worry. He must merely have a sense of destiny and a sense of himself. All this after all was only created by men. Not unlike them; not better than them.

He explained all these things by quoting from the Bhagavad Gita. It was the one book, he said, that had all the answers demanded by life. He said it was his father, a schoolteacher in the village, who had first taught him the great wisdoms of the song divine. That always men must act: they must both live their karma and make their karma—and all of it must be done without regard for reward or punishment. Lord Krishna said to the unequalled Arjuna, 'O Partha! In the three worlds, I have no duties. There is nothing I haven't attained, there is nothing yet to be attained, yet I am engaged in action. O Partha! If I ever relax and stop performing action, then men will follow my path in every way. If I don't perform action, then all these worlds will be destroyed. I will be the lord of hybrids and responsible for the destruction of these beings.'

Mr Healthy—he had been so named by a cruel English teacher when he was eleven: his real name was Sukesh Kumar—Mr Healthy did not believe in idols, temples, or rituals. All religion, except for the Gita, was skewered by him in his cool hard voice. He told Chaaku that all of modern Hinduism was a wasteland, full of hokum rites, festivals and places of worship, overrun by ignorant, corrupt priests. In contrast, in this mess, lay the heart of all profound truth, the Gita. And of all the great lessons of the Gita what was the greatest? The idea of detached action.

'Look at me. Look at me, my boy. Do you ever see me agitated, angry, emotional? When you slash skin with that knife, do it as if you are drawing birds in the air. When you gouge out someone's entrails do it as if you are digging soil in a flower-bed. And when someone puts a hard blade into you see it as a shower of sudden cold rain that you can do nothing about. When you feel pleasure see it as a passing breeze. When you feel pain see it as a passing breeze. Life itself is only a passing breeze. Detached action.'

The thin man from Amritsar with a cucumber for a cock had been sent to Delhi by Shauki seth to manage the soiled bundles, to buy the properties. This involved parsing the market, hard negotiations, doing numbers, checking papers, handling illicit cash, getting clearances, taking possession. The boy with the knife was there to protect him, and also to be a check on him. Shauki Mama had assumed his nephew's loyalty, the family bond. He had failed to see the boy was putty waiting to be moulded; he was not a finished product, just a tragic upshot of his circumstances. Anyone could seize control of him and bend him to his will. Shauki seth was also soon to learn the truth in the saw: never trust a thin man who thinks too much.

In less than four years, without cracking a smile, without Shauki seth's college-going son—in the next bedroom—having a clue, while getting his big cucumber regularly peeled and polished by Chaaku, the thin man with the ideal of detached action had siphoned enough soiled notes to set up on his own. With even greater cunning he had purloined several of the key papers of the properties he had acquired for his master. This meant that Shauki seth, instead of mounting a revengeful assault on him, had to come begging for truce and friendship. Without the missing documents his properties were valueless; in fact, he was vulnerable. A man as cunning as Mr Healthy could set the officials on him; and there was no way he could sell any of his properties without all the papers.

When his uncle came to meet his mentor, Chaaku sat in the inside room with the door ajar, playing nervously with his knife, opening and closing the blade. The renegade duo now lived in a tiny two-bedroom flat in Saket, a South Delhi colony. The thin man said this was where Delhi would boom in the future. Already this house was better furnished than the one they had first lived in. There was a proper red Rexine sofa suite in the drawing-room with a maroon durrie on the floor, a small dining-table with four chairs next to it, a two-burner gas stove in the kitchen, a white ceramic cistern in the toilet, which sat behind one's back and worked with a refined whoosh, box-beds with coir mattresses in the bedrooms, plastic shades over all the bulbs, and semi-transparent muslin curtains on the windows and doors.

From where he sat, with the lights off, Chaaku could see clearly into the well-lit drawing room. The thin man was sitting on the single seat, his pencil-thin arms spread out, his collarbones jutting out like wings, the big apple in his throat unmoving. Shauki Mama was on the triple-seater sofa, sitting on the edge. He was in a brown safari suit, wet patches of sweat under and around the armpits.

In the next one hour, the boy saw the thin man deconstruct the transporter. Everything his uncle threw at him—camaraderie, threat, blandishment; police, mafia, partnership—everything was dismissed with a cool demeanour and minimal words. Each time the thin man spoke it was as if he was cracking ice with a chisel.

The seth was free to do what he chose.

There was no reason to get all hot under the collar. Like the seth, they were only acting in self-interest.

The seth must watch his tone. Unlike them, he had a lot to lose.

They could all be winners. The world was a large place, with enough for everyone.

Would the seth like to go to jail? He could provide ten different tickets that could head him that way.

There was a civilized way of doing everything. He would hold the seth's papers in trust and pass them on periodically, as long as the seth kept his end of the bargain.

And Chaaku? Well, Chaaku was fine. Just fine. There should be a law against exploiting young nephews. Was he sent to him to be educated and prepared for life, or to be made into a small-time slasher? Why didn't he give his own son a knife and ask him to stick it into passers-by?

No, he could not see him. No, because he was not at home. And had he been, he may still not have wanted to.

By the time the thin man ushered Shauki Mama out and latched the door, Chaaku was giddy with adulation and pride. When he turned around, sombre and unsmiling, the boy fell to his knees and clasped his stick legs. Not one expression crossed the thin man's face as his cucumber was delicately peeled and consumed.

Later, he said, gravely, 'Every seth needs to have the key to his safe stolen once in his lifetime. Makes them into better men.'

Chaaku never left the thin man—and never fell out of love with him—till many years later, when he was dragged into jail for having conspired to murder a man.

7

THE EMPERORS OF AIR

By now the sparrow had become a full fluttering presence in Sara's life. His involvement with her had become a daily thing. If she was not seeing him, she was on the phone to him; else she was poring over his brown, string-strangled files, or she was talking to me about what they had lately discovered. Puny Bhandariji of the pencil moustache and stylized delivery, was, of course, fully infatuated by now, reeling under the Sara effect. As was her wont, she had made her own concerns the most important in his life, and it was obvious the one time I visited him in his house in Kalkaji that he was beginning to neglect his other cases.

In the one hour that Sara and I spent in the cramped room—a converted garage, partitioned with bad plywood into three tiny cubicles, and crammed with hardbound volumes of the *Law Reporter* and tottering heaps of mouldering files—in that one hour of repeated glasses of tepid tea and glucose biscuits, of dust particles hanging in the air, of a weird mishmash of white and yellow lights, Bhandariji's juniors came in several times, demanding with an exasperated tinge in their voices, his attention for other cases. They all looked at Sara as the bitch that had broken up the family.

I knew Sara was being derelict with her own organization too. Often she'd take a call from her rabid bunch at the women's advocacy group and start making excuses for not being able to travel out of the city—to Rajasthan, Himachal, Kumaon—for any length of time. Sara was a good liar. White lies, sure, but effortlessly essayed, without a crease of doubt in her tone. She was unwell; she had a key report to send off to Washington; her family was in town; a new funding contact had to be met; and, yes, there was a legal case she'd got stuck into. A couple of times she couldn't wiggle out of it, but I knew even when she was in the boondocks of Jaisalmer, she was burning the line to her sparrow.

The sparrow had, on her unstoppable urging, been taking her to the jail to meet the killers. It was how she was slowly piecing their stories together. I thought she had completely lost it. But I didn't care. Every visit to the jail was followed by a detailed, highly emotional narration, progressing to a colourful festival of abuse, culminating in a happy hanging on the wall. She was welcome to interview all the thirteen thousand prisoners in the jail—twice over if she chose—as long as she came back each time to be joyously crucified.

To be honest, as the weeks rolled into months I was surprised that the sparrow's affair with Sara had not petered out. I had imagined that the inevitable inertia of a court case in India would slowly sap the enthusiasm of both the do-gooders. Injustice, real and imagined, can be fought with red-hot passion for a day, a week, a month; you can picket, barricade, shout, scream, take on the tear-gas and the lathi; but if it becomes a somnolent waiting for a court date three months later, and a postponement and fresh date another two months later, and an adjournment and another date four months later, then passion can quickly dissipate.

There is very little that is stirring about collecting fresh dates from yoronour's clerk.

After the first two hearings the case had gone into characteristic limbo. In any case I had been informed that my role was consummately over. If I knew nothing about the alleged assassins, or about the conspiracy to kill me, then I was of no consequence to the proceedings. Sethiji—the king penguin—had said to me, beaming hugely, 'Go home and sleep peacefully. You are like the dead body in a mystery movie. The movie revolves around you, but you have only a guest appearance and it is now over. Your killers have now become the sons-in-law of the state, and will be fully taken care of.' We were sitting in his choked cubicle in the courts, around a small wooden table, sipping piping hot tea, with his junior penguins jamming the door. 'Look at them,' Sethiji said, taking a noisy slurp of his tea, 'do they look like lawyers? They look like extras in a film whom the hero will soon beat up!' All three grinned and flexed their arms and shoulders, their hair glistening with gel. 'See,' said Sethiji, 'they are the kind of extras who will keep smiling as they are beaten up!'

The oldest one among them—with trendy sideburns—said, 'Have you told Bhaiya what we heard last week?'

'And why don't you do it yourself, mister side-hero? Is my voice sweeter than yours? Is it my job to both argue in court and to amuse you with gossip?'

The convoluted story the boy told had to do with a huge sum of money that a business house had supposedly paid Jai to do a hit job in the magazine against certain bureaucrats and some businessmen. When I told him that it was not Jai who owned the magazine but a clutch of investors, the boy said he might have heard it wrong, the money then must have been paid to them. When I said they were already absurdly rich—with naked mermaids spouting water from their mouths—the boy said there was no such thing as having too much money. When I said that the investors did not even know about the story and only saw it when it was printed, the boy said, then it must be Jai who was being referred to. When I said the story was my idea and Jai had no role to play in it, the boy stroked his flaring sideburns and looked helplessly at his fat patriarch.

The king penguin snarled, 'Go on, James Bond, now tell him that it means that he only must have taken the money! All that day-night gym-shym muscle-phuscle has filled your brains with fat! If Mahatma Gandhi himself appeared in front of you, you'd kick him like a beggar! Now get out all of you before your foolishness makes me want to cry! And send us some tea and samosas!'

Grinning, the boys filed out, banging shut the steel door. Even after they left, the tiny cubicle felt cramped. It was barely enough for the fat lawyer. Stretching himself—no mean sight—and testing his suspenders with his thumbs, he now said, 'My father used to always say: "Son, don't do any bad but also don't do any good. In fact, if you do bad the people will fear you and respect you. If you do good they will be suspicious of you and attack you. Because in the depth of their own heart coils the serpent of deceit! Tell me, who killed Gandhiji? Was it the white man? This is not a country of men, my son, but of phuddus! Phuddus only understand the stick and the shoe." Sirji, my father was completely right. If I had my way I would impose military rule in this country and shove a stick and a shoe up each man's asshole, and I guarantee you each one would love it and bloom with good feeling and affection for everyone else!'

This was not the first time such bazaar gossip had washed up at our doors. Both Jai and I had been hearing wild theses from all kinds of sources for the last few months. Most of the stories had a predictable spin involving dubious motives and fat pay-offs, but some were truly outlandish, alluding to a cast of characters and conspiracies that staggered the imagination. These were a fevered mix of political skulduggery, the underworld, and big business—storylines generated from the deranged hyper idiom of Hindi cinema. To even conceive of them in jest required absurd credulity.

In the beginning they generated great amusement amongst us. Jai and I would strut around the room and loudly orate the grand attributions made to us. Jai would say, 'Maaderchod, I have a hundred million in Swiss banks—I am going to buy myself a yacht, and I am going to employ Chutiya-Nandan-Pandey as my butlers!'

I would say, 'That bugger, the transport minister, he's finished! Yesterday my car hit three potholes! I am changing him! D'Mello, it's over for you!'

And Jai would say, 'That paper guy, Arora, who cheated us and tried to threaten us—I've made a call to bhai in Dubai. By tomorrow evening he'll be in the crematorium.'

We would look at each other gravely and say, 'Shall we crash the stock market today, or start a border skirmish with Pakistan?'

This crap went on all day. There was little else to do. We'd drink endless glasses of tea and talk up our myth. The room was always echoing with hysterical laughter. But if any other staffer—less than a score remained—dropped by, Jai would shed all frivolity and become Mr Lincoln and deliver his state-of-the-nation address. No matter how many times I heard it, I was seduced by it. The fact is if there were still twenty-odd employees hanging around, it had to do with little other than Mr Lincoln's stirring orations. For all other purposes the place was dead.

In the crematorium, to use Jai's phrase.

Chutiya-Nandan-Pandey continued to stonewall us.

Jai had finally managed one meeting with them, in which they had categorically told him that they were way out of their depth, this was not the kind of thing they could afford to be associated with: it had the potential to damage everything else they owned.

When Mr Lincoln had made an attempt to talk about democracy, liberty and freedom, Kuchha Singh, raising his arm, had said, 'Everyone knows by now that we are chutiyas! But you really think we are the managing directors of the World Chutiya Federation!'

Jai was told we should expect no more help from them. As a gesture of goodwill they gave us one last cheque of five lakh rupees—to be used to buy time to find a new set of investors. They were willing to part with their own stake for a mere fifth of what they had so far invested.

Calvin Klein was going to have to sell a lot of extra underwear to white men to make up for the cost of democracy in India.

Asking someone to invest in us was, of course, like asking developers to put up a building on quicksand. Forget procuring a commitment, even getting someone to visit the site was nearly impossible. Jai had been steadily slipping down the scale of possibilities. He had long ago exited the category of what he called PLUs—people like us, the blue chip, public school, English-speaking scions, born rich and getting richer.

This category was now treating him like he'd caught some African disease. A couple of times I had walked in on him pleading abjectly on the phone with some friend to not be so fearful, to understand that the air was full of falsehoods and propaganda, and the truth really was that we were still a good investment. When he put the phone down he would revert to his usual bravura. There was no question that he was a chutiya too, but there was something charming about his cussed delusion. Now he was trawling territories that were totally alien to him—to both of us, actually. Shopkeepers from the old city; exporters of rice and iron ore; brokers from the stock exchanges of Delhi and Bombay; currency traders; mine owners and scrap merchants; government contractors and suppliers; small-town businessmen from Ludhiana and Indore looking for a positioning in the big city; and middlemen and deal-makers who closed the circuit between entrepreneurial desire and government largesse. Most of them he met at locations of their choosing. Hotel lobbies, coffee shops, their offices; occasionally even their crammed homes, with the bustle of children and servants. A rare few showed up at the office, wandered with suspicious eyes through our echoing rooms, and then settled down with Jai to monosyllabic inquiries.

All of them had an indefinable similarity. It wasn't girth—though most of them were obese—it wasn't clothes, it wasn't smoking or chewing paan, it wasn't the absence of courtesies, it wasn't language, it was something else altogether. I think it had to do with a kind of gift of clairvoyance they all seemed to carry around, an ability to walk into a space and intuit the true lay of the land. A quality of contained watchfulness, of shrewd assessment—vested in just their eyes—which saw them give away very little while soaking everything in. Of a piece with a commercial metabolism: always letting less flow out than was flowing in. Each had his own pattern of monosyllables. Theek hai. Bilkul. Barabar. Kyon nahin. Sahi bola. Karenge na. Bahut badhiya. Not one spoke expansively about what his own work was. Not one seemed to have any idea of what our work really was.

With these men, Jai was never Mr Lincoln. In fact, he was barely even Jai. Even a hard nut like me found it distressing to watch him negotiate them. These men existed outside the grand vocabulary of state and governance and citizenship and the ideas of privilege and responsibility. They were all men of the world, uncontaminated by any sense of larger agency or greater good. They were driven each moment by self-interest, by the primal need to protect and expand their turf and that of their families. It was very basic stuff, with narrow and insular horizons, and yet I could see these were not men to be dismissed: they shaped the world by the simple act of continual endeavour. Ants hoarding the grain, building huge silos, while the cicada pondered the seasons. Not one of them, I thought, would ever hit a state of stasis, or be crippled into inaction by the size and scale and unknowability of the universe.

Jai struggled to find the language that would connect him to them. His usual eloquence vanished and was replaced by a kind of wheedling manner, an attempt at rapping at their level. He spoke to them in a patchy mix of Hindi and English, cracking jokes, making cool comments on politics and business, attempting to exude the aura of a man who knew how to work the world, capable—like them—of sharp moves, of sleights-of-hand, of managing things. He dropped names, often in clusters, of people he may have met or spoken to fleetingly—often only once. Politicians, businessmen, bureaucrats, film stars, even fashion designers and TV minors: celebrities with whom he enjoyed virtually zero familiarity but whose wattage he imagined would dazzle these men.

He actually slumped low into his chair to make himself as small as he thought they were. I would come upon him giggling at their dumb quips, pressing their flesh, submitting himself to their laconic stories of power and pelf.

It was Bhalla, a smooth Punjabi, who for a time really captured our imagination.

Bhalla was in his forties and wore sharp shirts with monogrammed cufflinks, smoked acrid cigars, and spoke in a loud, filmi, gunslinger's drawl. He was flamboyantly and brutally dismissive of us, our opinions, our work, our plans. Jai had touched him through the king penguin, fat Sethiji, and over a six-week period Bhalla visited us several times. Each time I came upon him in Jai's office he was telling him a new story about some Bollywood starlet or the other and what her asking price was. He claimed there was a printed rate-list, and faced with our incredulity, dismissed us: 'You guys call yourselves journalists? You know nothing about the realities of this country! Nothing! A rate-list like in a restaurant, fully printed with menu and prices! Bread pakora, ten rupees; sandwich, fifteen rupees; chicken tikka, twenty rupees; full buffet, hundred rupees! All cash, no discount!'

He would mention names that sounded unbelievable, marquee names that fevered the fantasies of millions of Indian men. He spoke with a sneer, as if it were everyday material for him. The stuff was compelling, even without the hope of investment thrown in. But with that as a factor Jai and I were like panting dogs. Things went totally out of hand for us when he began to tell us about the ones he had personally ordered off the menu, at what price, and how they had sat on his palate. He referred to them always as 'line girls'. The first time that Jai ventured to inquire after the phrase Bhalla ignored the question. After that neither of us had the nerve to ask him lest we receive a merciless put-down. In any case, like good schoolboys, we were more interested in finding out who else was in this notionally available category.

'Is xyz a line girl?'

'Is pqr one too?'

'And rst? She couldn't possibly be!'

We'd be gawping, in our short pants, and he'd play us. Leaning back, he'd pull slowly on his cigar and say, 'What do you think?'

Jai and I would break into a babble, saying yes, no, maybe, all at the same time. After a long, amused, pause he would say, 'Yes.' The crazy part was it was always yes, and yet both of us needed to go through the process of denial and disbelief before we could savour the impossible lasciviousness of the confirmation.

Soon we knew the rate of every glittering star, and if Bhalla was to be believed all the truth—and lies—of their allure. In those days, inevitably, Jai and I laid bare our own cinematic fantasies as we made breathless inquiries. Nor was it beneath us to enter into heated arguments to protect the virtue or capacities of our favourites.

Cool Bhalla, who thought they were all overrated, that nothing matched the earthy delights of the ordinary EBM (ek bachche ki maa—the mother of one child), would say, through his thick cigar, 'While you are being chutiyas with each other about who belongs to whom, some slick rich dude is doing them!'

The voyeuristic roller-coaster was not the only reason we tolerated the man's disdain. He was, unexpectedly, quite a savant in other ways too. When he was not driving us mad with his menu card, he was giving us fluid dissertations on Hindu philosophy. He spoke of dvaita and advaita, mauna and maya, karma and dharma, Vaishnavism and Shaivism, sattva, rajas, and tamas, karma yoga, jnana yoga, bhakti yoga, raja yoga. Mr Lincoln, and even I, were kept reeling. Clearly the man had read—or received—a deep education in the scriptures.

Sometimes he would recite verses from the Gita—in the original Sanskrit, sonorously, and then render them for us in English.

One time, after he had finished inflaming us with stories about a glittering star with a fine pedigree who only offered herself by lying flat on her stomach, he suddenly challenged us to recite the Hanuman Chalisa. Then, as we were mumbling incoherently, he took his cigar out of his mouth and launched into a thunderous rendition of Jai jai jai Hanuman gosain, kripa karahu Gurudev ki nain. He belted out the long invocation to the fearless lord, a fail-safe charm against every kind of marauding djinn and spirit, without breaking for breath. We managed to catch only a few words and phrases, but that day after he left the two of us loped around the room, wielding imaginary maces, criss-crossing each other, loudly chanting 'Bhoot pisaach nikat nahin aave, Mahabir jab naam sunave', and 'Nase rog hare sab peeda', and again and again, 'Jai jai jai Hanuman gosain, kripa karahu Gurudev ki nain'.

Sippy, bringing in the tea, said, his eyes swimming, 'God will definitely help us, sirji.'

Accenting Bhalla's sway over us was his knowledge of the stock market. In fact, he presented an elaborate plan to us to raise some money for the magazine. Neither of us understood a word of it. Jai at least tried to make some intelligent noises, while I simply dove into the iron mask. In sum, what it seemed to entail was, we were to first hand over to him gratis one-third of the equity of the company, then he would reverse-merge the company into a shell company and take this entity to the stock market and raise fifteen crore rupees by first investing one crore of his own to ramp prices. And then he would give us ten of that for the magazine and keep five for himself, as well as the shares that we had given him.

We could make very little sense of it though he drew it all in elaborate bubbles on the white board, but it sounded great to us. We were sitting on a very big heap of shit. If someone was going to turn it into gold and keep half of it, we would gladly kiss his ass. But before I could ask, where should we sign, Mr Lincoln said, 'I hope you are not talking about some kind of insider trading?'

Bhalla stood up and rode into us with an angry sneer: 'You chutiyas, do you even know what insider trading is? You don't know the Hanuman Chalisa, you don't know how to fuck a heroine, you don't know dvaita and advaita, you don't know how to smoke a cigar, you don't know how to make money, and now you pretend to be Jesus Christs about insider trading! Motherfuckers, yes, it is insider trading—even though you don't know what it means! Motherfuckers, everything in the stock market is insider trading! In fact, everything in this fucking country is insider trading! What do you think politics in this damn city is? What do you think your fucking journalism is? There is no truth in this fucking country except for the poor bastard on the street who has to carry the load of all of it, and of you and me! Have you ever really looked at that poor bastard? Next time you are fucking around on the roads, look at him! He knows everything is insider trading! And he knows he's outside of it! And you know something—he's happy for it! He knows all of us great inside traders are doomed! We are busy scribbling out our misery! He's fucking happy, the universe is on his side. He knows the joke is on us!'

It turned out to be a cruel blow. We didn't see Bhalla in our office again. Jai made one attempt to thaw him, visiting him in his Hauz Khas house. Jai was thrown by the man he met in his own citadel.

The house was strangely unrefined, opulent in a crass satin-and-sunmica way, full of the claustrophobia of a joint family—the continual movement of crusty-cranky servants, the clamour of children of all ages, the hushed entry and lingering exit by doddering crones, the absence of any real individuality in either the furnishings or the shelves, the constant buzzing of intercom phones connecting different floors and units, the monosyllabic intra-house conversations.

Bhalla had no cigar stuck in his face and appeared a poor photocopy—faded, unclear—of the man who in the magazine office had for weeks held us in thrall. The handshake was loose, his booming voice low. The hectoring attitude was gone like starch from a washed shirt. Jai and he didn't sit in the main living-room but in a kind of alcove, just off his dark-doored bedroom on the first floor—approached from inside the house. It was a small cramped place appointed with a futon, two chairs and a small low table. On the table was a brown wood rhinoceros with its horn broken in half. It was only eight in the evening, but Bhalla was wearing a soft pajama and a loose nightshirt.

Bhalla spoke to Jai vaguely and softly, his eyes furtive. There was no talk of the 'line girls', no talk of the grand tenets of Hindu philosophy. He rambled noncommittally about politics and the economy, the likelihood of another war with Pakistan, the last film he'd seen. At one point the dark door opened and his wife walked in. Bhalla introduced her in an embarrassed way. She greeted Jai with folded hands and asked him in Hindi if he'd care to eat or drink anything. She was fat, dressed in a shiny salwar-kameez, and her fair skin had the bleached pallor that comes from too little sunlight. The bangles on her right wrist were heavy gold. She turned back at the top of the stairs to ask, in Hindi, what they were planning to do for dinner. He said in a very sweet voice, 'Whatever you decide.'

Her heavy tread could be heard down the stairs because of her payal.

Soon after, an older thickset man—balding, clean-shaven, chewing paan—came into the alcove. He didn't sit down, just shuffled around. He gave Jai a limp hand without looking at him and then proceeded to make cryptic inquiries of Bhalla in a gruff voice about stocks and banking details.

When it was done, Bhalla said, 'Bhaiya, Jai is the one I was talking to you about...the magazine...'

The brother looked at Jai with unsmiling eyes and said, 'Good to see you are still alive.'

Bhalla said, 'Bhaiya, remember I talked to you about the reverse merger and the listing...'

The brother said, 'Give him some tea and some biscuits. And I am sure there are some fresh kachoris at home. And make sure those Corporation Bank papers are with me before ten.'

Jai talked of this meeting for a long time. He said he didn't feel half as bad for himself as he did for Bhalla. In a moment of largesse he even said Bhalla deserved all the starlets he could possibly procure—including Jai's very own favourite, the one with an ass like a ripe pear—as reparation for his life in that joint family alcove.

After the debacle of Bhalla, Mr Lincoln began to lose his grand impulses even within the charmed circle of the office. In a desperate way we had begun to believe that the starlet-stocks-philosophy savant would somehow pull us out of our deepening pit. The joint family alcove was a crushing blow. Jai now stopped protesting the resignation letters that floated on to his table every other morning. Even those who had no other real options to this now occasionally paying job and came in expecting to be persuaded against leaving, were shocked to find a subdued Jai and a farewell handshake lying in wait for them.

In ten days we were down to ten people. For the first time I felt a touch of alarm. Without recognizing it, I too had assumed that Jai would somehow find an investor before it all wound down completely. But here we were now, undeniably on the lip of the precipice. The last two issues had been twenty-four pages each, and we had printed only a thousand copies—down from a high of forty-five thousand. Jai felt, rightly, that we had a chance as long as the magazine kept publishing, no matter how feebly. If we dropped even one issue, we were dead, beyond revival. The lip of the precipice: another seven days and there would be no issue.

I called Guruji. He had given me this privilege—of long-distance spiritual consultancy—to be used only in a crisis.

His laughter sang through the phone: 'What you make happen, son, will happen. It's the law of the universe.'

I said there seemed to be nothing left to try. There could be no doubt Jai had worked every opening he could contrive.

Laughing, he said, 'If you think that's the case, then it's over; if you don't, then it's not.'

I said, 'But what do you think, Guruji? That's what I want to know.'

He said, 'What I think is of no consequence. But I never think it's over till it's over.'

I said, 'So should we keep trying?'

He said, 'Is there anything else for you to do?'

I heard him chuckle softly. Then after a pause, he said, 'Look at the good side. All this is going to get your mate's head screwed on right. Maybe you should ask him to try some prayer now.'

I thought of Jai at the Hanuman temple, delivering an oration to the ascetic lord on democracy and the social contract.

We were sitting in his room, across the narrow corridor from mine. The scraggly branches of my laburnum wandered onto his balcony too. Through its bony brown fingers the sky was grey. The winter was almost dead and Holi was some days away. Already there were idiots on the road throwing water balloons at cars. Jai had things in his room, personal effects. Photographs on the wall, of his plump two-year-old son, his parents in a studio—father in a three-piece suit, mother in a saree with a big bun of hair. His wife was on his table, in a diptych, two close-ups, one fair and smiling, the other dark and pensive. 'So I never get deluded,' was his quip. There was a moulded metal ashtray of Arion and the dolphin, a sandalwood paper-cutter with animal engravings, a shelf of personal books (no *Naked Lunch* that a police inspector could have caressed), a slim wooden backscratcher in the shape of a naked undulating woman, a clock stuck into the side of a rearing horse, and a stack of CDs of Western classical music. On the table next to his sofa was a crumpled paper lamp. It looked clumsy to me but I knew it had some sort of designer origins. There was also a kind of large litho on the wall, in a heavy wood frame, of what seemed to me to be an Orville and Wilbur Wright airplane. It was the work of some guy called Laloo Shaw. Jai had said to me if all became debris, the litho would feed him and his family for six months.

In comparison my room had the personality of a McDonald's burger. If I walked down the stairs and never came back, anyone could get in and settle in my place, without a thought, five minutes after I had left. Sometimes I felt like that in my house too. I could walk out the door, past cavorting Jeevan, past pawing Mr Sharma, past the big peepul, and keep going, turning corner after corner, till there was no finding my way back. Anyone could, five minutes later, walk in without anxiety, settle into my bed and curve into the sleeping s of Dolly/folly. Later, dark-dank Felicia would fetch him tea on a plastic tray and he would use my toothbrush to shine his teeth.

I decided to tell Jai what Guruji had said. For once he didn't sneer or launch into a teasing harangue. The precipice can provoke unexpected faith. He got up from his chair and went and stood against the big window and put his palms against the plate glass. 'Actually, why not, there is nothing else to do. Let me for a moment remove this glass between god and me and see if it changes anything. And if it doesn't, we'll just put the glass right back!'

In the next week, in pursuit of an idea, Jai became a secular devotee. His zeal was to be marvelled at: it had the same intensity of his orations. With a schedule in hand, he visited as many major temples, gurudwaras, mosques and churches as he could manage. He meticulously followed the protocols of each, buying boondi and marigold garlands, cracking coconuts and drinking sweetened water, wearing white skullcaps and handkerchiefs tucked behind his ears, bending at the knee and bowing at the waist, lighting candles and parroting hymns, feeding urchins and amputated beggars, getting vermilion smeared on his forehead and sacred thread wound on his wrist, walking barefoot in the dirt and getting jostled by the believers. If there was a quota for spiritual genuflection, he had made up all the lost ground.

When I told Guruji, he said, through his happy laugh, 'You don't become a mahatma because you wear a loincloth. Else, every man in his bathroom would be one.'

And yet, despite Guruji's cheerful cynicism, something happened while Jai was still visiting god's showrooms—something totally removed from us—that altered our derailed fortunes. A few days after Jai began his quest, a couple of days after Holi, the hard colours still lingering on skins everywhere, irritating me because I hated that adolescent bullshit, on a lazy afternoon as I was slumped in my chair watching India struggling under the heel of the Australian cricket machine in Eden Gardens, Calcutta, my mobile buzzed frantically. I didn't recognize the number and I didn't recall the last time someone unknown had called me. It was several months since the hoopla of our exposé and the murder attempt had died down.

The voice belonged to a breathless television reporter. He wanted my reactions to a story. When I said I didn't know what he was talking about, he said, well, I ought to hotfoot it to my television set: if what we had done was the mother of all stories, this one was the motherfucking great-grandmom of them all. All hell was breaking loose; the government was about to fall; the skies were about to open; the Himalayas were about to crumble; the country was about to change. I clicked away from the Indian batsmen—abjectly on a follow-on, chasing a mountainous score—and found an exploding nuclear bomb of a story on the news channels.

A bunch of guys running a website had cracked wide open the rules of the journalistic game. Using spy cameras, they had hauled in footage of the rich, the powerful, and the animals who work the in-between, grabbing crisp rupee notes from reporters posing as arms dealers. The journos had sold the corrupt jokers a turkey as big as an elephant and, blinded by an endless influx of easy money, the jokers hadn't seen it. Now here they were—politicians, generals, businessmen, government officers, presidents of major political parties—all in Technicolor, emblazoned across tens of millions of television sets across the country with their pants down and scabs showing.

No one the fuck knew what to do. There were swarms of newsmen buzzing around like hornets, hitting on whoever they could find. There were politicians running around like headless chickens, raving and ranting every which way. Parliament had been stalled by screeching members filling the well and bouncing up and down as if they had roaches in their undies. Everyone was looking for a television screen. Everyone was looking for an explanation. Who was behind it? What was the motive? Was the government going to resign? Nothing like this had been seen before.

Jai barged into my room, his neck a swathe of Holi purple, his forehead freshly slashed with vermilion. Throwing himself on the single sofa in front of the television, he flung his legs over its arms, and said, 'They are fucked.' We both looked at each other, and knew what he meant. We'd been fucked for something that in comparison was the pop of a balloon.

At the moment they were on television, and they were talking big. Facing down phalanxes of cameras and thronging reporters, and talking real big. One of them in particular was grand—grand in the manner of Mr Lincoln. In fact, he was surreally reminiscent of Jai. He had a beard with a little more salt in it than Jai's, and the lofty cadences of Mr Lincoln. He was giving state-of-the-nation orations on corruption, morality, politics and the Idea of India. He was talking about illicit electoral funding and national security and the subversion of a democratic dream.

I looked at Jai, and asked, 'Separated at birth?'

Jai said, 'Boss, I am not in this guy's league.'

The bugger was dripping virtue like Christ on the crucifix. And he was smart enough to be loftily humble. No personal preening, no naming names. Just principles and values and morals and a whole lot of fucking hot air! Stuff that fills up balloons the size of buildings, but if you want to hold it in your hands you get nothing but your own damn palms rubbing against each other. Of course they would fuck him eventually, but it seemed it would take some doing.

The other guy with him appeared more all there, more my kind. Sort of a big, thickset, straight-seeming fellow with nothing overtly creepy about him. No grand design, no save-the-nation crap. There was shit out there in the world and he had gone and hit it with a solid club, a big bertha. And if it was now flying around splattering everyone, it was not his fault. It was not his shit. He was just the clubman.

Apart from hotair and clubman, there was a third specimen lurking in the corner. This one was like the bumbling hitman of a noir film, or the comic moment in a Hindi movie. He didn't seem like any investigative reporter one could have imagined. In comparison, Woodward and Bernstein were Citibank managers. This guy was rotund, clad in a loose bush shirt, with a shambling manner, and nothing he said made any sense. It was easy to see how devastatingly deceptive he could be. Men would think nothing of handing him their cheque books, and wives, for safekeeping.

I guessed he was the pitchman who'd sold the sod politicians the turkey bigger than an elephant. So all-pervasive was the hoopla around these guys that I, like many others, did not realize till a whole day later that India had turned around the Test match against Australia and were on the verge of their greatest-ever victory.

Though, like us, it teetered on the precipice for the next ten days, the government did not fall. The shit continued to fly—there were resignations, sackings, suspensions, inquiry committees. The cacophony grew by the moment but the citadel held. Within forty-eight hours the counter-attack began, and a hundred versions of everything rent the air. Soon no one knew the truth of anything. We had an eerie sense of déjà vu as wild theories of the underworld, business rivalries, stock market manipulations, Pakistani subversion, political skulduggery and Swiss bank pay-offs began to scorch the social waves. The only real difference was scale. If we had been mucking around in a puddle, these crazies had gone and fucked up the whole ocean.

For us the chaos created a sweet moment of reprieve. If it was owed to Jai's rush of eclectic religiosity, I was happy to credit him. And if it was the inadvertent doing of hotair, clubman and hitman, then they had my gratitude.

A few days later we were sitting in Jai's room watching the shit fly on television when his phone rang. I paid no attention, but when he got off the line he said, 'Do you remember that Kapoor?'

I did.

He had visited our office in a red Pajero, bathed in cologne, wearing a wide-brimmed hat. Delhi was full of weirdos struggling to manage their machismo. Chutiya-Nandan-Pandey had once talked about a friend who kept a ghariyal—illegally, of course—on his farmhouse, and often during parties, muzzled the antediluvian beast and lowered him into the pool as guests screeched in frightdelight. Kapoor had talked of holidaying in the south of France: 'Lousy beaches, skinny women, lovely blue waters; take your own women, ignore the beaches, sail the waters. Food and wine, just fine.'

Jai said, 'He wants to come and see us. Wants to carry on the investment discussion.'

We looked at each other, serious and expressionless.

I said, 'But do we want to?'

He said, 'No. Absolutely not. Not our type.'

By now both of us were standing, beginning to pace.

I said, 'Tell him we'll consider it only if he changes the colour of his Pajero and stops wearing that hat.'

Raising his right arm and his eyebrows, Jai said, 'Dhan dhana dhan dhan...'

Raising my right arm, I said, 'Mahmud di maa di lund!'

And then breaking into a slow dance—one arm raised—both of us said in unison, loud and ringing, 'Dhan dhana dhan dhan, Mahmud di maa di lund! Dhan dhana dhan dhan, Mahmud di maa di lund! Dhan dhana dhan dhan, Mahmud di maa di lund!'

We were still chanting and dancing, criss-crossing each other in front of the hyperventilating TV, when Sippy walked in, tea on tray, eyeballs swimming, and said softly, 'Sirji, you are right, Mahmud di maa di lund.'

When I called up Sara to inform her of the new glimmer of hope—there was no one else to tell: father, mother, Dolly/folly were imbeciles; Guruji I could dial only after eight in the evening—when I called Sara up, she was in the waiting room of Tihar jail. Before I could say anything, she said, 'You have no idea of the stories of these guys. Just no damn bloody idea. The bastards who run this fucking country owe an explanation to at least 800 million fucking people! A personal explanation and a personal apology to each one of the 800 million!'

I said, softly and slowly, 'Dhan dhana dhan dhan, Mahmud di maa di lund.'

8

KABIR M

i

The Science of Anonymity

His father named him Kabir to confuse all killers, amputators and arsonists of the ominous future. There was another perilous giveaway Ghulam Masood needed to account for, and for that he procured a medical certificate when his son was twelve years old. The certifying piece of paper was a letterhead that declared in bold black print: Dr Babban Khan, MBBS, Specialist in Diarrhoea, Fever, Boils and Ladies Problems. It stated in a typewriter's clear script, not a medic's illegible scrawl, that acute phimosis had necessitated the surgical removal of young Kabir's little skin of pleasure and pain. In effect, he was circumcised for medical reasons, not...

Carefully folding over the thick paper and encasing it in a robust green plastic pouch—fashioned from a smart shopping bag from the local saree emporium by firmly firing its new seams together—his father protected the document so that even the most torrential downpour could not breach its skin. Before he was thirteen, Kabir knew that he had to carry the pouch on his person whenever he left the house, and if the occasion ever arose, swiftly present it as his credentials.

Ghulam Masood did not stop at this alone. A hard-thinking, far-sighted man, quite unlike those of his tribe, he studied the past and cast the future and built in further safeguards for his boy in this forever unstable world.

When the padre at the local missionary school insisted he give his son's surname, Ghulam said, with his palms joined and his head bowed, that his son would carry his blood and his spirit but not his name. He had called his son Kabir to put him beyond the lines of community and religious lacerations that shredded the land. It had been the most thought-out act of his life.

Though this was most unusual, Fr Conrad was not thrown by it. The big burly priest from Kerala, dark as bitter chocolate and bald as an egg, had trained all his life for misery and the deformities it creates. The first case he had handled in his diocese as a young friar was of a middle-aged transport department clerk who got drunk and thrashed his parents every weekend while being a model son, caring and solicitous, all week. The old parents loved him and feared him; he adored them and hated them. He beat them with a seasoned bamboo cane either on Saturday night or on Sunday, sometimes on both days. Then on Monday morning he took them to the mission dispensary or to the government clinic and applied the poultices and mercurochrome on their wounds himself. Through the week, several times a day, he prayed at the altar of the crucified one, begging forgiveness for the beast that raged within him. And each night he heated a brick, wrapped it in an old towel, and pressed it for hours to his parents' aching bones. Then Saturday arrived, and the bottle was unscrewed. The brick was put away deep under the bed, and the cane was pulled out.

The young Conrad, attempting gravitas with a goatie—later he would sport a full flowing beard—had tried to talk to the entire family, in turn. The clerk's wife Maria had said, 'Better them than me! All men are animals, there's nothing to be done.' The old parents had said, 'He is a very good son. We forgive him his trespasses. The devil has ways of waylaying men that we can never know.' The clerk had said, 'I am a sinner. I deserve no mercy. There is no hope for me. Curse me, Father, curse me!'

The young friar had spent hours, week after week, talking to them all, fondly and threateningly, invoking man's law and god's law, till he finally understood the great truth of his calling. His task was not to talk but to listen. His job was to offer men the solace of god's ear. Men were what they were; very little could alter the darkness within them. Each man walked his darkness on his own, in his own way, feeling his way through. No lofty sermons, no stinging admonitions, no preceptor or padre, no policeman or pandit could help light the way. All that each stumbling soul wished to know was that there was someone out there who would hear him, hear the story of his darkness, and punish or absolve him.

So he began to listen, not preach. He became the representative not of a hectoring god but an empathetic one. It made him increasingly popular. The friar became a single gigantic ear—as in the gramophone boxes of another era, only this one sucking in sound, not issuing it. A single gigantic ear, into which could be poured all the misery of the world. His gift was quickly spotted by the grey hairs of the cloak and he was picked to work in the fine schools that the Cappuchian order ran across the spread of the country.

He proved a good teacher and a sound administrator, and as he moved from school to school, he left hundreds of malleable boys with lifelong memories of grace and godliness. Sometimes other things too. In time the friar had discovered the darkness within himself as well. Amid the press of boys, fresh-faced and supple-skinned, he had found torments that ravaged his senses. The lord above knew he fought it every moment, and each time he succumbed he fell in desperate penitence at the altar. He had come to learn that everyone failed the test of their own darkness. It was the lord's way of keeping men humble.

So Ghulam Masood was fortunate, in this critical moment of his son's life, to find Fr Conrad sitting across from him. The friar—now grown into a handsome beard of salt and pepper—understood this frail, tremulous clerk's area of darkness. Not only did he give the man's son admission to the school, but in a rare exception, he registered him as only Kabir M. In a crisis Ghulam knew the M could be Mishra, Mehra, Malhotra, Mallick, Mehta, Mahapatra, Modi, Mitra. Fr Conrad, who was a reader of modern literature, told his fellow brothers that it was a stylistic flourish sanctified by Franz Kafka himself, for hadn't he named his hero Joseph K. Ghulam told his kinsmen that he had shortened the Masood to the letter M so it could merge seamlessly with Mohammed, the one and only.

For the boy himself, in the universe of boys, there were no such easy explanations. Very early he was strung by the rope of the solitary letter. By the time he was in class four he had been firmly christened 'Muthal'—in recognition of the inherent delights of the stroking fist that his classmates were just beginning to discover. The name was to stay with him through his school years and beyond, to the point that many of his schoolmates never knew his real name. It also gave his wan, gaunt frame a different resonance: the provenance of the initial M was soon lost, and it came to be widely believed the boy's body was not delicate but wasted, thanks to an excess of self-abuse.

It's possible Ghulam did not know of the loss of his son's carefully chosen name, but if he did he could have derived relief from the fact that Muthal was no less secular a name than that of the wise unlettered saint he had chosen.

In any case, for Ghulam Masood, having his son named a masturbator was infinitely more welcome than one day having his organ sliced and his intestines gutted in a fleeting riot. Curiously, Ghulam was so incredibly timorous not because he had been savaged in some religious clash, but precisely because he had never been. It was the fear of it, the apprehension set deep in his bones, that had corroded him since he was a small boy.

Ghulam was not even a teenager when the rumours had begun to burn through their bastis like a forest fire in May: the new country

Gandhi was about to found was to be only for Hindus. They were to have another land, their own. The white man was definitely going, but he was going to leave two countries behind. In Ghulam's father's basti the dread word was that this land where they sat, where they lived, where they worked, where they prayed, where they fornicated, where they died, where they were buried—where they had done all this for time beyond recall—was not going to be theirs. Even to those used to being dealt random cards by the universe, this was an inconceivable thought. It sucked the sleep and peace out of every single person in the cluster of hutments.

Every single night of that scorching summer of 1947, as Ghulam and his friends played cops and robbers late into the night, their fathers sat in disarray under the tamarind tree, their vests patched with pockets of sweat, fanning themselves with flats of wood, smoking chillums and beedis and muttering to each other, as weak hurricane-lamps cast pools of shadows.

Inside the hutments, clustered together on their haunches like conferring vultures, sat their mothers holding their heads. Occasionally an old aunt let loose a hair-raising lament, cursing every man whose hand had ever steered the giant ship of India. This invariably provoked a chorus of curses—the arsenal of the ordinary. Till someone at the tamarind took his mouth off the chillum and told the whole bleating lot to shut the fuck up. Young Ghulam loved this moment of womanly excess and manly chastisement.

The basti had one battered battery-operated radio-set, which belonged to Hasanmian. From croaking once every evening under the tree for whoever cared to hear it, it had become a ceaseless mutterer. The men came by turns and put their ear to it, and if someone caught something that was vaguely intelligible, he set off a loud relay that had everyone in a fever of interpretation.

In that basti of artisans and craftsmen and cobblers and tailors, there was only one man who remained resolute about his position. He had neither much education nor the knowledge of the Book, but he knew his mind. The children called him Ali Baba, though his name was Ali Hussain, because of his long white beard and the wonderful stories he could tell. The tales he told were not originals nor gleaned from old texts. His material came from his workplace. Dramatic tales of emotion and intrigue and fantasy and history—with names like *Toofan Mail, Sikandar, Kismet, Hunterwali*. Stories that were absorbed by Ali Baba over days and unfurled to his young audience over weeks.

Ali Baba was the cleaner, usher, guard at Minerva, the only talkies in the nearby town. He unloaded and loaded the big steel cans of magic tapes when they arrived from Bombay and was always the first to taste their flavour. When Govind the projectionist rolled the spool for a check-out run and the fantasy beam cut through the dark, Ali would always be there, right under it, squatting on his haunches in the middle of the central aisle—never on the tin chairs, or the wooden benches, even though all of them were empty.

Ali Baba had seen enough cinema to know that life posed challenges, but in the end right always won over wrong, the good over bad, the fair over unfair. He had to only look at himself to know that this was beyond dispute: a man of such little worth—no learning, no culture, no artistry, no lineage—had been given a life of contentment, food, a roof, friendly neighbours, and a job that was not a job, but a rare gift, an endless feast of new and newer delights. Each time he squatted in that warm womb of stories he marvelled at the order in the universe, and he was deeply grateful that his simplicity and decency had brought him such rewards.

So Ali Baba refused to succumb to alarm or cynicism. Under the tamarind tree his position remained resolute. He was not going anywhere, and he saw no reason for anyone to go anywhere. This was where he had been born, and this is where he would die: his tenancy of his piece of earth was beyond dispute. The leaders of the Muslim League and the Congress and Lord and Lady Mountbatten and whoever else could divvy up whatever they wished among themselves—it had no bearing on the simple rights of Ali Hussain. If his patch was named Pakistan that was fine; if they called it India it would do too, thank you. He said, 'If someone passes an order, give us your wives, will you do it? And will anyone in his right mind expect you to do it? These are political games big men play, they have nothing to do with us in this Rohilla basti!'

Some of the men nodded in agreement and others scoffed: Ali Baba had seen too many films and lost all sense of reality. Also, unlettered as they all were, they could not really understand such things. Hashimmian had just been to Lucknow for his cousin's wedding and in that family of rich erudite lawyers he had heard long discussions on the new country that was being created for Muslims, where there would no Hindu domination, where Muslims would call the shots, where they would be safe, where they would live by their own religious laws, where they would prosper as they had never before.

Under the tamarind tree, the smoking men asked Hashimmian, 'Tell us, will Lucknow be in Pakistan? And Rampur? And Badayun? And Shahjahanpur? And Delhi? And Hyderabad? And Moradabad? And Lahore?'

Hashimmian sneered, 'And what will India be left with? Kabootarwali galli and Chachaji ka gol gumbaz?'

The fact was, Hashimmian reported, no one even in the big city seemed to know anything. Personally, he thought the whole debate was just the fanciful conjecture of the rich and educated. If every Muslim was going to be called Pakistan and every Hindu called India, then so be it. Changing names changed nothing. If Hashimmian was called Ali Baba he still remained Hashimmian. And physically, on the ground, how much could even rich and powerful men really change? Khichdi, he said, was made by mixing dal and rice, but once it was mixed could anyone separate them again? 'Can any of us, even with our needles, pick them apart? And if we do, what are we left with? Not rice, not dal, not khichdi. Just a chutiya mess not even a dog will put his mouth to!'

Ten-year-old Ghulam heard the squawking radio-set, heard the arguing men, heard the wailing women, and did not know what to make of it. All he knew was that the times were tense and this had some benefits: it allowed him to cut all his classes—school, the scriptures, and his hours at learning his father's trade of zari-zardozi. It was the last he hated the most. He attributed his father's cheerless disposition, his curved back, his scrunched eyes, to the endless, painstaking embroidery in gold-silver thread, on yet another tinselly ghaghra, put together for one more rich woman's wedding.

All the men in his family were embroidering drones—on his mother's side, his father's side, all the men married into the family, all the men earmarked for marrying into the family. And they all sat, hunched hopelessly, slit-eyed, ceaselessly snapping their wrists, fashioning tinsel. The only part of the process he found interesting was the old artist Abbajaan's drawing of the beautiful flowers, with curved leaves and winding stalks, on to the sheets of tracing paper. The old man drew up to ten different floral universes every day. Then the drones set to work.

The design was perforated, a dye of robin blue and kerosene run through it onto the fabric, and the satin cloth stretched taut on the wooden frame, the adda. His father and his fellow embroiderers, as many as five sometimes, all of them thick in the eyes with spectacles, sat down around it, as if settling in for a long meal on a low table. But this was not about moving jaws and easy talk. This was about the lightning dexterity of fingers as each of them picked their flower and leaf and began with blinding monotony to weave it with flashing needles and snipping scissors and shining baubles, into gold. They went on thus, hour after hour, tied down to the small low frame like tethered dogs.

Occasionally, some of the younger boys, working on adjoining addas, tried to crack jokes and make light conversation, but they were censoriously frowned upon by the older artists and craftsmen including his father.

Little Ghulam tried timorously to tell his abba that he did not want to be this kind of tethered animal. That the glittering garments weighing kilos and kilos, the shining threads, the sequins and cowries, the beads and shiny stones, the salma and sitara—none of them held any fascination for him. The thought of hunching over that low wooden frame for the rest of his life struck terror in his small heart. But so timorous was Ghulam's protest that his father—the artist without imagination—did not even register it.

Instead, the father only kept reiterating the inevitability of Ghulam's life. That he was fortunate to have been born into a family of craftsmen, to have his calling—and a dignified one at that—safely accounted for. He would never have to work crudely, in the scullery or the street. Never be a cleaner or a labourer, a guard or a barber, a cook or a gardener, a butcher or a cobbler. Nor would he have to labour at the crude crafts, as did many of his brethren in Moradabad and Rampur, hammering together iron tools or banging out brass vessels or weaving bamboo mats.

He was an artist, from an illustrious lineage of artists who had embroidered the rich raiments of landlord and warlord, nobles and kings, all the way back to the grand Mughals. Garments heavier than men, garments more expensive than houses. Such as the glorious robe of golden creepers that Akbar wore as he moved atop his gigantic elephant in the stirring royal procession of thousands of frolicking musicians and hundreds of cheetahs on leashes. Such as the sur coat of dark velvet with dancing flowers that Shah Jahan wore as he anticipated with growing arousal the arrival of his favourite wife, the soon to be memorialized Mumtaz Mahal.

The boy Ghulam could see none of this. All he could see was a tethered dog. So he was glad that the growing furore over the two countries and anxiety about which one they should pick had taken his father's eye off his son's zari-zardozi apprenticeship. And he was glad his instinct about the man from the Talkies, the teller of the moving stories, was being proven right.

Slowly, most of the men of the basti had begun to concur with Ali Baba's resolute position. This was their land, their air, their country. They knew no other. Nor wished to. Nehru and Jinnah could chop and slice the country as they pleased. They would stay exactly where they were, and go wherever the land under their feet went. If it was named Pakistan it was still their basti; if the name was India, it altered nothing, not even the latch on the front door.

Inevitably, the opposition to this philosophy of stasis came from the young. Those whose hair was thick and rich with oil and sharp in the parting; those whose flesh rippled with restless muscles; those whose hearts pumped hot blood; those whose lives lay in wait, ripe with hope—these young men, their eyes set on distant Xanadus, muttered at the inertia of their elders.

Among these boys in their late teens and early twenties, the excitement and hunger grew by the day. They paid no heed to the news of massacres and murders, of the dance of death, the gory tandav that had broken out between the Hindus and Muslims and Sikhs across the country, especially in the Punjab. They talked instead of their dreams—the promised land, brimful of new possibilities, where they would not have to hunch over the adda all day, where they would be able to do new things in new ways; start their own businesses, open their own shops, effortlessly acquire large lands and sprawling houses. A country was being born, it was waiting to be colonized by them. No more this choking basti on the outskirts of town; no more the interminable grind of the shining thread and traced flora.

Soon loud battles began to erupt within the basti as fathers and sons locked horns over the issue and mothers wailed the roofs off. The news from the big world—coming in ceaseless waves from the crackling radio-set, the half-anna Urdu papers, and heated word-of-mouth—did not help matters. All was not well. Wilful men had sliced the earth with no regard to the arteries of love, family, community, history, animals, trees that they were cutting. The news was that the blood from the severed arteries was beginning to flow everywhere.

Then news came that they were now free. That there were two new countries and two new flags flying across Hindustan. In the basti it felt no different. They felt no more free than before. Only Ali Baba, who spent every day in town, listening in to the educated and the knowing, said yes, there was something deep and abiding that had changed, but he too spoke without elation because the blood spilling from the arteries was colouring everything. Many of the stories were so gory as to defy belief. Of the wholesale massacre of dozens, scores, hundreds of people—on trains, buses, the streets and roads, fields and towns. The police was doing nothing, Nehru was doing nothing, Jinnah was doing nothing, the white man was doing nothing. Every evening, for hours under the tamarind tree, the men teased their anxieties, then dismissed them as improbable, hyperbolic.

A hush had fallen on the frolic of the children too. Inside little Ghulam the whispered stories were fast congealing into a hard splinter of icy fear that would not thaw for the rest of his life.

One dramatic muggy morning in the second week of September 1947 the basti woke to the knowledge that four of their young had packed their bundles and departed for Pakistan in the dead of night. Faisal, Wasim, Parvez, Imroze. Names Ghulam would not forget till his last day.

The one letter left behind by Parvez was passed from hand to hand, detonating ear-splitting grief. Only when the hysteria had eased did inquiries reveal that the great escape had been canvassed, discussed, rejected, accepted over many many days. Seven boys were to make the run, but finally in that fully dead hour between midnight and dawn, as the shadows began to slip away in the dark, three of them had lost their nerve. The three—Safdar, Rahim and Salman—were now being cosseted and assaulted in turn. Parents never can locate the shimmering line between love and domination.

All the children were interrogated, including Ghulam. They admitted that they'd heard of the plans, and when they began to be thrashed, they pleaded that they hadn't been sure. The elders of the basti went to the kotwali to register a complaint. The policeman in charge was sympathetic but professed helplessness. He said, twirling his big moustache, 'Mian, they are grown-up boys, they'll be okay. You know there are millions of people walking this way and that across the Punjab. If the laatsahib Mountbatten himself wanted to find his mother out there he wouldn't be able to! Do the only thing men can do at such an hour, pray to Allah and all will be well. You know what Sant Kabir has said, Jaako raakhe saiyan, maar sake na koye!'

None can bring distress to he whom the lord protects.

Towards the end of October, when the breeze under the tamarind tree had begun to nip the skin, early one evening, Imroze returned. The news electrified the basti; within minutes everyone had come tumbling out to meet the prodigal boy. Ghulam pushed through the legs of the adults to get a glimpse of the short, fair teenager. As a child Imroze had won jars and jars of shiny marbles, from which he gave freely—ten at a time—to all the young children. It was he who had taught Ghulam the correct way to strike marbles—left eye closed, knees bent, torso rigid, wrist tight, a soft kiss for luck and then a short sharp jab with the forearm to knock the striker in the right with the balancer in the left.

Because everyone was shoving and pushing and the hurricane-lamp was being moved about, it took Ghulam some time to sight his mentor. What he saw twisted the hard splinter of ice in his heart so brutally that his legs almost gave way. Lovely Imroze, beautiful Imroze, now had a thick scar running from the top of his forehead down his eye, across his right cheek, like an uneven bund dividing two fields. It had closed the right eye as it cleaved through it and near the jawline disappeared into a fuzz of brown-black beard that was freshly grown. The other eye, the left one, the one that was open, the one that worked, was also no longer Imroze's. It seemed like one of his cherished marbles: vacant, unseeing, without a flicker of recognition.

There was a policeman with him, in uniform, a hand on Imroze's shoulder. He was clearly waiting for the crush to abate. Surreally, all sound appeared to have been sucked out of the scene. Under the tamarind tree in the basti, at this hour, no one had ever known such profound noiselessness.

Ghulam watched the policeman carefully roll back the sleeve of Imroze's kameez, and a soundless scream rip through everyone. Imroze's left arm now ended at his elbow, where it was bandaged in rags. The master striker would never crash a marble from eight feet again. The cop moved it like the signal arm of a railway line, up, down, up, down. Then, like a forensic expert exhibiting a corpse to a batch of interns, the policeman lifted Imroze's shirt from the front to show a thick cable lashing his stomach. The knife's elliptical journey had been halted by the ribs.

In the shaking light of the lantern, the policeman then pushed the loose shirt up further to reveal Exhibit 2. A small hairless chest with a few vivid coils of rope. The policeman twirled his moustache and turning Imroze around, lifted his kameez from the back. Exhibit 3. The fair back of the boy was an emboss of dancing rope.

By the time the policeman had moved to Exhibit 4 and 5 on the soft buttocks and boyish legs, Imroze's parents arrived on the scene—straight from the whitewashed grave of the Abbasi pir where they had gone to seek the safekeeping of their absconding son—and the scream that his mother unleashed curdled the blood of every gawking child and unlocked every adult throat. A tidal wave of questions rose and crashed against the policeman and his mauled exhibit.

What had happened?

Where had they gone?

Who'd done this?

Where was Faisal? And Wasim? And Parvez?

Why wasn't he saying something?

Allahthemerciful, the arm! The arm! The arm!

The basti never fully recovered from Imroze's return. His story became engraved in every heart and mind, and in some, like Ghulam, it became a splinter of icy fear that would never melt.

Until Delhi the journey of the four friends had been full of banter and anticipation. Parvez, the writer of the letter, the instigator of the escape, had mimicked the reaction of each of their mothers on discovering their sons were gone. Even the other passengers had broken into smiles when they saw Wasim's mother beating her breasts with her fists. The four had sworn many vows of togetherness—nothing would come between them, not work, not wealth, and certainly never women. They had promised each other they would only return when they were followed by a train of gifts for each and every man, woman and child of the basti. They had amused themselves with what they would buy for whom, and how each of those wretched souls would react. The extent of their generosity made them giddy with pride and pleasure. Parvez had to remind them, 'Saale chutiye, if we eat one more meal without cooking it we'll die of starvation!'

The first foreboding surfaced at the New Delhi railway station. The station was suffocating with people but had the mood of a graveyard. Every face was drawn and watchful. It was easy to make out the large families cleaving together, often three, four generations clustered around their bags and bundles and trunks and hold-alls; endless tight circles, all looking inward, turning their backs to the backs of other circles that jammed the platform. A great stench of excrement filled the air. Scores of men, children and women—with their faces covered—squatted edgily in the dark low ravine beneath the platform, amid the sharp stones and steel tracks, continually startled by large rats.

Parvez's attempts at speaking to some of the men fetched blank stares and laconic responses. The few who were talking among themselves did so in funereal whispers. It seemed there had been trouble in the old city; every doorway was wet with blood. When the boys crossed the filthy tracks to the main building—holding their breath, dodging the bobbing bottoms—and stepped out of the grand facade to find some dinner, they got the first clear sense of the maelstrom they had landed in. There were uniforms everywhere: policemen and army men, khakis and olives, lathis and rifles. Instinctively, each one of them scrunched up within himself, smile fading, legs contracting to a mincing gait, stomach loosening.

They walked together in a tight knot, averting their eyes from the patrolling uniforms. By the gate they turned right and picked the first lean-to eatery, gravitating to a wooden bench away from the road. They shared the bench with a dozen others, all eating in concentrated silence. Most of them were Muslims, chewing with low heads and pushed out elbows. At the next table a young handsome boy, no older than them, with lush facial hair and red fiery eyes was snivelling loudly, his nostrils working angrily, like bellows. Every now and then he would begin to shake uncontrollably and start to rise and the two men flanking him would restrain him and murmur soothing words. At one point he let out a piercing wail, 'Ammmii!' and slumped into his curry-stained hands. The man next to him—wearing a Gandhi topi, not a skullcap—gathered him in his arms and held him close.

When Parvez asked the fat man running the eatery what was happening all around, he replied acidly, 'Do I look like Laad Mountbatten to you? And right now probably even he doesn't know what's happening.'

The burly man holding the crying boy said, 'Mountbatten ki maa ka bhosda! The white Englishman can make donkeys look like horses, shit smell like roses, and brothers behave like enemies. Let me tell you there is going to be no freedom, no independence. This is just one more game to make chutiyas out of us. India and Pakistan! They will wait for us to kill enough of each other, then they will step back in and continue to rule us as they have for hundreds of years. My grandfather used to say, if you are caught between a white man and a snake, run towards the snake. There is at least a chance you can kill the snake and survive its poison—with the white man there is no chance of either.'

The fat eatery man said, 'Inquilab zindabad! Haath mein loda, gaand mein paad!'

On the train, Imroze fell asleep on the rattling floor, curled against Wasim's soft buttocks, his head resting in the crook of his right arm. This was not how the four friends had imagined they would journey to the promised land, but given the run on space when the train had pulled in, this was not bad at all. As he slept he slid under the berth, along with their luggage. He had his arm around Wasim, and ahead of Wasim lay Parvez and Faisal, similarly tucked into each other. Imroze twisted the Idrisi pir baba's protective locket on his upper arm so that the metal wouldn't bite into his cheek. His mother had got it for him when he was eleven to ward off the fevers to which he was prone. It had worked to perfection and Imroze had not been ill since.

There were men, women, children, sleeping everywhere. Four to a berth, in the aisles, inside the toilets; sitting, standing, leaning—exhaustion and sleep melting and flowing into each other's pliant bodies. The train odour of sweat, dust, coal smoke, pickles, parathas, subzi, alcohol, fear, piss and vomit was everywhere. Jammed in that mess—in their own annexed space—the friends, before nodding off, had made playful jibes, accusing each other of harbouring dubious intentions. Some amount of jestful pushing and pulling had also ensued, with maybe a trace of seriousness. As they fell asleep the consensus had been that Imroze had the premier position, spooned into Wasim's feminine ass. Wasim's warning was, 'Saaley Imroze, make sure nothing escapes from your pajama! You know what they say in the basti, if you see a snake cut off its head!' Parvez said, from between Wasim and Faisal, 'That's the good thing about being a Musalman, the head is already cut off. Imroze, feel no fear! Let your headless snake go wherever it wishes!'

Imroze woke from a dream in which he was embroidering the sparkling zari with such frenzy that he had leapt past the holding frame of the adda and plunged into the spongy skins of the other craftsmen sitting around. Fountains of blood spurted as his needle thrust in and out of the screaming men and they began to thrash about desperately. Then one of the men pulled out a long curved dagger and plunged it into his speeding arm and he yelled out in pain, and when his eyes opened he knew he had tumbled into hell.

There was very little light, a great chaos of movement, and a medley of indescribable noises all around. Beside him, Wasim was reduced to a heap grunting softly like the pigs they used to stone as children, while someone drove the point of a spear steadily in and out of him. Over the sounds of grunts and moans and screams and pleading and keening was the clear barbaric sound of Hindi and Punjabi abuse. Maiovah, bahenovah, saale kanjar, phuddihondya, saale suar, kameene kutte, gaandu gaddaar, kutte katuay, kutte musultay, vaddho salya nu, vaddho, vaddho, vaddho. Hack them, hack them, hack them.

Curiously it was not the wild screams that were the dominant sound but the loud sighs. This was how—it seemed—people succumbed in sleep and half-sleep; with surprised, startled, grateful sighs. Deliverance following quickly on assault: the first sudden opening of raw pain; the second and third and fourth of relief—final, enduring relief—from it. The travellers to the promised land had been set upon like the herds of cattle of his childhood. In the moving light of lanterns he could see the herders had come in scores and were carrying swords, spears, axes and sickles. Actually—as with cattle—the herders were making more noise than the belaboured animals. The cattle just took in the blows with deep sighs.

Abuse, thud, scream, sigh. Abuse, thud, scream, sigh. Wasim next to him had ceased to moan. But Parvez was still sighing sweetly, softer by the moment, as the long-handled spear drove in and out of him. His hands were holding the bamboo shaft—and if you didn't follow the shaft to the man in the darkness who held it, it appeared as if Parvez in a frenzy of hara-kiri was steadily disembowelling himself. Faisal, true to type, was dying in an undignified way. All his youth he had been the crudest of them all—digging his nose, abusing, farting, masturbating in front of everyone. Now he was moaning and protesting and trying to get up, despite the steel buried in his stomach. When he had pulled himself halfway up there was the angry grunt of a herder, a slicing arc in the dark, a soft thud, and the gurgle of an opening tap. The herder pulled out his axe from Faisal's neck by planting his foot on the boy's chest to yank it out. Parvez and his blood became one.

Soon the sound of satisfied sighs and occasional groans had begun to reduce. From the berth above, lines of blood had begun to drip steadily onto him, wetting him warmly. The herders were now moving around looking to locate any animals that still needed to be taken care of. They spoke in the abbreviated grunts of herders, pointing out moving limbs to each other, encouraging the swift blow. Imroze had shrunk into himself, halfway under the seat, and stopped breathing a long time ago. Through his shut lashes he could see only the swinging lanterns and the anointed weapons.

Imroze thought of his marble collection. One more handful of milky whites and the jar would be full. A warm thick line began to drip down on the corner of his mouth. He pursed his lips tight.

Suddenly, he became aware that the train had not been moving all this while. Some faraway cries from outside the coach wafted through the window, riding on the gentle moonlight. There were sounds of many feet running along by the tracks, mixed with muffled verbal exchanges. He thought he heard the snorting of horses and the jangle of reins and stirrups. Now a rough voice called loudly, 'Are you done?' From behind a swaying lantern inside the coach a voice said, 'I think so.' Another voice said, 'Take a last look, laudu! These insects don't die so easily!'

Through the curtain of his eyelashes, in the moving light, Imroze saw the faceless herder pick his long steel-tipped bamboo, and like a river navigator, start prodding and probing the mounds of flesh lying splayed all about. Beside him there was another voice doing the same, with the edge of a warm-blooded sword. The axe-man had presumably moved on to further decapitations. Once he heard a low moan at the end of the spear, and it was swiftly cut off by a singing blade. The first voice said, 'Bloody insects! Don't die even when you've killed them!' The second voice said, 'Come on, this bunch were fucking calves! Not even one tried to fight back!'

Imroze's bowels had loosed completely now, and he lay on his side, trying to somehow bury himself under Wasim without making any movement. The angry-nosed spear was going thak, thak, thak—right through the spongy bodies—as the herders checked the carcasses. More voices called from outside the carriage, asking those inside to get a move on. There was no doubt that Allah the merciful would come between the steel of the infidel and the life of his faithful. Imroze squeezed shut his eyes to dwell on the glory of the almighty, the all-seeing, the all-protecting. And at that precise moment a fire raged through his belly as the spear slipped in the gap between Wasim and him, searing his flesh. The boy from the Rohilla basti screamed aloud, his torso jacking up in pain, his left arm shooting up to stall the assailant, and in the flash of that moment—in perfect time with the guttural abuse of the herders—the singing blade smoothly cut the air and the arm that came in its way. When the second swipe came it caught the wailing-collapsing boy across his face, opening his skin like a juicy tangerine, and the third and the fourth and the fifth scraped his ribs like a rake does the ground. When the herder's checking prod came soon after, the boy was too perforated and too far gone to twitch.

For the rest of his life Imroze lived within the tight confines of the basti, always within sight of his family—sitting against the mud wall while his father and brothers worked at the adda, or sitting on the dung-smoothed threshold of their hutments while his mother bustled around, her heart forever heavy. Always he carried with him his jar of milkywhites, scooping them out in the palm of his right hand, rolling them onto the ground, and striking at them endlessly, as he hissed, 'Vaddho! Vaddho! Vaddho!' Hack them, hack them, hack them.

Shaking his head sadly, Ali Baba said, 'Allah in his wisdom has put him on a train that will never reach its destination.'

For years after his country's independence, Ghulam slept next to his mother and never found the courage to go close to Imroze and try to speak to him. The news floating in from the Punjab only intensified the terror. Such rapine and savagery was afoot as no man could describe nor any god decree. The landscapes of Ghulam's nights were now full of swinging lanterns and jabbing spears and flashing blades and heavy-headed axes. Almost every night he came to with a start just as the steel was about to enter his flesh.

By never encountering the monster he grew more and more terrified of it. With every passing year it became more menacing, and Ghulam more fearful. When he walked the bazaar in town it was always with one eye over his shoulder. He avoided crowded buses, never boarded a train, and during festive occasions and marriage processions seized a position removed from the crush.

He refused to enter the choking galis of Kutubkhana or the Meena Bazaar where his friends spent their days buying and selling trinkets, artefacts, silver ornaments, black surma, diaphanous chunnis, shining zari-zardozi, sparkling glass bangles, cosmic bindis, particoloured kurtas, using it all to flirt with the girls who came to buy their wares, to hold a slim hand for a heart-stopping moment or caress an inch of fair skin. Ghulam knew that in the noisy intimacy of those alleys a single sweep of a singing sword could kill six people.

As he grew older he even began to fear living amid his brethren. Fretting about it at all hours, he realized that the basti itself was the biggest invitation to the monster. When its appetite was stirred, when its drool began to drip, when it wanted the blood of its choosing, where else would the monster head but for the basti? How obvious for the tiger to take the tethered goat.

Unlike the rest of his community he found no security in sticking together, in numbers. He wanted to shed his identity, to become anonymous. He had no quarrel with anyone in the world and did not want to lose an arm—or much more—for the absurd reason of his religion. It terrified him that none of the others in the basti seemed to think like him. They were continually full of religious assertions and the will of Allah. Every night by the tamarind tree there was someone high on ganja who mounted the horse of militancy and drummed up a mood of wild bravura. Every night they slaughtered trainfuls of infidels, chopping limbs like carrots, slicing heads like tomatoes.

Every night Ghulam raged to his mother, 'We will all soon become one-armed! That's when these people will be happy!'

His mother, old before her time, a bad hip giving a slow waddle to her walk, said, 'Men! Pay no attention to them. When they talk of killing elephants, they mean mice. Do you think the men who killed Faisal, Wasim and Parvez were killing elephants? They were killing trapped mice! Your father, those men under the tree, do you think they can kill anything but trapped mice? Just remember, my son, men are either brave and foolish, or foolish and brave. I have never yet seen a man who is brave and wise, or wise and brave. Never forget that we are small people and it is best for us to lie low—beneath the sweep of every marauding wind and murderous sword. We are not Hindu or Muslim, men or women—we are just small people who can only stay safe by making ourselves invisible.'

Shy Ghulam, timorous Ghulam—with a sliver of icy fear jamming his heart—resonated to his mother's words. The pursuit of his life became anonymity and evanescence, and later, for his son, the flattening out of all identity.

ii

An Alien Tongue

Before he turned twenty, Ghulam convinced Ali Baba to take him on as his understudy. Ali Baba had seen too many Hindi films to have a fanatic bone left in his body and he instinctively liked this timid boy's need to break away from the basti's narrow confines. Firdaus, the owner, didn't mind an extra hand—traffic at the Talkies was multiplying by the day as Bombay began to churn out more and more films, bigger, brighter, more irresistible. Ghulam was told to start working, and promised that one day some kind of a salary would come.

Ghulam's father flew into an abusive rage, screaming at the boy for abandoning the family craft for a menial job. For days, at every meal, he flung the food and utensils around. Mastering the lesson of lying low, Ghulam did not counter him with a single word and soon the fulminations settled into sullenness and the food was eaten and not thrown about.

Ghulam's working day began at seven in the morning with cleaning the stalls of the night show's offal—paper packets, beedi-cigarette stubs, the mud from a thousand feet, hair from the scratching of scalp and pubes—and proceeded to playing usher for the morning, noon and matinee shows. It was also his task to carry up glasses of tea twice during every screening for Govind in the projection room, and when the rolls of a new film arrived on Thursday it was he who helped cart them up. By six-thirty, once the matinee was over and he'd cleaned up, he was free to leave. It was Ali Baba's job to see the last two shows through, for now he only came in at noon.

However, when his day's work was done, Ghulam never wanted to go back to the basti, to the bragsters under the tamarind tree, to the hush of their hutment. Every night he stayed back at the Talkies till the last straggler had drifted out, the projection room had been locked, the footlights in the hall and the wall bulbs in the foyer had been turned off. Then, turning the big padlock on the front door and handing the key to the chowkidar, he would pull out Ali Baba's old cycle and slowly ride them home. All the way to the basti, forty minutes away, the old man on the back carrier and the thin young man straining at the loose pedals would discuss and debate every film that transited through Minerva Talkies. There would be the old man's slow, wise voice, often carried away by the wind and necessitating repetition, the rhythmic squeak of the cycle, and in between, the pant and push of Ghulam's thin-voiced assertions.

For a long time the caustic disagreement between the two men was over Madhubala and Nargis, and by extension, over Dilip Kumar and Raj Kapoor. Each gesture of those beautiful divas, each profile, the play of their eyes, the shape of their lips, the gaps in their teeth, the lilt in their voices, their nakhras and adas, the way they held their heads, the way they looked over their shoulders, the stretch of fabric across their fullness, everything was argued and contested. Ghulam's last word was if he had an option he would marry Nargis and take Madhubala as his mistress; the old man said he would do exactly the reverse.

One time, as they cycled home after the first-day screening of *Shree 420*, Ali Baba punctured Ghulam's heady elation—he was singing 'Pyaar hua ikraar hua' in loud, panting bursts into the velvet night—by calling Nargis horsey. His exact words, from behind the young man's singing-straining back, were, 'Oh stop singing this nonsense. In that sequence they looked like a clown and a horse standing under an umbrella. More circus than love.'

This upset Ghulam so viscerally that he threw his right leg over the front bar and jumped off the cycle. Ali Baba, riding behind on the carrier, had to scramble off to keep from falling. Dropping the cycle down on the road—its broken pedal pointing at the sky—Ghulam strode off in a huff. The old man stuck his foot into the still rotating wheel, picked up the fallen cycle and followed. The two men walked home on opposite sides of the road that night, in the dark blue night, a half-moon lighting the houses and fields in a dreamy glow.

Ali Baba said, 'Arre, stop behaving like she's your wife. Tomorrow your wife could look like a horse, what will you do then? Look at the women of the basti. They all look like strange animals. Amina is a pig, Shahnaz is a camel, Munni is an owl, and your aunt Shaukat is a splendid hippopotamus—the only one in all of Hindustan!' When the boy refused to relent, the old man said, 'This is why I don't like the young to go to the Talkies. They can never distinguish between real life and films. Now you think Nargis is your wife and you have to defend her even if it means walking home at one o'clock at night!'

There was some truth in what the old man was saying. Ghulam took the films more seriously than anything else in his life. He sat through two or three screenings of the same film every day, and with something like *Shree 420*—or any other film that starred Nargis—he saw every single show, sometimes for weeks on end. It was only in the inky dark, with the beam of divine light flowing above his head, that he felt safe and complete. Unlike Ali Baba he did not squat in the middle of the central aisle. He scouted for an empty chair anywhere in the hall, and actually revelled in the fact that he saw the same film from so many different angles. Sometimes he was in the first row up front, sometimes at the very back, sometimes he had a side seat and sometimes he managed dead centre. To see Nargis from so many perspectives was to fall more and more in love with her.

The laughing eyes, the promise of her lips, the strong straight limbs—often he chose to sit in the front row just to be overwhelmed by her beautiful immensity.

Minerva Talkies, the dark hall, the twilight zone between harsh reality and sublime desire, became his entire life. Four months into his job, when Firdaus gave him his first salary of five rupees, it was an unexpected bonus. This sense of money as an extra reward did not change in the forty years that he worked there—an endless access to the moving pictures always remained his main recompense. Only in the warmth of the hall did he feel a security that had been sucked out of his life in that autumn of 1947 by the departure of the four boys and the mangled return of Imroze.

Even when he rose, twenty-five years later, to become the manager of the hall—with Ali Baba dead and Govind retired—he did not stop slinking into the hall every minute he could escape his duties of accounting and paperwork and telephone calls to distributors, and the management of VIPs and the canteen stall and the cycle stand contractor. Only when he was in there, with the long-necked fans whirring, the sawing hum of the projector, the mega-sized stars in splendid motion—declaiming, singing, dancing, loving, fighting—did he feel safe and happy.

Ghulam had left his house and the basti soon after he had begun to earn a salary. Too meek to argue, he'd quietly ducked the utensils his father flung at him, taken his mother into confidence, and rented a tiny room near Minerva. It was on the second floor of a small, hundred-square-metre house and had a nice hole-in-the-floor toilet, a brick enclosure across the terrace with a tin panel for a door and no roof. There was no kitchen—the cooking stove was on a table inside the small room—and for bathing you used the open terrace.

The house belonged to Bhatiaji, a refugee from Rawalpindi who was piecing back his life by selling bolts of cloth off his cycle. Firdaus had to put in a personal word and stand guarantee for young Ghulam.

The first day the Muslim boy moved in, Bhatiaji—stocky, with unshaven jowls, and a Hitler moustache—Bhatiaji called him into his front room and without inviting him to sit took a leathery scabbard off the wall, unsheathed a long, slightly rusty sword and held it up in his pudgy hand. 'You put one step out of line, little boy, and I will chop into pieces all the bits of you that still remain uncut. Just remember this is not fucking Pakistan, this is Hindustan!'

All the blood drained out of Ghulam and he had to lean on the door jamb to keep from falling. For the rest of his stay on the second floor—four long years—he always climbed the stairs on animal feet. His endeavour was to never encounter his landlord. Coming back was fine—it was too late for anyone to be awake in the entire mohalla. But in the mornings he was very careful, glancing anxiously around for the refugee's cycle, before he sprinted out.

In contrast, the thuggish landlord's family was generally kind to him. On festive days they even left mithai and halwa outside his door. The young son, Pappu, no more than thirteen, occasionally made the trek up the narrow straight steps and chatted with him. Through him Ghulam acquired details of the family and understood their journey—the death of kinsmen, the rape of kinswomen, the hacking of limbs, the loss of everything, the neurosis of the rusted sword. The boy said, 'My father hates you. He says, "I am waiting for that katua to do something stupid so I can cut him to pieces."'

Inevitably, Ghulam was out of bounds for the wife and two daughters, but they always smiled at him warmly and coyly if he encountered them in the lane or at the grocer's. In turn, when a low-traffic film was running, Ghulam left complimentary tickets with the boy. Most times only Bhatiaji and Pappu came by—Bhatiaji's glare making jelly of Ghulam's limbs—but on a few occasions he was thrilled to see them accompanied by the wife and the two girls—filling out their kameezes, walking with tight thighs and darting eyes, the cowl of their dupattas creating a greater allure.

For some time he thought he was in love with Kamla, the older girl. She was fair with big liquid eyes and a strong nose. When he hummed the songs from *Aan* and *Awara*, *Baazi* and *Aar Paar*, he thought of Kamla looking at him. He paced the terrace practising passionate declamations gleaned from the movies on the inexorable nature of true love beyond the pale of border, caste, class and religion. He imagined the Hitler-moustached Bhatiaji breaking down in remorse and begging forgiveness. He saw the two of them embrace and the lovely woman in the middle—daughter of one, beloved of the other—shed tears that made her soft cheeks shine like morning dew. But he was also fearful that her father had sensed their romance and was whetting his sword. Ghulam took to firmly latching both the doors to his room—the one on the stairs and the other that opened on to the terrace.

The wordless romance ended when the girl was married off to a stout young man from Delhi who came on a seedy white mare with a frenzied band and troupes of wildly gyrating young men and patriarchs, wearing big pink turbans with cocky furls, who fired double-barrelled rifles into the air right outside the house, to lay claim to the bride. Ghulam was not even invited to the wedding and had to witness it peering over the parapet. Pappu brought up some food and goodies for the heartbroken lover on the terrace and reported what his father had said: 'I hope one of these bullets catches that katua sitting on top of our head.'

Ghulam did not eat the wedding food Pappu had brought, and sat up all night on the terrace under the shifting stars, listening to the pandit's rhythmic chanting of the wedding rites. When it grew cold, past midnight, he brought out his blanket and tied a gamchha around his head. Hundreds of tragic film scenes and sad songs played in his mind. He felt the sorrow of this night would weigh his life down forever.

When Kamla left in the wee hours of the morning, draped in jewellery and layers of red heavy with tinsel, amid the wails of her family, he craned his neck to see if she would glance up once, just once, to reaffirm the truth of their love. He knew this from the films: that even unsanctioned love, unarticulated love, was loaded with deep legitimacies.

In that hour before dawn the light was uneven and in the flurry of crying-hustling escorts it was not easy to see, but he would have had to be deluded beyond love to imagine that she even angled her neck in his direction.

The next day—and the next week—he wept in the privacy of the cinema hall through every show. The film playing was *Mother India* but his heart was full of scenes from *Pyaasa*. He saw himself as Guru Dutt, cheated of his love, in lyrical mourning, writing poetry, wandering the streets, rescuing abandoned prostitutes. The lump in his throat would become an unswallowable rock each time Nargis—her oxen dead, tears streaming down her beloved face—began to pull the plough herself, and all the images of her and Mala Sinha and Waheeda Rahman and Guru Dutt and the people from his basti and the lovely married-off Kamla became one tragic mush.

Some days later, Ghulam crossed Bhatiaji's younger daughter in the lane. Parvati's glossy black hair ran in a thick plait down her spine, like a splendid cobra. When she looked at him from the corner of her eyes Ghulam found it difficult to breathe. That was when he suddenly realized she was the one for him, the older sister had only been a decoy, a test of his true love. He knew this from the movies, of course, but now he had evidence of how incredibly devious the gods of love could be. To put forward Kamla when it had actually been Parvati all along!

After months of being in a daze of love, of exchanging burning glances and experiencing the whole hall light up like Diwali each time she visited it, one day Ghulam plucked up the courage to venture into Meena Bazaar and buy a dozen glass bangles—maroon and red with spangles of silver.

Two evenings later, he lured Pappu up to his eyrie for a conversation. When the boy asked him about the bangles spread out on his bed, Ghulam said his cousin who made them had sent across some and since he had no use of them why didn't Pappu just take them for his sister.

That night Ghulam could not sleep and from early next morning he waited for a sign. All day at work the conviction grew in him that she would show up at the Talkies, daringly wearing the bangles and her feelings. Through every show he lingered in the foyer, afraid he would somehow, tragically, as in the movies, miss the moment when she arrived at his doorstep. When the evening show began and she still had not shown up, he sought Ali Baba's permission and slowly walked home. Songs played in his head. He was Guru Dutt, lit masterfully in the shadows, questioning the universe.

He was sitting on his charpoy, eyes moist with heartache, when Bhatiaji kicked in the door, his Hitler moustache quivering and the rusted sword held aloft. Behind him were Hukumat Singh—the Sikh refugee from next door—and his two teenage sons in tight black patkas, twirling bamboo sticks. In Hitlerji's left hand was the set of spangled bangles, clutched so tight that they fanned out like the feathers of a peacock.

Ghulam's bowels became water. The first image that came to his mind was of Imroze's hacked limb bobbing up and down like a railway signal. He stood, transfixed by Hitlerji's burning eyes, when Hukumat Singh stepped forward. The sardar's slap exploded in his head like a comet, all coruscating light and noise. When the world cleared he was on the floor and Hitlerji was holding Hukumat back, as he slowly clenched and unclenched his ringing hand. When, out of politeness, Ghulam tried to struggle to his feet, Hitlerji kicked him in his stomach. The young man became a pretzel on the floor and began to spin. To complete the quorum the two sardar boys stepped forward and delivered a kick each. The pretzel spun faster, emitting a range of noises.

Hitlerji stopped the pretzel's spin with the tip of his rusted sword. The only sound emerging from the tightly rolled circle of pain and fear was a low mewl like the whine of a run-over dog. Leaning on his sword the refugee landlord said, 'Behanchod katuay, give me your hand!'

Through his tears Ghulam saw the railway signal arm Imroze had returned with: up, down, up, down. The older sardar boy kicked the pretzel where its buttocks were. Ghulam began to blubber incoherently for mercy.

The sardar—his beard corralled in a shining net—held Ghulam's left arm at its frail wrist and prised open his twig fingers. Hitlerji placed the flaring peacock of coloured glass in his left hand on top of it and slipped all the twelve bangles down the Muslim boy's forearm: 'Behanchod katuay, from now on you will wear these every damn day of your life! If I see you without them even once I will cut your entire fucking arm off! Maaderchod wants to be a Romeo!'

When they were at the door, the landlord turned back and said, 'And don't think of running away—I will chase you till the end of the world, chop your balls off and shove them up your traitorous ass!'

The pretzel moved slowly and moaned in response.

Ghulam was too scared to tell anyone of the assault and too battered to go to the Talkies next day. Yet, through the pain of his bruised body, he imagined Parvati weeping silently in the house below, begging her father for the gift of her love. In the morning he tore his old gamchha into two and took one half with him when he went down the stairs to go to work. At the corner of the lane, using his teeth and his right hand, he tied it over the clutch of bright bangles on his arm. To the queries of Ali Baba and his colleagues he said it was a good-luck charm given him by the mendicant who tended the pir's grave by the Nainital highway.

In the year that followed, Ghulam developed a permanent case of nerves—ready to whip off the cloth if he spotted the moustache anywhere. Each night as he entered his home lane he would untie the gamchha and let the bangles flash. When he walked up the steps he almost rattled them, hoping the landlord would see him holding fast to the covenant. Sometimes he did not have to because the refugee would be sitting in the tight porch by the gate whetting his sword bloodily on a brick, a steel glass of water next to him. He would look at the Muslim boy as if assessing how many pieces he could ideally chop him into. Always—always—Ghulam's stomach became water, and he had to open his door and rush to the roofless latrine on the terrace.

Through the endless fear raining on him, in delusory moments before he fell asleep, he sometimes imagined the landlord's heart melting at the unfair savagery he had meted out and the grace with which the young man had suffered it. In that moment of honour he saw the stocky marauder clasp him to his bosom, smash the humiliating bangles, beg for forgiveness, and put in his hand the hand of his daughter.

Yet, even in the confines of his room, in the cocoon of his bed, Ghulam did not dare remove the green and red bangles. Hitlerji was capable of suddenly breaking down the door in the middle of the night, or even glaring over the wall of the latrine. The fear ran so deep that he did not remove them even when he went to the basti. He told his family it was a putrid infection, being treated by the city doctor, too tender to be touched, too grotesque to see.

Through it all he retained faith in his love. How could it be otherwise given the smile in Parvati's eyes each time she saw him? He knew she had been profoundly moved by the gift of the bangles and the penance he was doing for them. On the other hand, Pappu never crept up the stairs any more and his eyes hardened in an unpleasant way when he saw Ghulam. One day when he handed him two tickets for *Naya Daur*, the boy threw them back at him, saying, 'We don't accept gifts from traitors.' Ghulam said, 'I am your friend!' The boy said, 'My father says you all are friends by daylight and in the dark you will stick a knife into us.'

Ghulam wanted to drag the boy to Minerva to show him Dilip Kumar singing the anthem of a new noble India, 'Saathi haath badhana, saathi re. . . .' But Ghulam was too weak and the boy was too small, and his father was pouring poison into him at a speed that nothing could possibly extract.

One evening Pappu came to the Talkies with a summons from his father. Inevitably Ghulam's bowels turned to water and he had to lean against the wall to steady himself. When he reached the house half an hour later, with night falling, he immediately noticed the bustle. Half a dozen men hung around the gate and in the thin veranda of the house several older people sat in what seemed like rented chairs. Everyone was eating and drinking—tea and samosas—and peals of laughter were doing the rounds. Curving his arms around his back—the right hand clasped tight over the jangle of glass on his left forearm—Ghulam stood by the gutter outside the house, self-conscious and afraid.

Long minutes passed and Ghulam had typically fallen inside the well of his own inner life and stopped seeing what was happening around when the landlord's rough voice hit him. 'Oye haramzade, come here! I've been waiting to show these fine people the specimen I have living up on the roof!'

The next ten minutes were raw wounds—never to heal. He could never bring himself to recall how he went into the room, how it arranged itself in a circle around him. All he remembered was his complete nakedness, the smallness of his incredible shame, as the refugee from Rawalpindi held up his left arm and shook it, jangling his adornments. 'See! Out there they pulled out our intestines and wrapped them around our necks, but here they wear glass bangles!'

Amid a great outpouring of noise and goodwill the assemblage left late in the night. They came back in a month—white mare, drums, crackers, rifle shots—to take Parvati away. This time Ghulam latched his door and crouched behind the parapet for twenty-four hours, listening to his heart hammer.

At the end of that week, Ghulam went to the basti and put his head in his mother's lap and cried like a baby. In disgust his father hawked and spat and walked off to the tamarind tree. 'His job has made him a eunuch! Marry him off before he becomes a dancing girl himself!'

The girl chosen for him was from Moradabad, from a family of brass craftsmen. Fatima had frizzy hair and was as scrawny like him, all bones and edges: not at all like the fleshy Kamla or the juicy Parvati. Yet the first time he sank into her he fell deep in love. The poetry of the Talkies had so primed him to the idea of romance that if he had found a statue in his room he would have discovered an intense passion for it. Fatima had never been inside a school, and knew nothing except cooking and cleaning and sewing and darning. She would have had trouble naming the century she lived in, or the prime minister of the country.

For a time Fatima lived with her mother-in-law in the basti, and Ghulam visited her every weekend for some frantic fumbling. Whenever he could, he also took her to the Talkies where they became all hands and moans. But soon he began to crave the comfort and security of her bony body on a daily basis. One day he persuaded Ali Baba to speak to his landlord. He stood outside the living-room while Baba went in. Strangely, Bhatiaji did not jump on to his horse and unsheathe his rusty sword. Indifferently, vaguely, he said, 'Yes, sure, let him. If he won't get his own wife whose will he get—the neighbour's?' Then when Baba had reached the door, he called out, 'But if he makes one more Musalman on my roof I'll chop his cock off.'

The boy, Kabir, inevitably then, was born to fear. To timidity, to trepidation, to caution. The first words he heard his father say to him were, 'Be careful.' And all the years he lived at home this warning was sounded out to him many times a day. Each time he used the stove to make a cup of tea, each time he moved a piece of furniture, each time he shaved his face ('I hope it's not too sharp!' 'No, father, it's blunt as my buttocks!'), each time he mounted his bicycle, each time he ate fish, and sometimes in winter even when he went to have a bath with hot water. 'Test it, first test it with your fingertips,' his father would shout from outside, and then wait by the door till his son made a splashing noise and declared it safe.

When he stepped out the threshold of the house, the cautions became even more feverish. Ride carefully. Don't talk to strangers. Steer clear of arguments. Never tell anyone where you live. You have no religion. You have no caste. You have no politics. You are just an Indian. Don't mingle with the poor. Don't mingle with the rich. Don't mingle with older boys. Don't mingle with younger boys. Never get into any tangles with girls. Actually, never talk to any girls. Be careful with the sardars, be careful with the vendors, be careful with the policemen, be careful with the padres. Don't scowl at anyone. Don't smile at anyone. Don't anything with anyone.

Till Kabir reached class eight, all this made him a rabbit. A very timid and lonely rabbit. He even had the large ears and big scared eyes of one. But his body was like that of a cricket's, thin and knobby, his legs and arms like burnt sticks—the legacy of his mother. He slid in and out of the missionary school quietly and sat in the front row of his class, eyes bulging, mostly in desperate incomprehension, his father's anxieties madly multiplied by the pressures of school.

The arithmetic and algebra he could manage, and Hindi he was good at. But English, and every other subject—all of them taught in English—fried his brains. He was not alone in this. The entire school was full of boys whose brains were being detonated by Shakespeare and Dickens and Wordsworth and Tennyson and memoriam and daffodils and tiger tiger burning bright and solitary reapers and artful dodgers and thous and forsooths and the rhymes of ancient mariners.

The first counter-attack Kabir M made on English was in class four when he learnt like the rest of his reeling mates to say, 'How-dudo? Howdudo?' The answer being: 'Juslikeaduddoo! Juslikeadud-doo!' It set the pattern for life for most of them. English was to be ambushed ruthlessly when and where the opportunity arose. Its soldiers were to be mangled, shot, amputated wherever they were spotted. Its emissaries to be captured and tortured. The enemy of English came at them from every direction: in the guise of forms to be filled, exams to be taken, interviews to be given, marriage proposals to be evaluated. The enemy English had a dwarfing weapon: it made instant lilliputs of them. Whenever it appeared on the horizon they seemed to suddenly shrink in size. Their weapon of Hindi was a mere slingshot compared to the enemy's cannon. Some of them understood that if they could somehow keep themselves from shrinking they would be able to take the enemy English on, beat it back, perhaps even show it its true place. But in practice it never worked: the English weapon was much too powerful and all their bravura and resolve dissolved in a moment, leaving them puny dwarfs. All they could attempt then were ambushes. And here too, many of them, in the course of their lives, would come to feel that the more enemy soldiers they killed the more they seemed to multiply. Some of them were so completely ruined by English, so shrunk by its brutal onslaught, that they never managed to regain their true size, not even when the enemy was not around, not even when they were in their own place with their own people. Many of them tried to broker a truce with it, but there can never be peace between unequals. Their attempts to cohabit with it—master such smatterings of it as they could—only left them open to further ridicule.

Of course there were some boys—especially from the army cantonment—who spoke English as if they were pissing in the bushes behind the school wall. A flowing, gushing, casual stream, laughingly delivered. In the classroom these boys chirped like budgerigars and answered questions with fluent orations that left Kabir and his mates scratching their heads. Turwant, the son of the motor-parts dealer, called them the 'chutterputter chutiyas'.

The chutterputter chutiyas monopolized the school dramatics society and the speakers' and quizzers' clubs; they were nominated class and school leaders and were gawped at by the girls. The chutterputter chutiyas seemed to have big engines of confidence humming in their bellies: they were always laughing and smiling and seemed to have private jokes about everyone else. Even when a teacher lost it with them, they retained a smiling, unfazed air. At least one teacher—the Hindi one, a Mr Pandey—hated them and was terrified of them. They would humiliate him by talking to him in English and making him struggle to understand them. When he would attack their betrayal to the foreign language of conquerors they would make him abject by questioning his betrayals of wearing English trousers, teaching in an English-medium school, using a toothbrush, and reporting to English-speaking Catholic priests.

In the presence of the chutterputter chutiyas, Kabir became a stunted dwarf scurrying for cover. Like Mr Pandey, he hated them and was terrified of them.

While Kabir, like most of his friends, rode to school on his father's old creaking Atlas cycle, the chutterputter chutiyas came in a green, shining, libidinous army truck. Many of them wore big black army boots, and all of them walked with a strut. Not only did they cut everyone to ribbons in the classroom with the merciless sword of English, they were also juggernauts on the sports field. And sitting in the last rows they talked of sports Kabir had never known or seen—squash, billiards, water polo, and something called dressage.

The bastards even masturbated in English. Crumpled copies by Anonymous were always being swapped between them and sometimes one of them brought a magazine with colour pictures of such provocation that even a fleeting glimpse of them sent you rushing to the toilet. The Mastram Mastanas—yellowed and hand-stapled and fraying—that Kabir and Co lived off were like the fare of beggars. They were read aloud by the chutterputter chutiyas and laughed at. It took the steam off Mastram's pages for a few hours.

Most days Kabir hated going to school, and hated his father for having admitted him there. Between his father's fearful cautions and the humiliations of the school, the boy found solace and wholeness in only one place, the same place that had worked for Ghulam: the warm womb of Minerva Talkies, with the reassuring solidity of its neat stories, its triumphs of Hindi dialogue, Hindi songs and the superstars revelling in Hindi exuberance.

Of course, in the perverse way in which parents will often deny their children precisely that which created and saved them, Ghulam forbade his son more than a film a month. Naturally then, the first deceit the son learnt was evading his father and conspiring with the Talkies staff to see every film that was released. Ghulam's colleagues never understood why he denied his son what he himself obsessed over. Ghulam said in defence, 'Does he have to also be a chutiya just because we are chutiyas? What have we learnt by watching films all day? To dance like Shammi Kapoor?'

The father wanted his son to be a child of the new India. Modern, rational, tutored in secular ways, a wearer of pants, a speaker of English, removed from the rumble and rabble of Bombay cinema and Bareilly's serpentine bazaars. He himself had moved very far away from the ties of the basti. He wanted his son to move even farther away, so far away that no shadow of its religion, rites, crafts, inheritances or dogmatic smallnesses could ever fall across his life. His son belonged to the city, to a life of hygiene and elegance and polished speech and educated work.

With a miraculous display of restraint and a generous use of free Nirodhs—the state-supplied condoms, thick enough to stop a snake—the timid Ghulam had ensured that he would not have another child. He needed all his resources to make a modern success of the one. To his wailing wife Fatima, who wanted to fill her yawning womb with the screaming train of life as her mother before her had, he said, in consolation, 'Bitches produce yelping litters. The tigress never gives birth to more than one or two.'

But no child is molten wax to be poured into a mould. Each is twisted inalienably inside its own genes. The truth was his son was concussed by the absurd alienness of English and quickly lost all talent for any textbook learning. By the time Kabir came to class five, Ghulam was on his knees in the padre's sombre office at the end of every academic year—the terracotta Christ on the cross looking down at him sadly—spelling out the litany of poverty and hardship against which his son's academic failure needed to be weighed. Schooled in compassion, the Cappuchian fathers pushed the boy along, giving him the grace marks the meek deserve. Till the rabbit-eared boy with limbs of stick reached class eight and made the first real friend of his life.

This boy came to school in the libidinous army truck and his name was Charlie. In the attendance register he was listed as Barun Chakravarty, and though he could rattle off English like the chutterputter chutiyas, he was not one of them. He didn't hang out with them, he didn't play sports, and he refused to take part in the character-building regimen of dramatics and elocution. Nor did he wear the big army boots or walk the strut. Yet he exuded a cockiness that was more potent than anyone else's. It stemmed from his mocking smile and his bludgeoning tongue. It did not cut and nick and slowly bleed its victims; it smashed their faces in. He called his fellow army boys Angrezi Laudus, English pricks. 'Unzip their pants and check them out,' he would say aloud, 'I can bet you they've painted them pink and white.'

Kabir never figured out why Charlie chose him as his friend other than the fact that he too was short and thin and had rabbit ears. The first time they connected was in the school auditorium where one of the army boys was elocuting Alfred Noyes's *The Highwayman* for an inter-class competition.

The hall had a stage but no chairs yet and the boys were crammed in disorderly fashion at the back while the girls stood in neat lines up front. Suddenly, beneath the dramatic monotones from the public address system, a mock thin voice was heard chanting:

Bal Krishan Bhatt,
dekho pad gaya putt;
boley lauda tana jhat,
boley bhonsdi ke hutt;
tera lauda hai ya lutth!

A titter snaked through the crowd and heads began to turn to locate the source of the doggerel. Next to Kabir a gnomish Bengali boy looked straight ahead. As Kabir stared at him, he slowly turned and gave him a smile. Meanwhile, the highwayman was continuing to ride up to the old inn door. To counter him, the same voice, now in a grave tone, slower and deeper, repeated the doggerel about Bal Krishan Bhatt's giant phallus:

> Bal Krishan Bhatt,
> dekho pad gaya putt;
> boley lauda tana jhat,
> boley bhonsdi ke hutt;
> tera lauda hai ya lutth!

Almost immediately a hundred adolescent throats thundered with laughter. The highwayman halted uncertainly. The padre who taught English, Father Michael, leapt up and roared like a provoked lion, frantically twirling the thick cord around his waist, which he used for whipping the boys. In the dead silence that followed, everyone sought the source from the corner of their eyes. The whirlpool of eyes slowly began to find its centre, and in the swirling heart of it stood Kabir. The padre caught him like a rabbit by the scruff of his neck and pushed him so that he went flying through the boys to lie sprawled on the floor.

Over the years Kabir had often witnessed this dance of penitence, but it was the first time he had a starring role in it. In a voice he had never heard before he shouted, 'No Father!' From the floor view he could see the padre's turned-up black trousers peeping from beneath his flowing white habit. His calloused feet were strapped in brown leather sandals. The padre said, 'Goonda boy! Rascal!' and sliced the cord across Kabir's back and buttocks. Kabir shouted, 'No Father!' and leapt up to run, but with one swift lunge the padre had his frail left wrist in his hand. Then the two dancers began to twirl in endless circles: the padre's left hand holding Kabir's left wrist, the boy running with jumps and skips, while Father rotated on his heels whipping the boy with the rope in his right hand.

No Father!
Goonda boy!
No Father!
Goonda boy!
No Father!
Goonda boy!

Round and round they spun with increasing speed—the knotted rope singing as it struck—while the assembly tittered.

Suddenly the yelping boy's thin wrist slipped out of the assailant's hand and the boy went crashing to the floor. Father Michael, giddy with the relentless circling, lurched towards him, and the reeling boy, frantic with fear, in a desperate attempt at escape, crawled between the padre's legs and disappeared under his flowing habit. Inside that dark secure place, the boy clung to a stout leg and refused to let go.

The father shouted, 'Rascal boy, where are you?'

A muffled voice screamed, 'No Father!'

Where are you? No Father! Where are you? No Father!

The maddened priest leapt and kicked and shook and twirled, trying to dislodge the infuriating boy clamped to his thigh. In a burst of fresh rage, the padre began to shout and wildly whip the habit between his legs with his rope.

'Goonda boy! Rascal boy! Where are you? Where are you? Come out! Come out!'

From the unseen place between his legs came the scream, 'No Father! No Father!'

Out I say! No Father! Out I say! No Father!

The assembly roared its approval.

Father Michael now began to stomp up and down in a manic fury. Hanging on in terror, getting banged against his knees and thighs, Kabir thought his life was about to end. Suddenly the father used the heel of his left foot to deliver a sharp reverse kick between the boy's bony buttocks. With a screech of pain the boy straightened up, hammering his head against the padre's swinging balls with the speed of a runaway train. The padre let out a long high-pitched scream—'Ooomiilorrrddjeessus!'—and clutching the hard head mashed against his balls keeled over like a sawn tree, taking the boy with him.

When Kabir emerged, scrabbling, from under the folds of the Friar's habit, like a cockroach from under a pile of bread slices, the assembly cheered and hooted and whistled. Even as he ran from there faster than any cockroach ever—without once looking back at the felled priest—and raced to the cycle-stand to jump on to his old Atlas, he remembered the laughing, approving faces of the packed assembly all around him.

For the very first time in his life he felt worthy.

The feeling—strange, novel, wonderful—did not desert him over the next week of pathetic grovelling in the principal's office. Ghulam weathered the storm of apologies, threats, and other abjections, while the boy insisted on his innocence. At home the fearful Ghulam implored his son to take the blame and end the stand-off. Revelling in this newly discovered sense of himself—a surging sense of potency that brought steel to his gnomish face, hardened his jaws and stilled his eyes—revelling in himself for the first time in his life, Kabir declined.

The bewildered father, imagining the worst—expulsion, police case, persecution—went and fell first at the feet of the crucified Christ and then at the principal's. 'Father, cane me instead! If the boy is bad, it is my fault. I gave birth to him. Cane me! Cane me!' And he grabbed the priest's slim cane and began to roll around the room flagellating himself wildly as he had seen his kinsmen do during the penitent rites of Muharram. The alarmed father had to grab him by his hair to bring him under control. Then Ghulam began to weep like a baby, squatting on the ground. 'None of this would have happened had I gone to Pakistan! No one would have thrown my son out of school had I gone to Pakistan!'

The principal thought the entire family was deranged. Father Michael was lucky the boy had not bitten his testicles off.

Looking on, Kabir thought his father was beyond idiotic. Profoundly disgusted, he did not speak to his father for many long years.

When he returned to his class a week later, he was no longer just roll number seven, the dumb and unknown Muthal—masturbator. He was the hero who had stopped the Highwayman and felled a full Father. Even the boys of class twelve now gave him a nod of recognition.

Charlie, of course, met him with a happy smile and a song—Bal Krishan Bhatt dekho pad gaya putt—and gave him a hug. That day Kabir changed his seat to the last row where Charlie sat. The irreverent Bengali boy cut open Kabir's head like a can of juice and began to stir it. Kabir had never seriously questioned anything in his life. Now everything was brought into question.

Why was he studying in this weird missionary school where English would humiliate him every day? Where he would always be a failure? Why did he know nothing about his community or religion? Did he want to be a floating fool, a deracinated chutter-putter chutiya? What was wrong with his father? Why was he such a coward about everything? Why did he treat Kabir like a three-year-old girl? And, by the way, why could Kabir not see as many films as he liked? Especially when his father could not stop seeing them? And what was this nonsense about getting home before dark every evening?

Charlie the anarchic Bengali told him all about the life of the cantonment. The gymkhana clubs, the officers' mess, the starch, the ceremony, the uniforms, the endless saluting, the spit and polish, the whisky and soda, the epaulettes and lanyards, the English films—*Mary Poppins, Gunfight at the OK Corral*—and the amateurish plays—gaudy bedroom capers with haw haw accents. He told him about hot fat aunties with moist cleavages and May Queen balls with Anglo-Indian bands crooning Cliff Richards and Neil Diamond. He told him about lean lieutenants hunting for any orifice and precious picnics during which soldiers used dynamite sticks to blast fish out of water. And he said he hated it all—the swagger, the affectation, the lack of intelligence. He said when he saw his father, a brilliant doctor, saluting and sirring morons whose only skill was parading up and down and firing rifles into the air, it drove him mad. He said he had once in anger in the middle of a dinner at the brigade commander's house pissed in his prize rose bed. He said it was the most satisfying piss of his life.

He said every time his father saluted some dumb senior in his presence, Charlie would loudly drawl, 'Bokachodaaa Battalion...forward march!' and stride off swinging his arms in a military clip. He said, actually his father was as idiotic as Kabir's father for suffering such shit.

Kabir was spellbound by Charlie. He could not imagine such an absence of fear, such chutzpah in the face of teachers, parents, the chutterputter chutiyas. In the Bengali boy's presence he found himself filling up with a crazy confidence too. To earn his approval, Kabir began to develop a manner he could once have barely imagined. He could still not talk smart—he was not clever enough to do that—but he could rustle up the outrageous act. As he had inside the habit of the fallen padre.

Once during an inter-house cricket final, Kabir commandeered an ass carrying sacks of sand from a line of animal transport trudging by the school, and rode it onto the middle of the field, pricking the beast's flanks with a pin. The crazed animal chased down Tora

Tora Vohra, the tearaway fast bowler from the cantonment, one of the chutterputter chutiyas. Tora Tora Vohra was running in to bowl, his windmill arms turning, when the maddened animal suddenly appeared behind him. With a scream of terror, Tora Tora Vohra kept running, ball-in-hand, down the pitch. The batsman facing him—called Mungfali, peanut, because of the size of his equipment: the boys insisted he didn't need ball guards since there was nothing to protect—Mungfali turned and ran, bat in hand, leg pads flapping. In front of him, running pell-mell already was Sukha the wicket-keeper—a sardar from Kichcha with no glove skills but a body of steel that he recklessly put behind the ball. With the presence of mind of a man of the world, Tora Tora Vohra slammed off the bails as he ran past the wickets, and shouted the question, Howzzat? Peter Massey, the history teacher—an Anglo-Indian so wedded to the perfections of the past, to Bradman and Ponsford, to rules and discipline, Peter Massey, whose trousers were so starched they did not break form even when he walked—Peter Massey, standing as umpire in a floppy white cap, raised his right forefinger. The benches of Green House exploded in screaming protest and began to infiltrate the boundary. Manjit Singh, captain of Green House and king jock of the school, six feet of moving muscle, famed for his brutal temper, ran on to the field and put his big fist into Mungfali's running face. 'Maaderchod, are you playing cricket or kho-kho!' Mungfali hit the ground flat on his back and stared up at the lovely blue sky with kites skating on it. Just then Sukha came running, big wicketkeeper pads and gloves aflap, and mighty Manjit swung his right leg and put his hard-nosed cricket shoes directly into his bum. Sukha actually sailed through the air for a few feet to the high-pitched whine of Maaaaaadiiiiiphuddeeeeee, before landing gracefully on his face. Frantic with fear, Tora Tora Vohra tried to change course but by now the furious Manjit had grabbed his bowling arm and was swinging him around like he did the discus at the nets, with Tora screeching, Obehhaanchoodddhhh! At that moment the jogging ass appeared with Kabir Muthal astride, and rounding on them Manjit kicked the beast hard in its belly, sending it hawing wildly, and careening off towards the teams now invading the field. A free-for-all erupted, and Manjit kicked everybody present at least once, and the runaway ass several times. At some point Peter Massey took off his floppy hat and declared the match abandoned.

Kabir's fame spread, and Charlie bathed him with attention and affection. For the first time since he had joined the school, the dwarfing effect of English was kept at bay.

This fame had a dangerous downside. He was now on the radar of the padres, and soon enough was singled out for Christian correction. The first time he was suspended from school for three days—for floating a gas balloon during a parent-teacher meeting with a carrot hung from it like a dangling dick—he panicked. But Charlie, in a display of true friendship, calmed him by bunking school to keep him company.

That day they rode his cycle out into the middle of the teeming market, consumed hot samosas and iced Fanta at Aggarwal's sweet shop, and then went off to see a film at Paras. When Helen began her cabaret number in her shimmering slit gown, Charlie pushed his hand up the leg of his school shorts, and began to rub. Helen and Charlie finished at the same time.

Kabir discovered another threshold of the acceptable.

Barring Minerva Talkies, the two boys now invaded every other movie hall in the city. On days when the prospect of entering the missionary school was too depressing, they turned back from the school gates, freewheeled their way to Aggarwal Sweets, drank endless cups of tea, ate samosas, and headed for the morning show. This was solace cinema, for the lowliest of the low, made by the lowliest of the low. The scattered heads slumped low in the seats, trembling with a transitory connection, were all busy pushing the threshold of the acceptable. Everyone entered the hall after the lights had been dimmed, and everyone exited the hall without looking at another.

There was always a second film, the gourmet morsel after the junk food. This was mainline stuff with marquee stars, thrilling music, and heroines so beautiful that they burned the imagination. Sometimes Kabir and Charlie stayed on in the same hall, and sometimes tore across town to another, desperate not to miss the opening credits. The atmosphere of the second show was very different. Happy chatter in the foyer, marble-sodas and samosas being consumed, women of all ages, eyes shining, restless with excitement. Standing at the edge of the snacks counter, sharp-eyed Charlie would study the women like a fine detective and elaborate on each one's possibilities. That one with the big red necklace? She'd only simper—you'd have to pinch her to make her move. The sharp-nosed one with a pierced right nostril and a tight mouth was a certain screamer—take her deep into a forest or put a pillow over her face. Purple saree, with those gold jhumkas—oh, don't look at her fat—would say no, mean yes, say no, mean yes. And that one in the green salwar-kameez—observe her high-heeled sandals—was to be mounted like a horse, and she'd neigh like one.

The gnomish Bengali boy was unstoppable—sociologist, psychologist, sexologist, all rolled into one, a committed researcher, gathering data. Soon, pursuing his research, he had his protégé testing new frontiers in the crush of the cinema halls. In the foyer, Charlie would identify the woman who badly wanted them, and then as the doors opened, Kabir would be right beside her and behind her, his loosely hanging arm and wide open palm—tactile vernier calipers—measuring flesh, calibrating response, verifying his master's theses.

Sometimes the crush was excessive, the subjects many, and the boy had to work overtime, using both hands as vernier calipers, measuring in every direction, working a variety of materials and apparel. The most cooperative were chiffon sarees, the least burqas, and the gathered folds of Punjabi salwars fell somewhere in between. The occasional trousers were a treat, but not if made of denim. As with all scientific endeavour, sometimes the boy brought back very precise findings and sometimes the results were fuzzy. Charlie, with the imperious distance of the academic, never ever participated in the data collection, but worked hard to juice every detail out of his field researcher.

It became the pattern of their friendship: Kabir acting to earn the approbation of his hammer-tongued friend; Charlie living vicariously all that he dared not do.

And Kabir, without registering it, crossed another threshold of the acceptable.

It was curious. For his father the movies had been about love and lyricism. For Kabir Muthal they were about lust and longing. For his father films had represented the quest for a more humane and refined world, removed from the poisons that made train signals out of men's limbs. For the boy it was an escape from the moral strictures of his father and the padres into a vigorous, vulgar world without any obvious boundaries.

By the time he came to take his class nine examinations he had begun to steal money from home. There was no other way to fund the films, the samosas, the colas, the extensive research. His father kept the folded five- and ten-rupee notes between stills of old black and white films—Raj Kapoor and Nargis and Dilip Kumar and Madhubala and Dev Anand and Guru Dutt—that he had collected from the Talkies over the decades. For some time Ghulam noticed nothing. He was more likely to miss a filched scene from *Anari* than some purloined rupees. But then Kabir became greedy and Ghulam's domestic budget began to spring sudden unknown holes.

The father was just beginning to round on his son when a new academic year dawned and it was time to go and genuflect in the Father's office. Kabir M had failed every subject except Hindi and maths. Thanks to the run of the ass through the inter-house finals, even the physical education teacher had given him a red entry. When Ghulam began his whine at the lofty Father's feet, the bearded padre picked up the report book and flung it at Kabir, standing in the corner. 'Forget the marks, Mr Masood! Your son is a goonda! He is a bad influence on all the boys! He will end up in jail one day!' Then, in a paroxysm of rage the padre threw his cane, the duster, two pens, a coaster, and the *Oxford English Dictionary* at the ducking boy.

Kabir had to repeat class nine, and Ghulam had to start keeping his money in the bank or in his pockets. When it began to vanish from his trousers hanging on the hook in his room—in the dead hours between sleeping and waking—he began to put it under his pillow. His son knew little English or history or geography or physics but he had the tread of an animal and fingers that were water, and Ghulam would lose a folded note or two from under his sleeping head every few days.

Though they were a class apart now, Charlie and Kabir remained buddies, doing the same things, bunking school, watching films, scouring the bazaar, tormenting other students and teachers with their pranks. Then Kabir was detained for a second time in class nine—the fucking impossibility of English, of Julius Caesar!—and something hardened in him irrevocably. The first threat of a moustache had appeared, and juniors who had once looked at him in awe now sat at his side.

Meanwhile, Charlie's father had been transferred to Kashmir, and with his board results out—he had done brilliantly—Charlie had moved to Modern School in Delhi for the last two years of his school life. With the ironic Bengali boy gone, Kabir—sitting in the last row of the classroom, the moustache deepening by the day—slowly lost his winning air of derring-do and outrage. He became a sullen brooding presence, refusing to talk to his new classmates, still trying to hang out with his friends who had moved on, increasingly maddened by Cassius and Brutus and Antony and the utter nonsense they spoke. Each time Father Michael strode into class and began to declaim, Kabir's head bloomed with murderous thoughts.

Soon the boy developed a tic that was not to leave him for the rest of his life. He began to mutter to himself, and every now and then—in the classroom, on the sports field, at home—he would break into a thunderous oration of gibberish. 'Haauu haaa, thouu thaa…lusheus dusheus chuseus…forsooth a geyser, in the gaand of Caesar…haauu haaa, thouu thaa…friends, romans, countrymen, meri murgi tumhari hen…ohhh brutus ki chootus mein balkishan ka jootus…haauu haaa, thouu thaa!' His father and mother looked at him in admiration, while his young mates brought up the chorus, 'friends, romans, countrymen, meri murgi tumhari hen…haauu haaa, thouu thaa.'

When the school decided to hold him back in the same class for the third year running, it was the principal who folded his hands in front of Ghulam and begged him to take his son to another school, a Hindi-medium one, perhaps the Islamia Inter College.

iii

The Peace of High Walls

In many ways, Kabir lived up to the promise of his sainted secular name. Over the years he travelled through scarred landscapes of religious bigotry and caste animus but remained untouched by them. Though the son could never see it, his father had—out of fear of the train signal arm—gifted him an unprejudiced mind. But he had also diminished him with the demon of fear and the poltergeist of English. Between the freedom and the crippling, the boy soon found his vocation in chaarsobeesi, the sleight-of-hand of minor thievery and deception.

Turning his back on the grand noises of the padres, turning his back on the whining aspirations of his father, Kabir joined the Islamia Inter College in class ten, and almost instantly felt the relief of an animal returned to its forest. Everyone spoke Hindi here and everyone called everyone else a chutiya.

The teachers chewed paan all the time, spitting red strings out of the windows and sometimes into the corners of the poorly white-washed rooms. Most of them wore sandals and frayed shirts. The school cricket kit had only two leg guards, and during matches the batsmen wore one each on their left leg. The football field and cricket ground overlapped, and on many afternoons parallel games resulted in pitched battles with clothes being torn and skulls cracked open. Lacking the armour of a padre's habit, the teachers looked the other way. Interventions in the past had invited fisticuffs, kicks and ambush as they pedalled home. In fact the student skirmishes were welcome—broken bones and stabbings thinned the ranks of the toughies.

Kabir embraced the crudity but steered clear of the violence. Unexpectedly, pleasantly, his elite background—amid the padres and the chutterputter chutiyas—opened up a niche of privilege for him. He brought with him stories of that other world, and his inadequate English was quite masterly for the rudimentary course requirements of the state board. Intrinsically he was still not terribly smart, but his time with Charlie had taught him the art of posturing, of seeming more than one was. Soon he had the patronage of young men who carried tamanchas—country-made pistols, welded from sawn-off pipes, capable of just one round, as likely to take off one's own hand as blow a hole in the enemy. These boys, laconic and angry young men with brooding eyes and a fine gift for abuse, moved in tight bands. They tied hankies around their wrists, and those who didn't have to conceal a tamancha tucked down their trousers, knotted their shirt fronts. Kabir felt these were real people, real men. Not cardboard cut-outs like his father, the padres, or the chutterputter chutiyas. In their presence he felt more potent than he had felt even with Charlie.

The leader of the main gang was a cocky youth called Babloo. It was rumoured he had access to the Lucknow don Sulaiman, who himself was rumoured to be a satrap of the great Mastaan of Bombay. Every once in a while there would be a phone call for him at Tewariji's cloth shop and a boy would come running with the message: Sulaimanbhai, Sulaimanbhai. Instantly, Babloo's expression would become urgent, and he would leap up and leave at a trot, Azam and Batti at his heels. Azam, an orphan, had a permanently skewed walk because he'd carried a tamancha in his groin since he was thirteen. And Batti's moniker referred to his particular specialization: shoving things up rival rectums. Pencils, pens, coins, fingers, marbles, sugarcane sticks, Fanta bottles, the hilt of his knife, the barrel of a tamancha. His stated ambition was to, one day, push a small frog up a victim. 'Nothing vile and poisonous like a snake or a beetle,' he would say. 'Just a little frog. To see if a man with a frog inside him will jump like one.'

Babloo himself had cultivated the look of a 1930s revolutionary. He had a rapier moustache that he oiled and twirled upwards, a maroon paratrooper's beret and an olive-green army shirt with epaulettes and flap pockets, bought from the service store in the cantonment. Below the waist, though, he was a 1960s revolutionary, a hell's angel: blue, locally tailored jeans and brown leather boots that zipped up his calves. The boots had iron studs in their soles so they clacked down every corridor of the inter college. The belt was a cycle chain with a canvas grip, which he sometimes trailed on the floor as he walked. His black Yezdi motorcycle had a high handle grafted on to it, and a special number plate: UP 0007. In a tin plate below it was stencilled, Live and Let Die. The silencer of the bike had been unscrewed and the gang leader's entrances and exits were salient affairs.

Babloo quickly warmed to Kabir. He liked the fact that despite Kabir's curiously elite educational background he was so willing to pay obeisance to him. It brought a kind of shine to the gang to have this boy from the missionary school in its fold. One of the first tasks allotted to him was to teach the gang some good English abuses. Very quickly, after fuck, cock, bastard and homo, Kabir realized there was no creativity in English expletives. In Hindi, by comparison—he learnt from the gang—you could string together virtual sonnets of singing abuse, like: Gaand mein gurda hai nahin, lauda karey salaam (crippled by fear yet flashing a hard-on).

Apart from his English, he earned respect for his knowledge of Hindi films. He could extensively cross-reference every film and hero for the gang leader, and Babloo, with a cinematic idea of his own life, was enthralled.

Soon Kabir and he developed a game.

Every morning when they met Babloo would ask, 'Jai or Veeru?'

Then they would toss a coin. If Kabir won, Babloo would be Veeru for the day—blathering away, playing the comic. If Babloo won then the gang leader would be Jai all day—sardonic, brooding, speaking in terse monosyllables.

Though he was a khalifa of the inter college, Babloo had put in enough repeat years to have acquired a reputation that had spread to the university grounds. During the annual student body elections his services were requisitioned by one party or the other—for mobilization, canvassing, managing the booths, and maintaining the balance of terror. It was mostly strong-arm stuff, but with his penchant for the outrageous act, with his need to please his mentor, Kabir quickly brought an element of artistry, of roguery, to the gang.

Shoplifting—which he had done occasionally in the past—now became a daily chore. He would sail through a few shops every day and bring his offerings to Babloo's court. The range was wide. Stationary, socks, hankies, jam tins, sauce bottles, booze, cigarettes, almonds, cashew nuts, spoons, forks, knives, crockery. Once he brought in a Racold mixer-grinder which the gang plugged into the classroom to stir up glasses of banana-shake. Another time he came in pushing an entire cart of ice-golas—having sent the vendor off to the police chowki on a fake summons—and proceeded to shave the ice and serve up endless combos from the coloured syrup bottles till every boy in the gang was speechless with a frozen tongue.

Babloo loved the audacity and the surprise. And the goodies were more than welcome. His gang had twelve people, and he took their welfare seriously. Now it seemed as if Kabir had put in a daily bonus plan for them all. Every freebie consumed multiplied the debt that the gang leader could call in. In pursuit of applause, Kabir soon progressed to hijacking scooters and motorcycles. Every day he would arrive astride a new one, and the gang would leap on it and ride it till its petrol tank ran dry. Sometimes he'd lift two or three in a day, working the growing bunch of master keys in his pocket. There were no police repercussions because the owners were relieved just to recover their vehicles.

In time he became such an adept he could swipe a scooter while its owner stepped into a shop, or once, even as the man slid down the road shoulder to take a piss. These capers were moments of wild amusement for the gang boys, and they often drove these scooters three astride, at screeching speed through the bazaars, whooping and slapping passing bottoms. Once they rode an antediluvian blue Lambretta straight into the Emergency room of the government hospital and handed it over to the duty doctor to save its blackened lungs that were collapsing from cancer. On the way out, they took the doctor's swish green Chetak scooter.

That year during the university elections Kabir became quartermaster general and did yeoman service for his gang and the candidature of Raghuraj Singh of the Independent Students Front. Instead of purloining from his own town, Kabir, in a brilliant move, led expeditions to Shahjahanpur, Rampur, Haldwani, Moradabad, bringing back vehicles from each town. Soon he had placed a fleet of eight scooters and three motorcycles, with fresh coats of paint and new number plates, at the disposal of the campaign. Babloo was elated, and in turn was acknowledged by Raghuraj Singh as the new strongman of the ISF.

The ISF swept all four seats that year and Raghuraj's victory procession snaked through the city on stolen wheels. Raghuraj presented Babloo a beautiful .32 Webley & Scott revolver with twelve bullets. In turn Babloo gifted Kabir his tamancha, with a fistful of rounds. This did not obviously excite Kabir. Ghulam's son had not yet been fully drained of a childhood soaked in fear.

In the gang he had always steered clear of the terror hardware, confining himself to the chaarsobeesi, the thievery and the duping.

Not even once—until Babloo handed him his own tamancha—had Kabir asked for or handled the guns and daggers the gang tucked away into their clothes. It was quite an interesting little armoury they carried around. Sanju had a Nepali khukri; Raja, a Rampuri flick-knife; Amresh kept a knuckle-duster, three iron spikes studded into a leather strap which he wrapped around his fist; Datun had a steel blade stitched into the toe of his boots, which he could open in a flash—one swinging kick could dig a neat hole in the flesh; Aziz carried a short-handle axe, only eighteen inches, strapped inside a brown leather jacket that he always wore, even in a summer of forty-five degrees; and Santokh, with religious sanction, openly wore a long kirpan, with an engraved handle, on a cross-belt at his waist.

It was Pandit, however, who possessed the most compelling piece, a lovely Luger, with its angled grip and slim sleek barrel. It had a magazine for 9mm bullets, but Pandit owned only two rounds. The weapon was a family heirloom, brought home by his grandfather who fought the Nazis in North Africa in the Second World War. It had last been fired in 1955—three shots in the air—when Pandit's father got married. Pandit kept the two precious rounds in his pocket in a polythene wrap, and fired the Luger every now and then by making sounds with his mouth—sometimes a single decisive phtak! and sometimes an improbable machine-gunning, diggi-diggi-diggi!

The fact is there were not that many brawls, and the armoury was seldom used. There was a great deal of posturing and brandishing though, and most times it was enough to settle growing arguments. The few times violence had erupted—with manic energy, screaming abuse, and flying fists and blades—Kabir had instantly backed off to the margins, refusing to participate. He had no stomach for physical pain, or even the sight of torn skin, broken bones and gushing blood. Each time a skirmish erupted he could feel his legs give way beneath him. Often it took him hours to regain any poise of speech or conduct. He had no way of understanding Sanju or Aziz or Datun, who sailed into battle emitting bloodcurdling yells—hammering and getting hammered, slashing and getting slashed—and regarded it all without anxiety or distress. Later, even as their own wounds oozed with pus, they laughed about how so and so had squealed when Datun's iron toe was wedged inside his testicles.

The gang was mockingly gentle about his squeamishness. 'We understand, Padre Kabir,' they'd say. 'There's no way you can punch or stab in English—you can only do that in Hindi. English is for refined things like robbing and cheating.' Kabir took up the subject of the violence with Babloo a few times, but found himself summarily dismissed. The gang leader said, 'Padreji, please remember that Gandhiji was shot! With a tamancha like this one! Just like cows eat grass, men assault each other. You can either eat the grass or be eaten as grass! Tell me, what would you prefer?'

So Kabir took the tamancha with butter fingers, and wrapping it in newspaper put it in a tattered cardboard suitcase crammed with old film posters on top of his cupboard. The rounds he poured into a thick khaki pair of old NCC socks and pushed the socks under the pile of musty woollens inside his cupboard. The chances of his parents finding either were remote since he aggressively discouraged their meddling in his space.

Six months later it was the police that dug them out, and as Ghulam and his wife wailed and lamented, put cuffs on their son's wrists and hauled him off to the police station.

It happened in the way these things do. One wayward thread unravelling the entire tapestry. In the course of courting a Punjabi girl, fair fleshy Rekha, with the haunches of a horse, wordlessly, of course, and from a distance, Aziz broke the jaw of a handsome young boy from first-year BA (English Honours), whom he saw walking by her side three days running. As it was, Aziz used the blunt end of his short-handle axe. Aziz did not know it, but the boy's name was Jaiwant and his father was Aakrosh Singh, the new superintendent of police, from the badlands of the Terai.

Aziz was picked up before night fell, taken to the backroom of the kotwali on Civil Lines, thrown face down on the floor, his leather jacket pulled over his head with his arms still in the sleeves and fastidiously beaten from ankles to neck with his own axe. No bones were broken, only ligaments and tendons torn. While doctors wired together Jaiwant's beautiful face in the government hospital and his mother wailed in the VIP waiting room, Aziz's sphincter was tested with the handle of his axe, and a pestle was rolled over his broken muscles to register and record the differing levels of pain.

Before Aziz broke his jaw, the young Jaiwant with beautiful long eyelashes had made a cautionary noise: 'You better watch it, motherfucker, you don't know who my father is!' To which Aziz had said, 'Well motherfucker, my name is Aziz! Aziz Kulhadiwala! And my father's name is Babloo! Babloo Black Lugerwala! And his cock is bigger than your leg! And all of it will be shoved inside you till your arsehole is so big that men can drive scooters through it with their helmets on! In this town if you fuck with us you fuck with the devil and the devil's father!'

Now the head constable screwing the handle into Aziz's anus asked, 'Is it bigger than this o great Kulhadiwala? Perhaps thicker? Or would you prefer your own father's, the great Babloo Black Lugerwala?' Aziz was beyond responding. He needed every bit of energy to cope with the agony. More than four inches of the axe handle was now buried in Aziz's asshole, like a flag on a mountain, at an angle, the blade catching the yellow light of the naked bulb.

The head constable said, 'Come here all you fucking laggards and salute the flag of Babloo Black Lugerwala!' And he gave it a ceremonial twist. Aziz barely changed the register of his low continuous whine.

Not much later Babloo was brought in. The iron flag was still at full mast. The gang leader, recalcitrant, squirming, giving lip to the cops, saw Aziz sprawled on the floor and went limp. To be locked in battle, however unequal, against another gang, was not a crippling prospect. To face-off against policemen in a police station produced utter hopelessness; there would never be a rescuing knock at the door.

Babloo's anus was first probed with the short barrel of his Webley & Scott, and later when Pandit had been brought in, with the sleek barrel of the Second World War Luger. By then a thick log had been rolled up and down his back and legs like he was a chapatti. No bone was broken; every muscle was pulped. The policemen took turns pulling the trigger of the Luger. One said, 'Oh don't fire any more! The bullets must be getting lost in all his shit! Fucking Babloo don! Black Lugerwala! A heap of dung bigger than my buffalo!' The other said, 'Shall we try the 303? Blow his arsehole to Kabul! Then he can become Babloo Kaala Kabuliwallah.'

That night they brought most of the gang in. Aakrosh Singh's son was still swimming under anaesthesia. Many anuses would have to be probed till he surfaced. Kabir was the last to be marched in, and he began to weep for mercy the moment he saw his friends on the floor, each with a different flag sticking out of his arse cheeks. He had never, he wailed, never lifted a finger on anyone. Never. The fat policeman who had done most of the plumbing early in the evening rolled the tamancha in his hand and said, 'And what do you use this for? Shooting ants?'

When they took his pants off, he cried like a baby. Then the fat cop lifted his cock up with the tip of the tamancha, and all four cops—their caps off, their belts unbuckled, their shirts unbuttoned, their shoes unlaced—exchanged glances.

One of them said, shaking his head sadly, 'No helmet...no helmet...very dangerous...'

The fat cop asked softly, 'What's your full name, my boy?'

Ghulam's son blubbered his name.

'Kabir Musalman,' said the fat cop softly to the others, in explanation, 'Kabir Musalman.'

The swarthy assistant sub-inspector, sitting on the lone chair of crude wood—the ASI said sonorously, 'Kabira baitha paed pe apna lund latkaye, jisko jitna chahiye kaat kaat le jaye...'

The fat cop took off his unlaced leather shoes and wore them on his hands like gloves. The ASI slowly repeated the obscene doggerel about Kabir sitting on a tree dangling his phallus, inviting his followers to chop off and take what they wished. At this, the fat cop caught Kabir's penis between his leather gloves and began to massage it. To begin with he did it gently, but the grit on the soles of the shoes was immediately lacerating. Kabir was crying like a child, with loud sobs and sniffles and pleas for forgiveness. His mouth and nose were choked with snot and he was finding it difficult to breathe. The ASI, slumped in his chair, had unbuttoned his pants, and had pulled up his khaki shirt to rub his hairy stomach. He said, 'Now boy repeat after me, Kabira baitha...'

When Kabir couldn't form the words through the snot and the sobs, the fat cop massaged his leather hands harder. Kabir screamed in agony and began to mutter the doggerel he had known since he was ten years old.

By the time the night ended, he was on the floor, sporting his own small flag, the black tamancha Babloo had gifted him and he had never used. Under him was his tiny piece of mashed flesh—to protect whose telltale baldness his father had once procured a spurious medical certificate. For the rest of his life it would be good only for pissing and little else.

By the end of the next day, Babloo's mentors managed to crank enough levers in Lucknow to stop the flag-hoisting ceremonies. But there was nothing to be done about the stretched rectums and the brutalized muscles. The rule of the police game was, you dealt with what happened on the field on the field, as it was played out. You could try and seize the advantage when the next game started; this one was over. To try and reopen the finished game was to ensure that the next time they got you they left you in no condition to protest.

By the time the boys were produced in front of the sessions judge, the facts of the case had metamorphosed. Except for two boys, the rest were arraigned only on charges of hooliganism, given warnings, ordered to pay fines, and let off. The crumbling courtroom with the roots of a huge peepul tree tearing through its walls and the high ventilators crammed with bird nests, was packed with students from the university, including Raghuraj—looking the concerned patriarch. When the weedy judge with a jumping apple in his throat mumbled the exonerations, Raghuraj and his army flexed their fists in triumph. Jumping apple looked at them with pleading eyes.

Only two boys were booked under the Arms Act and committed to judicial remand. The first was Aziz Kulhadiwala, now back inside his leather jacket, his face shining and unblemished, but every muscle in his body torn and his arsehole big as an exhaust pipe. The second was Kabir M—Musalman—whose every fear of pain, his own and his father's, had been now fully realized. In the screaming-pleading-begging-moaning night he had appealed not only to Allah—his birthright—but also to Jesus Christ—his schoolright—and to Lord Krishna—his nationalright. The secular pantheon was however clearly not interested in boys who didn't want to declare where their transcendent loyalty lay. This fact—that he was no god's responsibility—was ratified in the courtroom next day when only two boys were nailed: the one who broke the jaw and the one who wanted to escape his god.

Ghulam—the man who set this tragedy in motion, who imagined god would take the larger view of the equality of supreme gods—Ghulam, timid as ever, cowered behind his wheezing middle-aged lawyer whose slow arguments drizzled flecks of paan. The

Arms Act! Pistols! Bullets! Ghulam could scarcely grasp it. He had brought his son up to be afraid of hot water and fish bones. He had been taught under the majestic padres, with Christ on the Cross, in fine English, with Moral Science classes—fully prepared for the refinements of the modern world. To make it all possible Ghulam had cast his penis in rubber thick as a rain cape and left his wife's womb barren as the deserts of Rajasthan. Did this judge—who was not even listening to Rizvisahib's complex arguments, talking instead to some servant who had come in through the back door—did this judge even know all this? Did he know Father Conrad and Father Michael and Father Andrews? Did he know Ghulam had in nearly thirty years never even appropriated a single coin at the Talkies? Even when he knew others were doing so?

While Rizvisahib drizzled on, the judge sent off the two boys to judicial remand. Standing against the far wall, in a row with the six others—all leaning against each other in pain—Kabir did not even look into Ghulam's eyes. He could see his father still begging for a pretty place in the world, seeking some kind of approval that no one was ever going to give him.

Kabir took to jail like a deer fleeing the anxieties of a forest takes to a sanctuary. After the backroom of the police kotwali, the brisk leather rub and the flag-hoisting ceremonies, this was an oasis of peace and benign conduct. The yard of the prison was big with not a blade of grass on it. Its soul was a huge semul with many arms and many fingers stretching in every direction. Using a carpenter's plane the inmates had scraped off the semul's thorny flesh so they could lean against its trunk. At this time it was ablaze with scarlet flowers, and Kabir was surprised he had never noticed such a lovely tree ever before. Next to it, at half its height, a neem tree frothed green leaves.

It was under these two trees that the inmates hung out—squatting, sleeping, drawing out games in the dust, playing Lakad, in which the den could not snare you if you were touching wood. The best ally in this game was Ektara, the old man who had only a smooth peg below his left knee. It was not unusual, in the heat of the chase, to have a dozen men hanging on to Ektara's wooden stump.

Near the ten-foot-high wall were the communal baths: three handpumps, standing side by side, like a guard of honour. Everyone brushed, washed, bathed here. It was a selfless place—if you were under the pump, there was always some hand to keep the water gusting over you, and if you found someone under the pump then you immediately bent to the task. Kabir loved the cold water baths in the open, the camaraderie around the trees, the complete absence of expectation.

Contrary to anything he might have imagined, no one appeared particularly frustrated or irate or depressed at being corralled inside the high walls. Most of the inmates, in fact, seemed spiritually evolved, philosophically calm. There were some like Mootie Baba—he drank his own urine—who gave soothing religious discourses interspersed with sonorous chants, that even the jailors and warders came to hear. Aziz and Kabir arrived inside those walls seething, and in no time found their blood slowing down. Everyone lived the wisdom. There was the day, each day, and you simply dwelled in it.

They were roused before first light by the clanging of a metal plate, and ablutions done, were in the yard performing basic physical exercises of the jumping-slapping kind by six o'clock. Breakfast was a big steel mug of scalding tea and thick salted parathas, two apiece; and lunch and dinner, a runny dal with dusty chapattis and the occasional vegetable. There was tea in the evening, and once in a while, a hard mathi or a congealed laddu. In the evenings some fastidious ones hit the handpumps a second time and sang their cleanliness at the top of their voices, in bhajans or film ditties.

In between, during the day, the inmates divided into groups in different sheds at the far west end of the yard to earn their keep. The options ranged from tailoring, carpet-weaving, metalwork, carpentry, quilting, to bamboo work. There were no ustads, or teachers. There may have been once—but now it was simply the oldest prisoner, gently passing on his skills.

Kabir tried the split-and-weave of bamboo but he couldn't deal with the constant scything of his skin, the splinters getting under his nails, and he soon switched to carpentry. This involved the making of rudimentary chairs and tables, beds and shelves. To begin with Kabir was happy to just work the plane and see the crisp clean shavings fly, and the unexpectedly young, glowing skin of the wood emerge as he sloughed off the dirty old. But soon he discovered—the blood of his artisan ancestors, the zari-zardozi men, running in him—that he had a gift for chiselling the soft wood of mango into toy animals. It rapidly became an addiction and for the rest of his life he was to carry a hard knife and a slab of soft wood in his pockets, whittling out little figurines which he gave away to whoever would have them. His set piece would become the chooza—the chick of a hen—which he could cut and shape in less than twenty minutes, the easy curve of the belly and head, the gentle beak, and two twists of the tip of his knife for the soft eyes.

After the beasts of the kotwali, the warders were saints. Their attitude probably drew from the temperament of the head warder, Tiwarisahib, who was in his mid-fifties, walked with a slow gait and had a drooping grey moustache, and spectacles so thick that his eyes swam behind them. He always wore a white and maroon gamchha around his neck, and used it to wipe his mouth after every sentence. Tiwarisahib liked to say, 'In the world there are only two kinds of people, the jailor and the doctor, who know the truth—that most men are punished for no fault of theirs.'

When the two boys checked in, he looked at Kabir's papers and said, 'What a fancy convent school you went to, my dear boy! Your padres are good men, but now you are entering the greatest college in the world. Pay attention, son, and you will leave with a degree for wisdom which no other institution can ever give you.'

In the barracks, the duo's smooth induction was aided by the fact that Babloo's gang—and his mentors in Lucknow and Bombay—had a reputation. Ample space was made for them by the forty-two other occupants of Ward 3, and the king of that domain, Bhediya Boss—he had bitten off a patwari's jugular in a brawl—sent out the signal by sitting them next to himself at dinner and sharing with them his unfiltered cigarette.

One night, a week later, the Ward received some country liquor—for the scullery work the prisoners had done for the wedding of the superintendent's daughter. Kabir knocked it back and became a padre. 'Haauu haaa, thouu thaa...lusheus dusheus chuseus...forsooth a geyser, in the gaand of Caesar...haauu haaa, thouu thaa...friends, romans, countrymen, meri murgi tumhari hen...ohhh brutus ki chootus mein balkishan ka jootus...haauu haaa, thouu thaa!'

For years afterwards, in the city jail, prisoners wishing to savour a moment of anglicized grandness were inclined to strut about declaring, 'Haauu haaa, thou thaa...lusheus dusheus chuseus...'

By the time he got bail Kabir had come to understand the role the initial M and the missing piece of skin had played in his incarceration. Aziz's hard-on for the ripe Rekha had in the SP's khaki mind become an act of religious aggression. While Aziz raged about it every day, and swore religious and romantic revenge—also cursing Babloo and his mates for their betrayal—Kabir was sailing through the days peacefully, carving his wood menagerie—and had even begun to teach some of the inmates basic English.

It was strangely satisfying—that moment when someone finally understood a word and began to mouth it slowly: work—kaam; anger—krodh; peace—shanti; knowledge—gyan; balance—santulan; mad—paagal; hope—aasha; law—kanoon; strength—shakti; hard—mushkil; love—pyaar; sad—dukhi; thief—chor; rape—balaatkar;

justice—nyaya; fate—kismat; karma—karma. The students, many of them illiterate, many dropouts from government and village schools—in for crimes ranging from stealing poultry to assault and battery—looked at Kabir with deep admiration. He woke every morning wanting to see that look in someone's eye.

His lack of frenzy also had something to do with the truncating of desire. Over the months the wounds of the leather rub had slowly healed, but it appeared the nerves had been abraded beyond repair. Kabir knew his desires were now just a piece of dead flesh, his promise of eternity damaged forever. Those who get used to sleeping under the skies soon stop dreaming of roofs. The man who could not now know eternity found solace and then addiction in the sonorous sermons of Baba Mootie. Twice a week the bearded drinker of urine—he used his steel mug—read from the song divine. This he did under the soaring semul, sitting cross-legged on a low wooden slat, prisoner and warder sitting on the ground before him, as last light fell from the skies.

With the greatest armies of the world eyeball to eyeball, with ten thousand bowstrings stretched to twang and a hundred thousand swords unsheathed to sing, with mighty maces refracting the sun and a forest of spears tearing the sky, with a million men and beasts coiled to unleash mayhem, Kabir heard the unarmed blue god tell the peerless Arjuna, whose mighty Gandiva hung limp in his hand: 'He by whom other people are not disturbed and he who is not disturbed by other people and he who is free from delight, dissatisfaction, fear and concern, is dear to me. Without desire, pure, enterprising, neutral, without pain and one who has renounced all fruit, such a devotee is dear to me. He who is not delighted, nor hates. He who does not sorrow, nor desire. He who has given up good and evil, such a devotee is dear to me. Equal between friend and enemy, and respect and insult, equal between cold and warmth, happiness and unhappiness and without all attachment...Alike between criticism and praise, restrained in speech, satisfied with whatever is obtained, without habitation and controlled in mind, such a devoted man is dear to me.'

Kabir M looked at himself—within the high walls of the jail, free from delight, dissatisfaction, fear and concern—and he knew he was such a man. In his own mind, he felt he was slowly becoming like Baba Mootie, a realized being.

Soon, in fact, he became uncertain about what he would do in the great outside. Now each time Ghulam came to meet him and assured him the lawyer would have him released any day, Kabir abused him and told him to leave him alone. Each time his father mistook it for pique, and began to cry and mumble, promising to redouble his efforts.

By the time Ghulam paid the five thousand rupees that transformed the tamancha into a water pistol, more than a year had passed. None of the gang was in the crumbling courtroom when the judge signed off his papers finally and Kabir stepped out as a released convict and not a wronged hero.

He did not speak to his mother when he got home, and he did not leave the house for the next two months—lying mostly on his bed in his room looking at the roof. Often he found himself crying, weeping abjectly—as he had never done when he was incarcerated—and as the tears rolled off his face and soaked the pillow he knew he was sorrowing not for himself but for the nameless griefs of the universe.

In despair, timid Ghulam—the creator of the initial M, the seeker of the modern, non-aligned future for his son—went to the padres for help. He sought from them a counselling role, and the addresses of classmates who might be able to lend a hand. But there was no further purchase to be had in those hymn-soaked corridors, where eighteen years ago he had bowed and scraped to change the life of his only son. The padres were already overburdened with souls to save, and his son's peers had either moved on to the big cities of Lucknow and Allahabad and Delhi and Pune to pursue college or been syringed into the adult calculus of their family businesses, the factories and shops and hotels and petrol pumps. Of course they remembered Muthal who had disappeared up the padre's habit. It was tragic he had fallen on bad days. Sure they would try and help. And that was that. Generation after generation learns that the equalities of the schoolroom are a delusion. You pass through the greatest educational mixer-grinder and when you emerge on the other side what remains unshredded and intact are class, caste, religion and wealth.

Kabir, with neither money nor English, not religion nor clan, lay bare-torsoed on his back and looked at the peeling ceiling and the Usha fan twirling with slow creaks. Sometimes with his small knife he whittled a chooza, letting the wood shavings stick to his stomach and fleck his bed. His parents brought him food and tea and took the choozas away, lining them on the dining-room shelf, a chorus line for the kindergarten.

One day his parents packed him a bag and took him to Moradabad, sitting on each side of him in the state roadways bus. His mother's brothers had over the decades established a robust business in brassware, and as concerned families do, were open to accommodating the errant nephew. Given his background of the missionary school he was given a front-office job, talking up the wholesale clients who came from Delhi, Bombay and occasionally abroad, to place orders for jugs, ashtrays, vases, candelabras, peacocks, elephants, camels, dancing natarajas, long-eared Buddhas, tribal masks, sun faces, and even fat buffaloes in gleaming gold. 'Noorjehan Brassworks, Best and Brightest, Suppliers to All India and the World.'

Almost immediately the nephew proved a disappointment, struggling to converse in English, poorly informed of his wares, disinterested in closing a deal through the extra hustle. The first time a white man showed up he became clammy with the anxiety that would fill him each time the bell rang for the English class in school.

In a month, Syedmamu moved him to the backroom, to the preparation of the catalogues and sales pitches, and to help with the maintenance of the inventory. Kabir had no talent for either, and given his indifference, he soon earned the contempt of the old employees who had grown this trade through hard labour over the years. 'He should have been a carpenter or a poulterer,' the old accountant said, in derision, to Syedmamu, opening his palm to show him a chooza, many of which—open-beaked—filled the table where Kabir sat. Syedmamu said, 'It's his father's fault. He is a lost soul—not knowing god, and betrayed by men. He needs our compassion.'

Very quickly the uncle had noticed that the boy was bereft of all knowledge of the great religion he was born into. He didn't know where to look nor how to genuflect when the azaan sounded across the rooftops. Nor was he moved to imitate anyone. He would keep sitting on his chair, staring off, while everyone fell to the floor. Astonishingly, he knew not one kalma from the Holy Book, and it seemed he had never abstained a day during the great fasting.

Moved by the mansion of darkness his nephew had been abandoned in, Syedmamu sought the services of the old maulvi who had once tutored his sons. The maulvi's teeth were black with tobacco and mouth red with paan. He came from the old city, clad in soiled white, pumping his old cycle. His manner was gentle, and sitting in the room given to Kabir—on the roof, with a toilet outside, like his timid father thirty years ago—he spoke in a soft voice, eyes closed, rocking slowly on his haunches. The maulvi—instructed by the master of brass—exhorted the young man to understand divine design and to fulfil his destiny. Dread spiralled in Kabir at the spectre of fresh expectations...haauu haaa, thouu thaa...lusheus, dusheus, chuseus...

A few weeks later, from outside the brass showroom—so crammed with wares that nothing could be seen—he picked a shining red Maruti car, with a grip of faux fur, and drove it all the way up to Nainital. As he went ribboning up the mountain road, singing old Hindi film songs, he felt, after a very long time, free and elated. Leaving the car by the crowded bus stand, he strolled on the bustling mall and took a boat ride into the lake. All around were the glowing faces and telltale tinsel of honeymooning couples. Thanks to the leather rub, this was as alien a territory for him as English had been in school. Two days later, he slid into a white Ambassador at Mallital and drove it up to Ranikhet. The soaring chir-pines, the forests of oak and deodar, the cool breeze, the tiny red tin-roofed houses and hamlets—it was marvellous. The car however turned out to be the district magistrate's, and he was picked up in the bazaar while just beginning to eat a chhola-samosa.

A few days later, when the magistrate consigned him to judicial custody, a wave of relief swept over him. He refused to offer the name of anyone who could be contacted for the filing of bail.

He spent the next decade of his life sailing in and out of jails. Soon there was no town in the region that had not felt his thieving fingers, and hardly a jail that had not seen his gentle shadow on its walls. Bareilly, Shahjahanpur, Rampur, Moradabad, Haldwani, Almora, Dehradun, Mussoorie, Agra, Meerut, Pilibhit, Ferozabad, Farrukhabad, Lucknow, Kanpur, Varanasi, Allahabad, Amethi, Ayodhya, Gorakhpur, Barabanki....There was no design to the wanderings: the desire to see a monument, a town; the urging of an acquaintance in a dhaba; the pursuit of an unseen film; the mere fact of a road, tarred and uncurling, and leading somewhere.

Through it all he stuck to the minor sin of chaarsobeesi—the trivial deceptions of theft and con. India was changing rapidly and every day new fancy cars were scorching the roads. Japanese cars, Korean cars, American cars, European cars. They had power steering, electronic locks, stereo players, push-button windows, parking lights. Their skins glistened, their horns sang, their hearts purred. They started instantly, sped like rabbits, and everyone was busy banging into everyone. In the denting-painting workshops of every town master keys were being manufactured by the day. The pockets of Kabir's denim jacket were heavy with them.

Only two things propelled his capers: the search for something to do, and the necessity of finding food and a roof. He forged friendships that lasted a few days or a few weeks, at the end of which there was always a waiting car, a winding road, and happy incarceration. Not all jails were as benign as the first, but he discovered that each harboured a heart of deep wisdom; each had a tree that radiated calm; each a quiet corner where you could whittle the perfect chooza; and each a Baba Mootie who was in touch with eternal truths. Jailed men were free of things that free men could never be free of. Suffering men knew things ordinary men could never know.

Among the police force and the warders he developed a reputation for innocuousness. The small scarecrow-thin conman with big ears who never fussed when he was nabbed, and always gifted his captors lovely little wooden choozas for their children. Some of them knew that something had happened in a thana many years ago that had ensured he would never have any of his own ever.

In all those years he went back home only once, and found his father in a derelict state. Modernity had failed to embrace Ghulam with its promised enlightenments (it had in fact eluded his son too); and the religion he had rejected had kept from him its assurances. The magic of the dark theatre that had all his life absorbed his fears and given flesh to his dreams had also precipitously waned. The glory days of Minerva Talkies—of packed openings and new stars—were long over. Firdaus was dead—had been dead nine years—and his sons had moved on to Bombay and Delhi, mining new veins in advertising and trading. The hall was crumbling—the seats broken, the long-necked fans dysfunctional, the projection cameras dated, the screen in need of replacement, with tears at its edges and dirt all over. There was no air-conditioning and no new film opened there any more: it was now the haven of C-grade quickies and old cut-rates, and rank with the smell of labourers from adjoining constructions sites who squatted on the chairs to avoid the bounding rats. The Talkies was up for sale: a developer from Lucknow wanted to erect a contemporary shopping mall, with uniformed ushers, credit card machines, and walls of glass. Efforts were on to change the land use clauses.

Ghulam had no idea what he would do once Minerva Talkies was gone. The old basti had ceased to exist: its community had scattered, its rhythms were dead. In its place stood a government housing project with straight roads lined with mast trees. The cemetery in which his parents slept—as did Ali Baba and all the other grey-hairs of his childhood—had for the moment been cordoned off from the complex with a high brick wall. But negotiations were on to disinter and shift the dead to an area of lower realty prices and more breathing room.

The tamarind tree—where they had first felt the ground shift beneath their feet, where Imroze had returned alone, with just the one arm going up and down like a train signal—the tamarind tree was still there: a hoary man, its hair thin, its skin leathery, its scalp scaling with age. Some days, terrified by the echoing loneliness of his life, Ghulam went and sat under it and, closing his eyes, wept for himself.

Now the scarecrow-thin boy with large ears and quicksilver fingers, and the fearful man with hollow eyes and missing teeth, sat silently across the room and could not summon up a single redemptive word. They had both failed each other. Religion and language;

ambition and fear. When it was time for him to leave—the stolen silver Ford waiting outside—Kabir M—modern, muthal, moron, Musalman—told his father a lie. He said he worked in the State Bank of India in the faraway state of Kashmir, where he had the rank of an officer and filled ledgers in cursive English, and he gave him an address at which no letter could ever arrive.

To his wailing mother he made a promise: he would regularly send her and her husband enough money from his grand salary as an officer for them to not worry about the dying Talkies. And this he did each time a new car transited through his life, and in many ways the pledge became a tethering cord in a life of almost no meaning.

'He who is free from delight, dissatisfaction, fear and concern...without desire, pure, enterprising, neutral, without pain...he who is not delighted, nor hates...he who does not sorrow, nor desire... equal between friend and enemy, and respect and insult, equal between cold and warmth, happiness and unhappiness and without all attachment...alike between criticism and praise, restrained in speech, satisfied with whatever is obtained, without habitation and controlled in mind, such a devoted man is dear to me.'

This man then—indifferent to the passage of months and years—one day in the new year of the new century met another man in a jail near Dasna, who understanding his virtues—of heart and mind and hand—offered him a task that would take him on a long drive through beautiful roads. After the drive was over he would be given enough money to fill all his pockets and both his hands.

It was a long drive that would take Kabir M—defrocker of the padre, rider of the ass, hater of English, lover of ahimsa, chiseller of choozas, son of Ghulam, follower of Baba Mootie, dead of penis, quicksilver of hand, native of penitentiaries, prince of the road—on a journey that led to the murder of an innocent. Something his fearful genes had not prepared him for, and something he had never wished to do.

9

MONEYWORMS AND MENOFWATER

I had just taken Sara off the wall and was drifting in the happy place that I had never once found with Dolly/folly when she said, 'You know their lives are actually worthier than yours.'

This is what I hated. I had paid my talking dues in full before I'd picked her up and nailed her. We had talked for nearly two hours, telling and listening with great sincerity, as if we were really interested in what the other had to say—so this, now, as I floated in that place with no equal, was extortionate. Today in fact I had outdone myself, got her juices really raging.

After she had finished a long tearjerker about some weird fucker with a random initial and a smashed dick who thought jail was the Ritz-Carlton, I had filled her in on the cool horrors of Kapoor: his buying out of Chutiya-Nandan-Pandey for next to nothing, the draconian shareholders' agreement he'd made us sign, pretty much making over everything—life, liberty and lund. Our lawyer had warned us that such an agreement ought not to be signed even with a gun to our heads. But we said we were already dead, no agreement could kill us further. The lawyer said actually it could. We looked at the twenty-four pages the magazine had become, we looked at the eight people who remained, we calculated the debts the two of us had already incurred, we calculated them mounting as we spoke, and we just signed.

Life, liberty and lund.

In any event, all resistance had been drained out of us after witnessing the decimation of the garment trio. For all their wealth and business savvy, their equestrian dining-rooms and naked mermaids, they had appeared callow recruits getting their inaugural sizing-down from the boot-camp sergeant-major.

A Full Metal Jacket diminishment.

To begin with, Kapoor brutally spelt out to them the utter worthlessness of the publication they owned. This was done with hard numbers—accounting for the past, present and future. Jai and I in this time shrank into our chairs and vanished. Then he told them it was actually worse. The three of them had incurred financial and legal liabilities that would dog them for years, and some of these were actually criminal. Pay them for their stake? They would be lucky if someone even agreed to take it off them for free. And, to be sure, that someone was certainly not him! He said he had no idea things were so bad when he'd decided to examine the investment. And the only reason he hadn't fled yet was because Jai's uncle—Bhargavaji, a senior bureaucrat in the commerce ministry—was an old friend. But friendship had its limits. It did not include suicide. Jai's uncle would understand. He was a reasonable man.

The cool, classy negotiating-table toughness with which Kuchha King, Kuchha Singh and Frock Raja had tried to begin the dialogue collapsed quickly, like pudding. The attempt to stun the prospector with a display of opulence and style had ended badly. Walking through Frock Raja's excesses to his frock-shaped pool, Kapoorsahib had knocked the construction materials he'd used, the architect he'd used, the designer he'd used, and had pointed out all the zoning and building laws he had broken. 'Next time you build a house come and see me, I'll get you the right people,' he said. 'In fact, come and see mine and you'll know what's wrong with yours.'

The man was a master of bastardy. After the first few sentences of their sales pitch, Kapoor had closed his eyes. Irritated, the trio had stopped, but he'd continued to sleep. When one of them stood up in exasperation, he opened his eyes and said, 'Why did you stop? I was listening to everything—there was just nothing for me to react to.' When the trio began pitching again, he continued to remain expressionless. Immediately they switched to making whining noises: surely there was some value here; something had been created; something existed; it wasn't all *so* bad.

No, said Kapoor, it was worse, worse, worse. The worst. He felt for them, and he wished them well, but as far as he could see, the magazine was dead. They should just shut it down. Ah, but of course that wouldn't end it. There was still the legal shit. A lot of it criminal, trickily criminal. Some of it leading straight to jail.

When he got up to go, the threesome literally hustled him back into the chair. All three wheedled in tandem. Kapoorsahib must try and understand, they were garment exporters and had no means of figuring out or running this media business. It was a good business, a great business—so much influence and glamour and power—but they had neither the acumen nor the stomach for it. They were innocents in the big bad world of deals and dealmakers. Mere sellers of undies and frocks, lambs any wolf could casually slaughter. Kapoorsahib on the other hand was a man of the world. A man who worked Delhi's power levers; who understood politics and policy; he understood mega games and dined with mega players; he could take an ugly jab and deliver an uglier one. He could outwolf the wolves; he could outlamb the lambs; he could take the magazine to giddy heights; he could one day out-time *Time* and out-newsweek *Newsweek*.

Kapoorsahib drank in the supplications with sceptical eyes.

Jai was now the smallest I had ever seen him: the moralizing schoolteacher standing in front of the owner's boardroom, incapable of bridging the vast chasm between those who talk about the world and those who shape it.

His stirring words were harmless paper darts. I hoovered in the cashew nuts. My stomach had begun to move.

Kapoorsahib said, 'My answer is still no, and so it would be of any sane man. But I owe Bhargavaji many favours and so I promise to try and think about it.'

The trio walked him across the faux-stone driveway where the naked mermaid still spewed water and shook his hand with both theirs, bending low in entreaty. Then they came back to the poolside and alternately minced and pumped little Jai. He was a dog and had misled them and destroyed them. But, listen, he must convince his uncle to lean on this guy; it was clear he would do the deal with one nudge from him. Jai swelled and deflated at such speed that I thought he would have a schizophrenic spasm.

As I narrated this tale of immoralities to Sara, her rage and excitement had mounted. Sitting in the middle of the bed, facing me as I leaned against the headrest, her sarong had fallen open, beaming her readiness. The colour was already high in her cheeks, she was biting her lip. The abuses of money and power were shovelfuls of coal stoking her engines. Guruji could have been India's leading sex counsellor.

I had then ratcheted up the heat some more. I'd told her about all that we'd managed to unearth on Kapoorsahib. To every appearance he was in the furniture and carpet business. He had emporia in Delhi and Bombay, and he also exported to several countries in eastern Europe. These outlets were gleaming affairs—glass-fronted, wood-panelled, air-conditioned, worked by elegant women in silk sarees. Not Indian shops but international showrooms, with big glossy books on art and culture, piped Indian classical music and herbal tea.

A sneak visit to the one in South Delhi had left Jai and me breathless. It was so classy a place that no sales pitch was made in it at all. As we looked around at the carpets, the ornate, richly polished furniture with inlays of stone, a boy in grey livery, bending low, offered us several options of beverage and returned with flavoured hot water of a pale hue in handle-less ceramic cups. Perfect for gargling. The beautiful woman in a silk saree with black hair that fell below her waist and a black bindi shaped like a coiled snake asked us if she could do anything for us. I shook my head with a hard look in my eye, and when she had moved away Jai said, 'Yes, please. Take off all your clothes.'

Later, Jai made casual inquiries, pointing to dull carpets, nodding knowingly. Some of them cost more than a flat in Vasant Kunj. In the half hour we were there not one other client cracked open the imposing door and not for a moment did the beautiful woman stop smiling. Yes, please. Take off all your clothes.

It had taken us two days to figure out Kapoorsahib's real sources of income. The carpets, furniture, showrooms were all smokescreens. If they never made a rupee—and quite likely they did not, given the expensive overheads—he would not turn a hair. Kapoorsahib's real business was arms dealing. He was an agent representing several European companies and, it seemed, each time he closed a deal his bank accounts in Switzerland swelled by tens of millions of dollars.

From bullets to howitzers to submarines and flak jackets, Kapoorsahib sold everything an army could possibly need. Nothing terribly wrong there. Someone has to do the dirty stuff. Some kill and die; others provide the means for doing so. The problem was it was illegal. In a moment of mad political convulsion in the 1980s the government had, grandly, outlawed middlemen in arms deals. In other words, no commissions were to be paid or received, no deal was to have a facilitator. But as Indians know, nothing in the world happens without the greasing role of middlemen. Not jobs, not marriages, not access to god. If the law was to be strictly followed the Indian army would soon be throwing stones in battle.

The law was one thing. Reality was another.

So Kapoorsahib performed the invaluable and fraught task of keeping the Indian army well equipped. It was a spectral calling—for all purposes he and his work did not exist. Delhi was full of such people, who worked that surreal space between day and night, legal and illegal, government and private, national and international. For his labours, European companies dropped tens of millions of dollars into Kapoorsahib's many-numbered Swiss accounts, and he in turn generously dropped tidy sums into the many-numbered Swiss accounts of different politicians and bureaucrats. There were some who said there was more Indian money in Swiss banks than in the Indian treasury.

Father's friend, Bahugunaji, carper and crank, who had been a head clerk in the commerce ministry, used to say, 'Everybody has an account there! Everybody, prime ministers down, for decades and decades! If you string them all together, it'll make a poem longer than the Mahabharata!'

Aptly, Kapoorsahib's offices were staffed with armies of chartered accountants—moneyworms—who, all day, decoded regulations and constructed delicate webs that would make some of his riches available to him in India. We were told hawala transactions abounded, and unseen mounds of dollars travelled borders to become mountains of rupees. These bankers wore churidars and chappals, and ran a system even more foolproof than that of the suits of Switzerland. Most of these mountains of rupees when they suddenly surfaced in India went into property purchases. The very ground we stood on could well belong to Kapoorsahib or some merchant of arms like him.

Besides the moneyworms bent over desks, there were the liaison officers ranging the landscape. These were men of water, flowing smoothly everywhere, capable of taking care of any demand a man upholding the majesty of the state could possibly dream up—from Black Label whisky for a party to the canvas of a favourite painter to tickets for a holiday in Greece to admissions for a child in a posh

American university. Since the state did not look after its people, somebody had to.

This we were told was the sum of Kapoorsahib's professional staff: moneyworms and menofwater. All of them spectral creatures, working an unacknowledged business that produced very real military hardware and very big mountains of cash. Through the open sarong Sara's thick hair had shone in anger and anticipation. Now and then an inner thigh muscle flexed involuntarily, spurring me to a more eloquent account. The sheer potency of power and pelf! Easy to see why the great stories of the world are always about evil. Guruji was truly Masters & Johnson.

Then Sara asked the question that had been set up. 'So why you?'

This was complicated. We didn't know the answer either. I said it was possible Jai's uncle—given that he may have facilitated some of the spectral activities—had some leverage with Kapoor, but it was doubtful he would have used it to save a dead rag. Jai's Lincolnite speeches were not likely to have cut any ice with Bhargavaji, government servant extraordinaire, who lived deep in the belly of the beast and had no illusions about its nature.

'Then?' said Sara, the soft muscle twitching, the pupils beginning to dilate.

It was difficult to stay with the story. I was looking at the wall, next to the door, where she had to be crucified. So excruciating it was, the way she fought back, with just her hips, killing herself and me with deep stabs. Sometimes—her teeth clenched—she gyrated slowly, and reduced me to a babbling animal.

I said I felt that we were like the swank showrooms—Jai and I and the magazine. Like the silk carpets and the teak furniture and the beautiful woman with a snake for a bindi. Just another kind of smokescreen. And the reason we were needed could have something to do with the utter mayhem unleashed by the three crazies—hotair, clubman, and hitman—some weeks ago.

It was true the government had not fallen, but the chaos had intensified by the day: Parliament was still comatose; conspiracy theories, each worthy of a book, were bouncing off the walls; and everyone was shouting so much on television that every time you switched it on there were open maws staring you in the face.

Hotair—Jai's doppelganger—was in the thick of it all, delivering state-of-the-nation sermons that made Jai look like a classroom debater. In an eerie replay, the three of them had—like me, only multiplied manifold—come under the protection of the shadows. You couldn't miss the uniforms, the carbines, the men in bush shirts with hard iron tucked into their groins on television. Their protective cover, somehow, seemed more legitimate. If someone was out to get me, then these guys were up for being shot, hanged, poisoned and quartered all at once.

I felt—and Jai felt—that Kapoorsahib had come to us thanks largely to these three lunatics. These fuckers had shoved a large stick into the hornet's nest of arms purchases and stirred it like a glass of lassi. Of course everybody was going to get stung but none feared it more than the spectres, the moneyworms and the menofwater. Kapoor and the other ghosts stood to lose mountains of cash, the very ground everyone stood upon. They needed to set up more and more smokescreens so that the labyrinth of Indian legal and investigative processes took an eternity and more to arrive at their doorstep.

Jai, with his wily brahminical mind, said, 'You know when they come for him, when they try and nail him, what he's going to say? He's going to scream from the rooftops that he's being targeted because he happens to have an investment in this magazine. This magazine which in the past has annoyed powerful politicians and bureaucrats, this magazine which has taken on vested interests. And your sad fate, the fact of your killers, will be held up as an example. Kapoorsahib is going to be the victim, the man who was persecuted because he was doing the right thing, the honourable thing. The man who was upholding public interest. We will live yet, my friend, thanks to the wisdom of the crooked!'

Sara's breath was rasping in her chest and her eyes were completely dilated. I could almost smell her arousal. She hissed, 'What a dog! And you two too, what fucking dogs!' I almost sighed with relief: Ah, here comes the sun. I said, 'Madam, there is a real world out there, and most of us have to negotiate this real world. And unfortunately, the real world is run by men who have money and power.'

She said, face twisted with rage, 'You are just a dog! You would sell yourself to anyone! And that fucking friend of yours, the bearded one, he would find a rationale for it! And you would just echo it! Bloody maaderchods!'

I lunged for her, grabbed her slim wrists and plunged my face into her open sarong.

'That's right!' she screeched, struggling to free her hands. 'A fucking dog in every way! Saala kutta!' I shook my head like a dog inside her hot darkness, and she screamed and began to abuse me in English, porn film stuff. I shook it some more, my face slipping easily, and her invective turned to guttural Hindi, street-level stuff. When she began to repeat herself, I pulled my head out and unleashed a stream of such vulgarity that, in a public place it would have led to instant arrest. It made her face twist and her breath choke. She was trashing my prick in anglicized Hindi when I picked her up—so wonderfully light, so narrow in the torso, so full in the hips—and nailed her to the wall. At the precise spot I had been eyeing for the past hour.

When every syllable of abuse had become an endearment and we had reached the place where all arguments end and we were no longer on the wall but on the bed and I had no more legs left and hardly any arms and I was floating in that happy place that can only fleetingly be any man's, Sara said, 'You know their lives are actually worthier than yours.'

And their tools much longer than mine.

Contrary to our calculations, despite the abject surrender of Chutiya-Nandan-Pandey, despite our desperate genuflections, Kapoorsahib did not close the deal with any finality. In the world he came from—where spectres built hard-iron weapons and heaped mountains of cash—in that world men understood the true nature of power. They knew it didn't stem from the gracious handing out of assurances but from the breeding of uncertainty. The idea was to never let anyone, not even one's allies, not even the moneyworms and the menofwater, feel secure; the idea was to always keep a hand on the handle that flung open the trapdoor.

These men of the world understood that moral niceties, the rituals of honourable conduct, were for the feeble of heart. The men who were nice were the men who were afraid: afraid of being snubbed, afraid of not being liked, afraid of the law, afraid of others' disapproval, afraid of being alone, afraid of their reflection in the mirror. They were nice because they were afraid to be un-nice; they were nice in the desperate hope that other men would also be nice to them. But Kapoorsahib was not such a man. He was a man who was not afraid to be un-nice. He understood that the central principle of everything was neither decency nor ethics nor money nor love nor religion. It was power—and its acquiring and wielding. He understood that it was good to keep the men around you in continual fear: it made them into nice men. Afraid men. The path to power was smoothest when it ran through a forest of frightened men.

Men like Kapoor worked at growing sprawling forests of frightened men. In other countries, in Africa and Asia and South America, men were kept afraid through assault to limb and life. But this was a disappointingly free country, full of pretty ideas and retrograde policies that did not allow men to honestly sell a few weapons. Hard unsentimental guns that would guard the nation. In such a country you made men afraid by assaulting their minds, doing damage to the spongy lobes between their ears, left and right, back and front. You made them believe they did not live in a free country, you surrounded them with stories of assault. So that when they were alone, in the silver dark, they felt they were in Africa or South America, and there were shadows moving outside their walls, testing the windows, trying the doors.

As a master shadow yourself, you made them afraid of every shadow. You never took the police to them but you kept their eye on the door through which the police would soon come. You never took them to the courts but you made them aware of the spreading tentacles of the law everywhere. You never showed them the goon with his gun but you made them see the telltale bulge in every unshaven man's pants. You maimed the mind. You shrank the heart. You provided no certainty: of freedom, or of serfdom. Of death, or of life. You never said you would invest; and you never said you would not.

And that is how Kapoorsahib dangled us. He did not close the deal with Chutiya-Nandan-Pandey, baiting them continually with the absurdity of the offer, making them grovel to give away what they had started out wanting to sell. At the same time he extended us the thinnest lifeline, loaning us twenty-five lakhs, over forty-five days in five instalments, so we could hobble on for some time more. 'I know I am burning good money—but I owe too many favours to Bhargavaji!'

From that first meeting when he came to visit us in our office in his red Pajero and wide-brimmed hat, and we spoke to him as cool equals—the man of means meets the men of words—we had, in a few short weeks, reached the stage of sitting outside his offices, sometimes for hours, in search of a brief appointment.

The desperation was more Jai's than mine. I think he had delivered too many over-the-top orations to quietly fade away now. Somewhere along the way he had come to believe some of his own helium-pumped words and felt that we just had to survive, that all kinds of bullshit about democracy and freedom was tied to our sorry story.

Sometimes I watched him standing against the window with a set jaw and steely eyes and I thought, the fucker thinks he is in a film and everything will end happily before the curtain comes down. And then I watched him in Kapoorsahib's big office with its polished mahogany tables and plush leather sofas and golfing doodads everywhere, smiling ingratiatingly, making light wheedling talk, trying to discuss different kinds of golf clubs and courses, and I knew he knew that he was only a serf and would have to behave like one if he was to keep this gig alive.

I mostly kept quiet and, to tell the truth, I no longer cared a fuck who took over the magazine, whether it lived or died. It was clear by now that it was never going to make us rich, and the fame it had brought to us had been mostly dubious, fleeting, and inexplicably accompanied by some weird assassination conspiracy crap. The high of the shadows, the 9mms, the carbines, the walkie-talkies, the screeching escort car, had all thinned over the months. Even Dolly/folly's mother no longer rushed to the window when we went visiting, and the neighbours did not come knocking to discuss national affairs. All my relatives had crawled back into the holes they had leapt out of, and the media calls for random quotes and responses had fully died. The glory of the globe currently belonged to the three crazies who had stuck a javelin up the defence ministry's tight ass. All the shadows, all the security hardware, all the Z+ security and so on, were crawling over them, the media trailing them like a cloud of whining mosquitoes. Presumably their relatives were wriggling out of their holes and their mothers-in-law leaping in through the windows.

I had no time for Jai's save-the-democracy crap. I had done the story because it had fallen into my lap and because I loved the sweet rush of digging out some exciting dirt and plastering it all over the walls. What a reek is produced when the hidden dirt of pompous men is aired! It makes ordinary men's garbage seem so sweet smelling.

It happened like this. My cousin from the agriculture ministry had passed on some information, then many papers, and then some more. He was a disgruntled bastard, a cantankerous whiner whose career was unsurprisingly in abeyance. He was the perfect station for collecting dirt. The story was about a huge swindle—in subsidies, in grains. Fictitious invoices, fictitious transportation, fictitious handouts to millions of fictitious poor. Rivers of grain had flowed on paper, without a fistful exchanging hands. Ministers and bureaucrats had been colluding with fatcat traders to cream the exchequer of hundreds of crores.

We knew it was not unusual. It was how every government and department accounted for the poor. The pond was full of crocodiles, but we were only concerned with the one we had by the tail, and we were going to drag it out and string it up. We were stupid enough to not know that we had latched on to the biggest and meanest motherfucking mugger of all—the minister for agriculture—and he would take the government down with him if it came down to the line.

When we'd broken the story, making the charges, we were drowned in denials and threats of lawsuits. That was in week one. In what we thought was a smart move we had divided the story into two editions. The hard evidence, blowing holes in the denials, came in week two, leaving everyone looking really bad, marooned in their dirty underpants. In hindsight the strategy was not very wise. It's a dumb idea to leave a strong adversary—in this case, adversaries—with no escape route but to blindly hit back. When the crocodile snapped the rope it had nowhere to go but straight at us. With the second issue, the denials immediately turned into rabid countercharges. We were working at the behest of other political parties. We were on the payroll of a dubious business house. We were agents of the enemy, Pakistan. We were trying to destabilize the government, India, the whole fucking universe.

The media printed and repeated everything. They were like the man with a straight pipe for a stomach. Everything came out the asshole as it went in the mouth—unprocessed, undigested, nothing selected, nothing rejected. If required, you could have put it back into the mouth and pushed it out the asshole once more.

Unlike the internet lunatics who hung madly on to their quarry—the defence minister—through all the epic thrashings, our mean mugger flicked its tail out of our hands in no time and turned on us, its crocodile maw opening wider and wider. Who were we anyway? No one had heard of our magazine. No one had heard of me. Why had I done such a story? There had to be a sinister motive—it was only a matter of time before it was uncovered. The threats of lawsuits changed to threats to life and limb. Somewhere, hired assassins began to limber up for their next assignment.

Jai tried to keep us afloat with his orations, but words were not rupees, and here we were now, prostrate before the absurd Mr Kapoor, our magazine a twenty-four-page rag, our staff only eight strong, our trio of investors aching to slit our throats. I didn't give a twat about democracy and liberty and the glories of the Constitution but I did care about the debts we had run up. Some of Kapoorsahib's warnings of legal liabilities were true. Jai and I would not only be broke and in hock, but also likely to face criminal charges. Sharing a jail yard with Kuchha King, Kuchha Singh and Frock Raja was no solace—though the thought of seeing them there in their Calvin Klein boxers, under the gushing handpump, was a sweet one. Frock Raja, I am sure, had one with Dalmatian puppies frolicking on them.

So we went on our knees to Kapoorsahib every other day, and when he deigned to meet us, he lectured us about the journalistic carcass we were continually dragging to his door and Jai whinged about bogeys and doglegs and the hidden opportunities of media, and I sat quietly in the corner and imagined the merchant of arms naked, sneering at the beautiful woman labouring on him, telling her she needed to get herself a new vagina. This one was dead, and no one would take it, even for free. It was a physical, financial and legal liability. He was only sliding in it because of Bhargavaji—he owed him far too many favours.

It helped make him seem more farcical than sinister, and helped me feel less abject.

One stormy evening, with the wind ripping branches off neem trees and snapping power lines and the rain coming in waves of hard and harder, the house bell trilled. I was sitting in my cramped study—away from Dolly/folly, who was greedily swallowing some emotional family drama on television—and reading the part in the Mahabharata where Lord Krishna tricks the Kauravas with the illusion of sunset, allowing his favourite, Arjuna, to fulfil his dire vow and slay Jayadratha, when Felicia opened the door, flecks of water glistening on her coal-black face, and said, 'Huthyam.'

It had been a while, and it took me some time to realize what she was saying.

SI Hathi Ram stood outside the front door in a clumsy, standard army-issue rain cape, rivulets of water flowing off it, rubbing his cropped hair dry with the palm of his hand. Behind him, in the mouth of the open gate, was a white-coloured police Gypsy, its parking lights blinking in the soaked dark, with the silhouettes of four men dimly visible inside. My shadows stood at attention beside the SI, their feet hurriedly stuck into unlaced shoes. By now they had somehow managed to finish buttoning their clothes and recovering their weapons. A visiting assassin would have to wait for them to get dressed before engaging them.

With a smiling mouth and unsmiling eyes, Hathi Ram said, 'In the films, always, the bad man—the policeman—comes to meet the hero on a night like this. The wind is screaming; the rain falling in sheets; the lights have blown; every djinn and spirit has stirred from his hiding place; and then the bell rings. Ting tong. The audience's heart stops beating. It knows immediately that something dramatic is about to happen. Either the bad man will meet his deserved end, or he will trap the hero in a false case that will destroy his life.'

Wriggling out of the stiff canvas cape, he hooked it on the edge of the door where it hung stiffly, like a dripping corpse. 'You don't need to close the door,' he said, as I tried to push it shut as much as the cape would allow. 'We have enough fire-power outside to take on the Bhutanese army.'

I thought, only if it can get dressed in time.

His leather shoes squelched, and when I looked at them, he said, 'Don't mind?'

I didn't and I took him into the study, where he sat down comfortably on the chair opposite my table, and casting around, found and picked up *The Naked Lunch*. Caressing it tenderly with his fingertips, he gave me his first-ever critical appreciation. 'Naked lunch—that means nanga khana. Arre bhai, what an idea! Have you read it?'

I nodded.

He said, smiling only with his lips, 'Anything about the police in it?'

I said, only tangentially.

He said, 'You think I can read it?'

I said anyone could read anything.

He said, 'You know, sahib, that's not true. Most of us are fated to only mindlessly do. Like insects. Just do. We don't know how to think, we don't know how to read, we have no understanding of anything. We are just insects. The smallest of insects. Move our limbs, fill our stomachs; move our limbs, fill our stomachs. Day after day. And then one day we are dead. Just like that. Accidentally stepped upon, or flicked aside, or in our stupid greed we fall into a honey jar, or a bigger insect simply swallows us whole. Nobody mourns us, nobody remembers us. Insects like us are dying by the minute.'

I said, 'Hathi Ramji, have no illusions, that is true for all of us. We are all unsung birds of passage in this world.'

He suddenly held up the book and said, 'No sirji, we are both grown-up men, let us not just try and be nice to each other. The fact is, those who want to kill you are insects and those of us who guard you are insects. But you are not an insect. You are a killer of insects; you are a killer of those who kill insects. You are a man who challenges the world, shapes it, changes things. If you are an insect, you are a very big and important one.'

I thought of Dolly/folly getting wet watching some daughter-in-law scream at her mother-in-law on television. I thought of the eight people left at the magazine and Sippy swaying through the echoing rooms. I thought of Sara and me lunging and probing as we abused each other in accented Hindi. I thought of Jai and me performing a shashtang namaskar, fully prostrate in front of Kapoorsahib, whose dick pointed at us like the barrel of an AK-47. I thought of the five men, four nondescript, one a maker of brain curries, in a courtroom surrounded by a waddle of flapping penguins.

I said, 'So what happens in the film now? Is the hero trapped in a false case that destroys his life?'

The SI laughed with his mouth and said, 'Sirji, this is no film.

This is real life, and in this both the hero and the policeman are finally destroyed. And that is why I am here today, under the cloak of rain and storm. I am here not as SI Hathi Ram, but as a friend. You know we are pawns. We can only move straight, one step at a time. Someone pushes us and pushes us, till we die. But above us are bishops and knights and horses, and they can move right and left and up and down and back and front and jump over others too. There is no way of knowing what they will do. I have come to tell you that you must not trust anyone. No one. I know you are a powerful man and have friends in powerful places, but take this as the plea of a simple cop. Trust no one; nothing is what it seems.'

Trust no one? Fuck, I knew no one! The least powerful man I knew was Sippy and the most powerful was Kapoorsahib, with Jai in between. And of course Sara, who was a force of nature, beyond categorization.

The wind was howling in an almost continuous scream and sluicing through my closed window, making the bamboo chik thrash about. Right outside, in the alcove next to the entrance, sat the shadows, passing on their weapons from shift to shift, unbuttoning and buttoning their clothes, guarding a man against no one knew what.

I said, 'What happened to those five men? Did you find out anything about them?'

Just then the lights blew. In the dark Hathi Ram said, 'It's the question that did it.'

I could not remember being in such complete darkness ever. Always at night there was the seep of some light from the ventilators and windows. Now there was nothing. The storm had obliterated the skies, and the power cut had sucked out the streetlights too. Suddenly there was a rasp and the policeman's face appeared in the light of a match. In that wan light, with the rest of him missing, it came to me that he was actually an old man. His eyes were lined deep, and his jowls had begun to collect along his jawline. The skin on his neck was loose. More than hard and set, in that yellow light his eyes appeared tired and still.

I shouted, 'Felicia!' and almost instantly the door opened and she came in with a big red candle, thick as a coke bottle, its light glancing off her moist, coal-dark skin. Right behind her loomed ms fair and lovely, Dolly/folly, a vacuous white ghost, cut adrift from the squawking on the television. I refused to make any introductions, and she floated away soundlessly as ghosts do, after a perfunctory namaste. Now she would get on the phone and whisper to her mother for hours. I could never tell about what. Both were dumb and knew nothing.

The SI said, 'Very nice.'

I said, 'The men? Did you learn something from them?'

He fished out a pack of cigarettes from his trousers, held it up, and said, 'Don't mind?'

I found him a round green stone ashtray.

He said, 'I smoke less than a cigarette a month. Sometimes only one in three months. I bought this pack last year. Look at its state. I only do it when the stress gets too much. This weather—you know, this weather makes me nervous.'

He pulled on the cigarette with a theatrical flourish and followed it with an exaggerated cough. He didn't look nervous, just old. How many characters like me he must have negotiated in his long career, I thought. He thinks I am just a pup off the kennels who inadvertently landed the outsized bone.

He said, 'I should not be saying this to you, but I felt I had to. This Tuesday when I woke to go to the mandir I had a vision. I saw Hanumanji—he was carrying his mace on his shoulder, and he was so big I did not even come up to his ankles. His muscles were the size of mountains, and his tail was going through the sky. But he was smiling, and his eyes were shining with compassion and love. He said to me—his voice like a million megaphones though he was speaking softly—he said to me, "Hathi Ram, my son, you may be part of a vile and corrupt police force, but this week you will take a vow only to do good and to speak the truth, especially if you encounter anyone who is a devotee of mine." I clutched his mighty ankles, overcome, and suddenly he became as small as me. And before I knew it he had blessed me with his right hand and vanished. That day I took my wife out and bought her a saree, and I sent my sick mother and my daughter money orders of a thousand rupees each, and I bought boondi prasad for a hundred and one rupees and distributed it to my neighbours, and at the mandir I gave all the cripples a ten-rupee note each. And today, when I was sitting in my office and the orders came about the reassessment of your security, I knew immediately why Hanumanji had come to me. Tell me: is it possible that you are a devotee of Hanumanji?'

I nodded. There were probably two dozen entries in that red-cloth fold-over book recording my Tuesday evening excursions.

His face was in the dark. The candlelight was only a small pool on the table.

He said, in that flat voice of his, 'I knew it. There had to be a reason. Nothing in this world happens without a reason. The problem is, most of us never manage to find the reasons, or do so too late.'

I said, 'What did Hanumanji tell you to tell me?'

He said, 'To trust no one. Nothing is what it seems.'

I said, 'What did the men say?'

He said, 'I don't know. No one knows. They say one thing to the police, another thing to the media, and something else in court. None of it may be true.'

I said, 'What do the police say?'

He said, from beyond the pool of trembling light, 'That's even more unreliable. The police only say what someone wants them to say. They have nothing ever to say on their own.'

Just then Felicia materialized, soundlessly, from the dark, giving us both a start. Hathi Ram said, 'You should get headlights for her.' She handed out the cups of tea and set a plate of cream biscuits on the table. The policeman put away *The Naked Lunch*, stubbed out his cigarette, and picking up a biscuit opened its halves.

I said, 'But they did want to hit me?'

He said, smelling the cream, 'I hope so.' Then seeing my expression, he added, 'Sorry, that's not what I meant. I meant I hope they are not innocent.'

I said, 'So whom should I not trust?'

He said, 'Trust nobody. Believe nothing that anyone tells you. Don't go anywhere without your security. Avoid public places. Change the roads you take. Don't take the same route every day.'

I thought: Sara. The bastards probably had their eyeballs inside the chinks in her door.

I said, 'Is that all you came to tell me, Hathi Ramji?'

He said, 'I did what Hanumanji told me to do. But I had to also tell you that your security is being downgraded. They are pulling out the escort car and sentries.'

I said, 'That's good.'

He said, 'It's only good if it is good.'

Suddenly from the dark depths of the house came the sound of Dolly/folly singing a crap number from a recent Hindi film. She was desperately trying to pull registers out of her atonal voice. It was awful. Why wasn't she on the phone to her mad mother? Was she stupid enough to think no one could hear her because it was dark?

Hathi Ram said, 'The good wife? Good singer.'

I screamed, 'Felicia!'

Almost instantly, she emerged from the dark, spooking us again. Hathi Ram said, 'Big headlights, boss.' I looked at her and opened and shut the fingers of my right hand, and pointed a thumb in the direction of the bedroom. She disappeared in a blink. Hathi Ram said, 'Also tail lights.' An irate door slammed shut. The song died.

I said, 'If the risk is down, why should I be more careful?'

He said, 'I didn't say the risk is down. I said they've ordered a scale-down of your security. This is the time to be more careful.'

I said, 'What is it about the men that you are not telling me?'

He said, 'I don't even know if the men are who they are. Maybe your friend knows. The one who's always meeting the lawyers and going to the jail. Nice girl. Smart girl. Very smart girl. You must ask her to be careful too. This is a third-rate city. I would never live here if I had an option. Its surface is gold, its heart is grime. Every lamb in this city is a wolf; every flower is a bomb. And I would never take that forest road to Vasant Kunj at night. It turns and twists too much, and never ever can you tell what is coming from the other side.'

My mouth was tight and there was ice in my heart.

Banging the biscuit, he said, 'One of them it seems is a kung fu master and he can also sing a snake out of the deepest hole.'

The next evening when I went to the Saket sports club for my jog I found myself taking the long route across the IIT flyover. At the traffic light I stopped at some distance from the next car, and looked carefully at the cars parked around me. There was a fat woman and a child at the back of a Honda City and I glared at them so hard that the woman pulled her boy's eyes away from mine. The shadow in the back seat was dozing, and the one next to me was trying to make sense of the new mobile phone he had just bought. It was fluorescent blue with a glitzy keypad. If someone shot me now he would be able to quickly dial the mortuary. And then wake up the guy at the back.

Dusk was falling as I began to run. The cricketers at the nets in the club were packing away their equipment into their heavy kit-bags. Only a handful of very young boys slogged on. One smooth-faced Sikh boy, dancing forward on quick feet, was determined to put away two spinners in the failing light. He found the ball with the muscle of his bat each time—the voluptuous thwack cutting through the cawing and screeching of birds settling down for the night in the trees lining the jogging track. In another country the boy would have been earmarked for fame. But India was overflowing with such cricketing passion and talent. To go beyond the college and club stage, he would need luck, money, godfathers, and very cunning footwork that had nothing to do with cricket. As Huthyam would say, nothing in India is what it seems. As I jogged, and the light died, and the young boys too began to put away their gear, I felt a sudden inexplicable fear.

In the equestrian enclosure the last horses were being taken in by the syce, amid jangling harnesses and relieved snorting. The yelps of the rich kids, brought there by their fair, painted-up mothers or by dark, tired domestics to play out their horse-horse fantasies, had finally faded. By the time I was on my fourth round, only the tart smell of the animals remained, and the field held nothing but the surreal open embrace of the cricket net. The moon was fat enough to put a silvery light on the trees, making the trunks and leaves move. I looked around me as I ran, twisting my head to see if anyone was behind me. The wall along the big gutter was easy to scale. Swing off a branch, squeeze the trigger once, twice, twenty times, then grab the branch, clear the wall again, run stealthily along the gutter, in the undergrowth and rushes, out onto the road, walk briskly to the buzzing multiplex, catch a nice new film, with popcorn and Pepsi—in a jumbo combo—and perhaps a long hot dog with a pale pink sausage at its soft heart.

The shadows were sitting by the floodlit basketball court, where I always insisted they wait, watching the hectic half-court games that mostly ended in arguments and disputes. The young boys watched NBA games on cable television and were shod in Nike shoes and baggy shorts and bright piped vests. They were full of quick feints, loud abuse, and aggressive elbows. Some were accompanied by ripening girls who sat on the sides, taunting them for their fumbles. Later, they all huddled in a corner and shared cigarettes. Some knew of me and called me uncle. I wanted to slap their smug, confident faces. These were kids for whom India was just a vast amusement park, set up by some earnest geezers after kicking out some white men. They all needed a fucking crash course in the Vedanta and a stint in the army. Three months in Siachen, and six months in Imphal. Then they would gain perspective on the fadeaway jumper.

But right now I was wishing I had asked the shadows to accompany me to the centre of the field today, where standing back to back, cradling their cold hardware, they could have followed the entire track with their eyes.

I found myself running faster and faster, and soon galloping in a kind of panic.

Hanumanji had told Huthyam something.

And there was a kung fu master who sang snakes out of deep holes.

It was time to give Guruji a call. It was time to get a discourse from Sara.

10

KAALIYA AND CHINI

i

The Glue of Happiness

When the beautiful vapours filled their beings, they all heard different things.

Kaaliya heard the mesmeric whine of the pungi beckoning every serpent in existence to appear, dancing to its tune.

Chhotu heard his mother's voice singing a lullaby as she gently applied turmeric paste on the welts his father had just given him with his police belt.

Makhi Khan heard the reassuring sound of the mullah's call from the mosque near his childhood home before the riots began.

Tarjan heard the haunting Bhojpuri songs his skeletal father used to sing as he beat out a slow rhythm on an empty ghee tin outside their hut.

Gudiya heard the tinkling sound of the bells that hung around their sad-eyed cow's loose neck.

Chini heard the sweet music of rain on a thatch roof amid wet green trees at the end of a world he could never again find.

And Dhaka, macho Dhaka, with a grip of steel and hard-tipped army boots, heard the mocking words of Gabbar Singh. 'Jo darr gaya so marr gaya.' To be afraid is to be dead.

It was the divine gift of the solution. To give to you whatever you most craved. The boys knew that in the teeming world outside—the world of clean pants and shirts, and cars and houses, and gleaming shops filled with sweet-smelling women, and air-conditioned cinema halls with screens bigger than walls, and eating places where men wore uniforms to bring you hot intoxicating food, where policemen were smaller than politicians, where children spoke in singsong voices all day in school and were forced to drink tall glasses of spotless white milk—the boys knew that in that teeming world outside, the true virtues of the solution had not yet been discovered.

Out there, the boys had been told, it was used for other things. For prosaic stuff like erasure and correction, wiping out what had been written on a paper, blanking out one's mistakes, killing the error. These boys had no paper, and nothing to write, and nothing to write with, and even if they had all three, they did not have fingers that knew how to curl around the profound certitude of the written word.

But they knew the secret, the truth of the solution. It was meant for blanking out and erasure. It was meant to clean the dark blemishes in the mind. To blanket the ache of memory, correct the wring of emotion. It was meant to wipe out not just a sheet of paper, but the entire world. Everything. All the noise, all the stink, all the iron, all the piss, all the shit, all the policemen, all the rancid food, all the rags, all the scabs, all the offal, the offal, the offal. Everything. Everything, except the sound of rain singing on a thatch roof. Except the juicy green mountain slopes that came from the films but belonged to Chini's mind. Except the heroines whose eyes were full of kindness and whose mouths full of promise and whose skins glowed like the radiance of god.

Salushan Baba, the old man who came to the no man's land beyond platform six every evening, bringing them the magic potion, never said a word. No sales pitch, no hustling, no small talk. Selling water in the desert doesn't call for promotions. The thin hair on his head, with strips of scalp showing through, was pulled back and tied in a tight knot, but his beard flowed like water down to his chest in three shades of grey, dark like the rail tracks, lighter like gravel, and then dirty white like the newspapers. The beard was his obvious vanity, and he kept it oiled and washed, each strand gleaming, the breeze picking and running through it. Sitting on his haunches, the baba stroked it slowly with his left hand, smoking a beedi with his right, while his young clientele milled around, handing over soiled coins and notes and picking up a pair of bottles each.

The boys picked their wares from the baba's open-mouthed cloth bag and put the money down at his feet. He glanced down to check what each was putting, and when it was not enough he caught the boy's eye and logged in the debt. Nobody cheated the baba. This was a life transaction. You did not haggle at the door of the intensive care unit. And if you intended to come back to the life-giving threshold every day, then you played level and kept your accounts squared.

The first time a bewildered and fearful Chini had been taken to the end of platform six and beyond, the old man squatting on his haunches, stroking that hoary beard, had looked at him and then looked at Dhaka. The coal-dark, wiry boy with hard round biceps like cricket balls, had placed his index fingers at the ends of both his eyes and pulled them back into slits. 'Chini.' From China. 'Came off the Guwahati Express a few days ago.'

The baba put his rough hand on Chini's smooth cheek and gently patted it. Then he softly traced the little narrow eyes, the snub nose and the thin mouth with his fingertips. His gaze was steady but kind. Little Chini's panic ebbed. In a low hoarse voice the baba said, 'Cheen. Very very far away. It rains there all the time?' The boy nodded. The baba said, 'The king cobra there is longer than a train?' Dhaka, standing with his hands on his waist, said, 'Yes, and it can kill a man in ten minutes.' The baba said, 'There is a big animal there called the rhino and it can stop a speeding train?' Dhaka said, 'And if you fire bullets at it, they bounce back and kill you.' The baba said,

'The men there eat men?' Dhaka said, 'And collect their heads like toys.'

The baba reached into his open-mouthed bag and taking out a pair of small bottles put them in the little boy's hands. 'When you miss home too acutely, smell this, it will take you home. Ask Dhaka. Tell us, Dhaka, how often do you go to your Bangla home?' Dhaka, still standing, legs akimbo, his tight blue jeans streaked with many shades of grime, said, 'Every single day. Sometimes more than once in a day.'

The baba took Chini's little right hand and put it on his flowing beard. 'Go on, stroke it. Feels good, doesn't it?' It did. Long and silken. As the boy swam his fingers in the reassuring hair, the baba said, 'And when you don't want to go home, you can visit the gods. Go to Lord Shiva on Mount Kailasa and ask him for whatever you wish. But don't forget to tell him that the baba is his greatest devotee!'

That day, along with the magic potion, the baba also gave him a neatly folded ten-rupee note. 'On this first visit all of baba's prasad is free. But after this, when you come for baba's blessings, you will have to bring him your offerings. After all, the baba is old, and you are all young.'

The meeting with baba was one of the clearest memories Chini retained of his first few weeks in Delhi. The rest was a fog of tears and anxiety. He remembered he had not wept on the train, but when all the friendly men and women whose children he had played with, who had fed him their puris and bought him tea, suddenly picked up their trunks and holdalls and disembarked, and in one shrill spasm the big carriage that had been a warm chattering home for three days was completely emptied, he had begun to sob. All around him lay the silent debris of cracked tea kullads, stitched-leaf plates and rough napkins, biscuit and namkeen wrappers, newspaper scraps in different languages, plastic water bottles, and endless bits of discarded food—chapattis, bread, rice, subzi, banana peels, apple cores, flecks of chewed sugarcane. In contrast, outside the iron-barred window was pure swirling chaos. People without number were rushing around calling, asking, demanding. More people than the little boy had seen in all his life, more people than he could have imagined existed in the world.

At one point he spied the army man who had first taken him under his wing, given him a corner of his berth, a small yellow banana and the spread of his black blanket, thereby encouraging the kindness of others. The tightly shaven man with a pencil moustache had his green holdall on his right shoulder and a black iron trunk in his right hand. The boy called out, Uncle! Uncle! But his voice was weak, the noise was great, and the man was moving away, drowning in the vast crowd in a matter of seconds. He looked around desperately for any other familiar faces from the journey. The fat woman in a saree who had given him so many puris; the old man who had asked him about his parents; the young girl who had kept pinching his cheeks. But in that heaving mob he could spot no one.

Then terror filled his being when he saw, for the second time in fifteen minutes, a great multitude of people simply vanish as if suctioned out by a giant pipe. As he peered through the iron bars, the shouting screaming mob with all their luggage and children was suddenly gone. In the vast cemented patch from end to end that his eye could see, all that remained were a few static people, frozen behind food carts or vending kiosks. But then he focused a little farther away and he could see a line of tracks and another platform—which was run over by people—and beyond that another train, and when that suddenly moved, he saw another line of tracks and another platform, again run over by people. The place seemed to be packed with platform after platform, train upon train, a countless people in constant motion.

Hugging his knees, he closed his eyes and began to cry. Through his sobs he called out to his uncle who, three days ago, had sat him down in this very train before stepping off to get them something to eat. He was sure if he cried long enough his uncle would stop playing this game and come back and be sorry for having caused his nephew so much torment. Sure enough, soon there was the sound of footfalls, he heard his uncle coming closer and closer. He kept his eyes shut till the very last moment, wanting his uncle to suffer, to see the grief he had wrought. But when he opened his tear-washed eyes and looked up, he saw a face so black and scary and so close to his that he screamed aloud and flung himself back.

Kaaliya and his friends were used to such reactions. One of their favourite pastimes was terrifying the rich fair kids in the first-class compartments and watching them shout and shriek. The boys had a way of baring their teeth and popping their eyes that made them seem even more horrifying than they already were. At one time, for a few weeks, Kaaliya had got hold of a Domukhi snake, the harmless two-headed kind—ostensibly with a head at each end—and carried it inside his torn shirt, triggering panic and pandemonium inside the carriages and on the platform. Sometimes the passengers fled in terror, leaving behind whatever they were eating or drinking, which the boys then swiftly purloined. The lot of them had never laughed so hard, and often they were on the floor with a stitch in their sides and tears running down their cheeks. One time Kaaliya let the plump sleepy reptile slither out of his short pants as he squatted begging for a few rupees. The auntyji, clad in a tight salwar-kameez with dangling gold earrings, dismissive till that moment, screamed in such fury that a crowd began to gather and the boys had to make a run for it. In the night, Makhi Khan—so fair, so pretty, with not even a trace of down on his upper lip at eleven years—did an impersonation of the woman with pelvic thrusts that had the boys screeching in amusement.

It was Kaaliya—dark as night, skin shining like glass, a stud glinting in his left ear—who took the weeping boy home that evening, to be assessed by their chieftain. Kaaliya, Chhotu, Makhi Khan, Gudiya, Tarjan, all stood around while Dhaka, squatting at the entrance of their house, pulling on an unfiltered cigarette, took stock with slow scanning eyes.

Around Dhaka's stringy neck hung an assortment of beads and pendants—an ivory piece shaped like a claw, a rudraksha mala, a silver chain, a couple of necklaces of coloured seeds. They were all of varying lengths and filled the wide open vee of his big-collared shirt. On his wrists he wore red-and-blue wrist bands of the kind used by racquet players and basketballers. Whenever his cigarette was in his mouth, his hands repeatedly ripped and stuck the Velcro of the bands with a satisfying chirring sound. On his left upper arm, under his short-sleeved shirt, could be glimpsed an aluminium tabeez, tightly worn on a black string. There was faint stubble on the boy's darker-than-Kaaliya skin and it was tough to tell his age—anything between sixteen and twenty-six. The body was thin but muscled; the eyes full of experience and pose. His jeans were tight on his matchstick legs, and as he squatted they rode up over his ankles to reveal black leather boots with a glint of iron at the toes. The blue jeans were grimy like the shirt but the army boots had the gleam of a fresh rub. Washing clothes was an undertaking; getting the shoeshine boys to spruce up his leather every day was easy.

The weeping boy from the train had run dry of tears by now, but the fear inside him intensified as he looked at the squatting man-boy assessing him with menacing eyes. He noticed that none of the others who had accompanied him here was saying a word. Where in heavens had his uncle gone? His uncle whom he loved so much? His uncle who had come one night and taken him away when his mother did not return at the end of the day. His uncle who had said he would take care of him always. Maybe this squatting man knew about these things. Maybe he would know where his uncle was.

The man-boy got to the end of his cigarette, and lifting the tip of his right foot and placing the stub under it, killed its burn with a deliberate twist. Then in a mocking voice he said, 'Who found him?' Kaaliya raised his hand. 'What will you bring in next, chutiya? A hubshi from Africa!' Everyone tittered, including Kaaliya.

Looking at the little boy, the squatting leader said, 'Do you know your name, son?' The boy's narrow eyes pooled with tears. Kaaliya leaned into him and said with gestures, 'Naam? Name? My name is Kaaliya. Kaaliya the snakeman. What's yours?' In a barely audible voice the boy said, 'Lhungdim.' The squatting leader said, 'Aladdin!' Then turning to Kaaliya, he spat, 'And I suppose the djinns are also on their way!' Everyone tittered.

The little boy said again, softly, 'Lhungdim.'

Standing up now, the leader stretched and clicked his heels together. Then, putting out both hands, he slowly traced the little boy's slit eyes, his pug nose, and his small thin mouth with his forefingers. 'Listen Aladdin, from this day on your name is Chini. Get it, Chini! Because that's what you are, a Chini! Kaaliya will take you now to the waiting room and show you the mirror. And when you look into it, you will see who you are: a Chini! Just like Kaaliya is a kallu! What do you say, Kaaliya? Calling yourself Aladdin doesn't mean you become an Arabi sheikh, otherwise Kaaliya would call himself Victoria No 203 and become an angrez. The world is full of chutiyas who give themselves grand names imagining that this will make them grand, not realizing that we are only what our skin is and what our stupid faces are!'

The little boy's throat was a big lump. Throwing his head back, the leader now glanced to his left and said, 'Arre o Kaaliya, what is my name?' Kaaliya said, 'Dhaka, boss.' The leader said, 'Dhaka! Did you hear him? My name is Dhaka because my maaderchod father fucked my mother in Dhaka, and then threw her and me out into this country! And all my life since then, every day for the last twelve years, I have lived here, right here, but I am still Dhaka! Not Paha-rganj, not Delhi, not India, but Dhaka! It's our skin and our stupid faces! Nothing can change them! No names, no addresses! So just forget about all these wild fantasies of Aladdin and his magic lamp! You are a Chini! You were born a Chini and you will die a Chini! Think of it this way, I am from under the armpit of this chutiya country, you at least came from on top of its head!'

The boy looked on with uncomprehending, terrified eyes.

The leader said, 'What? You don't know any Hindi? Of course you wouldn't! You are a behanchod Chini! But don't worry, we'll teach you Hindi in no time. We'll teach you many things that no one in China knows anything about. You are going to be okay, little boy, so stop crying. And thank your bloody gods that you are from China and not from London, otherwise we would have called you Lund, and then you would have known what real trouble is!'

Everyone laughed, and Kaaliya clutched the crotch of his dirty short pants and sang, 'Naam nahin to kaam nahin. Lund nahin to thand nahin.'

The name is the game. The dick, the picnic.

For several months Dhaka did not lay a finger on the little boy. His troops were instructed to break him in, to take care of his needs, and to equip him with enough Hindi to work the carriages. He knew from experience that new entrants needed some time to claw out of the deep hole their minds and memories were trapped in. Blinded inside their own dark hole of grief and memory, they were incapable of even understanding self-interest. They could easily hurt themselves. Once they had crawled out, once they could again see the light and feel the air, once they had again tasted pleasure and laughter, then they were animals who could be trained, who could calculate the equations of profit and loss, of reward and punishment, who could be full members of the tribe, to do what needed to be done and be done to, in the ways that they were needed to be done.

Dhaka did not think this Chini boy, even though he had no Hindi and had such soft fair skin, would take unusually long to arrive at the point of existential equilibrium where there is no future and no past, just the moment and the day, the immediate exertion and the immediate fruit. In those first weeks the only thing Dhaka did himself was to take the Chini to the no man's zone beyond platform six to introduce him to the baba whose solutions, each night, collapsed the future and the past into a magical present. In the leader's experience the crucial thing was that the boy seemed no more than six or seven—the smaller the memory bank the sooner the animal learnt to celebrate the virtues of the immediate.

The only anxiety was that he might be purloined. A fine delicacy had been delivered to his doorstep; Dhaka did not want to wage war to retain it. Instructions were spelled out. Chini was never to be left alone. Not while eating, crapping, sleeping. He was not to be put to work yet. His tears were to be swiftly dried, his smile reclaimed and pasted back. He was to be kept out of sight of the Bihari gang from near the shunting yards, and not brought to the notice of the beat constables. As for the madamji who came from the hospice, her saree tucked hard into her waist, to suck children out into their centre—not a word was to reach her ears about this fair new flower that had bloomed in this squalor. His primary keeper was to be Kaaliya, who had first found him, and who was fully capable of managing him. Kaaliya was to guard him and cosset him, give him the best morsels, the occasional bottle of cola, the softer bed.

Kaaliya was a dodger and a scrapper, to the task born. Like the snakes his forefathers had mastered for generations, he could wriggle and he could strike. His first conscious memory, from the time he was three, was the feel of a rat snake slithering through his hands. For the toddler, shaking a serpent by its head was like waving a rattle. It was the way of his people, to let the harmless ones flow through their huts and tents, their clothes and bedding, their pots and pans, their sons and daughters. In winter, many of their folk slept with their snakes in their patchwork quilts, their fat fullness as reassuring as a mother's touch. The more lethal ones were kept apart, in a corner, in wicker baskets, lightly weighted down.

Before he learnt to walk, Kaaliya knew that in these baskets slept the reigning deity of their lives—the flared black one whose mesmeric swaying sustained his people and their wanderings. The world was full of serpents, but there was only one that was god, only one that had an equal measure of beauty, grace, rhythm and venom. No roadside trickster's sleight-of-hand, no prestidigitator's cheap illusions, no gambolling acrobat's twists of limb could match the magic of Lord Shiva's favourite as it rose to its striking stance and began to slowly sway, its sinuous head flared, its forked tongue darting. No sight in nature, no thunder, no cloudburst, no lightning, no storm, no gale, no hail, no flood, no fury, could stun the heart and fire the imagination like the dance of the divine killer. Loved by the gods, dreaded by men, for more than a thousand years, the dark dancing one had kept his nomadic people alive, travelling with them in their woven baskets, garnering for them food and sustenance, lending to them its own fearsome and celestial aura. Every hut in the cluster had its own embodiment of this deity, and each family treated it with reverence and care. For the deity gave, but could also take away.

Naag. Cobra. The very sound of its name stilled the heart and fired the mind.

Kaaliya knew his own name was a reminder of the power and magic of the black one. In high winter its basket slept under the patchwork quilt of his parents; and it was the one basket that always travelled with his father and uncles when they stepped outside the house. There were other coiled killers in the baskets, like the jack-in-the-box jalebia, darting to strike, its viper's sac heavy with death, but none of them were gifted with either majesty or myth. On the road they were a quick preamble before the pungi began to sing and the real show of the black lord commenced.

In the far corner, most often in the sun, there lay the muscular weight of the dozing python. This one was a bad deal: back-breaking to carry, incapable of turning a trick, with an appetite for chickens that was bankrupting, and impossible to hide or make a run with if a khaki or moral policeman suddenly appeared. Its size had an initial gasp-value but in no time at all the beast's sluggishness and lack of malice leached it of all excitement. Many huts, in fact, no longer kept the big one.

Times had changed and the followers of the timeless Baba Gorakhnath had fallen foul of democracy and modernity. New leaders, new laws, new fads had decreed that animals were more important than men, and that men who studied in colleges and wore pants and shirts and shoes knew more about being kind to animals than the men whose very lives and genes were entwined with the beasts. Had one of the men who pronounced these fiats ever slept with a serpent in their bed? Had one of them ever sliced strips of meat and lovingly fed them down a reptile's gullet? Had one of them ever changed the soiled clothes in their baskets, and bought them chicks and eggs with scarce money? Had one of them ever wandered the world with no one else as kinsman—no wife, no child, no parent—but the coiled one?

As they travelled through the burning plains of Gujarat and Rajasthan, the waving green fields of Punjab and Haryana, the badlands of Uttar Pradesh and Bihar, in search of a new town and clientele, seeking a vacant lot and an ancient tree under which to set up their tortoise-like tents of bamboo sticks and tarpaulin, little Kaaliya became aware of the cursed life that was their lot. This large, wide world had no place for them, and wherever they went—Kaaliya riding on the back of the donkey, the cow, his uncles, older siblings—they were unwelcome. Everywhere there was a landlord or a policeman to shoo them away, everywhere he saw his father and uncles beg and plead for a stretch of field where they could set up camp.

At such a time they were not the proud charmers of the dreaded black one, dressed in their resplendent saffron tehmat-kurtas, their regal turbans flashing their tails, their smooth voluptuous pungis issuing a music that identified them as unique in the universe; at such a time they were abject men, in soiled sweaty clothing, itinerant beggars, squatting on their haunches, their hands folded in supplication, asking for a temporary patch of the earth that no one was any more willing to give.

In the evenings, while the women and children and whippets idled about the wood fires and tortoise tents, the men smoked ganja and charas, drank any kind of alcohol they could lay their hands on, and talked up stirring stories of their past.

The story that never wore thin, the story a listener never forgot, was about the thirty-foot king cobra they had tracked thirty-five years ago in the dense jungles of Assam, ten of them for forty days, walking in tandem, working in tandem, pursuing a beast that had terrified entire villages and even felled wild elephants with the lash of its venom. It was said the very sight of the monster transfixed grown men and turned their bowels to water. This monarch of all snakes killed by rearing up to more than six feet—its swaying hood the size of four handspans, its forked tongue shredding the air at blistering speed—and striking between the eyes. It was said that most men were dead before their bodies hit the ground. Those who escaped the bite fell into a state of delirium for weeks, convulsed by the memory of the giant reptile. Every attempt to capture it had floundered. Hunting squads by the villagers, a contingent of the local police, rangers from the far-off rhino sanctuary, and even a platoon requisitioned from the army. Though gigantic, the beast moved like the wind, a blur of black, and it was gone.

On several occasions a volley of firing had convinced the trackers that they had their quarry, but it was as if its shining skin were armour and bullets glanced off it. And then some days later it was there again on a forest path, and a fresh body to be carried out. It was said the bodies were blue like deep water by the time they were brought back to the village. Finally word was sent to the great charmers of the north, and ten of them set forth, travelling by train and bus and jeep and cart for weeks. Kaaliya's father was the youngest, a mere sixteen, under instructions to always follow the lead. The oldest, over sixty, was a man they called Guru Bijli Nath. He had been given the moniker Bijli, lightning, before he was ten. It was said he was the greatest snake-catcher of his age. Small and sinewy, he was quick as lightning and as blinding. No serpent could escape his hands, and he had a hypnotic gaze that immobilized any snake that looked at him. One walk in the forest after the rains and he would come back with a sackful of serpents that he emptied out in the middle of the settlement, allowing everyone to take their pick. By the time he was thirty he had travelled far and wide—Burma, Borneo, Afghanistan, Iran, Ceylon, Indonesia, Japan—and been christened Guru. If there was anyone who could stop this black demon, this king of serpents, it was Guru Bijli Nath.

But as the nine men who witnessed it that day, in the deep forest slopes of Assam, in the small clearing under a canopy of leaves that barely let in any light, as the men recalled for the rest of their lives, for a long moment they all felt that the great Guru Bijli had finally met his match. In the dying light of evening, with their hurricane lanterns moving the shadows, with every looping creeper around them looking like one more stalking serpent, the black king rose to its striking height, more than six feet off the ground, towering over the magical snakeman. The peerless Guru Bijli was still as a stone, his unblinking eyes watching the great flaring head sway. Never in his long life had he seen a beast so ferocious, so evil—no big cat, no wild boar, no rhino nor wild elephant. He had tutored his squad to refrain from making a single movement once the stand-off commenced. It was a needless instruction—the life had drained out of each of the nine charmers. Kaaliya's young father was so without breath or heart that he was happy to die. He had no doubt the black king would dispatch them all after he had finished with the guru.

For a long time everyone remained frozen in that tableau, the only moving thing the swaying hood and darting tongue of the giant serpent. Not a sound of insect or bird broke the spell. And then in a flash—in a sequence so fast that none could fully follow it—the beast struck with its fearsome head, but Guru Bijli was no longer there. He was on the serpent's back, both his hands locked around the beast's thrashing neck. The great black one now began to hiss louder than a steam engine and in an instant had dragged the world's greatest snake-catcher to the ground, and was rolling him around and into his coils. Guru Bijli knew this was perhaps his last fight; he knew if one finger slacked from around the demon's throat, he was dead. Dead before it withdrew its fangs from his skin. This serpent was a poison factory—beyond the pale of every herb and potion. For the first and last time in his snake-catching life, Guru Bijli screamed for help. 'Save me, you fucking wastrels! Grab its tail! This is not a snake, you idiots, this is the messenger of the lord of death!' The panic in his voice—never heard before—galvanized the transfixed charmers. In a trice the nine of them were astride fifteen feet of thrashing, whipping muscle and struggling to stretch it out. With the guru screaming instructions—from a long way off, locked around the head of the heaving beast—two of the charmers shimmied up the closest tree, and slowly, with straining sinews, the rest of them began to feed the beast's tail to them. Soon four of them were strung out along the high branches, pinning down the lashing body by sitting on it. The black king was now in a place he had never been before, strung upside down, his body trapped at many places. Kaaliya's young father, who was up in the tree, struggling with strong thighs and hands to quell the thick muscle moving under him, and looking down at the apocalyptic scene beneath, said he knew even then that if he lived for two hundred years he would never see a spectacle so awesome. In that small clearing, in the flickering light of the lanterns, the great serpent and the little master fought a primal duel, locked head-to-head, fangs bared. Man and beast, skill and fury, death and life, without flintlocks or swords, magic or tricks. The charmers said it was if they were watching the child Lord Krishna battle the hydra-headed sea serpent Kaaliya. Like the villagers on the shore they knew the child-god must prevail but the scale of the tumult filled them with apprehension. Now only the great head of the scourge was near the ground, its black body a thick line going straight up into the trees. With the guru shouting encouragement, one of the trembling charmers knotted a twine around the neck of the serpent, leaving only a finger's slack. And then using only his two thumbs, millimetre by millimetre, the guru pushed the noose over the beast's brow and eyes, trapping the hood, clamping the fangs. When the snakeman leapt off its back—more battered than he had been in his entire life—the black king reared up with such menace that the charmers on the tree almost fell off with fright, while those on the ground almost fled into the forest. The guru's ringing shout restored sanity, and brandishing their forked sticks two of the charmers corralled the thrashing neck of the serpent while three others held wide open the large tarpaulin sack they had borrowed from the army; and with the guru screaming abuse and instruction, the head of the beast was pushed deep into the sack and held there with forked sticks, and in mere minutes, coil on coil, all of the great black king was nestled in its confines.

Kaaliya's father said no one spoke for the next one hour. They just sat in that forest enclosure, in the dancing shadows created by the lanterns, exhausted in limb, and tormented in the mind. They—ten of them—had subdued one of the great miracles of the world. In their bones they knew this magnificent creature, beloved of Lord Shiva, would not survive the custody of men. The greatest snake-catcher of the age, lying flat on his back, his eyes closed, said, 'This is it. There are no more snakes for me to catch in this lifetime.'

The presentiment of the men was well founded. On the fifth day of its capture and display, amid the rejoicing and curiosity of the villagers, in the dead of night, as the charmers slept high on hooch, vengeful men wielding heavy iron daos chopped the black king into a hundred pieces. The great head was put on a bamboo spike planted into the ground, and before the sun was fully up the hundred pieces were snatched away by the villagers as memorabilia.

Full of wrath, the guru said, 'I should have died and this king of snakes lived. These people deserved his terror.' Kaaliya's father said that true to his word the guru, though he lived fifteen years more, never snared another snake. But he talked often of the black king. He would say, 'In those burning eyes I saw everything—power and poison, divinity and death, magic and menace. We made a grave blunder. That was the greatest serpent in the world, and we captured and killed it. Ten cunning men against one magnificent serpent. Having seen it, we should have turned around and left—left the king alone to rule its forest world.'

There were other stories Kaaliya remembered, older, ancient, secondhand. A hundred and twenty years ago, near Agra, there was a charmer, Siva Jogi, whose knowledge of the anti-venom herbs was so complete that he could actually bring back to life the poisoned dead. The only condition was that the victim be brought to him within twenty-four hours of being bitten to death. He had a way of applying his mouth to the wound and sucking out all the venom from the blood in one long, uninterrupted breath. No disciple could master both—the knowledge of the herbs and the technique of siphoning out the settled poison without killing oneself. The art of reviving the poisoned dead was lost after Siva Jogi. Under the moonless sky, light with ganja and alcohol, the charmers also waxed on about the great patrons of yore—benign zamindars and bejewelled kings—who had given them and their serpents adequate land

and produce, and the dignity befitting an artist. A time when the charmers lived in plenty and were hailed wherever they appeared.

In a soft, deeply tired voice, Kaaliya's mother told her six children, of whom he was the youngest, that all this talk was balderdash. There were no benign zamindars, and there was no halcyon past. The king cobra was a fantasy, and Siva Jogi a myth. Their lives had always been rough, driven as they were from place to place, never more than a week's supply of grain in their sacks. And so it had been for her parents, and their parents. But she admitted it had never been so brutally tough. She said men had now gone to the moon, and these days there was a cinema set in every house. The fanged one no longer aroused awe or curiosity. The few rupees, the few fists of flour that still came their way bore the stamp of casual pity.

She knew that sometimes her man and his cousins had to sing the pungi for more than fifteen minutes before anyone above the age of eight would break step and care to linger. She knew that her man and his mates, several times a day, retreated under a tree to fill their heads with ganja so they could deal with the humiliation of being artists who had no takers. And that was not all. Not only were they artists facing rejection but they were also criminals now. Their work was outlawed, and it was not just the policemen they had to worry about. The real scourge was a new breed of fannekhans who came from the big cities of Delhi and Bombay and claimed to know what was best for their serpents and demanded that the local khakis enforce the law: take away their coiled beauties and threaten them with arrest. Some of these fannekhans—often young men and women, talking a broken Hindi—were also solicitous, promising that they had come to usher the charmers into a new way of life, that there would soon be other jobs waiting for them. Kaaliya's mother hissed like her snakes, 'Jobs! Yes, of course, my illiterate lord is now going to be put into a pant and a suit, and will sit in an office and sign papers!'

There was some money to be made as medicine men. Some

of them—the few sharp talkers—were dishing out herbs and potions in the small towns, mostly for aches and pains and boils and ulcers and impotence and virility and barrenness. The trick had a six-to-eight-week play. Three to four weeks in one spot to establish an air of permanence and reliability. Ideally under an old tree, at the crossroads of inner lanes, clad in full saffron and turban, an array of dusty jars spread on a piece of matting, a small iron pestle for customizing the treatment, and a few pictures of different gods to reassure every kind of follower. Some of the more desperate ones even displayed a monitor lizard pickled in oil. Sold in little bottles or tiny plastic vials, the yellowy lubricant when applied to the rubber of penis produced the iron of phallus. Like all cures it took time, like all cures it was mostly in the head. The medicine men did not stay around long enough to verify the results. The world was full of grief and there were other sufferers waiting. Three to four weeks to create familiarity; three to four weeks to milk the miserable; and then they were gone.

Every now and then there was some money to be made from panicked residents who had been visited by a harmless snake. Like the medicine men, they had to then embark on a charade, to multiply the fear, awe, relief. Kaaliya's father and his uncles had the acting abilities of a tree. They could blow the pungi to an aching sweetness; they could make the dark lord rise from the basket and sway to their rhythm; they could trap any snake from any hole in the forest with patience and quicksilver hands; they could snip fangs of poison and suture the venom sacs; and they could walk and walk and walk to the edge of the earth and beyond. But they lacked the talent to become conmen. They made a hash of pretending a rat snake was a lethal viper or a sand boa a python in the making.

There was one other way to earn a living, but it was absurdly sporadic. The rustic gujjars loved the haunting sound of the pungi, and invited the snakemen to play it at their weddings and festivities. It meant squatting in full regalia for hours and hours and blowing and blowing till their lungs were empty and their aching cheeks the size of apples. But later there was always good food to eat and enough alcohol available to stun yourself. Some of the gujjars did not mind the snakemen bringing their waifs along, though others could be insulting.

Kaaliya had done the rounds before he was six and suffered many wounds and diminishments. He had walked the inner lanes of dusty little towns whose names he was too young to know and seen his father and uncles toil and grovel—blowing, beseeching, squatting on the roadside like beggars—to collect a few coins and wrinkled rupee-notes. Their only succour seemed to be hashish; their only vent thrashing Kaaliya and the other small boys.

Kaaliya always saw his father either abject or angry. There was never enough to eat, and when any of his children fell ill, the father just looked the other way, doing nothing, waiting for them to heal or die. By the time Kaaliya was six he had lost a brother and a sister, one younger, the other older, to fevers that none of the herbs and potions could break. He had watched his father expressionlessly flow his dead siblings down the river, and then come home and embark on an orgy of intoxication.

His mother was no solace. She was exhausted beyond emotion. Apart from everything to do with the tortoise-shell homes, she went out for hours every day into alien fields to harness grass for their mule and cow—the two could not be let out to find their own food because they were their only valuable possessions. Sometimes she also managed to steal a few carrots or turnips or potatoes or gourds from the nearby field. And sometimes the odd fruit—a few green guavas or mangoes from a fruiting orchard. His father always abused and slapped his mother for her thieving, and then promptly proceeded to eat what she had stolen. Later, the mother beat Kaaliya and his elder sister—the others were much too old—before she dropped asleep exhausted on the floor between the hissing wicker baskets and her snivelling children.

When they moved, which was every few weeks, it fell to her, with some help from her small sons, to dismantle the house—the bamboo sticks, the shreds of tarp and plastic, the cooking stones, the rush mats and patchwork quilts, the many baskets filled with the coiled ones—and then some days later, outside a new town, in the vicinity of a defining tree and an enabling pond or tube well, set it up again. The father sat with the other men, looking from the corner of his eye, pulling on his chillum, the artist of the serpents who could not be expected to stoop to such mundanity.

Little Kaaliya hated his life, hated the endless trudging, hated being a beggar in every town and lane he ever visited. He felt they were the only houseless people in the world. Everywhere else he saw solidity, people living in firm, immovable homes. With each day Kaaliya grew into a very angry child, unafraid to shout, scream and protest. His exasperated father would say, 'This bastard's skin will peel off like a snake's with thrashings, but he'll continue to bark like a mad dog!' Every now and then the boy would arraign his mother, demanding to know when they would stop walking, when would they live in an immovable house, when would they begin to give alms rather than seek them, and when would his father stop behaving like a beast. The weary woman said all of it would happen when the sun swallowed the moon permanently and the rivers ran with milk and flowers bloomed all over the desert and men began to fly like birds and snakes began to talk like men and the gods began to look at everyone with an equal eye.

But Kaaliya knew there was another way. When he was eight, and they were camped outside a big town full of famous buildings and minarets, one evening there had been a sudden visitor who had created commotion in the group. He was dark like one of them but so beautifully turned out as to almost seem fair. The red shirt, the grey trousers, the shining black shoes, the oiled hair combed across the forehead, the gleaming gold-coloured watch on the wrist, and most dazzling of all, the ringing laughter and the smiling, confident manner.

Kaaliya and the other children had watched mesmerized from their tents as the young man sat amid the elders, regaling them with stories and talking to them as more than an equal. He was Shambhu Nath's second son who had fled the fold as a twelve-year-old and gone to the great metropolis of Delhi to find his fortune. Now he worked in an office that printed a famous paper, and his job was to rush around the city on a motor scooter, carrying important messages. He said he was called a Rider, and the outcome of many key events depended on his speed and reliability. Now he narrated ribald stories of the kind of cars the sahibs in his office had, and the things they did in them. The awed and amused charmers said, 'Arre saale Rider, at least we keep our snakes in baskets, these sahibs of yours carry them around inside their pants!' Rider, pulling on a cigarette, laughed, 'Theirs are not like ours, tau. Theirs are small—like a jalebia!'

Kaaliya dreamt of becoming the Rider, tearing around on motor scooters, wearing pants and red shirts, delivering crucial messages, and watching the sahibs in big cars taking out their small jalebias to give to the fair memsahibs. Rider said in Delhi there were joys and pleasures they could not imagine. Sweet-smelling restaurants and cool cinema halls and big shops with glittering wares and beautiful women clogging the streets and parks like paintings and buildings of glass and the amazing Qutub Minar, without a doubt the biggest jalebia in the world. For the rest of his life Kaaliya thought of the great minaret as a giant saw-scaled viper, head pointing into the sky.

That summer day in a small town in Rajasthan, in the searing heat of afternoon, when his thwarted father—with not ten rupees to show for hours of blowing and scraping—began to mercilessly thrash him, Kaaliya was filled with a black rage that knew no limits.

All morning at the top of his small voice he had canvassed the snakes, all morning he had held out his small hands seeking a hard coin, all morning he had felt thirst and hunger claw his insides, all morning he had seen men and women go about their lives asking for nothing, and with every passing moment he had known that his father's life could not be his. And when his father began to beat him, even banging the voluptuous pungi on his back, he knew he was running away from there. He was going to Delhi; he was going to be the Rider.

Spitting on his father, he tore away from his grip, and as the miserable charmer fell into the sleep of hashish, the little boy ran and ran, the blood pounding in his head. At the station a train was waiting for him and it left the moment he was on board. It took him three days, many queries, and three different trains to reach Delhi, where Dhaka was waiting for him—the black face in the compartment—as Kaaliya wept with fear like Chini would many years later, struck with terror at seeing so many people, so much bustle, so much noise, so many trains.

The charmer's angry little son never became a Rider, nor did he see rich sahibs in fancy cars showing their little jalebias to fair memsahibs, nor did he for many many years visit a fancy eatery or go to see the biggest jalebia in the world, the Qutub Minar, but he did take to the freedom of the platforms and tracks with a wild exuberance. He turned out an alley cat, snarling, spitting, scratching, biting, forcing respect out of others. He never begged for anything. He always demanded, stole, negotiated, cheated. If he ever came up against a tougher adversary, he located a harmless snake from the Paharganj alleys, and swiftly restored the balance of terror. He never thought of his family and the misery of those nomadic days, but every night when he soaked his rag in Shiva's prasad and stuck it under his nose he only heard one sound—the haunting, beckoning whine of the pungi—and saw just the one image, the flaring head of the black king as it rose above the rainforests of Assam, filling the sky and striking awe into the world.

When Dhaka's mentor Bham Bihari died some years later—many bottles of solution delivering him to eternally juicy green paddy fields—Dhaka became the keeper of his iron trident, the undisputed leader of the gang, and Kaaliya became his chosen henchman. Between Dhaka's violence and Kaaliya's cunning their gang never lacked for food or the solution. Only once did the snakeboy feel a pang when he saw a group of weather-beaten charmers alight from a train, their turbans soiled, their clothes frayed, their earrings dulled, their juttis torn, their eyes vacant, carrying little children, baskets of coiled serpents, bulging pungis, bundles of pots and pans, and remaining rags. And yet his instinct was to hide: among them could be someone who once knew him. But the group was sightless with misery, moving inside its own cocoon of aches.

Kaaliya liked Chini from the moment he saw him. He was so different from the rest of them with his smooth fair skin, his small long-lashed eyes, his lovely straight hair. A great maternal urge rose in him. This flower was not to be sullied by all the gutter rats around; this one was to be cherished and nurtured.

With Dhaka feeling the same way, Kaaliya took the little boy into his embrace, gently initiating him into their subterranean way of life, tutoring him in the deep joys of the solution, and earning his loyalty and love by telling him fascinating stories of the coiled ones—the spitters and the strikers, the two-faced and the hooded, the poisonous and the pliant.

The one story little Chini demanded to hear again and again was the tale from his part of the universe—of the great black king. Each time the peerless beast rose to its full striking height in the clearing of the rainforest and locked eyes with the greatest snake-catcher of his time, the excitement in the boy became so great that he had to clutch his penis to stop himself from peeing.

ii

Freedom at Midnight

Since the rains had not yet let up, Chini's first abode was above platform three, beneath the overbridge, wedged snugly between Kaaliya and Makhi Khan. At this point the corrugated iron roof sloped in gently from opposite directions, creating a lovely alcove that was secure and dry except during the worst storms. The breeze wafted in from both ends, day and night, and it was wonderful to lie there and watch the never-ceasing drama of travellers on the platform. It took him a few days to get used to fitting his body into the corrugations and to sleeping at an incline, but once he did, the comfort was complete. It also helped that the roof of their bedroom was only a few feet above their heads and resounded with the reassuring thump of human feet every minute of the waking-sleeping day.

This allowed them to play one of their favourite gambles: Madhuri. Mostly it fell to Gudiya to stand on the high point just outside the opening, peer onto the overbridge, and yell out the results. The wager was to intuit when Madhuri Dixit—Bombay cinema's reigning queen and everyone's fantasy—was right on top of them. Periodically a boy would shout Madhuri! and if Gudiya confirmed that at that very moment a beautiful woman had indeed walked over them, the others had to fork out a rupee each. There was an unspoken consensus on who qualified as Madhuri: any woman in jeans or trousers; fair women in churidar-kameez who had some make-up on, especially bright lipstick; newly married ones, in sarees with their glittering earrings and bangles and their freshly fucked aura. Dark skin was an instant disqualification. On days when something important was brewing at the station—a ceremonial function, a movement of VIPs—and the round-caps and khakis were out in a brutal mood, the boys would lie out of sight under the overbridge, playing Madhuri for hours. Ten per cent of the winnings went to Gudiya, and when Dhaka returned to his fold at night he would ask, 'Who did Madhuri how many times today?'

A week after his arrival there was a raging monsoon storm. Rain lashed their quarters mercilessly and lightning ripped open the skies. Chini went down with the rest of the gang to sleep above the juicewala's kiosk on the platform. Away from the screaming elements it was a cosy and secure perch, but Chini hated being there. A scooped-out space with tiny parapets, the juicewala's roof was dirty and musty, and the old newspapers they laid out under themselves crumpled and tore as they tossed and turned. Worse still was the flatness of the roof: without an incline, without corrugations, it was difficult to fit one's body into a comfortable position. And then there was that degraded feeling of being part of the platform, in the middle of the foolish swirl of passengers and vendors, their arguments and complaints, their hustling and screams. All through the night, right under them, they could hear people fighting over the price of bananas and oranges, juices and shakes. One unrelenting fair-price seeker was scared witless by an exasperated Dhaka who leaned his face out of the dark roof, and barked, 'Come up here, fucker! I'll give you a big banana for free!'

The juicewala, Ashok—Shoki—didn't mind. He hated asshole customers who behaved as though they were buying not an apple but the Kohinoor. The boys were his friends and allies; there was honour between them. They never stole from his shop and when they brought in fruits purloined or recovered from the trains he shined them up with an old rag, assessed their condition generously, and paid them fair and square.

Shoki was also their banker. Every night, before repairing to their rooftop, each one of them made their deposits at the shop. Shoki made his entries in a minuscule script in the school notebook that he kept above the juicer-mixer-grinder. Except for one boy, MD, no one could read with any facility. And MD too never dared ask to see the accounts. Shoki had a cluster of framed prints of the gods—Lakshmi, Shiva, Krishna, Hanuman, Santoshi Mata—in a tiny wooden alcove, and there were always incense sticks curling sweet smoke in their beatific faces. Pointing to the pantheon, he would say to new boys, 'If I decided to cheat your skinny ass you wouldn't know in seven lifetimes, but I have to make my final reckoning with them, and that's what I worry about!'

Shoki took twenty per cent as his banking charges, and if by any chance any of the boys were picked up by the round-caps or the khakis, he used their deposits to secure a release. There were a few boys on platforms five and six whose past was not a complete black hole. Living on the station was a career choice. There was one from Faizabad and another from Bijnor who had been there nearly ten years. These boys collected a wad from Shoki every few months to give to their families. They were never away for more than a few days. For one, they hated their homes and craved the freedom, the solution, the easy pleasures of the platform. For another, their domains could easily be annexed by new wayfarers. As Dhaka often said, 'A station boy's life is as fast as the trains. It's gone before you know it!'

It was true. Boys vanished routinely. The really tough ones were recruited by the criminal syndicates and dispatched to different parts of the country; some fell foul of the khakis and were condemned to reformatories, and others just suddenly died, their bodies discovered the next morning, killed by accident, drug, gang rivalry, or sexual abuse. If a boy was confirmed dead, Shoki transacted some sort of settlement with his closest buddies and closed the account; if a boy just went missing Shoki kept the page alive, often for years, till the entire ecosystem on the platform had changed, till no one retained a memory of the boy any more. Shoki made more money as a banker than as a fruit-seller.

It was the reason he tried to teach his son, Kishen, some respect for the boys. But Kishen, who had studied in a decent school in Rajinder Nagar and even done three years of college, was a fool. He had wasted six years studying and appearing for the civil services, logging up tuition expenses of tens of thousands of rupees. He had wanted to be a police or administrative officer. But Shoki knew his blood-line—the fucker didn't have the wits to be a clerk. Now at twenty-eight, washed up and desperate, he was laying claim to the juice shop. Shoki was okay with that, but Kishen spoke badly to the boys, and Shoki could see the boys doubted his honesty—they always looked at Shoki while handing over their money to his son. Shoki was fifty-three years old and had spent thirty-four years on the platform. He knew nothing was permanent. Big empires died, big companies died, big men died, every train eventually departed. His favourite cliché was, 'Arre, when Gandhi-Nehru have vanished, who the fuck are we!' He knew the boys could easily shift their business to one of the other bankers on the platforms—to Gulab, the smiling aaloo-puri vendor at the end of platform four who had lost ground because of his cash credibility; to Malhotra of the bookstall, who pulled out cellophane-wrapped pornography from under the self-help books, but whose cunning eyes forestalled trust. The boys could easily shift to them, and then his idiot son would have to shove a fucking banana and an apple down the throat of every single man who got on and off every train in order to merely survive!

Chini opened his account with Shoki by walking off with a red leather ladies' handbag from the two-tier A/C sleeper of a train about to leave for Patna.

His face scrubbed and shining, he was escorted into the bogey by Kaaliya, who sat him down at the edge of a berth beside a young mother struggling with three children. Then the dark-skinned son of timeless charmers went out onto the platform and stationed himself outside the window through which he could see the harassed mother jousting with her bawling brats. When the first preparatory tremor shook the iron, Kaaliya thrust his ugly mug in the window, bulging his red eyes and baring his teeth. The three kids gawped through the glass like animals in a zoo. As the train shook itself several times in quick succession, loosening its sinews to take off, Kaaliya pulled out a short fat domukhi from his sack and pressed it against the sullied glass. The children fell back in one motion, screaming. The mother leapt on them, gathering them in her safe arms, shouting voicelessly at the horrible black boy to go away. The train took its first step with a deep shudder. It merged with the shivers coursing through the family of four. The black boy and the fat snake on the glass moved alongside too. The train clicked its limbs more smoothly now as the mother put her hand over the eyes of the youngest to shut out the horror in the window. Soon the nightmare had passed, and there were only the bare buttocks of defecators lining the speeding vista.

When Kaaliya strolled back to the heart of the momentarily stilled platform, little Chini was standing there like an angel, clutching the shining red leather bag. Only one filled with vileness and canker could distrust a face like his. Since it was Chini's first proper kill, the group waited till evening for Dhaka to show up and unfurl it.

The leader was in a mellow mood; it was clear he had already been burning the foil. They were squatting in a semicircle on the sloping roof under the overbridge, around the central gutter where the opposing inclines met. Enough light drifted in from the platform at both ends. Dhaka said, 'Smart ladies' bag. The boy already has discernment. That's the difference between Chinis and you chutiyas!'

and he cuffed the ears of the boy sitting closest to him. Then he gestured to Kaaliya. 'Open it! There's no difference between a woman and a handbag—the exterior may have no relation to what's inside!'

From the many stomachs—small and big—of the bag emerged a mountain of jumble. Since it was an initiation, Kaaliya pulled out each item with ceremonial slowness and held it up for all to assess. Three sticks of lipstick, red, pink, and pinker. A round-handled hairbrush with sharp black plastic teeth and long hair twined in it (Tarjan pulled out a few strands and shut his eyes and smelled them). A small mud-brown bottle, its cap stained, its sharp smell pleasant. Two plastic ballpoint pens; one short pencil. A slim book of thick paper leaves which Dhaka said could be changed for money. A small yellow hand towel. A pair of dark glasses, with a touch of shining steel. A nail cutter, a nail file, a fat multipurpose knife. A small maroon leather diary held together with a string. Many thick black rubber bands. Many small thick paper cards with different kinds of words printed on them. Lengths of paper with words and numbers. The soft white length of a cotton pad; the bullet of a tampon. A shining compact of face powder. An eyeliner pencil. A small beautiful bottle of sweet perfume. A foil of some tablets, old and battered. Two thin silver bangles and two thick glass bangles. A tiny tin of some cream. A burst of white cotton in a plastic pouch. A bar of chocolate and a fistful of toffees. A stapled pamphlet that seemed religious—it had Lord Ram and Hanuman smudge-printed on it. A thick paper card with the picture of Goddess Lakshmi printed on one side, and on the other the year's calendar with many days darkly underlined with a pen. A pair of silver earrings with orange stone stuck in them. Another flat blue tin of white cream; a brown tube of more cream; another coloured tube of some sweet liquid. A disposable safety razor. A slim black flashlight that came on when its head was twisted. A litter of coins. A condom in black plastic encasing, the round ridge of its rubber inviting palpitation. And finally the bag within the bag—a tan-coloured wallet with credit cards, driving licence, small photographs of a man and some children, and seven hundred and twenty-two rupees.

Dhaka looked at the Manipuri boy and said, 'Motherfucker Chini, did you ever think so many things could come out of something so small? Learn! A woman's handbag is like her pussy—you think only piss can come out of it and then one day it throws out a whole fucking baby!' Then turning to the others, the leader said, 'And you chutiyas learn something from this little Chini! His very first time! And look at the heap he's brought in! No wonder he wanted to call himself Aladdin! And you fuckers! Come back every evening and say, "Guru, guru, I managed two bananas today—I'll eat one and sell the other!"' Everyone tittered aloud. The leader was on a roll. 'Look at this Aladdin! Just look at him! Seems like he's a fucking saint! Been praying all day, so god himself has given him this red bag for his devotion! Take it from me, this Chini will be the biggest maaderchod of all one day! He will yank your cock out, put it in his pocket and walk away, and you won't even get to know till you next go to take a piss!'

Little Lhungdim looked on in unblinking ignorance.

Dhaka set aside the rupees and the Swiss knife and started the divvying up. Gudiya got to go first. Since she had suddenly appeared on the scene less than a year ago, a feisty eight-year-old from near Indore, who had run away from a stepfather bent on abusing her, Dhaka had accorded her a special place in his band. For some reason—there had been an infant sister who had died of cholera before she learned to crawl; the fact that in his first days in Delhi he had seen *Hare Rama Hare Krishna* at Moti and been deeply moved by the love of the parted siblings Dev Anand and Zeenat Aman, and the poignancy of the song, 'Phoolon ka taaron ka', which he still hummed all the time—for some reason, Dhaka felt a great sense of fraternal responsibility and affection for the girl. Watching out for her was the only thing in the world that made him feel virtuous. On the station, where the pace of a boy's life was faster than a train and a girl's completely blistering—sometimes they vanished in days—the only reason Gudiya had survived was Dhaka's protection. She was under instruction to always remain within earshot of one of her band-mates and the boys knew that if anything happened to her Dhaka would take the skin off their bodies.

Once Gudiya had picked up the woman things—the earrings, bangles, lipsticks, lotions, nail polish; not the perfume or tampon—Dhaka gestured at Chini. The boy tentatively picked up the chocolate bar, hesitated, and then picked up some toffees. Dhaka said, 'See, I told you he'll grow up and fuck everyone's mother! I know you all would have picked the goggles or the torch, and lost or broken it in one day! He already knows the truth of the station—and of life: what you can consume today is all that you really have!' Kaaliya immediately picked out and put on the goggles with a glint of steel and, dark on dark with grinning white teeth, became an indescribable sight.

Despite Dhaka's fears, Chini never got nailed. His innocence shone like fresh rain. Cherub-like, he wafted through the crowded bogeys, snagging handbags, satchels, purses, rucksacks, whatever could be carried off with a twist of the wrist and a disarming smile. Given his unusual advantage, he was never reduced to the collecting and selling of refuse—newspapers, cardboard boxes, plastic and glass bottles, magazines, tins, tubes—the standard vocation of the other station boys. Even so, he could not do without the ubiquitous gunny sack. Inside each sack was a boy's life, all they had managed to grab from the world—plastic casing separating the rubbish from the intimate and the valuable. Chini's sack was unique in that it never dealt in the trade of refuse, and Kaaliya's unique in that it always hid a coiled snake.

Kaaliya and Chini quickly became an inseparable twosome,

eating, drinking, crapping, inhaling and operating together—the decoy shaitan and the thieving innocent. In no time at all, Chini acquired the perfections of platform Hindi, and learnt to gamble smoothly—with playing cards, coins, train numbers, Madhuri. When the rains were finally gone, the band moved house for the night to the concrete rooftop at the head of platform one. It was wonderful there: less noise, less fumes, and the incredible freedom of the wide open sky above and nothing around. In the night they lay on their backs, a soaked rag under their nostrils, talking about all the things they wished to do, till the vapours took away their stumbling words and filled their heads with a serene music. Right across, between the tracks, was the small green box of a masjid, with small minarets sticking out of it, like a child's hand. When the muezzin's call floated out and enveloped them, Makhi always fell to his knees. Nobody made fun of him. Sometimes those with him—mostly Tarjan or Chhotu—knelt alongside too. Religion deserved piety, they believed. When they went to the mandir by the Sheilapul bridge, Makhi Khan knelt to the ranged idols with equal fervour, touching his forehead to the ground. Given the odds against them, it was a wise approach to keep their divine arsenal as wide and varied as possible.

The most favoured religious spot was, of course, the mandir. The little masjid was too sombre. On the other hand, the temple, on a small rocky mound by an old ficus hairy with aerial roots, was littered with matted, half-naked sadhus who scratched their heavy-hairy balls and sucked in the truths of the universe through chillums filled with hashish. All around were the altars of the deities cut from stone, terracotta, wood and paper, painted in every lurid colour of the imagination. The entire trunk of one shisham, with a Hanuman idol embedded in it, was washed in saffron paste.

The sadhus were generally friendly with the boys, running

barters of cigarettes, soaps, watches, oils, knives, pens and food, in exchange for wads of hashish, ganja, smack and heroin. Occasionally one of the boys would get into a sexual tangle with a renunciate, but mostly it was about the exchange of drugs and chattel. For the more innocent, the lure was often just the need to align the almighty and to get to eat some of the sweet prasad of burfi, laddus, boondi and halwa offered by the more conservative devotees, rickshaw-pullers and railway workers from the nearby colonies. Sometimes, when someone had received the benediction they had sought for a job, a marriage, a child, or the defeat of a disease, there was puri and aloo and kheer.

The one cardinal rule Kaaliya quickly taught Chini was never to get into a scrap with the sadhus. The naked fakirs were always quarrelling among themselves, but if an outsider crossed them they instantly closed ranks and became god's own soldiers, brandishing their iron trishuls and spears. High on hashish they could do mad battle, impervious to pain or consequence. Station lore spoke of incidents in which boys had had their entrails ripped out and their eyeballs pushed in. Neither the police nor officials had been able to intercede.

Chini learnt to do his drugs in the shadow of the sadhus. Kaaliya and he would squat under the gracious arch of Sheilapul—the blocks of white sunlight at either end buzzing with flies and gnats, alive with mongrels and rabbit-sized rats foraging in the heaped garbage around them. When they had done some lines they would walk the tracks, masters of the world, the cold hard iron wonderful on their bare feet as they swayed forward, arms outstretched, daring any train to derail them. In this, they were inspired by the story of Tattua.

It was said that the greatest jaywalker in the memory of the New Delhi railway station, thin as a growing bamboo, quicker than a bird, was from a village outside Amritsar. His special act was darting across the track just as a train was about to pass. Sometimes he performed for the passengers cramming the platforms and evoked such a loud collective gasp that the pigeons were startled off the rafters. Though his hair was cut short, many thought he was a Sikh—nobody but a sardar would be so absurdly courageous.

There was no train that had not been challenged and vanquished by the Punjabi boy. He had done the mails and the expresses, the single engines and the Rajdhanis, the Shatabdis and the specials. Every once in a while, suddenly, the news that Tattua was going to walk such and such train outside such and such platform would burn like a lit fuse through the station. Every lowlife on the premises would scuttle to the spot; as also many of the karamcharis, the cleaners, sweepers, linesmen. The khakis knew too, but chose to look the other way: this was art, not the breaking of the law. As the train approached, rumbling the earth, Tattua would position himself by the track, right arm raised high, left stretched back, a big smile cracking his thin face. All around men and boys squatted, or stood, wondering if today would be the last crossing of the great Tattua. Then as the train drew impossibly close—always impossibly close—and many felt he was not going to jump today, he would launch himself across the trembling rails.

The uniqueness of Tattua's act lay not in its bravery, but in its grace. He never scrambled or ran; there was nothing ungainly about his flight from approaching death. Right arm thrown high, left arm stretched back, a serene smile on his face, he made the deadly journey with three swivels of his hip. This trademark move grew famous as 'Tattua ki chaal'—the gait of Tattua—and in his time and long after, the platforms were always full of small boys practising the legendary steps.

Tattua was said to have learnt to jaywalk in Amritsar, where all day long he scissored the narrow road leading past Jallianwallah Bagh towards the Golden Temple. Tattua said he had had a vision while kneeling in the sanctum of the temple in front of the holy book, in which the great Guru Gobind Singh, astride his magnificent horse, the plume of his turban riding the wind, his imperious nose sharp as an arrow, had told him that his life's task was to stop the flow of a mechanized mankind. Others claimed his jaywalking obsession came from the death of his mother under a rich man's car on a country road near Patti. It didn't matter what was true. What mattered was that Tattua ki chaal was a cheeky, graceful gauntlet thrown in the face of life, motorized transport, logic and odds, every day, several times a day.

Tattua had been forced to flee the city when a last-second dance across a speeding government Ambassador car led to a crash that killed four people, one of them the revenue commissioner's daughter. Surfacing on the New Delhi railway station, he then upped his burden to taking on a much more implacable adversary than a mere road vehicle. No one knew if Tattua did eventually die under a train. As with most of the station rats, he just disappeared one day. By the time Chini arrived on the platform, Tattua had been gone for years. Some said he had been cut to pieces on the track one night after hours of smoking the foil, and as was their practice, the railway khakis had collected his body parts, stuffed them into his gunny sack, and dumped them at the farther end of Paharganj, outside their jurisdiction. Some said he had been taken by the mafia to Bombay where he now worked the drug trail. A few believed he had gravitated to the next level of his pledge and was now jaywalking in big airports, trying to startle the big birds as they roared in to take off or land.

At the back, away from the tracks, right below where they slept, was a park—well, not quite a park, just an open dusty lot, fringed by anaemic eucalyptus trees and some bushes of yellow oleander. For two months every year, mostly in October-November, depending on what the priests decreed about the alignment of the stars, this lot became a veritable Kublai Khan's banquet hall. Each day the lot was taken over by a new group, who set up the same-looking red-and-blue striped tents, spread the same red-and-blue frayed durries on the ground, and arranged the same ugly iron and wood tables, covered in starched but stained white sheets. In the near corner, where the tallest eucalyptus grew, sat huge gas stoves and massive steel containers for cooking and serving.

During the day the rats avoided peeping down too often at the savouries that were being stirred. In the night when the lot stood transformed into a thing of light and beauty, and loud music beat up the trees and onto the roof, two of the band scrubbed themselves to shining and climbed into the cleanest clothes they could muster—some fancy export rejects bought for a few rupees from the pavements stalls of Sadar Bazaar. When the groom's army arrived, band blaring, horse frisking, men jerking, and tore a hole through the welcoming hosts into the heart of the tent, the two boys swept themselves in with the tide. At the tables, they dived into the middle of the biggest swirl of bodies and ate and ate till the food crept up to their nostrils; then they stuffed what they could into their pockets; and sometimes when there was no roofing tent, casually tossed food packets and cold drinks out onto the roof.

This gambit was not for everyone. Kaaliya never made the trip—he had intruder written all over him. Dhaka never went, partly for the same reason, partly because it was beneath him to scrounge. Tarjan was a risk. In a certain kind of wedding party he could merge, but there too his slow wit could wrong-foot him easily. The safest transgressors were Gudiya, who slopped on the stolen make-up, Chhotu, Makhi and Chini who, well served by their fair skins, were slow to arouse suspicion. Of them, Chini had to be the most cautious: though his innocence was completely beguiling, his slit eyes and pug nose were a giveaway.

Sure enough, every now and then they were caught out, and hunted down with a barrage of abuse. But it was not easy to snare a station rat. Working in tandem, they created diversions and chaos, blitzing under tables, over chairs, through gaps in the shamiana. Capturing hands received teeth marks, and the abuse was batted back with equal colour. The rats lived in a land way beyond shame. It was the first injunction of their catechism. In fact, baiting the swaying beaming fools pretending at marriage jollity was fun: sometimes when two of them had eaten well they would provoke a fracas just to generate a situation.

The finest days of their lives were the sweet weekends when a banquet in the lot coincided with a video night. The network would begin to hum by late afternoon, early evening. Yes, he was coming; yes, he had been spotted; yes, he had the latest Bachchan starrer. Everywhere the excitement was palpable. Their stomachs stuffed with matar-paneer and naan, gulab-jamun and rasmalai, Dhaka's gang would head for the large garbage dump beyond the end of platform one. Every path of the pathless station led there; the mood at the venue was already electric; the buzz of the rats like the hum of a million flies.

A 25-watt yellow bulb, hung on a pulled wire and looped around a nail, marked the entrance to the dump. On the left, against the far white-tiled wall sat a boxy television, hissing softly, emitting blue light. The heaped garbage on the right was cordoned off for the night with a length of discarded shamiana. Under the weak bulb, wearing a dirty white kurta-pajama, sitting cross-legged on a packing crate, pulling on a beedi that cut through the stench, was video uncle. He sported a long beard like Salushan Baba, but was different: fatter, younger, less patient, more authoritarian. Uncle would not start the film till the dump was packed, till every rat from the station's gutters had bought his five-rupee ticket and settled down. It angered him to rewind and repeat scenes, and he would not do it for anyone but the boys from the peepul tree. As it was, the peepul boys were never late. They loved the films as much as anyone else; in fact, it was they who ensured that video uncle gave them value for money through the night.

When the garbage dump was crammed and the chatter of the boys had startled every night bird out of the area, video uncle would send someone scampering to holler up the peepul tree. This ancient giant, once at the edge of the Raj-era outhouse that lay just beyond the main platform, had over the decades split the old brick wall and become one with the building. To access the roof you had to climb one of the tree's hundred knotted sinews. Over time, footholds had been scuffed out in the tree's flesh to make the ascent easier, and a thick iron stake driven into a crack just above head level to give the climbing hand a grip. Of course, you only went up there if you were invited in or dragged up. The rats referred to it as narak, hell. The stories of narak were aptly hair-raising: tales of violence, drugs, alcohol and sex. A casual summons to the peepul tree was enough to loosen the bowels of the most hardened rat.

The balcony—two back seats ripped from an old Ambassador car, the stuffing bursting through the green Rexine—was reserved for the peepul boys. They sprawled there with their strips of foil, cigarettes, peanut packets and beer bottles, commenting gutturally on the scenes, tossing emptied bottles in a high arc over the cloth wall into the refuse. Any rat daring to look back had his ears boxed. When they wanted to take a piss, when they wanted to see a scene again, they called out to uncle, who paused, repeated, re-repeated as ordered. If they disliked a film, they ordered it stopped. Uncle then rummaged in his duffel bag and slid in a fresh cassette.

The peepul boys were tough, shadowy, out-of-bounds; their numbers growing and dwindling, their reputation for violence keeping even the khakis at bay. At the time the group's leader was a youth called Shakaal—a reference to the shaven-headed villain of a 1980s' blockbuster. Every Saturday evening, Madhmudwa, the barber with a wall-side shop along the parking lot, climbed the peepul to shave

Shakaal's head. In the night, boys watching him from the corner of their eyes could see the light from the television screen glance off his oiled scalp. In Shakaal's pocket, it was said, nestled not just a katta made out of a sawn-off pipe, like the others had, but a real revolver.

Like everyone else, Chini fell in love with the movies immediately and the ardour never faded. Sitting on the durrie, arms tight around his folded knees, snug between Kaaliya and Tarjan or one of the other men, he sat riveted as one film after the other lit up the night. By the time the third film played itself out and the dark sky above began diluting into grey, he was among the few rats left wide awake.

When uncle began to roll up his wires and pack away the brick-like cassettes, Chini was always hit by a dreadful melancholy. Scattered hazy images drifted through his sad unslept mind. Of green hills slippery with rain; a bamboo and thatch house with low beds; big birds and small animals moving in and out; the continual swirl of people outside the open door; noises in a language he no longer knew; the arms of a mother with coal-black, defiant eyes; a man who came and went, patting his head, lying on his mother; many men who came and went, patting his head, huddling in whispers. Then the night of infernal noise: shouts in the night, screams in the night, flames in the night, dogs wailing, chicken squawking; someone hammering open the night with sharp cracks in nice rhythmic cycles. Thak. Thak. Thak. Thakathakathakathakathakathaka. A mother's arm pushing him under the low bed, followed by a thick shawl and full sack. Loud shouts in the room. A mother's defiant snarl. Thakathakathakathakathakathaka. Someone hammering open a mother in nice rhythmic cycles. Little Lhungdim sleeping. Little Lhungdim waking. Little Lhungdim travelling in an uncle's arms. Little Lhungdim on a train. Little Lhungdim on a train. Little Lhungdim on a train. Little Lhungdim, little Aladdin. Little Lhungdim, little Chini.

When Chini confided his fractured memories to Kaaliya, the

snakeboy assured him he'd had parents just like all the others did. Everyone has to come from somewhere. But it was good that he was rid of them. Parents were rarely anything but a burden. Kaaliya had had to flee his. And think: without losing them would Chini ever have found Kaaliya? And the band? And the solution? And the movies? Then Kaaliya took him to platform one where the baggage-laden hordes surged through the gates unarraigned by the ticket-checker, and pointed out to him glum child after glum child being dragged along by a snarling adult.

Chini had to agree that being a station rat was the only life worth living, and if the price of it was no parents, then it was not too much to pay.

Even so the shrapnel of memory kept flying in his head, and each time he sucked the rag, he heard the sweet music of rain on a thatch roof amid wet green trees at the end of a world he could never again find.

iii

From Bangkok to Hell

Dhaka was the first one to feel up his penis. It was his inalienable right. After all Chini was his catch, and his ward. By now winter had swept into Delhi, with fog, rising mist, and intermittent winds that spliced open the head and made it throb. Everyone's nose ran and everyone's eyes watered. The station, always cursed with fewer hours of sunlight than the rest of the city, now felt the fingers of night begin to clutch at it by four in the afternoon.

The band moved home again—the roofs had become killer glaciers—and was now snugly ensconced in the gutter between platforms four and five. It wasn't as bad as it sounded. The gutter was not more than four feet under the ground and was mostly dry. There was a trickle of sludge in the groove at the centre, but the boys had thrown old railway sleepers across it to bury its slime in deep. The iron cover of the manhole had been stolen and sold long ago, and now the entrance to their home was guarded by a cratewood trapdoor, the dozens of nail-heads in its flesh glinting in the midday sun. Most nights, unless there was unseasonal rain, the trapdoor was left to a side to allow the entry of fresh air and of reassuring station sounds.

It wasn't as bad as it sounded. The gutter pipe was in a generally good condition and did not run too many leaks even in driving rain. There were two big and many small perforations on the far left, but fortunately that section lay under the big sodium lamp that towered over the tracks—this meant that even on the darkest night a few sharp lines of light flowed into the subterranean den. In December and January and February when a single night without shelter could freeze your blood over and make you a corpse, the gutter was a great refuge, positively warm and comforting with bodies packed against each other, the rags of blankets and quilts wound tight. Sometimes you could even rig a small wood-fire on an iron grille set on four stolen bricks and a handful of sand.

It wasn't as bad as it sounded. As long as the boys stuck to their covenant of not bringing in and eating food in the gutter, the rodents—some the equal of small cats—stayed away. The occasional one that wandered through was grabbed by Tarjan and tossed like a cricket ball through the open hole. Passers-by were prone to be startled by rats suddenly falling from the sky.

That first winter there were nine of them sleeping in the gutter. They had to pay the round-caps on the beat, rupees fifty every day. Each of them pitched in with five and Dhaka gave ten. Sometimes a new boy could not put up his share and sometimes then the round-caps demanded other things.

It was here towards the end of December that Dhaka, descending into the gutter late at night, pushed Makhi aside and settled down next to Chini. It was the hour of vapours and the entire band had rags stuck under their noses. The rain was thumping the thatch reassuringly when little Lhungdim felt his mother's hand walk his skin. Soon it was up his shorts, palpitating his groin. This was good, very good, the best the solution had ever made him feel. Then his hand was taken and his fingers wrapped around something wonderfully hot. The baba, it seemed, had given him another kind of solution today.

Lying on the other side of Chini, Kaaliya read the contours of the dark—the pungi singing sweetly in his head—and felt a wrench of possessiveness. But he also knew that the new train that was leaving the station would soon stop at his feet too.

Dhaka did not do anything brutal or hurried. He was a young man who had dined well for years, and now had the approach of an epicure. The boy was still small, and he was a rare delicacy—pleasure lay not in consuming him abruptly, but in planting the seeds of arousal in him and seeing what grew from it. All the band boys, except for Gudiya who was his anointed sister, had had a period of initiation with Dhaka. It had been painless for all, except Makhi, with whose soft, fair skin and sharp features Dhaka had been besotted for a long time. With him too, eventually, the novelty had thinned, and sanity been restored.

Now Dhaka had two girls, one on platform two and another on platform nine. One from Calcutta and the other from Lucknow. He took them to the cushioned berths of parked carriages. Two boys from the band had to go along to keep vigil. Though Dhaka held on to his band and returned to it most nights, over the last year he had been moving away from the ordinary delights of the station to more serious concerns of drugs and crime. Kaaliya, for one, intuited that their chief was no longer cutting pockets; he was slowly getting involved with some big gangs in Sadar and Chandni Chowk.

On some days he had rolls of notes in his pocket, and instead of asking the gang to trot out what they had gathered during the day, he actually handed out crisp fifties to each of them. Two slim chains of shining gold had now appeared among the jostle of necklaces roped around his neck and he had put a hole through his left ear and jammed a gold ring in it. Grinning cheekily, Tarjan said, 'Dhaka has now become America!' Nor did the gang boss sniff the solution any more; he only smoked the foil. As they lay in the gutter in the dark, the boys watched him burn the lines at blistering speed and felt his growing sense of tranquillity envelop them all.

Dhaka's reputation had been built on his ability to strike with a screwdriver. A screwdriver demanded more rage than a knife. With a knife you could slash and scrape, undertake a skirmish and withdraw, engage in a tease and play. Not so with a screwdriver. A screwdriver demanded much greater commitment. There was no scope for whimsical engagement. It was something pure. With a screwdriver you had to dig deep: go all the way, go in with your soul screaming, go in with your whole body following your hand. A screwdriver could not live with doubt. If it did, it could never puncture skin, muscle and bone and reach the logical end of its iron tip. A screwdriver seldom afforded a second chance. It had to do its work in one unstoppable plunge. It was an iron pencil and what it wrote was unerasable. Dhaka said if you plunged it in right, you didn't even stain your clothes or splatter your boots. All you had to do was give your hands a good wash, and run the iron pencil under a flowing tap.

Dhaka said, 'Show-offs use a knife—all flick and flash and funtoosh! If you want to impress girls it's okay, but if you want to kill there's nothing like a screwdriver!' Dhaka said the beauty of a screwdriver was that it was aesthetic and it was a time bomb. No flesh flapping open, no entrails falling out, no blood gushing like a broken pipe. You made a small hole in the bastard and you sowed death. Many hours later, when he had gone back to whatever fucking hole he had crawled out from, death exploded inside him, and then everyone ran around looking for the hole it had crept in through. Those who did not die, lived for the rest of their life with a hole inside them full of pus and fear. They existed with the knowledge that deep inside them was a festering hollow that nothing could fill; and they lived in dread of getting another one.

Dhaka's arsenal of screwdrivers came from the hardware shops in Chawri Bazaar. A few were as long as his forearm; some had iron the length of his hand; and many were short, the rod only four inches, the wood handle rounded and smooth, with deep grooves for traction. These were the ones Dhaka preferred to use, and two of them were always on his body.

Chini liked the feel of the smooth round grip of the short screwdrivers, and when his hand was taken in the night by Dhaka he imagined what he lovingly caressed was the weapon's wooden handle. In time, over the months and years, he came to caress the handles of everyone in the band, especially that of his closest friend, Kaaliya.

From those initial fumblings to Bangkok was an inevitable journey. To reach Bangkok the boys exited from Ajmeri Gate and walked a straight line past old Delhi—through Asaf Ali Road and Daryaganj, to the power house behind Rajghat where Mahatma Gandhi's ashes still blew in the wind. The first time, they left the station at about eight in the evening and walked for two hours. Chini's mind was blown away by the sheer number of vehicles, the big buildings and the wide roads. He could not believe all of this—two hours of brisk walking—was the same city. His mates had told him that in Bangkok there lay surprises such as he could never imagine.

The jhuggi-jhopdi colony they entered was overhung by a mad skein of exposed wires and lit by naked bulbs. A line of sludge in a shallow groove ran alongside the tight mud lanes that criss-crossed it. In these lanes stood small pushcarts selling ice cream, chaat, tikki; modified bicycles selling rasgullas, cotton candy, aampapad, kulcha; large vendor carts for vegetables, sherbets, lunch and dinner ensembles; and aluminium carts for drinking water. Mongrels sprawled everywhere, and loud voices rang out from every loose brick and tin room—everyone seemed to be in the middle of an argument. No one looked at them with any curiosity as they threaded the lanes in single file.

They were deep in the bowels of the slum, and Chini was sure he could never find his way back, when the line stopped. Chini saw three small signboards on three one-room shacks, all in a row.

Tempo Video House. Manpasand Video House. Sweet Dreams Cinema Parlour.

For the next four hours, for five rupees, inside Sweet Dreams Cinema Parlour, packed in with twenty other boys, Chini saw films that blew his brain into kaleidoscopic fragments. Here were gora women prettier than Hindi film heroines, doing dirty things that could not be imagined. The genitalia of these golden-haired, red-mouthed white women was beyond fantasy. Breasts like balloons, thighs like pillars, vulvas like peaches. Kaaliya said, peering between their open thighs, they were like the muscular maw of a python, capable of swallowing any and everything.

In the translucent glow of moaning white women, Chini saw boys streaming in until, by midnight, the rough blue jute durrie, stained with a million happinesses, on which they sat, was completely packed. The bigger boys bagged the last row at the back, against the wall, and it was lit with glowing tips as silver lines were shared and burnt. It was the only row allowed to talk aloud; comments on the size, shape and colour of genitalia flowed steadily.

Chini had no time for such frivolity. He was not blinking, and his fingers were fluttering like a master weaver's. By now the sexual stench in the room was overpowering, blanking out the smell of sweat and dirt and cigarettes. Every boy was working his handle; some that of others. A few had fallen asleep, exhausted and sated. At some point they would wake and start working the handle again.

Malaria, the emaciated young owner of Sweet Dreams parlour, sat outside, intensely burning silver lines. When, with a loud click, the tape ran out and the boys erupted in a roar, he made a quick sortie to slip in a new cassette. Chini thought of video uncle and he thought of Malaria, and he marvelled at the endless wonders of cinema. At around three o'clock, Malaria staggered in sleepily to change yet one more cassette—the sex stench was thick as cheese now—and said, 'Fucking vagabonds, stop pulling at it as if there's a sack of gold coins at its root! Haven't you had enough for one night!'

The boys erupted, 'Fuck your mother, Malaria! May she get filaria!' He grinned and retreated.

Neither Chini nor Kaaliya slept a wink that night, and by the time the owner came in to finally turn off the player—warm as toast now—every body part of the boys, from eyes to limbs to hands to handle, was sore.

Outside, a red-grey dawn was opening the day. The lanes of Bangkok were full of bustle. Burnt-skin men in vests prepared their carts and cycles, rich food smells vying with the fumes from the sewage. A few privileged children in ragged uniforms trudged cheerlessly to school, weighed under their cloth satchels. In less than an hour the slum would be vacated of all activity. Every single denizen above the age of nine would leave to forage the city for every rupee they could find, while the night toilers, like Malaria and the sex and security platoon, would turn in to sleep off the daylight hours.

The slum worked hard every moment to discover new ways to make a living; new ways of any kind at all. Pornography was no less respectable than selling contaminated drinking water or looking after some rich man's dogs or soliciting funds for a fake orphanage. In fact, for years afterwards, Chini and Kaaliya argued that it was a positively wholesome pastime, compared to some of the other things their mates were doing. By the time they wound their weary way back to the tracks, the sun was beginning to singe the city, and the two friends had found in themselves a tacit commitment to the consumption of pornography that was to seal their friendship forever.

While Bangkok became a regular destination for the two boys, neither of them tasted any other part of the sprawling city for many years, except of course Sadar Bazaar, where they went once in two months to pick up a set of fifteen-rupee shirt and trouser ensembles, wearing them without break till every thread ran thin, returning in the winter for cardigans and coats for twenty-five rupees. Some of these clothes bore labels that would have dazzled the swank sets of Park Avenue and Mayfair; the gap between the white rich and the gutter boys was only a stitch insufficiently strong or a collar out of true.

While visiting Sadar was easy—you just walked the rails till you got there—the rest of the city remained alien. Different dangers lurked here: of policemen, government officials, the begging mafia, the eunuch tribes. Boys had been lost, with the accompanying mutilation of limbs and penises, to all of them. Then there were the spies of social agencies whose weapons were soft words and rosy dreams, who talked with sincere eyes about goodness and education, who wanted to pull the boys into their hospices and domesticate them into cooks and guards and gardeners. The few who managed to slave through school would end up as clerks and accountants.

Dhaka called them the 'fucking pimps of goodness'. 'I tell them to sit on my dick! They hate our freedom and happiness! They hate it that we don't live by their rules! They want to scrub our skins, teach us to write and read a few words, and then send us off to be slaves in some rich man's house or office! Clean some memsahib's shoes and wipe her children's ass! What happened to Ismail, to Kamal, to Doctor, to Pani? All serving tea and wiping tables and washing dishes! Has any one of us ever had to do that? I would rather die under a train than go with those pimps! Sit on my dick, I tell them!' To Chini he would say: 'You they won't even teach a few words! They'll straightaway give you a topi and a lathi and make you a chowkidar! You can spend the rest of your life awake every night walking around banging your lathi on the road!'

Chini, however, was in training to be not a guard but a crook. Dhaka had inducted him into the shaving blade. He'd said, 'Saaley Aladdin, you are too pretty to have the stomach for a screwdriver. You need something gentle, something dainty.' Given the innocence shining out of him, he was made for contact crime, charm crime—simple swindles, the theft of bags, the slitting of pockets. The stainless steel Topaz blade was snapped in two; it easily vanished between Chini's index and middle finger, the cutting edge flush with the palm. In the moment that Kaaliya banged up against the man, Chini's sweeping palm brushed past his pocket, opening it like a mongrel's mouth. If the man caught on, Kaaliya swarmed all over him, swaying and striking like the coiled black one whose blood-line was inextricably entwined with his, while Chini made a run for it.

There were times when they were caught and brutally thrashed. By groups of passengers, by the khakis, by the railway round-caps, by other bigger, meaner rats. There was nothing to do then but to lie on the roof or in the gutter and inhale the rag day on day till all pain had eased and every welt had healed. Sometimes one of the band would bring in a dark bottle of iodex, but it was more gratifying to eat it layered thickly on bread than to apply it to one's aching skin.

And so more than ten years passed.

Ten years in which everything, and nothing much, changed. In this time Dhaka was killed, chopped into pieces with a butcher's knife. When the news reached the station and the boys went rushing to the open lot behind Red Fort, they found parts of him strewn beside a small lantana bush near a sewer. Like a plastic doll whose arms and legs had been yanked out. His head, cut close to the torso, had rolled three feet away. The dismembered parts had bloated and discoloured to blue-green rust. There was no way anyone could have recognized him but for the trademark tennis wristbands. The short screwdriver he used to carry in his boot was hammered into his navel, the smooth wooden handle sticking out like a gravestone. When they had identified him, the policeman said, 'Motherfucking wastrels, this is how you'll all die! I hope someone will come to identify you!'

Dhaka's parts were bundled tightly in a sheet and burnt by the old cremation ghat by the Yamuna. Nobody from his sixteen years at the station came to watch him burn, except for three boys. Kaaliya, Chini and Tarjan gave seventy rupees to a cut-rate priest, who asked for a cigarette before performing some perfunctory rites. He mumbled incantations at a speed that did not yield a single word, and waving a clump of green grass and a brass lota, he threw some water randomly around the pyre. They paid another eighty rupees for three armfuls of wood. The priest said it was lucky the man had come chopped in small bits, else it would have never done the job.

The next day they went back and scooped the ashes and bits of charred bone into a small pot and caught a bus to Haridwar. Before they reached the ghat, Kaaliya had banged into two groups of well-heeled mourners, and Chini's blade fingers had opened up two crisp white kurtas. Now they had enough money to afford a young panda—a big steel watch on his wrist—to mouth some more facilitating incantations at a mumble and a speed that did not yield a single word. Bits of Dhaka were then floated down the great Ganga—to flow all the way back from where, those many years ago, he'd once come.

The three of them stayed on in the holy city for a few weeks, slitting flapping kurtas, observing the pilgrims and mourners, watching the evening aartis with the deafening chanting and the delightful floating of the glittering diyas, eating endless rounds of puri-aloo and halwa, studying the hustle and swindle of god's middlemen. They slept in the many buzzing ashrams, on the banks of the groaning river, and on days when the slit kurtas were fat with offerings, in one of the many cramped hotels dotting the town. They watched the muttering women dip themselves in the mother of all rivers—the blessing of Shiva, the cleanser of all sins—their sarees clinging to their rolling flesh, their white brassieres etched pointy against their white blouses, their nipples round and dark and liquid.

So more than ten years passed.

In this time, Gudiya was molested, abducted and raped. The boys from the other peepul tree, the one beyond the last platform, beside the tea-stall, near Ajmeri Gate, picked her up one evening as she trawled empty carriages for some left-behinds, and dragged her to the cave. The area was earmarked for crime—the last fingers of the big sodium lights stopped many feet away, and the khakis never ventured there. Inside the gaping hole, shaped like a cowl, under the grassy motte beyond the shunting tracks, the three of them fucked her by turns.

They were brutal and quick, spitting into their palms. None of them fucked silently. 'Enjoying it, bloody randi?' 'Now you'll want it all the time, won't you?' Almost as if they were lovers, seeking her approval.

Gudiya did not fight it after the first few minutes. It was late evening; she was high on the solution; and she had lived on the platform long enough to know this assault was overdue. When the fucking was over, they squatted in a semicircle, breathing heavily, dusting their forearms and trousers, and smoking plain cigarettes. On her haunches, Gudiya pushed her fingers deep into herself and scooped out all she could.

She was still wiping her fingers on her kameez, when Shankar, the biggest of the three, and the boss of platforms seven and eight, pushed her down again. He spat on his palm out of habit, though it was not needed. This time he was gentler and slower, and he did not shoot her with questions. Gudiya adjusted her head in the loose soil on the ground, and held her legs wide apart. She could hear the Jammu-Tawi Mail leaving with a piercing whistle. Afterwards he sent the other two off, and told her he'd been eyeing her for months, that he always thought she was Dhaka's and then he'd learnt the truth. Now she was his. He loved everything about her. He loved her name. He loved her beauty. He loved her. He shared a cigarette with her and gave her fifty rupees.

The next day he took her to Chandni Chowk and bought her a shimmering pink suit, tinsel jewellery, a pair of silver sandals, and a tiny bottle of ittar whose sweet smell filled the air like billowing smoke. They ate mutton korma at Karim's and he looked into her black eyes.

The next week he took her to his best friend, Abbas, behind Asaf Ali Road, and in his second-floor living-room, amid a clutter of stuffed and padded furniture, shared her love on the green Rexine sofa with him. Abbas was fat but kind, and called her the new queen—nai begum—as he wheezed away on her. Later, Abbas gave her chaat to eat and told her how much Shankar loved her. Shankar looked into her black eyes and she warmed to the deep love in them.

The next month he got on to the Rajdhani with her and took her to Bombay. He came back ten days later without her, and when Kaaliya and Chini and Tarjan went to platform seven to find out where she was, he said, 'What do I look like to you, you fuckers? The head of the missing persons' bureau? Can any of you even find your own missing mothers that you want me to find some missing bitch? You come here again and I'll slice your balls off! Maybe you'll feel like her then!'

The next night when Dhaka came to the gutter, they told him. Dhaka, burning lines of silver at blistering speed, said, 'Must be the best whore in Kamathipura by now. You hang around with Shankar, you deserve it. Anyway, where do you think we are all going to end up—the Rashtrapati Bhavan? Better a whore with cock between her legs than dead on some iron track!' Then he turned over and went to sleep and never mentioned her name again.

So more than ten years passed.

In this time Makhi Khan—once the love of Dhaka, the pretty boy from Malliana who had seen his family consumed by fire and sword, by slogans and screams—was cut into three by the thundering hooves of the Amritsar Shatabdi. By then the delicate boy had travelled way beyond the sniffing of the rag. He was now sucking the wet cloth like an ice lolly, and on days even tilting the little bottles like Coca-Cola directly into his throat. The mullah's reassuring voice summoning the faithful to prayer played in his head all the time, and just when the shrieking men, bandannas tied around their heads, steel slicing the air in front of them, were about to break through the door and grab his father and brothers, his sisters and mother, he quickly gave the bunched cloth in his palm a deep suck, and the mullah's soothing voice came sweetly rolling back.

Makhi had long ceased to beg or steal. He had given in to his inherent gift. It was difficult to look at him and not be snared by the soft flare of his hips, the full red mouth, the big brown eyes with long curving lashes. Unhappy men—young and old, married and single, sad and angry—poured through the station night and day, and it was gifted unto him to give them a fleeting moment of joy. Some hurt him and some did not pay him anything, but many were grateful and kind. Some came back, but if they did so too often then he learnt to avoid them. The khakis and the round-caps took him when they wanted. But that was okay. The station, after all, belonged to them.

Makhi used to say that because his mother begged so hysterically for her children, they killed her last, though they did not stop raping her. Her pleading excited them, made them laugh, fuelled their tumescence. He used that learning sometimes—in an empty carriage, bent over a lower berth, when the man was kind and had a fat pocket.

It always worked. The call to mercy provoked harder erections and greater arousal. Men, and power.

He had been wandering back from Sheilapul, pouring the solution into his throat. That day it had been two sadhus from the temple, high on charas, their long matted hair falling over his back as they grunted. They had paid him nothing, just fifteen rupees, saying he was fortunate to be doing god's work. And so he was, for he could hear the muezzin's sweet cry, loud and clear, filling the skies. When he fell on the stones, his legs over the smooth rails, and the Shatabdi thundered in, all flashing lights and faces, the muezzin's cry grew louder and sweeter bringing on more and more peace.

He was still smiling when the boys reached him. The khakis had put his legs in his gunny sack and were discussing what to do next. Kaaliya tried to bend down and cradle his beautiful head but a khaki uncoiled a kick to his side. 'Stupid fucking punks! Can't live cleanly, can't die cleanly!' he snarled. 'Get themselves chopped like vegetables, as if their mothers are waiting to cook them!'

They kept arguing among themselves till he was dead. Two rail karamcharis helped stuff him into a sack. He was left next to a refuse pile at the end of the Paharganj lane that fronted the station. Now he was the municipality's responsibility. They were good at disposing of assorted limbs and carcasses.

The next to go was Chhotu, chaser of kites, peeper into toilets, befriender of every rat on every platform, the laughing player of pranks, the boy who could not be caught. Chhotu's feet were running water. Dodging, feinting, taunting, he could elude three chasing men around a narrow platform for as long it took to exhaust them. Nothing slowed him down: not the beatitudes of the solution, not injury, not fever.

Some days, to amuse themselves, the rats would spot a smug group on the platform and say, 'Go screw them!' The creativity lay in the provocation: pissing at their feet, smearing snot on their baggage, dropping a kulhad of tea over their clothes, flashing their women. Then came the exchange of abuse, followed by the chase. Threading fatigued passengers, around kiosks and carts, up the stairs, leaping the banisters, over luggage—all the time the laughing abuse, and above on the roof the roaring audience. In every case the pursuers were doubled up on the floor grasping for breath in less than ten minutes.

But when the rag's magic vapours filled his being, Chhotu saw none of this. All he heard was his mother's sweet lullaby and all he saw were the flying kites. Soaring souls, in a hundred colours, in a hundred sizes, in their thousands, filling the blue sky, outfluttering every bird, skating the thermals, skipping and swerving, dipping and dancing, connected by the thin body of their threads to a thousand jerking fingers on a hundred shimmering rooftops.

Chhotu lived to fly the kite, to feel the life of the paper-bird flow through his grimy hands. In those years at the station anyone who saw a pair of bare feet silvering across the corrugated roofs, face tilted upwards, knew instantly who it was. On a windless day when paper was like stone, this runaway son of a constable could lift the bird with his wrists alone; and if the breeze blew he could sail the bird so deep into the heavens that it could no more be seen by the keenest eye. If the skies were crowded he could wield his flying bird like a warrior's scimitar to clear himself a wide space. His string was the edge of a blade, coated with crushed mirrors in the starch of rice; his palms roughly cross-hatched with lines beyond all ordainings of destiny.

Chhotu's champagne months were August and September. As the rains passed, leaving behind cool breezes; as Independence Day approached with the pale rituals of freedom speeches; as the bird-men emerged onto the roofs and streets of old Delhi holding their big kites like delicate porcelain, Chhotu became almost completely airborne. There were several other rats too—between the tracks, in the shunting yards, on the roofs—who put up their birds. But they were peasants amid a gladiator, and Chhotu never crossed his singing line with them. Striding the roofs of the station, he hunted the high-fliers, warriors like himself who could swerve and slash at several hundred feet, with power and precision, whose kites when decapitated were pursued by the peasants who ran and leapt pell-mell over everything to capture the trophy.

Kaaliya said it was apt that Chhotu died doing the two things that defined him—running and flying a kite. Aptly too, he died off the roof of platform four and in the middle of Independence Day celebrations when his father would have been on duty somewhere, guarding some leader or road against the vandalism of the spirit of freedom. On a midday when the air was buzzing with kites like flies on a heap of refuse, and Chhotu was slicing them down like blades of grass, his flying foot rolled on a dented can of Coke someone had flung on to the roof. The rats who saw him plunge said he bounced on the wires like a rubber ball while the wires sang and spat. The spectacle was so riveting that no one quite remembered if he screamed or said anything. But they all recalled that he held on tight to his big wooden spool of string. When he finally fell to the ground, nicely charred, and the khakis arrived to cart him away, he was still holding on to it.

That night Kaaliya said, lying on the roof, 'Chini, you are next! Take it from me. You look too sweet and innocent. Someone will do away with you just because of that!' Of course, by then, Chini was neither. He alone among the band had made the journey to the top of the peepul tree at the end of platform one. It was on a summons delivered one night at the garbage hall movie. The other band rats had stood at a distance while he climbed the knotted sinews of the ancient tree that had torn apart the building, grabbed the iron stake and swung himself into the dark leafy space above. Narak, hell, where you only went if you were invited or dragged.

Bizarrely—Chini said later—as he climbed up he was assailed by an acrid smell that he couldn't recognize, and when he emerged into the dark cave made by the peepul's lush canopy he was startled to see a large image of him staring back. He almost tripped back in fear and fell down the hole he had just crawled up. Then he realized it was a big stand-alone mirror in a tiltable wooden frame, of the kind found in old colonial bungalows. A voice cackled from the dark and said mockingly, 'See! We have a duplicate of everything!'

By now Chini's stomach was water, and as his eyes adjusted he saw a charpoy with a mattress and bed sheet and pillows and a bald young man lying on it with his arms folded under his head. He was wearing nothing but a black pair of Michael Jordan's Chicago Bulls shorts, the number 23 luminous in red, its crotch shaped like an igloo. But Shakaal was not the one who had spoken. There were also two wooden chairs and a small table, with young men sitting on all of them. One of them had a thick stubble and a wild grin. The boys called him Kumla Jogi—Mad Joginder—and he tended to blather and was prone to random acts of violence. He had a thick cigar stuck in his mouth and was grinning through it. 'You are a Chini?' he said. 'Do you like eating noodles?' Chini's voice had long ago drowned deep in the waters of his belly. When the boy didn't answer, Kumla Jogi cackled madly, then stopped dead and said, 'Anyway, take off all your pathetic clothes. We've heard Chinis have two cocks—one for pissing and one for fucking. And they can do both at the same time—that's why they have even more people than us!' He cackled madly again. 'Let's see if it's true.'

Nothing surprised the boy because he was an aficionado of Bangkok's cinema. But it certainly hurt. Shakaal was the first in, without taking off his Michael Jordan shorts; then Kumla Jogi, cackling and talking all the while; and finally the third man, who first brutally used his mouth. Later, he kneeled the boy on the edge of the table and simply would not stop. Chini could look through the beautiful peepul leaves and see the lights coming on in the outer reaches of the station, some white, other yellow. He wished he had the rag—it would have soaked up the pain.

The other two were talking among themselves, discussing some new film. The table was screeching rhythmically on the brick floor. Dhaka had told him to stick close to the path of no resistance. Boys had gone up that tree, and come down as cripples. Sometimes even as corpses. There were no reparations possible. Hell and the khakis were one team. Now there was no pain; just the banging. He held on hard to the edges of the table. Finally Shakaal said in his filmy baritone, 'Stop it now, chutiya, unless you are trying to make India and China into one country!'

Afterwards, Kumla Jogi put the barrel of a big black pistol in his mouth and slowly moved it in and out. 'My little Bruce Lee that one gives a hot fuck, this one gives a cold fuck! That one shoots life into you, this one shoots death!' And he cackled madly. 'So be a good obedient boy always so that you always get life!' When the boy stumbled down the tree he saw his shadow move in the big mirror.

For five days Lhungdim lay in the gutter, face stuffed into a dripping rag, hearing the sweet sound of rain falling on a thatch roof amid wet green trees at the end of a world he could never again find. From then on, in the garbage hall during the weekend shows, he hid himself, covering his head with a cap, lying low between the rats in a dark corner. But hell knows how to find those it chooses.

Lhungdim. Aladdin. Chini. Catamite. The summons came periodically, and in time he mastered every sinew of the tree, scaling it in a jiffy even in the dead of night. He learnt to relax the tight muscles, and he remembered to take his rag along. The canopy regularly unveiled new bodies, and occasionally he felt he was part of some transaction. Sometimes when he was being banged he'd hear a voice ask, 'Does he know any Hindi? I have to say Chini ass is better than Indian ass!' Occasionally he was surprised when someone would pull on a cap before starting on him: of course he realized it was to protect themselves, not him. Its abrasions tore at him for days.

Kaaliya always waited in the platform below, often falling asleep on the undulating concrete bench. He had grown into a wiry young man full of the sullenness of the unfairly relegated. On the platform, colour of skin was fate. The night-dark son of snakemen loved his friend, and was his guardian and keeper, but he was also forced to stand in the wings and to share him with the masters of the world. In the beginning he would rage, threatening to unleash cobras up the tree. But as Chini's own anxieties tempered and the hell boys began to hand him hundred-rupee notes, Kaaliya began to see it all as one more line of work. You could collect waste, you could steal, you could sell drugs, you could get fucked, or you could, as most of them did, do a bit of everything. It insulated you against the vagaries of the marketplace.

So more than ten years passed.

In that time they discovered there was a city beyond the station. It was full of a real opulence and a real beauty. For too long they'd imagined these were only attributes of the films they saw in their garbage hall. In Connaught Circus—a mere slingshot away from the gutter they'd always lived in—were dazzling glass-fronted shops and big glowing signs. There were cinema halls with screens the size of a thousand televisions, and on the road big cars that shone like diamonds. In the colonnaded corridors walked women—and men—so beautiful, so sweet smelling, that one felt faint in their very presence. And that was not all. The city, in a similar way, stretched on and on for miles and miles, to an end none of them had ever seen.

In that time they discovered the big world was not for them. They had no tools to take it on—no language, no knowledge, no contacts, no money. On the other hand the station was no longer big enough. New young boys were filling the holes and roofs. They were insolent, energetic, scrappy. To contest them for space and spoils was a diminishment—for Kaaliya and Chini lacked the authority or the wit or the violence to generate awe. And the hell boys of the peepul tree had no interest in the turf battles of the platforms—they were players in the big stakes of the larger world.

So when they were summoned up the peepul tree one evening, and Shakaal did not unbutton his Jordan shorts and no one took off their pants, and they were offered a new line of work, they were fully ready. Kumla Jogi cackled madly and said, 'What a pair! Black and white! Night and day! God and demon! It's perfect!'

They were not put on the drug route, or the arms line, or the fake currency racket. A new con was being tested, and the maibaaps of the hell boys had demanded a few novices, with no police record, and innocence in their eyes. A new revenue stream in white-collar swindling was being opened—no knives, no guns, no blood, no gore, just go to the bank and collect some money.

The maibaap, the government, in its infinite mercy had started a loan scheme for the illiterate handicapped. Kaaliya and Chini were handed medical certificates, sheathed in laminate, declaring them deaf-and-dumb. They were then taken to a small branch of a nationalized bank in Gurgaon. Benighted Mr Lhungdim and Mr Nath applied for a state loan to set up a scooter repairs shop. Billa, the broker, held their thumbs and stuck them into various documents; then he heartily backslapped the thin manager, Mr Pareenja, making the claustrophobic plywood cabin shake. Two weeks later, they collected and cashed a cheque of two hundred thousand rupees. Shakaal gave them four thousand each out of it, and stroking his oiled scalp said, 'Lucky dogs! Didn't have to spill a drop of blood for it! Like working in a motherfucking office!'

The next one was a cooperative bank in Najafgarh. The broker Sehwag, fat and unshaven, wore a soiled white kurta-pajama and drove a red battered Maruti. The manager was a young man with a fine moustache that curled upwards, and he gave the two deaf-and-dumb illiterates one hundred fifty thousand rupees to buy buffaloes and set up a dairy milk project. Handing out four thousand each to the serial entrepreneurs, Kumla Jogi cackled madly and said, 'We've always cursed the motherfucking government for not doing anything for poor people. The fact is you have to just learn to ask nicely!'

Eight months later, Chini and Kaaliya had moved out to a room in Rajinder Nagar. It was above the second floor of a tiny house and you had to climb endless narrow steps to get to it. The toilet and bathroom were out on the small terrace, and each was the size of a large cupboard. They both slept on the single bed and lay low in the neighbourhood, not talking to anyone. The only time they went back to the station was when they had to report to the hell boys. Or on the odd night when sleep would just not come unless they heard the rumble of the trains.

But going there now was an unhappy experience. Most of the rats of their time were dead or gone; even the khakis were unfamiliar. Shoki too had died some years ago, and soon after, they had closed their bank accounts at the fruit mart. The rail lines still lived by the rag, but Salushan Baba's place had been taken by a younger man—sharply dressed, not wise, not a fakir, just a salesman. Worst of all the movie hall had been cleared out: the garbage dump was now only a garbage dump—stuffed to overflowing—and no video uncle appeared there every weekend with magic in his duffel bags. As terrible was the onslaught of Dhaka's dreaded 'pimps of goodness'. Men and women with saintly smiles were crawling all over the station trying to snare the rats into morbid hospices and spiritless schools.

The new life was welcome. Every few months the handicapped duo were shepherded to a new bank to mop up a loan. Kumla Jogi cackled and said, 'We should buy them suits and ties! Look at them—Mr and Mrs 55! Fultu sahibs, going to banks! Their parents would be proud of them!'

In the long spare hours they sniffed the rag and burnt the silver lines. Sometimes, for days, they were too much at peace to even walk down the stairs. When they could they went to Bangkok, spending entire nights there, inhaling the musk of male desire, finding the perfect peace of oblivion. Even when they got their own Akai TV and

Panasonic video player, they did not cease to seek out the collective frisson of Bangkok.

In October 1996 they were arrested in Ghaziabad while trying to collect a five-lakh loan from the State Bank for a machine-tooling unit. After seven heists the word was out on them. The cops beat them systematically, hurting every bone in their body without breaking it, and pulping every muscle without tearing it. For weeks they were crumpled heaps. No one in more than ten years at the station had hurt them so badly. The cops were in a fury: for one, the two of them had no money to fork out; and then clearly they were street labour, totally dispensable, and their maibaaps, whoever they were, would have no interest in salvaging them. Kumla Jogi bailed them out four months later, and took them back up the peepul tree. Chini's left cheek had a scar now, from a fight in Dasna jail. The horny Jat who had given him the scar had had a chunk bitten off his chest by Kaaliya. Shakaal rubbed his Michael Jordan crotch and said, 'Good! Now you've finally graduated! Now you are ready for the next level. Tell me, what comes after sahib?' Kumla Jogi cackled and said, 'Shaitan!' Shakaal cracked a smile and said, 'And after shaitan?' Kumla Jogi cackled, 'Sant!'

Sahib. Satan. Saint.

Conformity. Rebellion. Enlightenment.

Shakaal said, his voice sombre, 'Do you know what Bhagwan Krishna told Arjuna when he was standing around like you looking stupid, in front of a million armed warriors? The great lord said, "Even a wise person acts according to his own nature. Nature drives all beings. Why should you use restraint? Attachment and aversion are certain. But don't be overcome by those. They are obstacles. Your own dharma, even if followed imperfectly, is superior to someone else's dharma, even if followed perfectly. It is better to be slain while following your own dharma. Someone else's dharma is tinged with fear."' At this Kumla Jogi cackled, 'And what is your dharma, boys?'

To carry and to fetch.

So the order of evolution was laid out for the two former rats, and they were inducted into the life of carriers and couriers: delivering packages, collecting packages, asking no questions, seeking no answers. Knowing no one beyond the hell boys; knowing nothing beyond the next address. In this way in the next few years they travelled all over the country, from Kashmir to Bombay to Guwahati to Calcutta to coastal Gujarat and coastal Tamil Nadu and the frontiers of Pakistan and Nepal and Bangladesh and Burma. Sometimes the cargo was a mere envelope slipped in between their vest and skin; sometimes a smooth cylinder nestled in Chini's supple ass; sometimes a truck laden with sacks and crates, lashed down tightly, and the two of them in the co-driver's cabin, sharing a rag, burning a silver line. Only once did Shakaal offer them a pistol—beneath the green canopy of peepul leaves, before sending them on a collection to Ganganagar in Rajasthan—but when they hesitated, afraid, Kumla Jogi took it away and cackled, 'Oh don't! Not to Mr and Mrs 55! Look at them! If your hands shake like that you should masturbate, not hold guns!'

They stayed with Dhaka's legacy of screwdrivers, blades, scalpels, almost never needing to use them, till one day Shakaal summoned them up the tree and twirling a brand-new silver-coloured mobile phone in his hand, said, 'This whole country is changing, everyone is full of new excitements, don't you want to do something more with yourselves? Or are you happy being postmen all your life?'

The two of them kept quiet, knowing well that the decision had already been taken for them. Kumla Jogi, who was wearing a green balaclava over his face, its edges sticking out like bunny rabbit ears, cackled and said, 'Chutiyas, he's going to make you James Bond! Zero zero seven! Cars, guns, and a licence to kill!'

Chini, lost son of a distant land where the slopes were green and the rain always fell, and Kaaliya, coal-dark offspring of a bloodline that never stopped walking and was forever entwined with the scaled one, were given a piece of paper with an address where they were to meet a man more fearsome than Dhaka, more fearsome than the hell boys, more fearsome than any they had known, whose chosen weapon of mayhem was an iron hammer, who was dreaded by men whose illicit empires ran across states, who made holes in heads that no surgeon could ever hope to suture.

11

THE RODENT IN THE CASTLE

For some reason Jai decided to accompany me. He didn't need to. The summons was for me. But it was the kind of showy gesture he occasionally indulged in, to show he really cared. I don't think he did, for anyone, but it flowed with his self-image. Also, I knew he had been dining out on these grimy state-versus-citizen stories—they held a macabre fascination for the kind of well-heeled precious fucks he socialized with; men and women who would pull up their pant legs and stop breathing if you dropped them on a village road. He embroidered into drawing-room theatre everything that I told him: the sinister shadows, the Kafka courtroom, the slippery Sethiji, the menacing Hathi Ram, the clinical assassins led by the brain-curry man, the lethal Kapoorsahib, Bhalla's line girls. The fools he regaled never realized that, actually, they were part of the same chorus line—the state-and-the-system that had a finger up everyone's ass. The moment we entered the building, I knew Jai was soon going to command a new silence in the margarita rooms.

It was a concrete block off Chanakyapuri and it rose nine storeys high, featureless and opaque as a cardboard box. A guard in khaki sat near the main entrance on a wooden stall, carefully punching a blue mobile phone, and he didn't look up as we went in. The foyer was tight and dimly lit, the terrazzo floor and cement walls thick with grime. There were two lifts, next to each other, with steel doors. When you punched the buttons you heard, somewhere in the distance, a deep groaning and cranking followed by a thick whine. The narrow glass consoles over the doors were playful, displaying some floors and ignoring others. When the lift hit the ground there was a big bang and shudder. But the men in it walked out alive, all nondescript, all in bush shirts and trousers.

It was six in the evening. Only the two of us were going up. When the doors had juddered shut and we were enclosed in the semi-dark, Jai said nervously, 'You think we should take the stairs?' Before I could say yes, someone up there pressed a button and with a deep groan and jerk we were on the move.

We emerged on floor eight into a cramped corridor littered with government-issue furniture—iron-frame tables with shiny wooden boards screwed on, chairs with the plastic mesh torn in several places, dented steel almirahs, broken wooden cupboards, even some aluminium trunks with thick locks. The area was badly lit with a few lopsided tubelights coated with streaks of thickly settled dust. The lift went no further, but we had to go to the ninth floor. A pot-bellied man emerged from a door, jostling his crotch. He stopped and looked at us. We asked. He pointed with his free hand to a stairwell behind us.

The winding staircase was reasonably broad but giving way at the edges and without air or illumination. It had banks of windows with latches that ought to have allowed them to open six inches but they were all jammed shut and the panes were so caked with dirt and pigeon shit that not a shard of light could penetrate. A cement banister wound alongside but there was no way we could bring ourselves to put a hand on it. We walked in tandem, me ahead, feeling every step, Jai behind, mumbling abuse at the state of the state.

The ninth floor landing was much like the eighth with the same clutter of third-rate furniture and the same crooked flickering tubelights, except that at both ends of the corridor there were unmarked wood-board walls with doors cut into them.

A faux confidence suddenly seized Jai. He took the lead, wrenching open the door to our right and marching in. A stout man with a big moustache and a bush shirt open to the fourth button sat behind a small shiny table—wood-board pasted with sunmica—writing in a fat cloth register. He looked up at us without expression, jiggled the back of his pen in his right ear, and went back to writing. Jai asked for the man we had come to meet. He pointed over his shoulder without lifting his head. We went through another wood-board door, flimsy, unpolished, unsteady on its hinges, with a shiny chrome handle stuck into it, and immediately waded into what seemed like a small work hall, with tables and chairs at all angles. Every one of them empty save one at the far end. Two men sat there, facing each other, comparing the text of two documents. One read out a sentence softly and the other read it softly back. Then the first one said, 'Check!' loudly. Both officials were clean-shaven, in cream bush shirts, identical in their nondescriptness. If they went back to each other's homes their wives would not notice.

We went and stood by them, but they did not look at us till they had done about fifteen checks and come to the end of the typewritten page. They had the same incurious look the man outside had worn; weirdos probably pranced through these rooms by the hour. Jai asked, and they wordlessly thumbed us on to another door behind them, immediately returning to their task.

Inside this door we found ourselves in a dark vestibule, hemmed in on all sides by plywood walls. The edges of the strips of ply, painted a dull cream-yellow, were peeling off, like skin from nails. There were three doors in front of us: one on the left with a silver lock fat as a pomfret stuck in its latch; one right in front with a big brown signboard with 'No Entry Without Permission' stencilled in white; and one on the right, out of true with its frame, saying nothing.

Inside, a man leaned back in his chair, the fingers of his right hand splayed over his forehead, listening to a small radio softly singing Mukesh's maudlin 'Jeena yahaan marna yahaan. . . .' He looked at us through the slats of his fingers, then closed his eyes. He was in a moment of sadness; his head moving slowly, one with the song. Jai closed his eyes and began to hum the song too. This fucking country was awash with sentimental fools. One turn of a radio knob could conjure up weeping hordes.

The song finished. The man rubbed his eyes and sat up. He had a too-perfect mop of brown-black hair, with a parting clean and sharp as a knife. Probably a cheap toupee. Jai said, 'There's no one like Mukesh.' The man agreed, eyes shining, holding his left hand like a small mirror before his face. 'Before god! First Mukesh, then god! When I hear Mukesh I stop doing everything. I don't care whose work it is—my wife's, my children's, or my boss's! After all, if you are kneeling in the temple in front of god's image, do you jump up because a senior officer walks in?' Jai said, 'Your god is truly great, and you are a true disciple!'

The man patted his toupee sombrely—his hair was definitely nylon—and looked at me. I told him my name. The light went out of his eyes. He nodded impassively, and opening a register, turned it around and pushed it at me. The entire double-page spread was a scrawl of different hands, most of them illegible. I filled in our names, the name of the person we'd come to meet, the purpose of our meeting, our address, the time of arrival, and signed. He peered at it without turning it around, then putting a steel foot-rule on a white sheet of foolscap, neatly tore out a small square of paper and wrote my name on it with a ballpoint pen tethered to the desk with a string. Then he shut the register, got up, buttoned the waistband of his trousers with an audible suck, opened the door, and left.

Jai said, 'The song lover meets the commissar in a moment of melancholic intelligence sharing.'

The song lover returned, loosed his trouser button with a sigh, and sat down, expressionless. Then he turned up the small radio again. Mohammad Rafi's voice floated out. 'Yoon toh hamne lakh haseen dekhe hain, tumsa nahin dekha....' Immediately he grew agitated. 'Junk! Junk! Junk! Is this a song! A hundred thousand lovers! Shammi Kapoor jumping up and down!' Jai said, 'Will it take time, boss?' The man just held up a hand, his face full of distaste. We waited, talking to each other in whispers. He diddled the radio knobs, unleashing static, hunting for Mukesh. A boy came in carrying tea in small glasses in a wire holder. The song lover raised his eyebrows at us. We raised ours back. He raised them at the tea boy. The tea boy gave us a glass each and left.

A low buzzer rang somewhere in the room. The song lover got up, buttoned his trousers, and said, 'Come.' Gingerly, he cracked open the door with the signboard, and ushered us in.

The room was big, with enough space for a sofa suite with a coffee-table, and a big work desk with four chairs in front of it. Behind the desk was a high-backed chair, with an unsmiling man with a thin moustache sitting on it. The collar of his white shirt was pushed open to accommodate a small towel wrapped around his neck. He acknowledged us with a curt nod, making no effort at getting up. His spectacles were black and thick, and he bent down to his papers again, as we took a chair each.

On the wall behind the officer were four framed pictures. Gandhi, Nehru, and the incumbent president and prime minister. The only place those four would ever be found together was on a government wall. Gandhi was grinning toothily at the man below, while Nehru had a faraway tryst-with-destiny look. I turned slowly in my chair and scanned the room. Thick green curtains on the windows, two slim black briefcases on the floor with gold-coloured number locks, a heap of dirty-brown files tied with cord on the table next to the single sofa, some photographs on the wall of the man puffed out in police uniform, some thick books on a shelf, prominent among them the *Indian Penal Code* and *Gray's Anatomy.*

And then my eyes fell on Jai, and I was terrified. He was going into full Lincoln mode—the self-righteous clasp of the lips, the moral tightening of the eyes, the squaring of the ethical shoulders. He was poised for an oration. Fuck, the bugger was mad! These guys ate Lincolns for breakfast. If the real Abe showed up, they'd make him fill forms and wait in a corner till his beard touched the floor. Only the Sethijis of the world were a match for them. I put a hand on his knee. He turned and looked at me as if I was standing between him and the eradication of poverty. I pinched his flesh hard till the pain took the nobility out of his eyes. 'Say nothing!' I hissed.

The man looked up from his papers, the glasses low on his nose. I said, 'His name is Jai. He's the editor.' Not a muscle flickered on the man's face. He looked down again and continued to read with the tip of his pencil.

They were all Huthyams, inscrutable bastards, whether they prattled like schoolgirls or stayed silent like monks.

After a long time he threw the pencil down on the table, making it bounce, shut the file, and took off his glasses. Then he chucked the file on top of several others lying on the floor. On cue the song lover appeared, stooping at the waist, in response, no doubt, to the press of an invisible buzzer, and falling to his knees, picked up the files and vanished. The man lifted one end of the towel around his neck and without removing it dabbed his forehead and chin, his eyes shut. Then he opened his eyes and turned off the table lamp, pushed back his chair and scissored his hands on his belly. 'So why did they want to kill you?'

I said, my hand tight on Jai's knee, 'I have no idea. I have been hoping some of your men would let me know.'

He said, 'You know the killers?'

'No.'

'You have met them?'

'Saw them in the courtroom once.'

'Did you think they were killers?'

'I have no idea at all.'

He dabbed his upper lip with the end of the towel. It was like a small python coiled around his neck. Then he looked at Jai.

Jai leapt on to his horse and said, 'I think it's a complete set-up.'

No hand on the knee was going to restrain the march of the human spirit.

The man said, steepling the fingers on his belly, 'Interesting. You mean like a frame-up?'

Jai said, 'Yes. The truth is definitely something else. It's quite possible the arrested men are not the killers at all.'

I loved this. So wonderfully easy to declare other men's killers innocent! Sara and he were probably sharing morning walks at the Lodhi Gardens!

I said, 'Why don't you tell us what you know? We are just conjecturing.'

The man ignored me, and said to Jai, 'So what do you think could be the reason for this set-up?'

What was the fucking academy of dark sciences that all these cops went to! They were meant to be brutal breakers of bones. But they all behaved like master psychoanalysts. From lowly Hathi Ram to this portly DIG. No pounding; just slow dicing.

Jai said, at full gallop now, 'To protect the minister, to protect the government, to protect all the contractors who may be involved.'

I wanted to move my hands up from his knees to his testicles and squeeze them till they became one. It was really time to shut down missionary schools and elite education in India; they bred fucking aliens who knew nothing of Indian reality.

The man with a towel for a neck said, 'But they are the obvious suspects. This would directly indict them.'

Jai said, 'Ah, but that's it, precisely. It's so obvious that it cannot possibly be taken for the truth. The basic law of false obviousness. So everyone will say—they couldn't be that stupid. So everyone argues the innocence of the killers, they go to jail, get bail after four years, are acquitted after twelve—and forgotten by now are the contractors and the politicians and the siphoning of hundreds of millions!'

He was just making it up as he went along. The basic law of false obviousness! He was a star. I should have plunged to touch his feet.

The man slowly rubbed his chin against his towel neck and said, 'Interesting. So the crooks get some petty killers to launch an operation to shoot you, but to not actually shoot you?'

Jai said, waving his arms now, his voice thick with wisdom, 'Absolutely! But it doesn't actually matter whether they really shoot him or not. If they do, end of story; if they don't, still end of their part of the story. In any case, no one can ever trace the killers back to these guys. The shooters, you can be sure, are just cheap labour, picked from the villages, given ten thousand rupees and a country-made iron each. More disposable than plastic bags.'

Looking at me, towel-neck said, 'Would you agree with him?'

I said, 'I know nothing.'

Jai said, 'Nor do I. I am just making plausible conjecture.'

Do men with big words do big things, or do they just dig bigger holes in their path of life?

I said, 'But the security sub-inspector seemed to suggest that you all knew the true story.'

The man said, with no movement or change in expression, 'The contract to kill you was taken out by the ISI.'

I said, 'Of Pakistan?'

He nodded.

Jai said, 'You are not serious? This sounds like bad Indian propaganda. Blame everything on Pakistan. Why would they care about him?'

So now I was a geopolitical pawn. Fuck, what would Guruji make of all this? Would he convert it into a mango parable or a sea parable?

The man said, 'They calculated that killing him would indict all the political men he exposed. It would cause a public outcry. The government could even be destabilized.'

Public outcry! Every bugger in this mad country was a fantasist. At best, three women would have cried. My mother in a continuum of wailing that had been going on forever; Dolly/folly with a mix of self-pity and coy winsomeness at the cremation; and Sara for the poor killers who would now be arraigned.

Jai said, 'So the government is protecting him to protect itself?'

I said, 'The arrested men have confessed to this? This ISI thing?'

The man was now holding the towel at both ends and slowly working it back and forth. The way my grandmother in the village used to churn butter. Maybe it was a way of getting his cerebellum to rise to the surface.

He said, 'It's only a matter of time. They will.'

Mahatma Gandhi grinned down at him. Nehru looked nobly into the distance.

I said, 'You know it from other sources?'

He said, 'The government of India is a big organization. It works all the time.'

The fire had gone of out Jai's eyes. He was a mortal once again. He said, 'So you are still not sure?'

The man ignored him now. He said, looking between the two of us at the exit door, 'So you know nothing at all?'

We looked at each other. How Jai would spin this story in margarita living-rooms lit by perfumed candles!

The man stood up—he was short, his waist barely reaching the edge of the table—and extended a short arm with a small soft hand. Despite the neck towel the hand was clammy. The door behind us opened and the song lover appeared. The man said, 'Take them to Dubeyji. Then he sat down, put his glasses back on, and began to read from where he had left off with the tip of his red-and-black striped pencil. When Jai said, goodbye sir, the man without looking up waved his pencil in erudite dismissal.

Outside the door Jai said, 'The government of India is a very big organization with very small men! He probably sees Pakistani plots in the colour of his piss!'

Turning to him, the song lover said, 'Which is your favourite Mukesh song?'

Dubeyji was a mouse. Actually, he was more like a squirrel. He was tiny, with a rodent's nose and darting eyes, but his air was playful, not furtive. Under the rodent's nose was a bristly moustache, quivering, full of friendly cheer, like a squirrel's tail.

The road to him had led through another maze of cardboard walls and doors—no windows—and empty rooms with unoccupied chairs and desks. Everywhere the furniture was in disarray, as if the occupants had rushed out at short notice. Either the intelligence armies of the state were scouring the landscape for priceless information, or they had concluded it was a hopeless pursuit in this mad sprawling nation and simply abandoned their stations.

Dubeyji shook our hands heartily, and said to me, 'Good job, sir.'

Like everyone else in the building he wore a creamy-white bush shirt and dark trousers. On his thin left wrist was an enormous steel-link watch, and on his right many strands of frayed pink-red mauli. Around his neck a tight black cord with a tin locket. Inside it, I was sure, nestled a picture of a holy man or two.

Dubeyji was the officer on the case, with the rank, perhaps, of sub-inspector or inspector. In this department of spooks there was no place for uniforms. This was not policing through authority; this was policing through stealth. Dubeyji was obviously a field man, the swordarm of this central citadel of investigations and intelligence. On his humble gleanings would grand cases live and die, grand governments plot and move. In this job, his size and his rodent's nose were definite assets.

The room given to the swordarm was so tiny that I had to half pull one chair out to let Jai through before dragging it back in. It was intimate, like being together on a bed: the small steel table, the three iron-pipe chairs tight around it, our bodies tending to touch at the feet and the knees. Nailed to the corner of the wall was a small fan, whirling noisily, moving its neck with arthritic clicks. Jai looked at it malevolently, and Dubeyji got up with some difficulty and poked it dead. This closet room, unexpectedly, also had a window. But in keeping with the mood of the place it was a thin slit, a gun embrasure in a castle wall. When he saw us looking at it, the swordarm said, 'In the beginning, once, someone jumped out during questioning and killed himself. Now no air, no light, but also no suicide!' He had his own briefcase too—shiny Rexine, dark brown, a bit dented, standing next to his chair. It too had a numbered lock. Presumably 007: licence to inspire suicide.

Smiling happily under his bushy moustache, Dubeyji said, 'So tell me, sir, what all do you know about your murder.'

I said, 'I only know what the police has told me.'

He said, 'The DIG sahib?'

I said, 'Yes. And what I saw and heard in the courtroom.'

He said, 'You saw them? They look so innocent, don't they?'

I said, 'Sure, some of them.'

He said, 'It's how it always is. God is the best suspense film-maker in the world. He always gives killers innocent faces, so that the audience has to keep guessing and the police has to work twice as hard.'

Jai was paying no attention. This rodent was too low in the food chain to hold his interest. He was punching away at a searing pace on his mobile. Probably sending the first bush alert to the margarita club about his latest adventures, wetting depilated ladies with tales of Kafka's castle.

I said, 'So it is true—this ISI thing?'

He licked the tip of his forefinger and carefully pulled out three sheets of white foolscap paper and two sheets of creased blue carbon from his drawer. Setting the carbon between the white sheets, he pinned them together neatly and pushed them towards me. 'Please write an account of all you know and sign it.'

I said, 'I told you. I know nothing.'

Dubeyji smiled happily and said, 'Of course we know you know nothing. Just write that. It's a formality. Paperwork. Just like a buffalo needs grass, the government needs paper.'

I looked at him blankly.

He said, grinning, 'Like a buffalo it will chew and chew and chew the paper endlessly. And finally there will be milk!'

I pulled the paper towards me, and slanting it for ease of wrist, in a large scrawl wrote: 'Apart from the information given to me by the police, I have no knowledge whatsoever of the five men who it is alleged had plotted to kill me. I do not know any of them, and have only seen them once in the courtroom at Patiala House.' I signed with a flourish and put the date, my phone number and address, and pushed it across the table. He read it slowly, mouthing the words, once, twice, three times. Then with a grin he said, 'You don't want to write if you suspect someone?' I said I suspected nobody.

The rodent removed the pin, separated the carbon sheets from the foolscap, and carefully put everything back in his drawer. Jai was still hammering away on his mobile. His eyes were squinting and his lips were bared in a rictus of a smile. The margarita girls were probably in a senseless froth by now. Was the rodent so despicable that he did not deserve even a fleeting oration on liberty, equality, fraternity?

Turning the key of his drawer, the happy officer said, 'There is a girl. A very smart girl. She is helping these men. At least trying to. You know her?'

Jai looked up sharply—his fingers kept moving of their own accord. I thought of Sara and felt myself stir. It had been many days.

I said, 'Who? No, I don't.'

He said, 'She's a troublemaker, it seems. The kind who looks for rallies to go to. Lives in Vasant Kunj. She's been visiting these men in Tihar jail. Has also got them a lawyer. She has friends in the press too.'

I thought, another few minutes and there'll be photographs on the table—my hairy naked buttocks nailing Sara to the wall. The Crusader's Crucifixion—a four-colour poster. Maybe even a videotape—with both of us singing a bilingual duet of genitalia and abuse.

I knew Jai was looking at me. I stayed inside the mask and said, 'This Pakistani thing—have these men confessed to it?'

Grinning till his bushy moustache quivered, the officer said, 'Confessing means nothing. In lock-up we can make them confess to anything! Even the murder of Gandhiji! But it doesn't have any value in court. We have to collect hard proof.'

I said, 'And you have it?'

He said, 'We have the truth. The proof will come.'

Behind the inspector's head the wall was bare but for a lurid green poster. There was the image of a handsome man in a peak-cap, and he had spelt out an equation in bold letters.

Small minds: discuss people.

Average minds: discuss events.

Big minds: discuss ideas.

Great minds: work in silence.

We opened and shut many plywood doors before we made our way back to the cramped landing and groped our way down the dark stairs to the equally cramped eighth floor. Jai pressed the button for the lift, then we looked at each other, remembered the shuddering impact with which it had descended, and decided to walk. It was like a stroll through a slum. There was offal everywhere. Big dust balls, blackened banana peels, membrane-thin plastic bags, shiny chips and biscuit packets, stones of pickle, bits of bread, cigarette butts, matchboxes, rags, torn papers. In the weak light seeping in from the landings you could see the cobwebs festooning the corners, and every sooty wall had splashes of paan juice, layers upon layers, dulled with time. We walked in line—Jai before me, carefully staying away from the walls and the banisters. Every now and then the stench of rancid food and sour piss hit us like a fist stopping our breath.

The lift was a better idea. Plummeting down a shaft a safer option.

Down eight storeys and sixteen flights we did not exchange a single word, trying to descend quickly, focusing on where to put our feet, holding our breath much of the time. By the time we hit the ground floor and emerged out into the dark, we were totally winded.

My shadows peeled away from the wall they were leaning against, dropping their lit cigarettes and grinding them underfoot. The man on the stool looked up from his mobile phone and said, 'What? It's broken down again?'

Jai said, 'Yes, it has. Not the lift, but your fucking government!'

The man said, 'Not mine, sahib, yours. I am just a watchman outside the walls—you are the sahibs inside.' The big parking lot was empty but for our cars and a few official white Ambassadors. High above, on the top floor of the shoebox building, a few lights glowed dimly through slim windows that only allowed suicidees below forty kilos to squeeze through. All night the man in the towel and the squirrel would track the enemies of the great Indian state.

With his car door open, Jai turned around and said, 'Who's this woman, boss? Sounds quite something.'

I said, 'The government has an imagination no one gives them credit for. Hasn't it worked out that Pakistan's taken out a contract on me?'

Jai said, 'You are such a desperately secretive bastard! Won't let your balls know what your dick is doing!'

And you, maaderchod, are the messiah of the drawing-rooms, pissing margaritas and morality in a fine balance! Elvis Presley speaking in the voice of Mahatma Gandhi.

She opened the door and I wanted her. Her face wore a sullen resistance—her natural mien—that was immediately arousing. I had driven here directly from Kafka's castle because I didn't want to go home, and there was nowhere else to go. I had briefly contemplated heading to the sports club for a jog, but the thought of talking to Sara was more appealing. Then she opened the door wearing a thin white cotton slip, a red wrap with yellow flowers and a petulant look, and all I wanted to do was to pick her up and hang her on the wall.

The problem, of course, was that to hang Sara on the wall you needed first to argue with her. Or, more accurately, have her shout at you. Today I had fresh fuel for her rage. But my ardour cooled the moment I stepped in and saw she was drinking rum with water. The squat glass was less than half full, and I could see it was strong with the dark alcohol. I hated her rum mouth, the sourness of the flavour. A fat bottle of Old Monk sat on the dining-table, freshly opened, dipped to just below its neck. Next to it, cap-less, sat an empty bottle. The signs were bad. The rum assault meant she was in a roil about something serious. Not the kind that would lead to a shouting match and a nailing. This one seemed like a simmer: few words, the shutters down, a melancholy aloofness. Occasionally—very rarely—even self-doubt, though that was so alien to her condition.

Without asking me she went into her untidy kitchen—food stains on the burner, disorder in the cupboards, unwashed dishes in the sink—brewed me a big mug of tea, and walked into her bedroom. I followed. The heap of newspapers, books, magazines, printed sheets and loosely strung brown files heaped on the bed had grown out of control. Adding to the mess were an open packet of potato chips, an open packet of glucose biscuits, and a steel ashtray studded with cigarette butts. One of these days we'd be lying on the floor. The bedside lamp, angled on to the pillows, had clearly been burning for a long time. It was pulsing a slow heat. Napoleon was silent, dead till next April.

She sat down against the pillows, and I had to find a perch near her feet. I could look up her wrap but did not dare do so. That kind of vulgarity she never forgave. Cheap, roadside stuff. Our symphony of abuse was different. It was intellectual. It was an art form. So I looked her in the eye, and she glowered back. Her frail shoulders—the bones cutting the air—were truly sensual. It was a pity I could never get past her full hips.

In as flat a voice as I could summon I slowly led her through our visit to the ninth floor. I omitted the allusions to the mysterious woman. There was no point in alarming her. Also, I did not want her storming up the stairs and pulling the plywood walls down. She didn't interrupt me even once, alternately pulling on a cigarette and glugging the rum. When I finished, she tilted the last drops into her throat, got off the bed, and came back with a replenished glass. I hated it when she was like this.

I said, 'Do you think they are telling the truth?'

About what, she asked with her eyebrows.

'Pakistan,' I said.

In a toneless voice she said, 'Listen, you are a stupid schoolboy. They know it. They deal with fools like you every day. They know you are thrilled at having become so grand. Killers after you, policemen guarding you, judges studying your case. It's your ultimate wet dream, isn't it? Well, they are making it wetter for you, much grander—an international conspiracy, Pakistan commissioning assassins, fancy officers in multistoreyed buildings decoding complicated plots. You are finally starring in your own pulp novel. You are dying to believe them. So just do.'

I wanted to pick her up, slam her against the wall and twist her neck till all the smugness was squeezed out of her like coils of toothpaste. Guruji was right: too much reading, too many books, were a dangerous thing. No conversation could be simple; no response uncalibrated. Everything had to be fashioned into an elaborate construct: of motives and postures and neuroses and failings. I wish I could have told the crazy bitch that I wasn't even interested in what she thought. I just wanted to feel her exquisite chocolate skin and perish with her voice ringing in my ears in that deep dark place that she kept so madly moist.

I said, 'They seem to know about you too.'

She pulled on her cigarette—her third since I'd arrived—for so long that I could see the burn run and crackle. 'And what do they know, mighty peashooter? That I drink rum with water and allow you sometimes to stick your toothpick into me?'

What did her parents do? Wean her on quinine?

'It makes sense to be careful,' I said. 'Can't trust these guys.'

For the first time a kind of smile cracked her face. It was the kind of smile that accompanies the final stab. 'Oh, now you can't trust these guys! For the last one year you've diligently listened to whatever they had to say—these are policemen to guard you, these are the killers, there's Pakistan handing out the contracts! But now that you know they're getting into the details of your adulterous poking, you begin to not trust them! What do you think they'll do to me? Name me as an accomplice of the other five? Accuse me of dangerously draining your body fluids?'

The huge mug of tea had filled my bladder like a water balloon. I got up and went to her loo and poured myself into the sink in a splatter that lasted forever. When I came out, she had pulled on her jeans and was standing in the living-room, her house keys in her hand. Anger burst in me in a flash and I elbowed her aside and without a word was out the door. I was down the stairs when her voice came: 'Time to go home and fill ms white's pinkie-winkie. But when you are done, mr peashooter, look at the ceiling and think about yourself.'

So I did what she said. When Dolly/folly opened the door and asked if I'd like some dinner, I pushed her into our bedroom and onto our bed without saying a word. She was so thrilled at this rare assault that she immediately flung up her long legs—the cherubs on her nightie taking a dive—and mewled softly. The rage was still moving in me and I was deep in her with the first thrust. It was like being in a mug of warm water. She was a weeping mess. So like her; not a trace of subtlety.

I buried my face in her neck, away from her mouth, and began to swim. She locked her ankles around my back like a pair of handcuffs, and began to pant and moan my name. It was unbearable. The lights made it worse. I tried to shut out her voice, her body.

For some reason I found myself thinking of the grinning squirrel in the closet room on the ninth floor: great minds work in silence. Did he really know more, or was this how all these guys worked? Never letting on that they knew more, and always pretending they knew more than they actually did? And ought I to care? Wasn't this a typically Indian situation, full of fevered fictions and forked tongues? As Guruji often said, 'Most of the time we are like ghosts moving in the mist. We can barely find ourselves, leave alone others.' I had always taken advantage of being a ghost in the mist, so why should I worry now? Just because a woman with an unequal body had ordered me to stare up at the ceiling and think about myself?

I suddenly realized that Dolly/folly was agitating under me. Probably because I was swimming poorly. It didn't look like I had much stroke left in me. At this rate I would soon drown. Her heel was digging into my back. She was prodding me like a horse! What happened to the ideal of the demure Hindu wife? Her loud panting was mystifying too. The action did not support it. If I were Guruji now, I would have said, 'Don't mix up things. Never work out the ire against one woman on another.'

I noticed her earrings. They were tiny silver tennis racquets! We were really a country without hope. I closed my eyes tight and tried to conjure up a red wrap with yellow flowers. Without warning the woman below me gave a loud grunt. It was an animal sound. In disgust I bit hard into her shoulder. She read it wrong and began to buck even more, her heel banging me rhythmically. I tried to think of things that would help me finish this. I could dredge up nothing.

For some reason, the grinning squirrel kept grabbing all the space: the bushy moustache; the no-suicide window; great minds working in silence.

Three muffled beeps sounded. I stretched my hand down to the floor and felt around in my peeled-off trousers for my mobile. I held it away from her head and opened the message and instantly felt a charge. It was nothing short of a book. Much too long to read and fuck at the same time. So I rolled off her and sat up against the backrest. She looked at me with an abject mix of self-pity and rebuke, as if I'd stripped her naked in the middle of the road. The flying cherubs bunched around her waist looked pretty forlorn too. Grimly, without looking her in the face, I said, 'Police', and began to scroll. Dolly/folly! She was foolish enough to believe the police was writing me novellas on sms in the middle of the night. The best thing I'd ever done in my life was to have never given her the right to ask questions. Two scrolls of the screen and I'd forgotten there was a half-naked woman with a mug of warm water inside her lying by my side.

Sara was distressed because the sparrow had finally flown from her side. For the last two months I knew Bhandariji, the tiny melodramatic lawyer of Patiala House, had been giving signs of waning interest in Sara's case, or rather in Sara. I had not been told this, but had gathered it from the drift of her conversation. Today it seemed he had not taken her calls, and when she'd shown up at his office—in his residence—he had refused to meet her. Of course you did not stop Sara so easily. She had hollered so loud and long that all the doors had to be flung open. In the presence of his juniors, and with his sour, prematurely ageing wife hovering in the backdrop, Bhandariji had declared that there was no case. The five men were doomed. He had done his best. He could not give it any more time.

When Sara attacked him for being money-fixated, he said—and I could just see him, with a cinematic cock of his head, his fingertips priming his collar—'Madam, who doesn't like money? But here there is no case and there is no money! I have studied it and I know. We are both wasting our time. These men are like random stalks of sugarcane. Powerful men cut them, chew them, and spit them out. No one pays to kill them; no one pays to save them. You must spend your time on better things. Bride burning, child labour, witch-hunting, sati, dowry deaths, female foeticide, cholera, tuberculosis, polio, tree-felling, pollution...'

Yes, the whole fucking world waiting to be saved. From itself.

Sara was not one to take anything at face value. She was too full of grand education for that. The American university had taught her things like deconstruction and subtext. Instead of the cunning of the sub-literate she had the suspicion of the overeducated. And like most Indians, with two hundred years of colonial genuflections running in their veins, she was born bawling conspiracy theories. She said: clearly, the sparrow was either being leaned upon or had taken money from someone. She was going to find out and she was going to fix him. The sparrow's strange about-face made her even more certain that the assassins were innocent.

I became aware of naked legs lying next to me, the cherubs congregating at the waist. How well she'd trimmed herself, as if she were about to star in a centrefold. She was doing what I had been ordered to do—stare up at the ceiling and think about oneself. Sensing my gaze, she turned to look at me. Her pleading cow eyes filled me with revulsion and I leapt off the bed, picked up my trousers, and went into the bathroom.

I pulled the car out of the lane, took two turns and parked under the old semul tree by the park.

The shadow had been sleeping on his fold-out bed inside the veranda's overhang when I emerged from the house, and had poked his head out of the blanket. This was a new one, a young boy called

Munna, only six months in the business. He was not made to be a cop. He had done a BSc and an MSc in physics from Rohtak (one degree more than me) and had a soft face that belonged to a bank clerk or a chemist. Someone—some frantic family member: in Indian families breeding insecurity is a favourite pastime—someone had pushed him into enlisting. His ambitions lay elsewhere. Often he could be seen reading thick blue-coloured tomes, preparing for the civil service exam that he hoped would give him a desk job and other cops to order around. The fool held his 9mm as if it would explode in his hands. I knew he never kept it loaded—the magazine was always in his right pocket. If I was ever attacked I would be killed, cremated and drifted down the Ganga before he got his pistol and ammunition aligned. I answered the question in his eyes by saying I was just going down the road for a paan and he could keep sleeping. He had slumped back gratefully.

Under the semul tree, I turned off the car lights, locked the doors and dialled Guruji's number. It was not yet ten, but the colony lanes were empty, with not a single after-dinner stroller visible. Only one-eyed Jeevan was moving around, and had jumped out of his nest amid the dried leaves in the gutter and headed towards me and the car. He was a determined bastard, with a saint's faith in humanity. For some reason I didn't kick him away as I tended to, and he stood next to me, wagging his weak tail, as I opened the door and fired the engine.

Guruji was relaxed as ever when he came on the line. 'What trouble have you got into now?' he said, with the hint of laughter in his voice.

I told him the story of Kafka's castle.

He said, 'Just as the temple stands between man and god, in India the government stands between man and justice. Don't let it worry you.'

I said, 'But how does one get to know what the truth is?'

He said, and I could see him sitting on his charpoy under a

billion stars, bare of torso and smiling, 'The truth is what it is. It doesn't change whether you know it or not. So why let it worry you? Men chase the truth as if it's Aladdin's djinn, and will solve all their problems—instead of doing the right thing, secure in the knowledge that the truth is unalterable and will remain what it is whether we know it or not. What is it about all this that is worrying you now?'

So like Guruji. The large wisdom, and in the same breath, the small tactic.

I said, 'All I want to know is whether I should worry at all. While they are saying these are killers contracted by Pakistan, she says she's been checking and they are fully innocent, and have been trapped in all this.'

Of all the people in the world, Sippy staggered by. His sparse hair was standing on end, and his pants were dangerously low, getting in the way of his stagger. I could almost smell the stench of booze through the closed windows. He went past without noticing me. How could he possibly push up the shutter in this state? One of these days he was just going to die on the veranda and we'd be dealing with another hundred conspiracy theories.

Guruji said—I could almost see him beaming—'If she means innocent because they are the victims of their circumstances, then of course they are innocent. Just as the police are, and she is, and you are, and I am!' He laughed, and added, 'And Ravana was, and Duryodhana was, and Pakistan is!'

I said, 'This leaves me no wiser.'

He said, 'Of course it won't. And in any case this is not what she means. This is not the way to look at the world. Only holy men and fools are supposed to find everyone blameless. And you all are neither. Trust is not like love. It is good to give love freely to everybody, but trust is like good karma—it must always be earned. Men must remember that they live among men. There is no wisdom in forgetting that. For men, we know, are the least reliable of all animals.

For money and power they can forsake the womb that birthed them, slice the loins that spawned them, murder the friend that sheltered them. Remember, Gandhi was killed by a Hindu, and Issa betrayed by his followers and nailed to a cross. The universe manufactures more bad than good men so that the good may be continually tested. Because it is not enough to be good once or twice; it's not enough to get the better of one bad man—the warriors of god need to best battalions of the bad in the course of their lives.'

Fuck. I was regretting I had called. This was not the sermon for a man transporting his tumescence across town. By the time I got to her she'd probably have reverted from Durga to Mahakali. Somewhere behind me I could hear the jangle of steel. Sippy was wrestling with the shutter as if with an oiled snake.

I said, 'I understand, Guruji.'

The laughing voice said, 'You are wondering why Guruji is dribbling big words like spittle at this time of night. But you know, gurujis too have to fulfil their karma. Just remember, if you are not a holy man and not a fool, and your destiny is neither to forgive nor to laugh, then the men are not innocent. All of them have crossed the lines men draw among themselves, and one of them was cracking open heads like eggshells at an age when you were still cycling to school in your half-pants.'

12

HATHODA TYAGI

i

The Sprinting Master's Journey

His mother insisted he was benign of heart. It was just his head that was hot. His father, spitting a scattershot, a frayed datun poking out of his mouth, said that his head was not merely hot, it was in flames, and that one day the flames would char his heart, and perhaps everything else around him. His siblings said they loved him but needed protection from him. His friends at school said they loved him but needed protection from him. His teachers said they doubted they could teach him anything, especially the fundamentals of non-violence.

The shastri—the astrologer-cum-pandit from the neighbouring village—who had made his birth-chart, peeled open the roll of yellow parchment and scratched his head. Going up and down the garish blue-and-red hexagons, pentagons and triangles with the blunt end of his pencil, he said slowly, 'The boy's chart is full of good signs. He is born under the sign of the ruler. He will have strength, and he will have power. Men will fear him, and men will follow him. He will never lack for food or for money. It will come to him whenever he wants it, and like a king he will give of it freely to others.' He then stopped, and from over his thick black glasses, looked around the yard.

These were people fallen on bad days. The dung-washed yard was clean but spare. At the far right end were tethered one milch buffalo and her thin-legged calf, and a little removed from them, two dirty-white oxen with starvation bones jutting out. A single rectangular mud trough, its edges crumbling, served them all. At the moment it was flecked with snatches of dry hay. On the left side of the yard was a clunky handpump with an unusual square mouth, and just behind it a small, screening mud wall, behind which the women of the house bathed. Draped over the wall he could see women's clothes drying.

The shastri, who lived two villages away, had been visiting this family for a lifetime. He bore witness to its gathering distress—the land disputes, the brutal face-offs, the police interventions, the resort to the courts, the ensuing impasse, and the shrinking fortunes.

The house comprised one large room, made with rejected bricks—their nakedness displaying their defects. The solitary door was always open, letting in a shaft of sunlight during the day, and in the night, a shimmer of moon. The two windows, at opposite ends, were always closed, their sills loaded with chattel, the frames hung over with dusty old clothes. The floor was polished dung. Chinks of light burst into the room from the imperfect wall, the loose frames of the window, and the clumsy roof, which was always alive with the traffic of rodents.

Two big iron trunks sat next to each other against the far wall, piled high with bedding—mattresses, pillows, quilts—all the same faded dirty brown. Both the trunks sported big locks. Inside them were secured everything of value the family possessed, most importantly wedding jewellery passed down the generations. Often years rolled by without either of the trunks ever being opened. Standing on their side, stacked into each other, were five rope charpoys with crudely carved legs. In the summer they were dragged out at night as the family slept under the stars, and in the winters laid out inside cheek-by-jowl till the room was a sheet of charpoys and everyone had to climb over each other to find their appointed place. In one corner stood two long spears, their bamboo torsos stout and strong, their iron heads blunt and rusted. A naked sword, its metal black with neglect, hung from a nail next to them. Heaped in the far corner were big brass utensils, some of them large enough to stir up meals for a hundred people.

Gyanendra Tyagi had a handlebar moustache and big shoulders but only one good leg. His left knee had been shattered by an iron-tipped lathi six years ago during the last land-grab. Gyanendra had only fifty bighas of land left. One hundred bighas were in dispute, and hundred and twenty more had been wrested—over many invasions—by his older cousin Jogendar and his five strapping sons.

For six years now, the shastri was aware, Gyanendra had held the peace, simmering in rage but scared to provoke another physical skirmish. The boy whose horoscope he had come to read was named Vikram and he was already two years old. Gyanendra had spawned him after a succession of girls. All hopes of levelling with his cousin rested on him.

Weighing his words carefully, chewing on the pencil, the shastri said, 'For his father he will be like a tangerine—sweet and sour at the same time. For his mother he will be like a guava—always tasty even when it has too many seeds. And for the world he will be like a pineapple—very thorny outside but full of juice inside.'

To Gyanendra Tyagi, sitting cross-legged on the charpoy opposite the shastri, it all sounded good. His wife, squatting on the yard floor, veil pulled over her forehead asked, 'Will his coming help end this endless land row? Will we have peace finally? And will there be enough once again?'

The shastri rustled his parchment. Every damn parent hoped a new child would bring a change in fortune. In his experience all they did was add one more mouth to be fed. He had seen birth-charts like this before. They presaged a stormy life.

He said, 'Yes, he will be a warrior who strikes fear into his enemies. He will bring you material well-being, and he will bring you protection. But it will take a heavy toll of him.'

In alarm the mother cried, 'Shastriji, you are hiding something from us! What is wrong with my son? Is he ill-fated?'

The astrologer, his grey hair thick over his ears but gone from the top of his head, said, 'Oh, don't start getting worked up. It's just that, because of his work and his strength, he will have powerful foes. You do know, mataji, that only powerful men have powerful enemies! But it will not be easy to harm him. His stars are like Hrinyakashyap's. He can only be harmed in a place that has both sunlight and shade; he can only be harmed when he is moving and not still; he can only be harmed when his belly is full; he can only be harmed when he is hidden from view; he can only be harmed by a slain enemy; and he can only be harmed when he is trapped between friends. For all these things to come together is a near impossibility. So you must not worry. Remember, to kill the evil Hrinyakashyap, Lord Vishnu had to appear himself and bend the elements. And as you know, the gods don't descend into this country any more.'

Despite the shastri's reassuring odds, the mother could not stay her anxiety. And, sure enough, the signs of trouble surfaced early as the boy grew strong and tempestuous with every passing year. He talked little and never argued, but he was prone to sudden explosions of temper. It was impossible to tell what triggered the outbursts, but it was mostly something said, not something done or denied. It could be a casual remark by one of his sisters, his mother's nagging, the sour undertone in his father's voice, a farmhand's jibe. When he was small it would result in him flinging things around—pots, pans, slippers, clothes, food, anything that his hands found. If an attempt was made to restrain him he would become a ball of fury, lashing out with his fists and feet and teeth.

In a big city, in a rich house, he would have been taken to a counsellor. He would have been offered sweet words and coloured pills. In the village, in the one-room house amid the fields, the problem was first redressed with systematic thrashings. But soon it became clear that this was a medicine designed to aggravate the disease. The beating would scarcely be over than the ball of fury would erupt in a fresh round of destruction.

One time, when the father had been particularly excessive, laying into him with the short bamboo stick they used to goad the cattle and then tying his hands together, the enraged boy—who never cried or begged for mercy—banged his head against the wall till his skin split and the blood ran into his mouth.

The terrified family was forced to change tack. The best way to keep water still is to not stir it. In a declared—and oft-repeated—consensus, it was agreed, 'Don't say anything to him. Just let him be.'

Very early then, he fell out of all conversation and emotional commerce with his sisters, and with his parents there arose a distance that would never be bridged. The boy did not seem to mind. He never sought anyone out—for company or assistance—and was quite happy to escape the family by plunging into the sugarcane forests that began, literally, from the edge of their yard, and lay all around them. It was not unusual for him to spend hours exploring and roaming them. He would peel and chew and peel and chew stalk after stalk of cane, as he picked his way through the crowded razor-leaves.

Sometimes he would walk for so long that he would enter other men's fields and lose his bearings. Then he would need to make an exit from the forest, locate his position—by a homestead, a tree, a tube well—and slowly saunter back over the bunds.

Sometimes he would imagine that he was surrounded by armed dacoits, and he had to evade and slay them. He would then wreak havoc with the juicy weapon in his hand, thrusting it like a dagger and brandishing it like a sword.

The sugarcane forests were alive with surprises other than the rustling dacoits. Snakes were not uncommon, nor were hares. Occasionally you could see a jackal slinking away, head low to the ground, and rarely, very rarely, a wild pig or a hulking nilgai. Once he found the neighbouring thakur's son wrestling with a woman who worked in the fields. He had managed to get on top of her and was thrusting her hard into the ground. The boy watched—unseen—for some time, but when he thought the man was about to kill her he scuttled away. Somehow the woman survived. A few days later, he saw her squatting between the cabbage rows, diligently turning the soil.

Another thing to watch out for in the cane forests were the defecating bottoms. The trick was to walk close to the heart of the thicket—the crappers seldom went in farther than three rows from the edge. Deep in there he discovered two things: the profound peace that lies at the heart of rustling nothingness, and a matchless hiding place. Both were to provide him solace in the years to come.

He had another source of comfort. The cattle tethered in the yard. He liked stroking their heaving flanks—the buffalo's fleshy but rough; the oxen's spare but silky. It calmed him to rub down their bony heads, to grip their hard horns. Their startled stomping when he pulled and played with their ears and tails was the only thing that made him gurgle with amusement. And sometimes, when no one was watching, he slowly caressed his face with the hairy end of their frayed tails, making his nose tickle, giving himself shivery giggles and bouts of sneezing.

Since everyone said his head was too hot, he also discovered an unusual way of cooling it. When the buffalo—called Shanti, peace—had settled on her side to ruminate, he would lie in front of her, head propped on his elbows, and offer her his severely cropped head (his father's strategy for keeping it cool). Shanti would then proceed to systematically lick it with her thick wet tongue. He would move his head slowly under the lapping tongue and in no time his scalp would be drenched. The boy loved this massage and anytime he was sure no one was watching he would seek it out. Sometimes he would actually nod off to sleep as Shanti lapped his head.

At his naming ceremony the shastri had pulled out the letter 'V'. To begin with the family named him Vinod, after a couple of film actors of that name, one of them a macho Punjabi hero with a cleft chin. The boy's pet name was, of course, Guddu; the formal Vinod was never used. Then, when he was six, and was taken to the local government school, the headmaster ran his hands down the boy's shoulders and arms and said, 'He looks too big to be six. Are you telling the truth about his age?' Soon after, his father changed the boy's name to Vishal—huge. And though he did not grow up to be unnaturally tall, he did develop the torso of a lifter of weights and the rolling gait of a professional boxer.

In school they began to tease him early. He was big of size but not quick of wit. He spoke little and haltingly and had slow eyes, which in later years would turn into an unflinching gaze. The boys called him chacha, daddu, oonth, bhainsa, khachchar, mule. In every school skit he was given the role of the demon. Thick black moustaches were painted under his nose and rolled over his cheeks, and he was he made to strut the makeshift stage with a wooden club, before being slain by Rama or Bhima or Shiva. His maths teacher called him Bakasura.

When he was nine, and strong enough to be fourteen, he began to bang the heads of the teasing boys together. His behaviour was no different from what it had been when he was younger. He'd let the jibes slide for a long time, paying no heed, not responding, looking the other way, carrying on in his slow fashion, and then suddenly something would snap and he would grab whoever he could lay his hands on and hammer them till their wails for mercy filled the school.

The headmaster took it up with his father more than once. Gyanendra Tyagi, exhausted by a lifetime's legal and physical war with his cousins, sick of his son's intransigence, simply said, 'Why do you think we've sent him to you, masterji? What is the meaning of this big school in this small village if finally I am left to kick him into shape? You come and run my house and fields and I'll run this fancy school of yours, if that's what you want!'

The school was certainly extravagant. Sixteen concrete rooms, in an L-shaped block, ten and six, all the rooms twelve by twelve feet, with two windows and two doors each. Twelve years ago a local village man had become the MLA of the area and had then become a minister in the state government. The school was his gift to his kinsmen, though the village was too small to fulfil the criterion for a high school. Once the minister lost power, the school grew derelict. Maintenance funds were scarce and most villagers didn't have the patience to walk their children down the long tortuous education road that would most likely end in a blind alley. Now the bricks of the boundary wall were being continually purloined, several rooms had become living quarters for the teachers, and the playing field behind the building was grazing ground for cattle.

The headmaster, who ran a small cement sale agency alongside, actually didn't give a damn about the school. His only concern was avoiding a scandal. He didn't want a death on his hands. Times had changed. There were small and big newspapers everywhere, some like *Sanjhi Khabar*, Twilight News, no more than four smudged sheets, always on the lookout for a juicy story that they could drum up and parley into a deal. This was a comfortable posting. His village was just fifteen kilometres away, and the cement agency was doing brisk business. Any controversy, and he could well be on his way to eastern UP, or worse still, to some godforsaken hamlet at 8000 feet in the Kumaon—an hour's walk from the road and so cold in December that it froze your piss.

This boy bothered him. Either he was going to be dead before he was eighteen, or he was going to be a legend. The headmaster had spent a lifetime thrashing bullies and brats, and he had learnt to identify their varying thresholds. The most common ones gave you lip and played to the gallery: they could be easily silenced with some precise insults about their caste, or their physical features, or the sheer meanness of their family conditions. There were others, more thick-skinned, inured to insult, who needed to be caned to within an inch of their lives before they understood the obedience–punishment equation. There were still others, physically strong, more resistant to authority, carrying the threat of counter-violence in their bodies. For these you called in their fathers: between master and patriarch they could be taught the meaning of piety.

This boy was different. He didn't give lip, and he didn't play to any gallery. Most times, he just exploded disproportionately to someone's provocation. Then there was no restraining him till his fury was spent. And physically he was an ox. On a few occasions he had mercilessly beaten up as many as six-seven boys, while scaring off another half a dozen from interfering. Since class seven, the headmaster had not risked assaulting him. Matters were compounded by not knowing what would trigger his violence. His Hindi teacher, a thoughtful man who chewed on his sacred thread, always said, 'Inside his head is a jwalamukhi. A simmering volcano. Does anyone ever know why and when a volcano will erupt? Even a geologist? Even the volcano itself? It's the same with him.' And when he was asked what should be done, the teacher would say, thread between his teeth, 'What do men do with a live volcano? Keep a watchful eye on it, and maintain a safe distance.'

Everyone took that advice as an injunction—at home, in the school, in the village. Except one man—the one man who was to shape and define his life.

Rajbir Gujjar had done twenty-four years in the state constabulary and was now employed in the school as sports-master. In his youth he had been a sprinter, but not good enough to go under eleven seconds, and then in police camp he had graduated to becoming a lightning-quick right-out in hockey. He had made it to the state police team and had played the national police games and endless other regional tournaments for five years. Rajbir's role on the field was simple: run down the long pass on the right flank, trap the ball, and centre it swiftly for the forwards. He had to do this endlessly: explode from the half line, heart and muscles pumping, stick in his right hand, and somehow intercept the speeding ball and swat it to the top of the D. His mates called him Bhagbir Gujjar. For doing this well, he had been excused from all policing duties for seven years. He lived in a separate, special barracks with the team, close to the playing field. They had to be on the ground before the grey of morning broke; during the day they rested and oiled their bodies; and at four in the afternoon—rain, sun, or storm—they had to be back on the field till night fell and they were guessing at the ball by its running sound. Their extra diet included a litre of milk, three eggs, and a dozen bananas each day, and chicken three times a week.

These long years of no policing and pampered, sportsmanlike conduct ensured he was a bit of a deviant by the time he was trucked into the job. In no time his colleagues discovered he was a liability. On the beat he was sincere, full of the self-importance of his uniform, and inside the station he was fastidious, with an eye for rules and procedures. But leaving him alone was dangerous. It took months to just get him to understand that you did not file a First Information Report each time someone walked in with a complaint. The FIR, the case diary, all these were lethal legal documents, and it was critical to manage them right. The repercussions of one unmeditated entry could play out over years and ruin entire lives and careers. There was also the business of balancing the statistics. Rape, theft, murder, riot: there was a historical legacy to them all, and you worked to keep the numbers along the running line—not too over, not too under, nothing that could attract praise or damnation, nothing that got you on the radar.

In his first year in Allahabad, three police stations parcelled him on. As a former star player he had access to senior police officers. He sought and obtained a transfer to Lucknow, imagining in the state capital it would be easier to work as the rules stated. It is the universal affliction of all athletes: struggling to level with the infinitely more complex rules of life outside the playing arena. Of course Lucknow was worse, a rabidly political city, with no scope for errors. In less than a year, the speedy right-out was in Meerut, then Gorakhpur, then Shahjahanpur, then Faizabad. Everywhere he discovered he was sprinting one way with the rules, while all the other players ran the other way. The rules, he realized, were not what were written in the book, but what everyone had agreed to follow.

It was not about wanting to be just, or honest, or different. It was just that he had poor instinct. Within the esoteric circle of khaki, he never seemed to know what the required word or action on any given occasion was.

By the time he reached Gorakhpur he had decided to leave his wife and daughters permanently in Ghamond, his village near Muzaffarnagar, with his parents. It was a village of Tyagis, but his forefathers had lived there for generations without too much trouble. There were enough stories of the Gujjar peasants being oppressed by Tyagi landlords, but that sort of thing could happen anywhere on the Gangetic plain. Anyway, now new awakenings were afoot and new political alliances were being forged—the Gujjars were becoming big landlords themselves and a strong vote block. To begin with, whether all this would improve or worsen matters remained to be seen.

Eventually, Rajbir Gujjar—lightning-quick right-out but third-rate cop—was transferred to the security detail in the state capital. This was a battalion that provided armed personnel to luminaries perceived by the state intelligence cell to be under serious physical threat. The men in this battalion were of two kinds: tyros, straight out of police academy, full of bristle and ignorance; and the older flotsam of the force, dysfunctional men who lacked the savvy and pliability to be smooth and valuable cogs in the great police machine. The men they were tasked to guard were mostly politicians, and sometimes businessmen who were friends of politicians. It was a dumb, mechanical job. For eight hours every day the Personal Security Officer hung around with the Protected Person with his pistol stuffed into his crotch, and then he went off to sleep and watch television. If he was part of a larger contingent of guards, it was even easier. Everyone worked their timings around to suit themselves: sometimes one could work two days without a break, then take four days off and go home to the family.

In some ways this was a job for a writer. If you wished to see human degradation at the highest levels, you needed to become a PSO. Most of the politicians they guarded were themselves mafia dons. They had their own armed men from their villages, carrying double-barrels and pistols, hovering inside the rooms, speaking rough, guarding the last mile of access and transaction. Through their hands passed criminals, bribe givers, political fixers, and comfort women. The policemen were needed to establish an official cordon, to provide the curtain behind which the grimy business of public office could be conducted. Like many good men, as long as he didn't have to sully his own hands, Rajbir Gujjar was happy to play the curtain.

The man Rajbir was to protect for many years was a legislator from Chitrakoot. Bajpaisahib was a high-caste, a brahmin who had correctly intuited the forces of modernity and politics and aligned himself with the lower castes. His father would have taken ritual dips in the Mandakini if an untouchable's shadow touched his body, but Bajpaisahib sat with them, ate with them, embraced them, and even deferred to their supreme leader—never contradicting her in public, never speaking out unless she invited him to. Behind closed doors it was a different story: he was more than an equal, disagreeing with her, upbraiding her, using the legendary brahminical wiles honed over millennia of manipulating kings, warriors and laity, to help her chalk her next move.

Power is a greater principle than family, friendship, race, colour, religion. But caste is skin, caste is indelible. And so Rajbir knew, like everyone else who was part of Bajpaisahib's entourage, that every night, without exception, when all the business of the world was done, when he was finished with the pollutions of the material life, of power and commerce, of blood and flesh, he withdrew to the fastness of purity that had been occupied by his forefathers for hundreds of generations, cleansing himself with mugs of Ganga water. The holy water travelled with him wherever he went, in an army jerry can that was latched tight and strapped to an iron frame welded into the back of his Willys jeep. Each month the sacred water arrived on a Matador van, in four drums from the ghats, under close supervision, and was stored in the garage.

The supreme leader was not unaware of this, and she understood. In public, caste was a badge, but in private caste was skin. Once you were naked, you were who you were born. In birth, marriage and death the greater truths prevailed. Not money, not politics.

On the other hand, in his swift transit through numberless police stations Rajbir had learnt that policing was not about good and bad, law and order, rules and regulations: it was only about politics and money.

Now, in the entourage of Bajpaisahib, detailed by the state to guard the brahmin leader, his 9mm iron tucked into his crotch, the former athlete learnt that there was very little difference between those who broke the law and those who upheld it. It was like a hockey match in which both the teams were on the same side, but were putting up a show to please the spectators. As long as the audience was fooled the match was a success. Occasionally the spectators caught on, and then an elaborate charade had to be undertaken, of blame and inquiry, arrest and bail, crime and punishment.

In his years with Bajpaisahib, Rajbir saw every crime lord, drug don, property king, gunrunner, bootlegger, currency smuggler show up at the suave politician's door—often bringing in satchels of currency or taking them away. Many of these were famed men of the region, feared and revered. All of them had scores of cases registered against them; some of them had even done fleeting time in jail. They were only moved against when they fell adrift of the party in power.

Rajbir watched them arrive, mostly after dark, in thick entourages, gun barrels sticking out of the jeeps like party flags. Everyone salaamed them, even the policemen. In bad times, they were a better bet than anyone else. They could give you money for a daughter's wedding, or a father's operation. They could get you a transfer to a safer post, or a more lucrative one. They could tell an enemy to lay off, or a friend to be more friendly. They could arrange a lawyer and bail. They could organize flight and a refuge.

All you had to do was to remember the favour. To never lose your sense of gratitude. It was not like in the films where, eventually, the day would come for the laconic godfather to call in his dues. Most of the time, no favours were ever called in. There was little that the majority of the beneficiaries could possibly give in return. In truth these dons were like powerful men everywhere. They wanted not just money and influence, but also the affection and admiration of people. Like the best kings and chieftains they wanted to be known as magnificent patrons, as givers and grantors—more considerate than the police, more humane and generous than the state. They wanted the streets and gallis of the villages and towns to buzz with stories of their terror and their munificence. Not different from the gods. Feared and adored. Clasped to the heart and placed on a pedestal.

It was here, in the outer cordon of Bajpaisahib's circle of security, that Rajbir Gujjar first met Donullia Gujjar. Along with a score of other servants, supplicants, and guards the former athlete was sitting on the ridge-like roots of the ancient banyan tree near the bungalow's front gate, sipping tea from a glass, listening wide-eyed to the story of the acquisition of a new foreign car worth forty lakh rupees by the supreme leader, when a Trekker and a Willys jeep screeched in through the open gate, burning grass and gravel. The Trekker had an iron roof but no doors while the jeep had a canvas top with its back flap rolled up. It was the hour of last light and the sound of nesting crows and screeching parakeets filled the air.

Nearly a dozen men spilled out of the vehicles, shawls and blankets slung over their shoulders. Half of them were armed with rifles, and at least two of them wore brown buttoned-down pistol holsters across their chests. They were in the rough pants of police khaki or in army olives. Their boots were either thick leather clompers or green canvas jungle shoes, made for thorn and scrub.

They stood around in a loose cluster, with forbidding self-assurance. Then one of the men, in a white turban, with a broad swarthy face and no visible arsenal, grunted an order. Two of the men peeled away and went and planted themselves by the gate. None of the others made any attempt to move towards the bungalow. Under the banyan tree the murmurs began to rage, and Rajbir stood up, adjusting the pistol lodged inside his crotch. He was after all the police guard on duty.

Finally the mesh door on the side of the bungalow, away from the main entrance, under the porch, opened and Pandeyji came out, wearing his fur-lined astrakhan and rimless glasses. The man in the turban spoke to him. Pandeyji nodded and went back inside. Rajbir sidled closer to the group, angling for an opening, but the men ignored him. Soon glasses of tea appeared for them from the kitchen.

Rajbir retraced his way to the ridge-roots under the banyan, and the word echoing there was, Donullia! Donullia was here! This was Donullia's band! Everyone was craning to figure out which one he was, which one. It was difficult to tell. Night had fallen, and all the men had their faces masked by shawls and blankets. Also, none deferred to another. In any case there were scarcely any people in the world who even knew what the man looked like. There was no photograph of him in police records, and the only time he had been captured was twelve years ago; he had escaped while being transferred from the police station to the court. Of all the dreaded names of the region, his was the most charismatic.

Donullia had become a brigand at the age of sixteen, shooting dead his thakur landlord and his ruthless son. The story went that the peasant boy, enraged by the regular rape of his sisters by the masters, had run them down in the yard of their own house, and his last words to them were: 'Motherfuckers, you have never treated anyone as equal, but I am treating you both equally—one barrel and one bullet for each!'

The donulli—double-barrel—gun was the thakur's own, and the Gujjar teenager had blown one nulli each through both their hearts. Two days later, the thakur's brothers had picked up the boy's sisters and raped them repeatedly before decapitating them and hanging their heads on the palash tree. Only great terror can restore order. A week later, one brother had a hole blasted through his spine as he squatted by the long rushes next to the Gupt nullah early in the morning. The note found stuffed into his nostril warned that any further act of retaliation against the Gujjars and every member of the thakur's family would be hunted down.

The thakurs exploded with fury and the repercussions were felt all the way in Lucknow. In those days the thakurs were still a political force. Soon after, a special police party comprising two dozen men led by an officer of the rank of assistant superintendent was dispatched to bring the young brigand to book. A picture of the police party armed with SLRs and carbines was published in the local papers, accompanied by a short write-up in which the officer leading the group said they would bring the killer back in a week, on a leash, like a house dog.

But the boy had vanished—into the forests and ravines of Chitrakoot and from there perhaps into the adjoining badlands of the Chambal in the state of Madhya Pradesh. Nine months later, the special party called off the search and went back to the capital.

The word spread that Donullia could slip through men like a shadow.

Eight months later, the boy ransacked a marriage party of another thakur family of village Habusa, killing the groom and his father and decamping with cash, jewellery, and arms. The note lodged in the dead groom's nostril warned that any thakur family marrying without paying him his cess faced similar consequences.

The state assembly in Lucknow was convulsed with anger as legislators thumped desks and uprooted microphones. A second police party was assembled under an established sharpshooter of the state police. For more than a year the entire district was combed, the boy's house kept under watch, informers paid and put on the road, every criminal of the area questioned and aligned, other Gujjar families threatened and tortured, but there was no sign of the young bandit.

It became known that Donullia was not only fearless, and not only liquid as a shadow, but also a bahurupiya, a man of a thousand faces. The featureless peasant sitting next to you at the tea shop could well be the two-barrelled one.

Around this time a young man from Habusa who had been brutally interrogated by the special group suddenly vanished. His name was Kana Commando. He had been sent back from the army after he lost his left eye in an insurgency operation in Nagaland. Soon news came that the one-eyed infantryman had joined up with Donullia Gujjar, and was adding his vast knowledge of arms, terrain and tactics to the outlaw's cunning and courage. Then on, every few months, there would be reports of another young man gone missing.

Between the police, the upper castes and the landlords, there was enough oppression going around to fuel endless platoons of angry revenge-seekers.

Donullia offered dignity, vendetta and the matchless pleasure of a metal-spitting gun. For men who had spent a lifetime cowering under a lathi, this was an offer made by the gods.

Donullia, it seemed, was also a secular modernist. He ran a casteless and religion-free gang. Anyone could join up, everyone was free to worship their own gods and follow their own rituals, and everyone ate and drank from the same pot. Another of his key deputies was Hulla Mallah, a low-caste boatman who in a moment of rage had drowned two high-caste Pandeys whose feet his ancestors would have kissed. Hulla Mallah was reputed to be so big and strong that he could jog through the ravines with an injured comrade on his shoulders without breaking for breath or falling behind. On the other side of the caste spectrum there was Kana Commando, a high-caste Tyagi, who was treated by the gang as a mentor, providing instruction in marksmanship, the maintenance of weapons, and shoot-and-scoot tactics.

The job also had the perks of a modern corporation. Not only did the organization take care of you in injury and in ill-health, it also ensured that your family and clan were protected and provided for. Ruthless retribution was visited on anyone—official, policeman, or moneylender—who dared to pose a threat. The recruits poured in, and at its apogee the Donullia Gujjar gang numbered more than a hundred. When they moved into an area they were like a locust swarm, feasting on whatever they chose.

For many years there was not only a big price on the head of the chieftain but also, individually, on nearly a dozen of his gang members. Hulla Mallah's life alone was worth a lakh of rupees, and Kana Commando's one-and-a-half.

Local lore was that the leader wielded the same donulli gun that he had started his career with, and that he carried scores of red cartridges in a waterproof canvas pouch inside the haversack strapped to his back at all times. All alone, it was said, he could hold off a posse of ten armed policemen for a few hours.

Sitting under the banyan tree, Rajbir now looked for the telltale double-barrel. He spotted a couple, jutting out from around the wrapped blankets, but the men carrying them did not seem possessed of any centrality. It was quite likely that the double-barrel rumour was false; just another smokescreen used by the bahurupiya, the man of a thousand faces.

It had grown dark now, the street lamps were dimly yellow, and clouds of mosquitoes were building spirals in the air. An occasional vehicle rumbled past on the wide road as temple bells loudly tolled the evening prayers. None of the men had moved to enter the house; no one else had come out to talk to them. Bread pakoras had arrived in a large paper packet and were being circulated.

Bajpaisahib, of course, was inside the house. Visitors and petitioners swung steadily in and out of the mesh door by the side of the driveway. Occasionally some important town official, or local businessman, or religious leader, arrived encased in a crowd of hangers-on, and was ushered in through the main porch into the room at the front. A narrow connecting door allowed the politician to switch from the hard-nosed business of his office to the expansive deal-making of the living-room.

Rajbir picked a man with a gentle face—no handlebar moustache, no obvious scorn in his eyes, just a deep scar that ran from the edge of his left eye to his mouth—and sidled up to him. The man squatted on the edge of the driveway, chin resting on his knees, a rifle between his thighs and stomach, both ends sticking out like sharp elbows. Rajbir dropped on his haunches next to him and told him he was a policeman attached to the leader. It was the surest way of gaining some purchase with the brigand. Policemen did not scare these men; they knew how to use them.

The man said, from the corner of his mouth, 'You want to quit?' The scar was deep, even in the dark. Someone had tried to carve his face as an example.

Rajbir said, 'Not yet.'

The man said, 'Then come back when you do.'

Rajbir said, 'This is not a bad life.'

The man said, 'Nor is a eunuch's or a gravedigger's. One is cockless while servicing others cocks, while the other is alive while serving the dead.'

Rajbir said, 'But being hunted day and night can hardly be the recommended life?'

The man replied, still as a tree, 'Donullia Gujjar's men hunt, they are not hunted. We are from the country of free men. We do not follow laws made by rich men for rich men, and we do not follow men who say one thing and do another.'

Rajbir said, 'But your captain comes here. Why?'

Turning his head to look into the policeman's eye, the man said, 'He comes as a king. To talk things; to extract his tithe. Not as a supplicant. Ask the man whom you guard—if you ever have the courage to—ask him if he could survive without Donullia Gujjar.'

Rajbir thought of Bajpaisahib. Alliances with untouchables, alliances with bandits—how many gallons of Ganga water would he need to cleanse himself?

Rajbir said, 'I too am a Gujjar.'

The man said, nodding at the house, 'Then when the high-caste fails you, you can come to Donullia. Even a dog never forgets the gutter that spawned him. The kaptaan is committed to helping any Gujjar who seeks his help.'

Rajbir said, 'But where is he? Can I meet him when he comes?'

The man suddenly grinned, the ravine on his face making him

look diabolic. 'He is inside the house you are guarding, shaking down your rich seth for the money he makes off the poor.'

Rajbir said, 'When did he get in?'

The man said, 'He moves like a snake through water, like a shadow through the dark. If there were a hundred of you with four eyes each, you would still not know when he went past you and into that house. In fact I could be him and you would not know.'

In panic Rajbir peered at the squatting man. Fuck, was he in the midst of the crowning foolishness of his stupid career?

The man laughed aloud. 'He can be a snake through water, a shadow among shadows, but never a fool talking to a fool! I couldn't be Donullia if I lived seven lifetimes. You didn't see him go in and you won't see him going out.'

Rajbir said, 'But will you get me to meet him?'

The man said, 'Well, if we all stay alive, and you be a true Gujjar, and you come to him not as a policeman but a true kinsman: a dog from his own gutter, blood of his blood.'

Rajbir said, 'I am a policeman for the salary, merely one more whore in the whorehouse of the state. No matter how much you pay the whore, she never belongs to you. She is always only the child of the mother she was born to.'

'Well spoken,' said the man. 'The kaptaan should meet you. First let us see, stellar policeman, if you can recognize him at all.'

Rajbir said, 'Are you a Gujjar too?'

The man laughed, the tin-shade light on the bungalow wall making his scar dance. 'If the captain is do nullia, double-barrelled, then I am ek nullia, single-barrelled. If you ever go to village Bhasodi, ask about Katua Kasai and see them scurry like rats. On the peepul tree in the square I strung up four of them naked and alive, after putting a cross on their chests with my knife, and dared the milling bastards to cut them down and take them away.' The squatting man broke his narration and spat to the side in disgust. 'It took them fifteen hours to bleed to death but not one villager had the guts to even fetch help. That's why we are a country of serfs, we are scared of everything! If we see the shadow of a cock, we think it's going to bugger us!'

Rajbir said, 'So you are a...'

The man said, 'Yes, I am cut not only on my face, but also down there. My forefather was Akbar the great, emperor of all of Hindustan, but I am only Katua Kasai, king of whichever tree I sleep under every night.'

At some point, around nine o'clock, when the crowds under the banyan had thinned and most of the petitioners had received their moment inside the bungalow, the gang of men spread out over the driveway and the gate, jumped into their trekker and jeep and drove off. Rajbir was not quite sure what had happened. He reconnoitred the front porch. He could hear low voices in the living-room, including that of the leader. He walked to the other side, looking for a staffer who could give him some information. There were only two peasants there: unshaven, dirty turbans wound loosely around their heads, coarse black blankets wrapped about their shoulders and chin. One of them had rheumy eyes and was coughing like a tuberculosis patient, bringing up phlegm, spitting all around. They clambered awkwardly onto an old Atlas cycle leaning against the wall—the smaller, thinner man on the carrier at the back—and with a weaving start, slowly cranked their way off.

A minute later, he knew. Beneath the dirty white pajama the tuberculosis patient had been wearing sports keds with thick rubber soles. The kind you got in swank shoe shops; the kind that absorbed thorn and stone; the kind that gripped in mud and slope. By the time he rushed to the gate the street was empty. Around the big yellow lights were a million night insects committing hara-kiri.

A snake through water; a shadow in the dark.

He was still standing there, reflecting on his slow-witted life, when the Willys jeep came and parked across the street. The scarred man leaned out from the co-driver's seat and said, 'Oh policya, I have something to show you.' When Rajbir walked up to him, the Muslim bandit put his hand behind Rajbir's head and shoved it into the jeep. Inside, in the dark, he could dimly register the shapes of several men, and the light through the canvas sparked on the barrels of guns.

A quiet voice said, 'Gujjar?'

'Yes.' The grip on the back of the policeman's neck was firm.

'You want to be a friend?'

It was too dark inside. 'Yes,' said Rajbir, 'it would be an honour if I could ever do anything for you.'

The voice said, 'Do your given job well. Keep a good eye on the brahmin. You may be a whore of the state, but it is only men like us who truly appreciate you.'

Rajbir could now make out that there were three men in there, on the back seat, but he couldn't even tell which of them was speaking to him. He said, 'I am there for you.'

The voice said, 'For the people, for the people. Always for the people. Not for me. Your service rules say you have to serve the people. My service rules say the same. Serve the people.'

ii

An Asshole of Iron

When he was seventeen and in class ten, two of Vishal Tyagi's sisters were savagely raped. They were not killed. The aim was not pleasure, but leverage. A hundred bighas of land hung in the balance. Joginder was not so stupid—or so crude—as to have his sons rape their cousins. The men entrusted for the task were from Meerut. Karimbhai, the small-time don and truck transporter who sent them, said they were the best in the business. They did precisely as instructed: chhota kaam, small job; bada kaam, big job; poora kaam, full job. The small commission was a strongly intimidatory molestation—the tearing of clothes, the squeezing of breasts, the insertion of fingers. It was a warning, a call to action to some errant party. The big brief was full intercourse, to its conclusion, with the violate seed firmly implanted. It was a warning and a punishment to someone who had earned it. The full job was rape followed by murder, with established degrees of brutality. This was warning, punishment, and the closing of old accounts.

Joginder had contracted for the second degree.

Early one morning, with the mist rising off the fields like vapour off boiling milk, the two girls, out for their morning ablutions, were dragged deep into the sugarcane fields and professionally raped. At seventeen and nineteen respectively both were betrothed; the older was set to be wed in three months.

When they returned their mother held her head and howled

like a jackal, but refused to allow Gyanendra to go to the police or to visit his cousin. The police, she knew, would fill up some papers and do nothing, except confirm to the entire world that her girls were irretrievably damaged. If they played it astutely, the information might be contained till the marriage was over. The most difficult part was stopping her husband from heading out to confront his cousin. He had a single-barrel gun and a few old red cartridges in the tin trunk, but she knew Joginder and his sons would bring him to ruin before he brought off a shot. The mother and raped daughters clung to his legs, pleading with him for his life, imploring him to not widow and orphan them. Gyanendra—aware he would be walking out to his death—finally relented, shrinking, with this decision, to a husk of himself.

Driven mad by the screaming and crying, Vishal Tyagi went into the yard, lay down in front of his buffalo, Shanti, and had his cropped head licked again and again. He said nothing to his sisters, nor a thing to his parents. He had nothing to say. A week later, walking to school in the evening for his body-building exercises—iron dumbbells, push-ups, sit-ups, rope-climbing, sprints—under the tutelage of Rajbir Gujjar, he crossed Joginder's three sons by the stone shrine under the peepul tree. One of them said, 'How lovely his sisters are and how ugly he is! Think how much more it would have cost to get him fucked!'

The inside of his head exploded like a bomb. He tried to leap on them, but armed with iron-tipped lathis they menaced him back. Vishal Tyagi then ran, head on fire, straight to the room of his mentor, and the first thing he saw there was a long-limbed hammer. It was a nice hammer, with a smooth handle and a small hard head. One side drove in the nails; the other was hooked and split to wrench them out. Before Rajbir could mouth a word, the boy had snatched it up and was out the door.

The boy caught up with them just as they had entered their own fields and were walking on the bund, sweet fresh water from the throbbing tube wells running in the channel on one side, the cane fields dense and rustling on the other. The eldest, bringing up the rear, went down without a word as the hammer pistoned through his skull, fusing his circuitry before it could form a word. He fell with a splash into the channel, the water gurgling into his open mouth. As the other two turned, Vishal Tyagi's weapon was already swinging. It went through the centre of the second brother's forehead and nose like a spoon through an eggshell, collapsing his eyes into each other and taking down his upper jaw. They would have to cremate him with his face swathed in bandages. The third brother began to babble incoherently from behind his extended lathi, by turns begging abjectly for mercy and threatening him with great punishment. In an act of creativity, the rampaging boy swung his right hand in a smooth round-arm while blocking the counter-attack with his left and exploded the iron head through his cousin's left ear. A second, redundant, blow caved in his temple. Like his brothers he too slopped into the channel, damming the flow of the water, making it spill out onto the bund.

The boy washed the blood and brains off his hammer and hands and returned to his homestead where he lay in front of Shanti and submitted his scalp to her loving licks. The only witnesses to the carnage were Joginder's three curs who snarled and barked and circled the scene, but had the good instinct not to take on the foe.

It was not late but everyone had eaten dinner. They were working the handpump for the last cleanings when Gyanendra's dogs began to bark. It was Rajbir Gujjar and he was alone. In his right hand was his single-barrel, the canvas strap looping low, like a garland. His face was set. He sat down on the edge of Gyanendra's charpoy and accepted the glass of boiling milk handed to him. The moon was thin, and it was a night of a billion stars.

The former cop said, 'Joginder's sons are dead.'

Gyanendra, pulling on his last hookah for the day, said, 'Why, what have they done now?'

'They are dead, tau. Dead. All three of them. Too dead to be even taken to a hospital. Somebody pulped their heads, as if they were animals.'

Gyanendra pulled the bubbling pipe out of his mouth, and said, 'It cannot be. I saw them this morning in the village, their chests puffed out like a cockerel's. The bastards said to me, "Hope you are well, tau, and your children. We haven't seen your daughters around for some time now."'

The cop said, sipping carefully from the burning steel glass, 'Tau, no one in these parts has seen a killing like this in years. Even their mother couldn't recognize one of them.'

In the dark, Vishal Tyagi sat by his buffalo on the ground, slowly stroking her sandpaper flanks. He felt calm. His father now gripped his tutor's shoulder and said, 'Have you seen it for yourself? I don't trust that low-caste and his satanic sons!'

Sipping loudly, the cop put two fingers on his eyes.

'God be praised! But who?'

'Nothing is known yet. The police say it looks like the work of a gang, five-six people. But nobody seems to have seen anything. The farmhands went to investigate when the dogs wouldn't stop barking.'

Gyanendra said, 'Finally we can be sure there is a god! There is justice!'

But his wife, squatting on the ground near the handpump, shook her head slowly. 'This is not good. No one deserves such an end. Now there will be a new cycle of bloodshed. Joginder will not keep still.'

The cop had seen the boy's bulk beside the buffalo, sunk into the shadows. He called out, 'And what do you plan to do now?'

The boy did not reply. His raped sisters sat in the open doorway of the house, squatting on the threshold. They picked at their hair in silence. The death of the cousins meant nothing to them. They were inside their own cocoon of taint and unhappiness. All their lives they would have to live in dread of their husbands discovering they were used goods. That's if their marriages went through at all. The killing of the cousins could start a police investigation that would lead to the disclosure of their torn flesh.

The cop said, 'So what did you do with the hammer?'

He had buried it behind the house, between rows of cabbage, tamping the mud down on it neatly. Watching him dig it out, his mentor said, 'The police would have found this in less than two days. Don't ever make the mistake of underestimating a policeman. Their sources and resources are infinite. When they want to get to the bottom of something they do so easily. And they can get information out of anyone, if they want. Even me.'

The family watched in admiration and horror as the cop and the boy washed the hammer under the handpump. The father said, 'You have avenged me, my son. You have given your father back his fallen turban.' The boy said nothing. He could have popped another three skulls had the occasion demanded. It was a sweet sensation: that moment when the iron exploded through flesh and bone, ending all argument, settling all dispute. How the last one's words had died on his lips as he went through his left ear. He had always felt people fussed and complained too much. Today he knew it was easy to resolve discord if you had clarity of purpose.

Once the excitement had abated, Gyanendra asked, 'Will they find out?'

The cop said, 'Without a doubt. He has to leave this place. If they catch him they will hang him three times. After which Joginder will take a hammer and break all his bones. The villagers have just begun to stream in to see the bodies. No one has ever seen anything like it. There are going to be no exonerating circumstances, no sympathy from any quarter.'

'But where? He has a maternal uncle near Varanasi. Shall we send him there?'

'All relations are out. Two wireless messages and he will be picked up. Also, don't forget Joginder. He will get to know soon, and he will be on the hunt too.'

Looking at the boy, now leaning against the wall—his frame so powerful—the cop said, 'You come with me. The hare must cover as much distance as he can before the hounds begin to run.'

Thanks to a senior officer who had been passionate about hockey and to a Gujjar legislator from the area, Rajbir Gujjar had managed to get a job as a physical training instructor in a government school close to his village when he had been pensioned off from the service. The school, like the police, was in a shambles, the chasm between the idea and the reality vast enough to sink a thousand students. Many of the schoolrooms were occupied by the staff as private residences and the holding of classes was a ramshackle consensus between the students and teachers. Some of the key teachers there actually worked on a proxy. The men appointed by the state lived in Muzaffarnagar while other men nominated by them came and taught in their name: the salary was split between the two. It was a kind of subletting. The government was aware of this, but it had more important things to worry about.

As far as Rajbir Gujjar was concerned, he had nothing much else to do. He could have, had he wished, brokered a deal with the headmaster and never shown up at all. Teaching was a luxury here; the idea of sport, a joke. Village children in India are not born for the affectations of academic accents and athletics: they go to school to escape oppressive fathers and unrelenting toil. The playing field behind the school building had very quickly become broken ground, used by the villagers to graze their cattle. The iron-pipe goalposts at the two ends looked eerie, like doorways into nothingness. No ball had ever rolled through their mouth. At one point, equipment of all kinds had been bought: hockey-sticks, footballs, javelins, badminton racquets, cricket bats and wickets. Now nothing remained except a fat, heavy iron shotput. It was the only sport left for the schoolboys. Each day boys wagered on their ability to throw the heavy ball. The ground in front of the line, drawn in the front yard of the school, was heavily dented.

It was in this arena of grunts and soft thuds that Rajbir Gujjar first met the young Vishal Tyagi. Already he could heave the shot farther than his older classmates, and the flex in his big shoulders suggested he could do better still. There was also an intensity about the boy that he found attractive—in his time he had had it too, as did the best players he had played alongside. It was what he had missed the most when he'd finally become a journeyman cop, the hard focus on getting something done. The boy also appeared unusually calm and generous. He did not talk much or backslap, and he was happy to give other, more puny boys a chance at tossing the shot while he waited. Often he also saw him exert his huge strength to back someone who was being mocked or short-changed.

The former cop, when living in the sports barracks, had seen the athletes work out. He was familiar with the rotating swivel that was used for propelling the shot. The schoolboys just threw it with the shuffling momentum of a few short steps. Vishal was the one to teach it to. In a few weeks the taciturn Tyagi boy was spinning and heaving the iron ball farther than anyone had even seen. Now there was one patch of dented ground at thirty feet, and more than ten feet farther, another patch, wholly attributable to the young Tyagi. Rajbir felt this boy could go all the way to Lucknow to the state championships; in fact, with a bit of training he could make it to the national school games. No one from this entire district had ever gone that far.

As is often the case with coaches and mentors, his entire life, all his personal ambitions, became focused on the young athlete. He set the regime. Hundred sit-ups and fifty push-ups twice a day; twenty chin-ups on the football goalpost five times a day; a five-kilometre run every morning, the last kilometre with a brick clasped in each hand; and two hundred puts of the shot. Once a week he would take him to his fields, unyoke the oxen, and while he sat in the shade and shouted instructions, watch him work the plough till the water ran off his body in a cascade and he could move no more.

To supplement his exertions, Rajbir Gujjar argued with the headmaster till a special diet was sanctioned for the promising athlete: two litres of milk, a dozen bananas, and four eggs each day. He also convinced the boy to defy his parents and eat chicken once a week. 'You are not trying to become a priest! You have to eat flesh if you want strength in your flesh!' With each week, the boy began to dent the ground farther and farther. When he was at training the boys would come and watch, and marvel at the voluptuous biceps and big shoulders.

On Saturdays, the mentor would give his protégé's body a mustard oil rub, and as he massaged him they would talk. Rajbir Gujjar told the boy thrilling stories about his playing days—the breathtaking runs he made to trap and centre the ball; the cliffhangers they won; the newspaper mentions; the trophies; the luminaries they met. The boy talked of the only two he loved: his mother and the buffalo, Shanti. He spoke of his resolve to reach the nationals and win a medal there. In his quiet, halting way he would say, 'The name of this village will become famous because of me.'

Later, as he came closer to the master, Vishal talked about the family feud. How his father's cousin and his sons had seized their lands, how they intimidated them, and how they had broken his father's kneecap. He felt his father was weak. 'He should have shot them. He has a gun in his trunk.' He asked the former cop, 'If the police does not help you, what should you do?' Rajbir had to agree there was a case for taking matters into one's own hands.

As anticipated by the coach, the boy swept the district and zonal championships, breaking the record at every level, and by the time they reached Lucknow he already had a name. At the stadium, while other boys and girls guzzled soft drinks, ate aloo tikki and lurid ice lollies, flirting with the burning heat of adolescence, Vishal drank his milk, ate his bananas, pumped his muscles, and threw the shot to a record distance. That night Rajbir took him to Hazratganj and fed him a lavish dinner at Gaylord's. 'Remember, son, the final seat of all achievement is neither the head nor the heart nor the muscles. It is the ass. Courage and determination lives in the ass! When the odds stack up against men, when the challenges mount, it is the ass that gives way first! All my life I have seen it. The asshole opens up and bleats like a goat. The head and the heart and the muscles see it, and follow suit!'

In saying this, Rajbir Gujjar was able to bring himself to confess to his protégé that his own life and career had been diminished because he had not enough strength in his ass. 'I was a good player on the sports field, but when I came to the police station my sphincter could not hold. Every time there was something bold to be done, I had to sit down to save my ass from weeping. There was a man with us, from Bulandshahar—Chuchundur, we used to call him. He was not more than five feet tall and was dark as a crow and scrawny as the neck of a vulture. You would treat him as a sweeper if you saw him on the road. But he had an asshole made of iron. I saw him at work at the station. If you wanted finger-bones crunched, kneecaps broken, ligaments wrenched, testicles twisted like toffee wrappers, you turned to Chuchundur. Big men, huge men, feared him. He could in a flash put a pistol up your mouth and have you suck it like a lollipop and wet your pants at the same time. Later, he rose to become the best cleaner of garbage in the state police. Anyone who didn't deserve to be sent to the courts was sent on a ride with Chuchundur. Because he was tiny they all tried to run away from him, and had to be shot. At one time he was also called Chuchundur Pacheesi, because his score was twenty-five. Later, he went far beyond it. From a mere constable, the little runt rose to become an inspector faster than anyone else, and summons for him would come from inspector-generals of police and powerful ministers. So remember, my son, you can throw a shot very far with muscles and heart, but to win in life you need an asshole of iron!'

The boy, working his way through a second plate of chholabhatura said, 'And where is he now?'

'Dead. Found by the riverbank with his kneecaps splintered, his penis spliced off, and his tongue pulled out. They had to identify him by the rings on his fingers.'

The boy widened his eyes in silent query.

The former cop said, 'It's much better to have an asshole of iron and lead a splendid if short life than to be like the rest of us, our backsides bleating like goats, fearfully rationing out our small pathetic lives. Life gave Chuchundur nothing—no caste, no money, no education, no height, no muscles, no looks, no connections. Nothing! Nothing, except an asshole of iron! And with that he changed everything.'

The boy said nothing, but he understood the message. He'd been born with an iron asshole, anyway; now it was only a matter of reinforcing it some.

Even by the standard of iron assholes, the former cop and present coach was taken aback at the brain-curry spree his protégé had embarked on. Defending his ward's very occasional excesses from irate school authorities and the headmaster was one thing, but with this carnage Rajbir was totally out of his depth. Three dead men, heads caved in. To protect such a killer you needed to be a very powerful politician or a very rich man. Or you needed to be someone who feared neither.

There was only one he had ever known.

For most of his four-year tenure with Bajpaisahib, the personal security officer had been Donullia Gujjar's man. At the time, the mighty brigand was in the process of starting to legitimize some of his wealth. He had lived beyond the line of the law for long enough to know that the greatest bandits worked inside the line as much as outside it. It was only then that you went from being a mere dacoit to a legend. It was only then that you survived beyond the swift cycle of seven years of glory and death.

Donullia Gujjar knew that while men like him worked from the outside in, there was another class of men who worked from the inside out. Bajpai was such a man. When men like Donullia and Bajpai fell into a marriage they became the masters of all realms, heaven and earth, city and field, money and power.

Donullia's brother, Gwala Gujjar, became a civil-works contractor. He was so good at his work that he began to get a slice of every new and old project in the district. Repairing torn roads, laying new ones, building rural schools and primary health centres, culverts and bridges, bus stops and night shelters, clearing drains and gutters, planting power poles and stringing telephone lines. The shrewdest men in India have always known that money lurks not in the dazzle of the markets but in the dour corridors of government. Laying macadam is paved with greater—and quieter—riches than all the hustle of the high marketplace.

The benign politician blessed the contracts and Donullia's severe shadow ensured competitors sewed their lips and stilled their fingers.

But Donullia and Bajpaisahib's relationship went deeper than macadam. It was also tied to the high rituals of democracy. The brigand was a persuasive canvasser for the public man, and at every election his word would scorch through the district, urging the peasants to vote wisely and in their best interests. On voting days his men would trawl through the booths—armed and alert—ensuring fair electoral processes were not derailed by money or muscle. Bajpaisahib never lost an election, and Gwala Gujjar's businesses diversified to include shops, petrol pumps, gas agencies, cinema halls, a small vegetarian hotel, and an English-medium school.

It was only proper that Gwala Gujjar, who was older than Donullia, was a small, mild man. He beamed the terror of his two shadows, but he spoke softly and without aggression. Too few people understand the potency of the big fist that presents a soft face. Gwala Gujjar then was the man to whom Rajbir reported. Mining the minister's bungalow continually, he took to him news of Bajpaisahib's movements, the men he had met, and the way the political winds were blowing. He provided details of the comfort women who brought solace to the public man's stressed life, and of the traders and businessmen who were opening up new and novel mines of moneymaking.

The brigand's brother always met him with humility and grace, bending and smiling. He met him at the door of his house, sat him next to himself in his bed-cum-sitting-room, fed him well with snacks and tea, and walked him out to the gate. Sometimes he gave him an envelope thick with gratitude, and sometimes a warm hug. Often he would say, 'You are my Gujjar brother. Donullia always says, in the gang there is no caste and never can be, but in life caste is family. He has ordered me never to turn away a Gujjar from my door.'

There were always supplicants crowding the front of the house, seeking jobs, referrals, financial aid, justice, and sometimes the road to the famous brother. Gwala Gujjar performed every good and generous deed with utter humility in Donullia's name, and always he told the grateful, 'Seek blessings for him. He lives in the jungle and sleeps on the hard ground, often eating uncooked food, with the open sky for a roof, and wild animals for company—and he does all this for you, for the cause of justice, for the salvation of the poor. So pray for him every day, and on Tuesdays offer prasad to Hanuman so he may protect him and, by extension, us.'

In the four years that he lived in Chitrakoot, Rajbir saw Donullia's empire expand and his wealth multiply. New jeeps and big cars, new properties, a movie hall, and a motorcycle agency. More of his men could be seen overground, transiting through the town, creating a stir. Often there were rumours that the man himself was visiting, but for some reason Rajbir had never met anyone who said he had actually seen him. It was always a second-hand story, and it was always couched in vagueness. Few even knew any more what he looked like. Though he had been a legend for fifteen years, the police did not possess a single image of the man. He had turned an outlaw much before the government had started snaring all criminals in passport-sized photographs, and in all the years since, he had never once been captured. Nor had anyone betrayed him and lived to tell the tale. There were stories of defecting gang members whose body parts—eyes, tongue, ears, heart, testicles—had been systematically removed and set in a line, like a modular toy. Donullia gave his life for his men; the least he expected was some gratitude.

He was a master of disguise who practised his craft at all times; growing moustaches and beards, changing hairstyles, tying turbans, affecting lisps and limps. The great bahurupiya—man of a thousand faces—had a vast collection of false whiskers, wigs, robes, glasses, caps, and moles. Once, he had terrified and excited his men by appearing in their forest clearing, suddenly in the dead of night, dressed in an electric-blue saree with red lipstick full on his mouth. Even when he came to meet Bajpaisahib, his political partner, he never came as himself. In the end the world is a shifting place, and political partners can be trusted with cracking deals, not with one's life.

The few times Rajbir asked the brother for an audience, Gwala said, 'Of course, of course. He would love to meet you. He always speaks so affectionately about you.'

But that was never to be. On a couple of occasions, he reached Gwala's house only to be told that he had just missed him; he was in the jeep that drove past him as he entered the driveway. When his tenure ended and he was transferred back to Lucknow to work in the records department, Gwala assured him that Donullia was sad to see him go. 'He told me to tell you that he is there if you ever need him. In the world of the gods he can do nothing for anyone, but in the world of men he will do his best.'

As it turned out, Vishal Tyagi did not get rid of the long-stemmed hammer. It was still in his bag when they arrived at Gwala Gujjar's house and the armed men outside insisted on frisking them. Too many years had passed and there was no one on that outer periphery who readily remembered the former policeman. The house was the same, but Rajbir could see it had grown, adding on several floors. The boundary walls were also much higher, with blue-flowered creepers running over them, and there were now shisham trees encasing the walls. Rajbir recalled a much gentler cordon. Now the men were rude and aggressive, flaunting their double-barrel guns and their privilege.

Inside, however, the man was the same. Gwala Gujjar recognized Rajbir immediately and met him with the same bending humility and grace. But this time they did not go into the inner quarters; they sat in the living-room, which had become a fine place, with upholstered chairs and sofas and shining wood tables with brass and glass artifacts set on them. While Gwala's hair had turned silver and his face was softer than before, the long red tilak on his forehead was fresh and thick as ever. Rajbir noticed that now there was also a holstered gun under his white kurta, the concealed brown belt running diagonally across his chest. The stakes had obviously risen over time.

Rajbir said, 'How is Guruji?'

That's how Donullia was now known. The years had taken him beyond the categories of outlaw and terror. His name still froze the blood—and his men slaughtered a few times a year to keep the fear coursing—but his deeds of generosity and kindness, of giving and facilitating, had altered the account books. In the current audit he was more patron than predator.

Gwala said, 'If you had come yesterday, you could have met him…'

'Is he keeping well?'

'Well, he is no younger, as you know. But he still runs through the jungles and ravines with the youngest of them, and still sleeps on the ground with the stars above, and often with uncooked food in his stomach. Meanwhile, we who do nothing and exist by his grace live in these pretty cake-like houses, eating motichur laddus and oiling our bodies.'

Rajbir said, 'It is the way of great men. To suffer for the good of others.'

Gwala said, 'He is opening a hospital and an orphanage. He said to me, "Gwalabhai, the government can say the worst about us and they need to do so all the time because they need to look good in comparison. But we know what our duty is. It is to always serve the people, the poor and the needy and the suffering. Do I live the life of a fakir in a jungle because I enjoy it? I do it because it is my karma. It is the will of Shiv-Shambhu—the lord of all creation and destruction, the richest ascetic in the world, the keeper of insects and animals, of djinns and men. If he wanted me to be you, Gwalabhai, he would have made me you. He made me Donullia so I could fight against injustice and protect the weak. He made me Donullia so I could do his work in this transitory world. When I run in the forest with the rifle in my hand I feel him running by my side."'

Rajbir said, 'He is a great man. And it is the way of great men: to suffer for the good of others.'

Gwala said, 'And what can I do for you, our old friend?'

Rajbir grasped Vishal's wrists and said, 'I have an offering for Guruji.'

Gwala said, 'Is his heart as big as his body?'

Rajbir pulled out the thin-stemmed hammer from the boy's bag, and said, 'He just made kachumar of three heads. Even their mother couldn't recognize them. They had raped his sisters.'

'And he will strike in the service of others as he has done for himself?'

'Gwalabhai, he is a boy unlike any other. I would not bring you a mule dressed up like a horse. You know I have seen the world, of men and of boys. Guruji will find in him all the virtues of the Alsatian dog—strength and courage, love and loyalty.'

Gwala looked at the boy sitting upright on the edge of the sofa, the fair broad face expressionless, the eyes steady, the muscles bulging. His great brother could tell the truth of a man in a single look. But he himself had no such gift. He had to feel his way around, make risky guesses, hope for the best.

Gwala said, 'This is a life of no pleasures and no rewards. It is a life of daily danger and hardship and selfless service. It is Shiv-Shambhu's work. Can you do it?'

Vishal Tyagi nodded.

'Can you kill, not out of anger and enmity and greed, but for the greater good?'

Vishal Tyagi nodded.

'You do know that once you become a soldier of Guruji, a devotee of Shiv-Shambhu, you cease to be detained by other ties of family and friends.'

Vishal Tyagi thought, this is such music to my ears.

For the first several weeks, his allotted space was a charpoy in the garage that lay at the end of the short tight driveway. At the back was a bathroom, and a small windowless store stuffed with weaponry. Swords, spears, axes, several substandard rifles from Indian ordnance factories, nearly a dozen tamanchas, unreliable local pistols, the barrels made of sawn-off water pipes. There were also a few .303

Enfields, taken off the police, heavy and destructive; one black carbine, hung on the wall, its holes sinister, its magazine clamped into place; one Webley & Scott revolver and two 9mm pistols; and in a small wooden box kept on a high ledge, half a dozen plump grenades.

The store was kept locked, the key under the soap dish in the bathroom. It was only after two weeks that one of the men, Gainda—rhino—opened the door and showed Vishal the tools of the trade. The three men did not know how to work the entire armoury, and were under orders to not stupidly fiddle. Their comfort zone spanned the non-firearms and the local rifles and tamanchas. Each of them carried one of each. Not a single piece was made available to the boy.

Rajbir had left two days ago, but the boy was calm. He was happy to sit at the gate and watch the street flow by, to observe the line of visitors who streamed in and out of Gwalabhai's house. Many were questioned, most frisked, but a few strode in as if they owned the place. Beefy Gainda, his neck thick as a thigh, would often try and impress him with the significance of some of them. Director of public works, chief engineer, subdivisional magistrate, deputy superintendent of police, the local president of the low-caste party, the local president of the high-caste party, the local president of the national party, the chairman of the temples committee, the imam from the local masjid, the seth who presided over the grain mandi, the principal of the local inter college, the businessman from Lucknow who was whispered to be worth five hundred crores.

The boy was not impressed by any of them. He only stayed alert for that one man who might suddenly show up—fully aware that he might come in any manner of guise. Each time a visitor arrived, he scanned him carefully—looking for other signs, of weapons, accomplices, anything that might give a clue to his true identity. In the beginning, Gainda and his two buddies pretended they had seen him and met him, but soon it became clear to the boy that they too were still awaiting their first sighting. And they had been there for years.

Gainda told him hilarious stories of the false sightings at the gate. Once, he said, the three of them had fallen at the feet of an ochre-robed mendicant convinced that it was Guruji. They had been told the telltale sign was that he always wore keds, and since the mendicant was also carrying an iron trident—Shiv-Shambhu's weapon—they were carried past all doubt. Only when Gwalabhai dismissed him with some alms did the three of them stop grovelling at his feet.

Gainda said, nodding at the house, 'I don't think even he has seen him for years. Some say there is no Donullia Gujjar any more. That he was injured in a police encounter five years ago and died in the ravines. His name is kept alive so that the fools of this area keep their pricks inside their trousers and don't start getting grand ideas about themselves. Didn't Gwalabhai tell you he was here just the day before? He says that to everyone who comes and makes an inquiry. It shrivels up your testicles some more. The thought that he was just here, that he can so effortlessly pass through the lives of men, like a shadow in the night, like a wispy djinn from a magician's lamp. If anyone asks us, we too say that he was here just the other day. The truth is we have seen him as often as we have seen Alexander the Great! Listen, there is no Donullia any more. Gwalabhai and Bajpaisahib keep him alive, and it is our job to do the same. You may have made brain curry out of three men's heads—and you look like someone who could—but just remember that, like us, you will stand at this gate for years, and you will be looked after well, and whenever anyone asks you will say, he was here just yesterday, but you will never see him because he has already gone where we are all headed soon.' And he looked up at the sky and waved his right hand cheerily.

Gainda was wrong. Six weeks after Vishal's arrival, Gwalabhai summoned him and said, 'The sub-inspector came by, son. It seems the police have some idea of your whereabouts. It's time for you to move out of here.'

A man waited outside on a red Yamaha motorcycle with two big rear-view mirrors, like an insect's antennae, on its steering handle. Gainda gave the boy a farewell hug and said, 'If you see him, tell him you can punch out thirty-two teeth in one blow, and can suck the blood of a man like Coca-Cola!' Then he laughed aloud—the veins in his thick neck jumping—and said, 'And don't fall at the feet of any old man wearing PT shoes!'

The man driving the motorcycle was not young. His crew-cut was grey. He wore a white dhoti and a blue shirt and his sock-less feet were encased in rough leather juttis. He said, 'Hold on tight,' and then sheathing his mouth and nose in a white bandanna, roared off in high gear, zigzagging through the busy streets, blaring a power horn worthy of a big truck. Soon they were out of the town and on a narrow country road, shooting past small villages. The man drove them deeper and deeper into the country, rattling and scudding over semi-tarred lanes, fields and throbbing tube wells on either side, meeting only, as the evening waned, the odd ploughman, lines of shuffling cattle, or a struggling bicycle. Soon the last tarred road was behind them. The dust was now a moving cloud, choking Vishal's eyes and mouth and nostrils. He shut his eyelids tight and held on, feeling the machine's heart move through his muscles, aware of the man's holster digging into his wrist.

He was jolted out of his rhythmic trance when he realized the bike had come to a halt and the engine had died. He first heard the barking of dogs, in several registers; followed by the clucking of hens. In the supernatural light of dusk he saw that the farmhouse in front of him was made of naked brick and mud and dung. There were two ageing trees to one side, a shisham and a neem, both with spare branches and fraying leaves. Unusually the house was two-storeyed, and the small open windows were like watching eyes. On the flat roof, like a single hair, stood a television antenna.

All around the house, for several acres, were open fields, clear of all vegetation. Beyond that, to one side, green blocks of sugarcane rustled. On the other side, much further away, the tree-line of the jungles was visible. It was not possible to sneak up to the house without being seen; at the same time, it was possible to make a run for the cover of the cane and the forest if the need arose.

There were five dogs, and they were all around the visitors, sniffing and assessing. The motorcycle driver gave the snuffling-growling canines a hard push away from himself, but Vishal found himself running his hands over their graceful brows and napes, feeling their rough warm tongues lick his skin. The tall old man who had emerged from the house in a white dhoti, wearing wire-rimmed glasses, a turban around his head, holding a short stick, said, 'The love of the beast! If they don't love you, they won't let you survive, and if they love you, they won't leave you alone! My friend, you are in trouble!'

The motorcycle driver said, 'Shall I leave?'

The old man said, 'Unless you want a cup of tea.'

The driver wrapped his scarf around his face and said, 'Old man, there is much better company in the world than yours! Keep him alive till some use is found of him!'

Vishal Tyagi was given a charpoy and bedding in a room on the first floor. There were nails on the wall for clothes to be hung. There were two other charpoys in the room, but they were propped on their side—this was clearly a transit space. In one corner stood a few sacks of grain, one of unshelled peanuts, and one of black-brown gur. On the wall next to the door was a big smudged mirror, which caught and reflected the sunlight blindingly during the day. On the other wall was a calendar with an image of a smiling Shiva, sitting on a tiger skin, hand resting on his trident, the Ganga flowing out of his matted hair. The calendar was four years old.

Placing the long-stemmed hammer under his pillow—for no

reason other than a vague sense of security—he looked out the window. The boy could see the forest-line. At night he heard the baying of wolves and jackals fill the air. From that day on, on nights that the moon was high, he would sit by the window for hours and imagine the animals moving in the thick forest cover. The old man said there was a time when tigers routinely wandered through, but now that men were mice, tigers too had become jackals.

As far as the boy could tell the only permanent inhabitant of the house was the old man. He cooked in a makeshift outdoor kitchen, much like his mother did, to keep the woodsmoke from filling the house. Each day, early in the morning, he put a dal to simmer in a burnt pot, and they all ate it, with raw onions and mango pickle, with parathas for breakfast, rice for lunch, and rotis for dinner.

There was also milk to be drunk, but it was cow's milk and Vishal didn't like it. He was used to Shanti's thicker buffalo fare. It made even the tea taste wrong, and it took many days before he could adapt his palate to it. The old man told him he had it wrong: 'Buffalo milk gives you flab, cow milk builds your muscle and bone.' Then he looked at the boy's huge shoulders and rolling biceps, and said, 'Twice as big. You would have been twice as big, if you'd been drinking cow's milk.'

Leave alone the milk, Vishal found the cow no solace either. He tried to get it to lick his head—kneeling in the dust and offering up his scalp—but the beast had no gift of empathy at all.

Instead, the boy found friendship with the dogs. He stroked their throats and caressed their flanks till they fell asleep; he fed them rotis soaked in dal with his own hands; and occasionally, when the old man was not looking, poured them some milk to drink. Soon they were licking his hands and face, and trailing him wherever he went. Then they began to clamber on to his charpoy in the night and array themselves around him in various ways. The boy loved it. Their warm bodies, their steady breathing, the sudden shake of their head and the whisk of their tails, bred in him the same sense of calm that Shanti's tongue baths once had. One morning, as he walked down the stairs covered in dog hair, the old man said in disgust, 'It's only a matter of time before you open your mouth to talk and begin to bark! Bowwwww!'

The days turned to weeks, and the occasional visitor transited through. The dogs would begin to bark and sprint as soon as anyone set foot in the penumbra of the open fields—on foot, or cycle, or motorbike. The old man would welcome him after his acerbic fashion. The stacked charpoy in Vishal's room would be dropped on its feet and a heap of bedding unrolled. The protocol was to keep conversation down to the minimum. To the weather, the dogs, the food. Always, the transiting men carried firearms, but they remained unremarked, like routine articles of clothing.

One evening the dogs barked wildly as the motorcycle man with the white bandanna arrived. Gruffly, he said, 'Gwalabhai wants to know if the boy is okay.'

The old man cackled and said, 'Tell him he is doing very well, and is growing bigger and tougher on cow's milk and dog hair! Next time he will crack open six skulls with his hammer!'

The motorcycle man ignored him and continued, 'Gwalabhai says the police has put a sum of twenty-five thousand rupees on his head. His uncle is baying for revenge and is trying to target Rajbir.'

Vishal said, 'So what should I do?'

'Do?' snorted the motorcycle rider. 'Do nothing! Plunder the old man's dal, and pull at your small willy! You don't need any help with that, do you?'

Later, the old man said, 'He puts on arrogance because he is actually Guruji's uncle—his mother's brother. But in reality he's like the rest of us, only a disciple.'

Vishal said, 'Have you ever met Guruji?'

The old man laughed. 'What do I look to you? A chick hatched yesterday? I knew him before he was Guruji, and I knew him before he was Donullia! His father was my cousin. I knew him before he had learnt to stand up and piss!'

As he saw the boy assessing the information, he quickly added, 'But now I am like all of you—merely a disciple. Just because you knew the foal before he could walk doesn't mean that you will still outrun it when it's a horse! Today he's my Guruji too, and we all live on his generosity and mercy.'

Vishal said, 'When did you last see him?'

The old man said, 'Just the night before you arrived.'

Vishal looked at him sceptically. He was at peace in this lonely farmhouse—especially with the dogs—but his arms had begun to ache with inaction. Near the tube well he had found a smooth, heavy rock to use as a shot and spent long hours twirling and hurling it, but he found himself missing that moment of high when his hammer had smashed through the skulls of those three bastards. Never in his life had he felt more pure, more powerful, as he had then. Even as he was fleeing to Donullia Gujjar's realm, his head was bursting not with the prospect of escape but with the excitement of meeting the famed brigand and being commissioned into action.

But the weeks had rolled into months and all he had done was strain different charpoys, eat heaps of dal, sleep with the dogs, take long excursions into the cane fields, and hear endless accounts of the man who had a thousand faces. Maybe Gainda was right: maybe there was no Donullia Gujjar any more. He was merely kept alive by those who needed his protective shield.

The two of them were sitting in the front yard—on charpoys opposite each other, their feet tucked under them. Above, the sky was bursting with stars, and every few minutes one left its mooring and burnt a path through the dark. It was late September and the breeze had begun to sharpen its cold teeth. The moon was slow in rising, but the forest was beginning to howl and move.

The boy said, 'So when did he die?'

A beedi in his mouth, the old man said, 'Who?'

'Guruji.'

The old man pulled the beedi out of his mouth and said, 'You should stop sleeping with those dogs. You are beginning to bark. When you have lived long enough you will realize it is not a good idea to talk loosely about Donullia Gujjar! You will see him when he wants to see you, not when you want to see him! At this moment, of course, he is more alive than you and me! But remember, even when he is dead he will still be alive!'

iii

Swordarm of the Guru

With his days so barren, Vishal Tyagi's dreaming had acquired a kaleidoscopic fecundity. Every morning he woke with the residue of busy images floating in his head. Most days he liked the dreams. They were full of action—double-barrelled guns, flying hammers, galloping horses, baying dogs, running policemen, a moving shadow. Having woken, he would scrunch his eyes shut again, in a futile attempt at recapturing the storyline. Then he would pull out his slim-stemmed hammer from under the pillow, caress it, and know that his life fell in that unknown space between dreams and reality, and he did not have the tools to make any sense of it.

One night, as he lay buried in the depths of his quilt, amid the slumbering dogs, the dream became unusually vivid and menacing. He found himself suddenly surrounded in the dark by numberless shadows. The shadows had no faces but had lines of guns sticking out of them. There were two by the door, barring escape. And there were two flanking the window, which was now open with the moon shining through. In the middle of the room was a huge shadow whose head seemed to go through the ceiling, and who had shoulders that could have hurled the shot into the next country and beyond. Next to its thick legs was a lumpy one—as if it were sitting on a chair.

Soon the boy realized there were more shadows than he'd first thought—they were clinging to the walls and filling the corners. This was a dream unlike any he had ever had. More vivid, more sinister. Suddenly he began to hear mewling sounds. The dogs were burrowing into him, pushing themselves under the bedding, into his feet and thighs. This too was odd. He didn't think his dreams had ever had a soundtrack.

Okay, he thought to himself, if this was going to be about battle, he'd better get on with it. He pulled his hand out of the warm quilt and reached under his pillow, and in that very instant he found both his wrists grabbed and held tight. In the last couple of years Vishal had not met anyone who could physically match him or contain him, but now no matter how much he flexed his arms, they were trapped in a stronger grip. It had something to do with the position. Someone very heavy was leaning his whole weight down onto his wrists, pinning them to the bed. It was a dream, after all—unlikely things were allowed.

The boy relaxed, letting the struggle drain out of him, and in the next moment his dream exploded in a flash of blinding light. Someone was shining a powerful torch into his eyes, and he suddenly knew he was not in a dream but awake, and he was in deep trouble because the police had found him, and all the shadows looming around the room had come to pick him up. With a loud roar he snapped his wrists free and banged the torch away from his face and jumped up from the bed, scattering the quilt and dogs, but before he had found his feet something slammed him hard on his chest and he was flung back onto the bed, the breath knocked clean out of him, the mad baying and whining of the dogs ringing all around.

When his head cleared the light was still on his face, and the whimpering of the dogs had gone into diminuendo. A low gravelly voice said, 'So, boy, you are very strong, are you? And did you really hammer in the skulls of three men all by yourself?' Vishal knew that his uncle Joginder was most probably in the room too, and the police were going to bump him off once they had his confession. When he said nothing, the low voice asked, 'Did Gwala say he had no tongue?' The shadow in the middle of the room, with his head going through the roof, said with a chuckle, 'Most tongues quickly slip down into the stomach in your presence, don't they!'

Vishal exclaimed, 'Guruji!'

The voice from the roof said, 'He has a tongue, and it says the right things.'

The torchlight had dipped from his eyes a little and Vishal could once again see the shadow lines. Yes, there was someone sitting on a chair in the middle of the room, next to the huge silhouette. In a low gruff voice it said, 'You want to work for the people? You want to fight for justice? You want to swing your hammer to help the poor?'

Vishal said, 'Yes. Yes. Whatever you tell me to do.' He was straining to make out the face and features of the man, but all he could see was a dark lump, swathed perhaps in a blanket, with a kind of beret on its head.

The low voice said, 'What I tell you to do, boy, will come later. First, what is that you'd like to do? Hulla, do you want to ask him if he's made of sand or steel?'

The man with his head in the roof and shoulders like a cupboard said, 'Tell us, boy, did you kill them to gain money or respect?'

Vishal said, 'Respect.'

The man said, 'There were three of them. Did that scare you?'

The boy said, 'I had the hammer.'

'And suppose there had been six of them?'

The boy said, 'I would have swung the hammer faster.'

'And suppose you had a gun?'

'Then I would have taken down twelve of them.'

'Do you even know how to use a gun?'

'I know how to point it and how to squeeze a trigger.'

The man in his practised baritone said, 'Do you know what happens when you come under the grace of Guruji?'

'Yes.'

'Then on, you belong to him alone. No family, no friends, no other allegiances, no other loyalties. Like a true bhakt, you give yourself up to him, doing only the good that he commands. He works for the weak and the wronged, and you work for him. Your days are his, and your nights are his. Your life is his, and your death is his.'

The boy's skin prickled with excitement. He said, 'I understand.'

The man with his head in the roof said, 'But first, how do we know that you are not a police informer? Some of us here think you're not to be trusted. The old man says you say nothing but observe everything, and you are always asking questions about us.'

The boy looked around to locate the old man, but none of the shadows seemed to be him.

He said, 'The old man is a chutiya. Far stupider than the dogs.'

A few of the shadows tittered.

The man said, 'So give your guru dakshina and prove yourself.'

The boy said, 'Whatever you want.'

The man said, 'What did Eklavya give?'

'His thumb.'

'Well, you can give your little finger.'

The boy held out his left hand, all the fingers curled in but the smallest.

The man said, 'Katua, you don't need to take it—just brand it as Guruji's. Use his hammer. Let's see how good it is.'

At the edge of the torchlight, the boy saw a face appear with a big scar running down its side. He knew it instantly from the stories of his sports mentor. Katua Kasai. So it was all true. All of it! The one with the head in the roof had to be Hulla Mallah, who had drowned a boatful of upper-caste landlords; who could run through the forest with a man on his shoulders. And somewhere amid the shadows must be the one-eyed armyman, Kana Commando—a Tyagi like him. And, yes, that dark shapeless silhouette in the middle with the beret…

The man with the scar had pulled out the hammer from under the pillow. He caught the tiny extended finger and put it on the wooden bar of the charpoy's frame. The man from the roof said, 'Are you sure, boy? Guruji does not want any reluctant warriors. In Guruji's army there are only true karmayogis—who fulfil their duty without any regard for recognition or reward. If there is any fear or avarice in your heart just pull back your hand, get back into your quilt, close your eyes, and it'll all be over and you can go back to your life.'

The man with the scar waited, poised with hammer and finger.

The boy thought of his mentor and the story of Chuchunder. An iron asshole. Men who stood apart had an iron asshole. He said, 'I am sure. I have nine more. And you don't need this one for hammer or gun.'

The silhouette said in a low voice, 'Do you know what the great lord Krishna said to Arjuna as he stood there, head sunk low, bow flung to the ground, unwilling to fight? The lord said, "I envy no one, nor am I partial to anyone. I am equal to all. But whoever renders service unto me in devotion is a friend. He is in me, and I am also a friend to him. Even if one commits the most abominable action, if he is engaged in devotional service he is to be considered saintly because he is properly situated in his determination. He quickly becomes righteous and attains lasting peace. O son of Kunti, know it verily that my devotee never perishes. O son of Partha, those who take shelter in me, though they be of lower birth, of any birth, can attain the supreme destination." It is what I say to you, son.'

Overcome, the boy merely said, 'Guruji.'

The voice from above said, 'Accept his gift then, Katua. Brand it with Guruji's love.'

The last thing the boy remembered was the light sparking off the kneeling man's rich scar and the whirl of a forearm, and then the world blew up in an explosion of pain that wrenched a scream from deep inside him and hurled him into a blackness darker than the silhouette with the slanted beret.

The first job he was given was to eliminate a contractor in Jhansi. The man was young but had amassed a large fortune by annexing government contracts. In city circles he was known as an unstoppable trident. One tine of his power was his father's youngest brother, a senior official in Lucknow, who had six times been voted among the most corrupt bureaucrats in the state. The second tine was his mother's maternal uncle, who was a legislator and minister from western Uttar Pradesh, a chargesheeter, who had been named in several cases of abduction and murder. The third tine was the man himself—ruthless, crisp, wielding money, men, gun and influence to sweep all before him. His fate was further sealed by the fact of his good looks. It completed the cocktail of arrogance, encouraging him to the kind of excess a more plain-faced man would have balked at. Before he was thirty he had been named in half a dozen FIRs for the abduction of girls. In time, all of them had withdrawn their complaints.

Vishal Tyagi was sure Guruji had nothing personal against the contractor. The man who came to brief him at the farm wore a white kurta-pajama and spoke with a lisp. He said the contractor was an oppressor. Complaints about him had heaped up at Guruji's feet and it was time to bring his terror to an end. Then he proceeded to show him pictures of the man, and explain his location and habits. He made the boy take down directions, names, addresses, and the modus operandi. Vishal was distracted by the man's childish voice and had to struggle to concentrate.

Later, when he had left on his Bajaj scooter, trailing a line of dust, the old man, squatting by the cow and pulling at its teats, asked, 'What did you get—a tamancha or a pistol?'

Vishal replied, 'Neither.'

Stilling his bony hand mid-spurt, the old man said, 'Ah, test run! The last one who was sent out without either never came back. But enough money was sent to his home.'

Rolling the flesh of his boneless little finger like putty, Vishal said, 'Old man, you like money, do you?'

'Not more than my life.'

'Have you ever killed anyone, old man?'

Resuming a slow massage of the udders, the small brass bucket held in place by his feet, the old man said, 'I do something even more important. I collect the bones and flow them down the Ganga. None of you would get moksha without my hard work. I am the brahmin Guruji keeps to send you all safely on your way.'

'So now you are going to wait to collect my bones, old man?'

Hopping on his haunches along with the shuffling cow, the milk frothing warmly in the bucket, the old man said, 'Don't say such a thing. There is no pleasure ever in collecting the bones of the young. And I have done enough of that in my life.'

He met with his accomplice in the tea shop at the bus stand. The accomplice called himself Ali and was clean-shaven with a bright red mouth wet with paan. Ali took him to a hotel in the crowded bazaar, called New Delite. The entrance was through a narrow staircase between a saree shop and a kirana store, and upstairs there were many dimly lit corridors and a small windowless room. Ali barely spoke. The only thing he muttered when he learnt it was Vishal's first job was, 'What will they send me next—a schoolboy in half-pants? The only one they are going to get killed soon is me!' Vishal, anyway, was not inclined to speak. The two of them ate dinner in silence at a small dhaba in an adjoining lane, and then Ali left, saying he'd be back early the next morning.

Ten minutes later, Vishal went down to the pale, thin, swollen-eyed man sitting on the first-floor landing behind a stained plywood desk with a cellophane-bulb lit picture of Goddess Lakshmi behind him, and asked for another room. The man who'd probably not been out in the sun for the last ten years had some peanuts spread out on the counter and was fastidiously picking them up one by one and popping them into his mouth. 'Why, the palace is not good enough for his lordship, the Nawab of Siraj-ud-Daulah?' he asked, not bothering to look up. When Vishal leaned into him, blocking the light of the bulb overhead, he quickly said, 'Well, let me offer his royalty the Hawa Mahal then.' Prostitution, drugs, guns, it all happened here, and it made sense to not provoke trouble. You never knew which crazy was transiting through. Few wore the name of their gangs or their homicidal records on their foreheads.

The Hawa Mahal turned out to be a room with a small window at the back of the second floor. The window had no bars. Halfway down was the discoloured hulk of a desert cooler. By its side grew an electricity pole that rose from a narrow back lane filled with refuse, dank water, and the steady hum of mosquitoes. The boy latched the window, then latched the door and pushed a small table against it. Then he lay down fully dressed on the bed, and pulling out his thin-stemmed hammer from his small blue shoulder bag, placed it next to his pillow.

He slept badly. All night the corridors were alive with hushed voices and shuffling feet. The sad world was trying to fuck itself out of unhappiness. He waited for the one footfall that would stop outside his door. The sky was beginning to lighten outside his window before he finally fell asleep, and was immediately woken by an infernal banging on his door. In an instant he had the hammer in his hand.

It was Ali, and he came in ranting, flecks of paan flying out of his mouth. Who the fuck did the boy think he was! Changing the room he'd been put in! He'd just had a row with the man downstairs about it! Was it Ali's fate to spend his life chaperoning adolescents and chutiyas! Allah gave men wife, children, and livestock. Unto him had been given only chutiyas, chutiyas, and more chutiyas! Some with small useless brains and some with small useless fingers, and some with both! And what was that damn hammer in his hand? Was he here on a killing contract or to make a sofa set!

That old red light exploded inside the boy's head, and in one quick move he caught Ali by his shirt collar, lifted him with one hand till only the points of his sandalled feet were on the floor, and banged him against the wall. Then he swung his hammer hard and smashed it against the wall next to Ali's left ear. Shrapnels of white plaster flew. Through his choked windpipe Ali screamed inarticulately for mercy. The boy held him there for long minutes, with Ali clawing at his arms and kicking his legs, till the red light in his head dimmed. When he let go of him, Ali slumped to the ground, holding his head, gasping to fill his lungs. Then he croaked, 'Maaderchod, have they sent you to kill me?'

Vishal Tyagi said nothing; the boundaries stood redrawn. Ali had come on a yellow Chetak scooter with a Donald Duck sticker on it. He took his partner on it to check out the house near Civil Lines where their quarry lived, with new care.

The front wall of the house was about seven feet high, topped with iron rods and coils of barbed wire. The iron gates had a beware-of-dogs sign, big light globes on the pillars, and an assortment of men in white uniform. In the driveway, through the bars of the gate, he could see several cars and at least two jeeps. Ali said that in the small guard hut next to the gate, the men had a couple of local weapons, including a rifle.

At night, after dinner, Ali rode Vishal through the road once more. Now the gate was ablaze under the fire of floodlights and one of the guards had a rifle slung on his shoulder. Ali said, in his high-pitched nasal twang, 'When we fire the first shot, this one will shit a trail from here till Lucknow!'

Later, at Hawa Mahal, Ali said, 'My dear King Kong, now please stay where I am leaving you, so that I can find you in the morning without calling in Inspector Eagle!' The plan was to be out before five in the morning to scope out the contractor's morning walk and badminton routine. They had three strike options. The morning walk; in his very lair, in the house, where he had an office to meet visitors; or at his hotel construction site near Orchha, at the point where the tarred road turned off onto a narrow dust track that could be accidentally blocked. They had been given ten days to decide, plan and execute.

That night too Vishal slept with his shoes on, and was waiting, all ablutions over, sitting on the lone wooden chair, when the knock came. Ali wore a green monkey cap pulled down low over his face. 'Hah!' he whined. 'Didn't recognize me? Not even my wife would! Might even open her legs because of that!' He rolled up his cap till it was a thick cream band on his forehead. Even at this first hour before light, his mouth was full of paan.

The halwai shops were the only ones stirring in the bazaar, when Ali kick-started the scooter. Just out of the bazaar a tea-stall owner and his underage assistant, a boy in loose torn shorts and close-cropped hair, were putting out their biscuit jars and setting a pan to boil. Ali tried to slow down, hoping to grab a hot glass, but Vishal knocked him on his skull with his knuckles and hissed, 'Go!'

The shotput champion with the long-fuse and big detonation never learnt to speak much, but he always had an instinct. It would see him survive many a perilous situation. Ali would be dead before long, and so would most of the hitmen he worked with over the coming years. As a rule, triggermen were picked for their dispensability. Conscripted raw, with no police records, no faces, they were expected to run a job or two before they were eliminated by the police or the commissioning gang, or by an understanding between the two. For sheer evanescence there wasn't a career to compare. A rare few rose to be leaders, escaping the hitman's fate. Fewer still were those who refused to become leaders—managing gangs and managing money—and refused to die. These were the true artists of the business, the legends, in sweet harmony with what they practised, warriors from the Gita, concerned little with reward and recognition, capable of audacious strikes and survival, again and again.

From the start, Vishal Tyagi was such a man.

When they halted by the big banyan tree at the corner of the road, the morning mist was still lifting from the ditches and grass. The birdsong all around, like a manic Kishore Kumar yodel, was occasionally flattened by the plangent lowing of cattle that many affluent families kept in their compounds, pursuing the Indian obsession with pure milk. Ali dropped to his haunches and popped open the engine guard of his sweetly plump scooter, exposing its iron entrails and plastic veins. The area was often patrolled by the beat policemen.

All down the wide street, gate lights and veranda lights glowed weakly, about to be killed by daylight. The brightest by far, at the end of the street, was the contractor's spotlight. A milkman went by, head bent low, humming a popular song to himself, his big steel canisters hanging on both sides of his cycle, clanging away. From his low crouch, Ali spat out a stream of red juice and whined, 'A cup of tea! That's all I wanted! A cup of tea! Even a man about to be hanged gets a cup of tea!' A newspaper vendor rattled by on his cycle, the rolled-up rubber banded newspapers bunched in his front basket like cobs of corn. The first thud came soon after; then the thuds diminished quickly down the road. Ali whined, 'Shall I continue to polish this engine till it becomes a diamond while you survey the battlefield, General Dyer?' The boy thought, it's a miracle this Ali is not already dead. He has way too many nerves; he talks too much.

The last smudgings of mist had blotted away, and now you could see clearly to the very end of the street. A gate opened down the left side and two young boys, shiny with privilege, pedalled out on red cycles, wearing rich white cricket clothes, their bats in plastic sheaths slung across their shoulders like guns. They pedalled with their heels, keeping the studs of their cricket shoes clear. Moving in the blindness of their privilege they did not even register the two men crouched by the scooter and later could tell the police nothing.

Another gate opened on the left, and an old couple, wearing thick spectacles, white tennis shoes and stern expressions, the man with a short stick in his right hand and the woman in a green saree, walked out, looked left and right and then briskly set off—pumping their arms as if in a race—in the other direction. Later, they too could tell the police nothing.

Ali said, 'Shall we go?'

Vishal said, 'No.'

Ali said, 'Shall I stand up?'

Vishal said, 'No.'

Ali said, 'Another five minutes and I'll never be able to! My knees will be more jammed than my grandmother's. Instead of Ali the killer, your partner will be Ali the frog! Graaon! Graaon!'

Vishal banged his knuckles on Ali's head to stop his croaking. How had this man survived in the business?

Another gate opened at the end of the street and a lone figure staggered out with three dogs on leashes and began to walk towards them. The dark stringy servant boy was in someone's hand-me-downs—loose khaki shorts and a frayed Saturday Night Fever tee shirt, John Travolta stretched like a bow, arm up, back curved, staying alive. The dogs, frisking away in front of him, pulling in different directions, were two golden-brown cocker spaniels and a precious white Pomeranian with a snub nose and a sharp yip. As they reached them the dogs converged towards Vishal's feet, suddenly yanking the servant boy along. Ali shouted, 'Saaley chutiye, take these bloody rats away!' Vishal knuckled him on his head, and bent down to stroke the dogs, cooing to them. Later, the boy would give the police a precise description of the man who had stroked his dogs—a description that would reverberate through the police stations of the state and set rolling the legend of Hathoda Tyagi.

When the servant and the dogs were gone, and the street was empty, Ali spat out a red stream and said, 'Let's go. Maybe he is bending the limbs of his old lady this morning. We've seen enough for today. Hopefully we'll get a glimpse of him tomorrow.'

Vishal said, 'Ten minutes more.'

Ali said, 'If I bark like a dog, will you listen to me? Boww, bowww, bowwww!' Vishal was just considering rapping him again when the gate he had been peering at opened and a man walked out stretching his arms and swivelling his shoulders. He was tall and well-built and dressed in a shiny blue track-suit, the top rakishly unzipped to his stomach, revealing a white polo-neck tee shirt with the collars pulled up. He stood outside the gate loosening his limbs: flexing his arms, lifting his knees high and crunching them in his interlaced hands, touching his toes.

Vishal hissed, 'Move!' Ali was up in an instant, slamming the engine guard shut, pushing the scooter off its stand, kicking it alive. Two men—one of whom they had seen the day before at the gate—now appeared behind the young contractor, single-barrel guns on their shoulders. The contractor went still, as if waiting for the starter's gun, and then turning towards them began to walk briskly, moving his arms hard across his chest.

Ali said, 'Fuck his sister! He's coming this way! Let's get out of here—we don't want him to notice us yet!'

Vishal said, 'No! Drive past him. I want to take a closer look.'

As the scooter jerked forward in second gear, Vishal hissed, 'Right by him, Ali!' The distance between them was less than hundred yards. Within seconds, jumping into third gear and being given full throttle by a nervous Ali, the scooter was on the contractor. The contractor, who was swinging his arms briskly and moving inside the unseeing cocoon of his privilege—like the cricket boys and the old couple—did not even notice the scooter and the speeding twosome till almost the very moment that the hammerhead smashed through his nose and forehead, instantly turning off all his lights.

To Ali's credit, he did not break the acceleration, and by the time the guards had taken the guns off their shoulders, the killers had turned the corner and vanished. Into the rushing wind, Ali wailed, 'Fucking butcher, couldn't you warn me! I could have pulled down my fucking cap! I was flaunting my face as if I was in a cold-cream advertisement! I am dead! By tomorrow every policeman in the state will know my face! I am dead! My wife is a widow! My children are orphans!'

When the guards came back to pick up their ward they found a long-stemmed hammer buried in his face in a pool of warm blood. The men did not panic or scream or run for help. They stood there looking at each other. The boss was dead, beyond all repair, and they were out of work.

With the killing of the contractor, his own name died too. No one called him Vishal ever again. He became Hathoda Tyagi for everyone—the police, the media, Donullia's gang. Four skulls had cracked under his hammer now, and the state police placed a reward of fifty thousand rupees on any information leading to his arrest.

When he returned to the farm four days later, the old man said, 'Son, you're making many of the old gang members look bad. Some of them took ten years to hit fifty thousand.'

A few days later, early in the morning before the sun was up, a jeep pulled up at the farm in a cloud of dust. It was Gwalabhai, whom he had not seen in months, wearing a crisp white pajama-kurta, a thick gold necklace, and smelling sweet. He embraced him with the warmth of a father and called him his son. He said Guruji was thrilled with his work, and had said that after a long time they had found another worthy warrior of the people. He said in the

Bundelkhand area people were sending up prayers for him for saving them from the menace of the oppressive contractor. He said it was the blessings of the people that they all worked for, and it was what kept them safe and alive.

Sitting on the charpoy in the frontyard as his gunmen sauntered idly in the fields beyond, sipping the scalding tea the old man made, Gwalabhai said it was true the police was under huge pressure to find and nail him, but he mustn't worry. In Chitrakoot, a few kilometres from the ravines and forests of Madhya Pradesh, they were very far from the fiefs of the contractor's influential relatives. This was the realm of Bajpaisahib and of Donullia Gujjar, and nothing could happen here without their assent. Gwalabhai added that Bajpaisahib too was fully aware of his exemplary deed, and was full of praise for his courage and dedication. In fact, he had asked for the boy to be brought to him one of these days, when the heat had cooled somewhat.

Hathoda Tyagi sat humbly and quietly, caressing the dogs leaning into his lap with their front paws and nuzzling his feet. His mind was cool and still, and nothing Gwalabhai said held any real meaning for him. He had only one small inquiry—the same one he had had the last time Gwalabhai's man had come to visit him. Was his family okay or was it still being harassed?

Gwalabhai said, 'Let's go to the tube well and wash our faces with fresh water.'

One glance from him ensured no one followed except the yipping, frisking dogs. Gwalabhai said, 'Guruji also loves animals, especially dogs. He says, if a man likes dogs he's a good man; and if dogs like a man he's a good man.' Nurse-white egrets took wing as they walked the narrow bunds between the fields. He went on, 'He saw it that night. More than the gift of your finger, it was your love of the dogs that brought him to trust you. You must know it is almost impossible for Guruji to trust anybody. He has survived so many years only because he is fully awake even when he is asleep.'

They used their palms to slice a thin layer of water from the throbbing gush of the tube well and splashed their faces with it. When both had done so several times, Gwalabhai put his hand on the boy's back and informed him that twenty-five thousand rupees in cash had been delivered to his parents. The man who had gone there had told them that the money had been sent by their son. He had left his mobile phone number with them and said they were to call him if they ever needed anything. He told them that he had also paid a visit to their relation, Joginder Tyagi. He had condoled with Joginder about the loss of his sons, and had talked about the world and the way in which men ought to conduct themselves. Gwalabhai's man had assured Vishal's family that Joginder would not be bothering them ever again.

When the boy said nothing, Gwalabhai turned him around and patting his shoulder said, 'Is it insufficient? Do you want me to send some more?'

The boy said, 'No. You have done too much already. I did it for Guruji—and for you—not for the money. I expected nothing.'

Gwalabhai said, 'You are just as Guruji was when he was young. A true karmayogi. You know that is why Guruji worships Shiva—because the lord of snakes and djinns, of beasts and yogis, the all-powerful creator and destroyer of the world, has everything, and yet he lives like an ascetic. The most powerful men in the world, my son, like you, have no needs. They only live to give.'

Vishal Tyagi—hammerman, shotput champion, lover of animals—was deeply moved. As he looked down at his dusty sandalled feet, his eyes filled, and he felt a rush of love and kinship for Gwalabhai that he had not felt for anyone ever. Finally someone had intuited the man he truly was, recognized the beauty of his inner being. Yes, he was like Guruji. He had an asshole of iron; and he wanted nothing for himself. His great strength and courage were there to be used only for the protection of the weak and the oppressed. He experienced the peace of the lost wanderer who has suddenly found home.

In instinctive gratitude and happiness he bent down and touched Gwalabhai's feet, and when he stood up the gentle don was holding out a gift for him. It was a beautiful stainless metal-frame Smith and Wesson 908 pistol. It had a black plastic grip, and was a prohibited bore, 9mm, with an eight-round magazine. It was sensuous. It demanded to be held, caressed, used. 'Guruji has sent it for you. It is the finest he had. It is a token of his love. Now you are under Guruji's immense umbrella. No one has been accepted by Guruji so quickly. Never betray him—in action or in word.'

Standing by the shuddering brick wall of the tube well, looking down at the first light of sun glancing off the pistol, the boy's big muscular shoulders began to shake. Slowly, as if the strength had drained from his huge frame, he settled back on his haunches, put the pistol at his own feet, and cupped his head in his palms. The older man waited, consummate in the handling of emotions and servitors and loyalty. The boy finally said, in a choked voice, 'Tell Guruji I will kill myself before betraying him.'

After Gwalabhai had left in a burst of dust, the old man fondled the shining 908 in his palms and said, 'Hmmmm, they are readying you for bigger things. Well, certainly beats going around swinging a hammer. But I suppose it also gets you to the cremation ground that much faster.'

Yet, remarkably, month after month, year after year, Hathoda Tyagi kept licking the odds. His natural reticence; the absence of any avarice or driving temptations like booze, drugs and women; his sharp instinct for survival; and his unflinching loyalty to Donullia kept him alive. In that time he became, outside the home district of Chitrakoot, the very swordarm of the brigand. Periodically, information would reach the farm, of an oppressor and a tyrant who needed to be cured or crippled or killed. The courier would inform him he had come directly from Guruji and would pass on the great man's blessings. Each time, a great tide of warmth and affection and pride would surge through the warrior.

Calmly and meticulously, Hathoda Tyagi would make his plans. The explosion in the head, the avenging frenzy, he would trust to the moment. Sometimes he would work with an accomplice, or several, but most often he'd go it alone. Sometimes he would exercise the hammer—for old time's sake, to create confusion—but most often he would wield the beautiful 908. Sometimes he would fail in the first attempt, but always he would succeed eventually.

His strike range was rare in its spread. Donullia had never had such a man at his command. Without too many questions, without any fuss, some days after the information had been delivered to the farm, Hathoda Tyagi would get into a car, or onto a bus, or hitch a ride on a truck, or climb onto a train and disappear. Some days, a week, some weeks later news would reach Donullia that the living names he had sent out to his man on the farm were now only obituaries.

Over the years Hathoda Tyagi struck not only in several outlying districts of Uttar Pradesh but also as far as Ludhiana in the Punjab, Asansol in West Bengal, Jorhat in Assam, Nagpur in Maharashtra, Bhilwara in Rajasthan, Shimla in Himachal Pradesh, Vadodara in Gujarat, and once even in the very citadel of the underworld, Bombay. Many of these killings were never attributed to him, but enough were for his name to acquire a dread ring.

All his killings displayed a trademark violence, a certain brutality of assault. It came from that explosion in the head. If it was the hammer, the skull was caved in, the face smashed; if the exquisite 908, the barrel was inserted through the ear or the mouth or the nose and the brains blown out. Some said there had been cases where the barrel had been put up the ass and the bullet travelled into the brain. Those post-mortems, they said, were many pages long.

If it was curing or crippling that was called for, Guruji's words to him would be 'make him wise'. Then he only used the hammer or his rough hands. He was big and burly and still running with the daily regime of weights and push-ups taught to him by his sports mentor, and he could delicately break bones for hours till the recipient had become fully 'wise'. Fingers, toes, ankles, knees, elbows, teeth, nose, ears, testicles. Sometimes by just twisting an arm he could help men find instant wisdom in an operatic wail. He did not personally care too much for curing and crippling; it was Guruji's great generosity that he often chose it. Hathoda Tyagi preferred the explosion in his head, that heady moment of pure potency and vengeance, the finality of the stilled brain. Only dead men were wise men. Cured and crippled men could once again become unwise.

In those years, even though he had no personal needs or demands, the upper storey of the farmhouse became his exclusive domain, and the old man was reduced to nothing but an old man serving him. Each time Hathoda Tyagi returned from an operation—successful, unscathed, taciturn—the old man said, 'Behanchod, you are definitely the favoured messenger of Yamraj! He alone knows how many souls he has ordered you to dispatch to him! I know you are here to see me off too!'

In his room with his many dogs—never less than five wrapped around his legs—he woke each morning covered in dog hair. When the old man's cow died, he got him to bring in a young buffalo and soon tutored the gentle animal to lap his scalp. He christened her Shanti too, and felt he had rediscovered an old elusive peace.

That was the closest he came to connecting back to his life as a boy. He never went back to his home; never met his family again. Every now and then a man sent by Gwalabhai went and delivered a sheaf of rupees to his parents and checked on their needs. His sisters were married with children. The last one's wedding had been a flamboyant affair, befitting the sibling of a growing legend. Besides bundles of currency notes, Gwalabhai had sent three sets of gold ornaments and four armed men to ensure that all went smoothly.

On that occasion—as in Hindi films—everyone expected the feared brother to suddenly show up. But Hathoda Tyagi was too removed from his family, and Gwalabhai had cautioned him against going—Donullia's gang had thin purchase in western Uttar Pradesh, and the number of his enemies were growing in direct proportion to his victims. A marriage, a sentimental, showy moment was the perfect place to find and nail him. It was not for them to know that Donullia's most effective hitman was neither showy nor sentimental.

Unable to contain himself, Joginder had had an episode some years ago and once again turned on his cousin. He was now dead. Lesser hitmen from the gang's stables had done the needful. Apart from his standing, Gyanendra Tyagi's holdings had grown—close to two hundred bighas. A red tractor worked his fields, and the house they lived in had piped water and sanitary fittings in pink bought in the town.

In those years Hathoda Tyagi came to know several members of the gang. Some nameless, transiting through; some regular couriers and informers, who brought in ammunition, money, news, and the death warrants Guruji was writing up. Prime among the regulars was Kaka, a dark, thin, optimistic Sikh with a wasted left arm, who told him a new story of the great Donullia's exploits each time they met. Beaming with pride he would say, 'Fighting Aurangzeb's armies, Guru Gobind Singh had declared, Sava lakh se ek ladaoon! That's exactly what our Guruji does!' Each follower of mine will vanquish a multitude.

It stirred Hathoda Tyagi immeasurably. He could see himself astride a big white horse, slicing through ranks of oppressors, restoring the balance of good in the world. More stirring still were his encounters with some of the key associates of the great chieftain. Hulla Mallah, big as a door, with a gentle voice, and hands so big they could crush a man's skull like an orange. Kana Commando, blind in the left eye, sharp in the tongue, capable of taking apart and putting together a weapon by flickering candlelight, full of deep analysis and strategy. And the man with the ravine running down his face, Katua Kasai, the real cool killer, with blade or bullet, mostly by Donullia's side, laconic, wiry, capable of drinking an entire bottle of country liquor—Shiva's prasad—and remaining cogent.

These men would arrive unannounced in the dead of night, and the old man would scurry about cobbling together food and bed for them. They came trailed by many armed men who hung around the yard, smoking and talking. Sometimes they came merely to convalesce from infection and wound; at other times for a meeting with Gwalabhai, or Bajpaisahib.

The farm, flush by the forest, far from the town and village, an indistinct dot on the great Gangetic plain, was a key and permanent outpost and was not exposed to other associates. The meetings with policemen, arms suppliers, traders, businessmen, and local politicians were held in shifting locations in the forest and the town.

If it became necessary to bring someone to the farm, the blindfold was deployed. Often it was used with medics who were brought in to treat fevers and injury. There was a regular doc, Srivastavji, with a Hitler moustache and thick glasses, on the rolls, but sometimes he needed to bring in assistants, and even other doctors. At such a time he too was brought in blindfolded. In a small room downstairs was a big wooden table used for surgical procedures. Directly above it hung three fat 200-watt bulbs, which when switched on necessitated the turning off of all the farm's lights.

Occasionally this was done with traders with whom terms had to be negotiated. It was not about the usual protection money, but new deals, including the commissioning of actions to neutralize enemies. At such a time one of the big boys from the ravines—Kana Commando, Hulla Mallah, Katua Kasai—was always present to provide a whiff of the authentic and to strike terror into the heart. Every negotiation was done in the name of Donullia Gujjar; every twist of the screw carried his name.

Hathoda Tyagi, with his growing reputation, was a hulking

presence at these summits. He never spoke and he seldom followed the train of the conversation. What he did was to observe with fascination the fear that gripped rich men in the face of physical violence. Men who would have been ruthless and dismissive with underlings, men with fortunes they could not burn in three lifetimes, wheedled and whinged in the presence of Donullia's men. And yet, the moment they had to commission the killing of another, they acquired a rare bravura.

The assassin understood that wealth and station do not finally provide freedom from fear; only physical courage does. He felt truly free, blessed by one who was also truly free. Yet, in all those years, for all his special status, for all the wonderful missives Donullia sent him, Hathoda Tyagi did not once catch sight of his great and liberated patron. Each time he made an inquiry he was told the meeting was soon to take place; that Guruji was no less eager to meet him; that a new crisis, a new danger was keeping him occupied.

Often rumours floated up to him from the old man. Of expansions, alliances, political manoeuvrings. A new plant to make aerated drinks; a twenty-room hotel with air-conditioning; another cinema hall; an engineering college; differences with Bajpaisahib; a brewing axis with the new dispensation in Lucknow; perhaps a legislator's ticket for Gwalabhai. None of it held any interest for the assassin. He knew none of this had anything to do with the great brigand. These were the petty material concerns of the men around him, including his brother Gwalabhai. What excited Hathoda Tyagi were the stories of Donullia's latest strike, his most recent escapade.

And the brigand kept his legend alive by striking ruthlessly several times a year. In one brutal reminder he sent back the nineteen-year-old son of a Yadav landlord in nineteen pieces over nineteen days—in polythene bags, like stale meat—after having abducted him from the midst of his nineteenth birthday celebrations.

In September 1997, Hathoda Tyagi sensed an opportunity to finally see his Guru. That month the entire district was feverish with expectation. In every house and office, on every village chaupal and town corner, the question was: would he really risk it?

Two years before, Donullia Gujjar had decreed a massive temple to Hanuman—avatar of Shiva, protector of Rama, lord of strength, courage, celibacy, purity. It was built in granite and marble, with pillars and steeple of cast iron. The plinth was set at an imposing six feet, and the huge central statue of the god carrying the mountain with the Sanjivini herb had been carved by a team of master craftsmen from Rajasthan. The bell hung at the entrance of the sanctum weighed nearly a ton and had been strung on a thick girder. The sound of it tolling vibrated the floor and could be heard for miles and miles. The brigand chief had paid for it all, and now that it was complete, a date had been set for its consecration.

Sadhus, mendicants, fakirs, priests had been invited from everywhere, not just Chitrakoot and Varanasi. Donullia wanted to feed and honour at least one thousand and one holy men to commemorate its inauguration, and he wanted to do it himself. His intention had been announced and thousands were planning to turn up to catch a darshan of the god and the legend. So was the largest complement of policemen ever assembled in the district for a civil action, led by the superintendent himself.

On the evening of 24 September, when Hathoda Tyagi and the old man turned off the highway onto the link road that led to the temple that lay at the foot of a hillock, they found themselves swept up in a surging sea of humanity. Men and women of all ages, riding cycles, bullock-carts, motorcycles, scooters, horse-carts, overflowing tempos, walking, were on a determined pilgrimage. As they slowly negotiated their own motorcycle through this moving mass—their feet stabilizing rudders on the ground—they became one with the charged atmosphere. Everyone was coiled with the expectation of action; everywhere were policemen, in uniform and in plainclothes. The hammerman avoided looking any of them in the eye. In preparation for this excursion, like his leader, he had grown a beard. It was a risk, but he had his exquisite 908 in the pocket of his jacket. If the occasion required, he could, in an instant slip off the back of the motorcycle and melt into the crowds, pistol cocked and ready.

The river flowed to the rhythm of dholaks and single-stringed mandolins and chants to Shiva and Hanuman. Old men and women shuffled along with the aid of sticks, children travelled on the shoulders of the young. Threading through them were hawkers selling chana and chiki and pink candyfloss and besan burfi from aluminium boxes strung around their backs.

Long before they reached the temple, the river's flow had slowed to a gutter's sludge. The old man had turned off the motorbike engine and they were now propelling it forward with their feet. The ardour and tension was thickening around them as the chanting grew louder, swallowing up all small talk.

The temple on the foothills was like a big piece of cake overrun by thousands of ants. There were people up the hill, on the banyan trees, in the barren fields all around. Lights and lanterns were everywhere: in the hands of the faithful, strung up on poles and trees. The chorus of a loud kirtan, with clashing cymbals, ringing bells and the boom of dholaks, was powering out of the inner sanctum—festooned with moving lights—and was being echoed by the concentric rings of fevered devotees that went all the way out and beyond.

Along the plinth of the temple sat a long line of beggars and alms-seekers—cripples, lepers, the blighted and the cursed; limbs missing, limbs gnarled, eyes gouged out; men, women, children. They had travelled from all over, some from adjoining districts, to collect at faith's altar. Hathoda Tyagi walked down the hellish ranks doling out ten- and twenty-rupee notes, sparking a ripple of cries and blessings. It was what he did whenever he got the opportunity. He had no real use for his money. What went to his family went to his family, the remaining bundles were squandered on meat for the dogs, doles to the old man, and alms to all manner of fakirs and beggars.

Hathoda Tyagi knew the prophecy about himself. As did Guruji and the others in the gang: the boy was blessed. The priest had said, 'It will not be easy to harm him. His stars are like Hrinyakashyap's. He can only be harmed in a place that has both sunlight and shade; he can only be harmed when he is moving and not still; he can only be harmed when his belly is full; he can only be harmed when he is hidden from view; he can only be harmed by a slain enemy; and he can only be harmed when he is trapped between friends. For all these things to come together is a near impossibility. Remember, to kill the evil Hrinyakashyap, Lord Vishnu had to appear himself and bend the elements. And as you know, the gods don't descend into this country any more!'

Hathoda Tyagi also knew that all blessings need to be secured and kept whole by continual acts of generosity and kindness. In the company of vileness the greatest boons were leached of their potency. He gave what he had little need of—his money—and tried to keep what he needed—the benedictions of the wretched—which were the benedictions of the gods.

As the two of them wandered through the crush, they began to spot the men of the gang threaded in the crowd. No one acknowledged the other; blank eyes gave encouragement to look the other way. Gwalabhai stood at the entrance to the sanctum, welcoming the luminaries of the district, who pushed through a narrow path kept open by volunteers for men of privilege who had a first right to the divine. Government officers, landlords, rich traders, media-men, politicians poured through this narrow pipe, greeting Gwalabhai and being ushered in. This was an obeisance to god and a legend. Both would make a reckoning with them—one in this life, the other in the next.

Bajpaisahib arrived amid a flutter of his supporters and policemen, their elbows and shoulders widening a pathway for him. His appearance was significant. For some time rumours had been rolling that the romance between Donullia Gujjar and the wily brahmin had begun to sour. Many felt the new police action and the cordon at the temple's inauguration was his doing. His appearance here was an alibi, to allay these suspicions. He was a brahmin. He would never take on the brigand in the town square. He would mug him in some warm and intimate alley.

Gwalabhai touched the politician's feet, and on his way out fifteen minutes later, Hathoda Tyagi caught his eye. When the assassin reached for his feet, Bajpaisahib said, 'Should you be here? I am told they want you in five states now.' Without straightening up, the young man said, 'Guruji needs me here tonight. I will always be where he needs me.' The old man said, 'Well, be careful. These are not good times. And this place today has as many policemen as god's men!' Folding his palms, the assassin said, 'I carry my life in my pocket, and am happy to give it away.' The politician filed away the information as he vanished into the heaving crowd.

Just before midnight there was a sudden uproar as a manic band of sadhus and fakirs pistoned through the mob. In flowing beards and flowing ochre, wearing multiple necklaces and wristlets of exotic beads, high on god and high on hashish, they came chanting the glory of Shiva, clacking their castanets and beating their dholaks and banging their cymbals and strumming their ektaras.

Immediately, as the crowds made way for the soldiers of god, the soldiers of the state closed in. In this swirling noisy whirlwind of orange, somewhere, without a doubt, was the man they were looking for. Hathoda Tyagi too dissected the swirl. Could it be that one? The not-too-long beard, partly grey; the prominent hook nose; the firm wrist holding the ektara; swaying with two big men close by him. No, more likely this one. A big turban twirled around the head; strong shoulders; and even in the delirium of devotion, eyes that were open and watching. Yes, this was him.

Hathoda Tyagi mowed through the crowd to stay apace with the dervishes as they powered their way to the shrine, not losing sight of his mentor. All around, he could see and sense the policemen working the sieve, looking for signals from their informers. The assassin's hand hovered near his waistband. This was the day he had lived for. When he would kill to save Donullia Gujjar, display he had an asshole of iron, become part of folklore.

Then his eyes met the eyes of the man and he knew it was not him. Yes, they were open, but they shone with an empty abandon, a foolish immersion in the moment. The noisy frenzied orange blob was now squeezing through the main portal of carved sandstone, beginning to dance up the short flight of wide steps. At the head waited Gwalabhai, hands folded, delighted at the appearance of god's armies. With his big shoulders Hathoda Tyagi pushed his way through, in parallel, up the stairs, and he spotted Guruji at the precise moment three pairs of policemen's hands reached into the heaving bodies to unobtrusively pull him out. The giveaway was right there—the sneakers! The big unruly white beard with streaks of black, the dark skin, the wiry body!

The assassin reached into his waistband for his 908, poised to unleash mayhem, but suddenly found his wrist gripped in iron. He tried to hit out with his elbow, but the hand holding his wrist had trapped the arm too. By his ear, a firm voice, said, 'Stay still, son. The world is an illusion. Nothing is ever what it seems. Those who adore the gods are taken care of by the gods.'

From the corner of his eye, in the shoving-screaming crowd, he saw a bent-over tired-looking man with a salt-and-pepper stubble and a bushy grey moustache, wearing wire-rimmed glasses and a loose maroon turban. On his forehead was a wet red tilak and in his ears round gold earrings. The assassin said, 'Guruji!' The bent-over man said, 'If you call someone guruji, then he becomes a guru. Surely you know this. It's written in our scriptures.'

Before the assassin could think of something to say, the bent-over man said, 'Like the immense Bajrangbali, you are a man of purity and purpose and strength. Take his blessings, son, and become twice the man you are, and be quickly gone. Today is not a day to linger. Our friends are behaving like our enemies, and you have many important things to do.'

Hathoda Tyagi said, 'But Guruji, I am here to protect you.'

The bent-over man said, 'I do not build monuments to the gods only to be then scared of men. There is only one mighty Hanuman and there is only one Donullia Gujjar! The policeman has yet to be conscripted who can pluck a hair from his body. Go now, son! Go!'

By the time he realized the iron grip on his arm was no longer there, the bent-over man had vanished, like a shadow in the dark, and the cavalcade of delirious sadhus and fakirs had swept into the sanctum, and the thousands of peasants and townsmen, the old and the young, the poor and the affluent, men and women, upper caste and lower caste had ascended into a crescendo of chanting, one with the gods, elevated into the divine.

For the next ten days the local papers quoted dozens of devotees who had seen Donullia Gujjar, and even touched him. No two descriptions matched.

The man who had been pulled out and arrested was revealed to be a harmless panda from the sangam at Allahabad. The sneakers were a gift from an American tourist.

The police superintendent received a public rebuke, two inspectors were transferred, and one sub-inspector suspended.

The district buzzed with speculation about the growing estrangement between Bajpaisahib and Donullia Gujjar, based on the shifting alliances in Lucknow.

The temple's reputation soared, and hundreds of devotees began to visit it daily.

Hathoda Tyagi walked on air.

The old man at the farm said, 'He called you son? He touched you? What do you have that the rest of us don't?'

Courage. Loyalty. Asceticism.

Like the great god Hanuman. Servitor of Lord Rama. Embodiment of strength. Eschewer of all pleasures of the flesh.

For the next few years, as Donullia Gujjar's swordarm outside the ravines, Hathoda Tyagi, with unemotional efficiency, battered and slaughtered the foes of his chieftain and of the people, sending brain and bone flying like confetti. Working alone, working with teams, he never asked questions and he seldom failed. Once a name was delivered unto him, the man was, for all practical purposes, dead.

He continued to live on the first floor on the farm—the old man, growing older, merely his vassal now—and lavished all his money and love on his multiplying dogs and had his scalp lapped daily by the buffalo. A few times his sports mentor, Rajbir Gujjar, came to visit him, but there was little left in common between them. The protégé had entered and colonized a space whose boundaries the teacher had dared not touch. With characteristic generosity the young man gave to his tutor more money than he had ever seen. It was after all thanks to him that he had found his asshole of iron, and found meaning in the shade of Guruji.

Thanks to Guruji he also gave up the eating of all flesh, and took to fasting on every Tuesday. Continually Guruji sent him gifts. Little personal things, a Rolex watch, Nike shoes, a Denim deo. Also new weapons, pistols, revolvers, even two grenades. He locked everything up in the steel trunk, and lived solely by his 908 and hammer.

Hathoda Tyagi was content. He had a mission. He had a guru. He had a god. He had his dogs and a buffalo. He had a roof over his head. And he had an asshole of iron.

He needed nothing else.

Then one day Gwalabhai drove up in a cloud of dust in a new blue Gypsy and told him about a man who was working for forces inimical to the nation. For the enemy. Pakistan. This man posed as a journalist and was cunning as a fox. He lived in the country's capital,

Delhi, and was guarded by the police. A team would have to be assembled. Gwalabhai would help do that.

Guruji sent his blessings. And from the ravines, the others—Kana Commando, Hulla Mallah, Katua Kasai—their admiration and love.

This one was for the country. This one was for all Indians. They knew he would not fail.

Hathoda Tyagi—from the sugarcane fields of western UP, brain-curry man and ascetic disciple of Hanuman and Donullia—was overcome with gratitude and a sense of purpose.

13

THE SCALES OF ETERNITY

'Kafka!' Jai said, slurping a mouthful of tea. 'Read Kafka, read Miller, read all the business newspapers. That's it! And pay no attention to god, and pay no attention to love! Power is the engine of the world, and sex and money its oil and lubricants. God is at best the invocation before you start the engine—meaningless if you have no engine to start! God is a goli, a multi-flavoured pill, invented by those who have power, money and sex, to give to those who have none! Love is another great goli. Some days we too swallow these golis. They feel good, like a joint, a temporary high! But they are not the reality. The reality is power, money, sex! And yes, there's another goli—morality!'

And, I thought, the revolution. Sara, Kafka, Miller and Che Guevara. Power, sex, and the revolution! All in one unequal body, nailed singing to the wall.

We were sitting in his swank new office. Glass walls shaded with wooden venetian blinds; recessed white lights in the ceiling; a big desk heavy with stationery and books and magazines and papers and a gargantuan tea mug and a computer; a black-and-white picture of his wife behind him, her eyes and mouth in happy laughter; and a round table with four chairs tucked into it where important decisions about shaping the world could be taken with speed and intimacy.

Nearly three years had passed since we finally shed ourselves of the magazine. His beard was greyer, his hair thinner. Little else had changed. He was still at the pulpit, his passion and eloquence undimmed. But the discourse was no longer state-of-the-nation, no more about democracy, liberty, equality, public interest, Gandhi, Nehru, and the idea of India. Now was the time of the philosopher of realism. In a flawed world, flawed humans pursued flawed dreams—the real triumph lay in being a master negotiator of this journey, whose engine and lubricants were power, money and sex.

'Kapoorsahib! Remember him? We used to knock him, but he knew how to read the world! Kapoorsahib ran the world, Kapoorsahib is the world! You must understand, Kafka is not power, Kafka only understood power! Power is the Castle! Kapoorsahib is the Castle! You and I can only write about the phallus, but Kapoorsahib *is* the phallus!'

With a typical sleight-of-words Jai had made a virtuous thesis of his humiliation, our humiliation. In reality, Kapoorsahib had stripped and buggered all of us, Chutiya-Nandan-Pandey included, for many months before sending us on our way.

Kapoorsahib had taken on the financial cross of the company but had made each of us sign hillocks of documents higher than our knees, ensuring we initialled each page (we had to take breaks to rest our wrists). These documents made it clear that every legal liability for anything the magazine had ever done was ours. The three original investors had their high-powered lawyers read their agreements and argue about them, unsuccessfully, but Jai and I just signed wherever we were told. There were no lawyers we could possibly hire, and to attempt to read those documents was to enter a labyrinth of language and possibility that could fry your brains.

There was no point in contesting anything, either. If we had once signed away our life, liberty and lund to Kuchha King, Kuchha Singh and Frock Raja, then we were doing it a hundredfold now. Kapoorsahib's lawyers had pioneered endless unintelligible ways of laying claim to them.

At the final signing at the lawyers' offices in Connaught Place, in a sombre meeting room with video-conferencing screens and dark teakwood furniture, the three original investors had not even cast a look in our direction. We had sat at the opposite end of a table huge enough to negotiate the buying of America, and signed our respective hillocks, one junior attorney by each one's side to ensure we didn't skip a single page. Just before the ceremonial disembowelment, Jai had attempted one last stand at Kapoorsahib's feet. Should the two of us not be given some kind of severance fee, given all we had done to create the magazine? 'You should be caned! For creating this fucking shambles. Across your dirty buttocks!' Kapoorsahib used the Hindi word—chootad. 'For taking on this garbage I should get the two of you for free! Put a leash on you and tie you to my door!'

Within the month, Jai had lined up a job for himself as a consultant with a television news production company. The money was real, and way more than anything our wretched enterprise had ever produced. It was also the key that once again unshackled his eloquence. Since then, in the last two years, he had floated on his soaring rhetoric to two job changes—the cabins getting swisher, the cheques heavier, the philosophy of realism more robust. Now he was astride a zebra, a round-the-clock news channel. Depending on the call of the hour it could be posited as a black animal temporarily painted white, or as a white animal temporarily painted black. Realism never dressed better, and Jai was the master of such dressage.

India had more such zebras now than in five millennia. And more masters of such dressage than ever before.

Of these, Kapoorsahib was an exemplar. Kapoorsahib was the phallus.

Once we were out the door, he'd brought in an old washed-up beast from the watering hole of the India International Centre. The city was awash with such animals: vaguely familiar names whose eminence was a mystery. Men who had once thundered morals on the editorial pages of the dailies, and now dissected Delhi over whisky and soda in subsidized bars. They were all also zebra riders, and could be used by anyone wanting to dress up realism better. So the magazine had chugged on, now full of political and strategic bombast, and hardly any reportage. Jai said, 'You can see what it is? It's an iron poker kept in the fire. When it's needed—if it's needed—it will be taken out for a quick jab! It's another Afghan carpet venture complete with the herbal tea and the lovely woman!'

After signing off my hillock of papers I had tried to quit the business. An old-time book publisher from Daryaganj, full of the excitement of new glossy jackets and perfect spines—foreign imprints and dollar signs—had offered me a two-book deal. One on the story of our food scam sting operation; the other on the politics of modern India. The advance was enough to sustain me if I ate grass from Lodhi Gardens and drank water from the Yamuna. But I gave it a shot. I threw Dolly/folly out for a month, banishing her to her mother's, and locked myself into my tiny study and hammered the keyboard till it developed a list and I had to put a chewing-gum plug under its left leg.

In six weeks I had sixty thousand words hammered out, a title in place, and a dedication in mind. I stuck to the details of the scam and left out our own sorry story of the aftermath. Jai thought it was a stupid decision. 'Human drama! That's what people want! The scam is finally a bore! What's interesting is what happens to the people because of it!' The publisher, a thin, refined man, with a pencil moustache from forty years ago, was delighted by my efficiency. He shook my hand hard and long.

I called him a week later. He was terse. He needed some more time to finish reading it. I gave it ten days and called again. He said books were not newspapers, and publishers had hundreds of books to deal with. He would call. Another ten days went by. In that time

I played around with the text some more, chopping and adding. Fair, tall Dolly/folly looked at me in soft-eyed adoration, as if I'd just written the Mahabharata. And she hummed songs of courage and determination. Felicia passed through the day like a dark ghost, bearing tea and toast.

This time he didn't take my call. His phone kept playing the Gayatri Mantra till I began to believe I had given my book to a temple priest not a publisher. I called one of the editors he had introduced me to. A middle-aged Bengali whose virtue seemed to be sensibility, not language. He wore thick glasses and had a twitch in his right eye. Laughing nervously he said, 'The lawyers have raised some issue. But I cannot tell—only boss will know for sure.' I drove into the hellish lanes of Daryaganj and had three angry arguments before I could find parking space.

Mr Sahgal showed no sign of panic when I stormed into his room, brushing aside his assistant—a traumatized aunty in a blue saree who kept bleating, please sir, please sir. He was wearing a sharp black suit and his sharp black moustache, and he calmly hung me out to dry with a shower of legal objections raised by the attorneys. The manuscript lying in front of him had so many yellow and pink Post-its sticking out if it, I knew I would have to rewrite every page. My only counter-argument was that lawyers are alarmists. He said, so refined, 'Lawyers send people to jail, and keep people out of jail.'

And make sure no one ever does anything worthwhile.

I tried to be like Jai, talking the grand stuff: public good, clean governance, et al.

He only said, smooth and plain as vanilla ice cream, 'I am just a publisher sir, not Mother Teresa.'

He gave me the manuscript with its pink and yellow ears as a take-home gift. On my way out I stood on the back fender of his old white Mercedes till it crashed to the ground. Then I used a sharp stone to run a loving line through its steel flesh and draw an uncircumcised cock at its end. As my assassin Kabir would have said, 'Bhosdi ke hatt, tera lauda hai ya lutth!' When I returned home I put the festooned manuscript on the shelf in the study beneath *The Naked Lunch*, and addressing the ceiling fan, announced my retirement as a writer.

The very next day I drove off to see Guruji.

He calmed my nerves and told me what to do. On my way back I began to call old acquaintances for a job. I didn't call Jai. I needed work and money, not one more oration on the big picture.

Truth is, there was no big picture. There was just Kapoorsahib and his labyrinth and Bhalla and his line girls and Chutiya-Nandan-Pandey and their flowing mermaids and Huthyam and his shadows and the assassins and Sara's stories and Kafka's castle and Dubeyji and ms fair and folly and Felicia, and lurking in every corner with arsenals of paper lawyers and lawyers and lawyers. There was no big picture. If there was one, it had died fifty years ago, or five hundred years ago, or five thousand years ago. Maybe Gandhi was the last man to have it; or maybe it was the guy who rattled off the Gita, sitting under a ficus, a deerskin draped over his loins.

There was no big picture. There were no grand connections. There were only endless small pieces, and all you could do was to somehow manage your own. And everyone was struggling to do just that, uncaring of the other. And all of it—the careening, colliding small pieces—were plummeting the world down the chute. My pieces too were in a fine shambles: wife, Sara, shadows, killers. Only Guruji was fine. But he was not a piece. He was Guruji, the answer to all this crap.

The one piece I knew I could put right was job and money. In two weeks I had it. An investigative reporter's job in a daily that was modernizing with such speed and determination that its graphics and font sizes were growing by the day and white bimbettes from Los Angeles famed for having their private sex videos leaked were jumping on to its front pages, screaming their skins. I asked the man heading the bureau—fat and affable, hands in his pockets tossing his testicles like salad—to let me know the red lines. He smiled expansively and said there were none; then proceeded to reel off so many names that I lost track. Among them were the prime minister, the leader of the opposition, several political dynasties, and enough business houses to host a grand summit. 'You can go ahead and hammer everyone else,' he said, with a smile.

Yes, slaughter the rabbits. They were way too many, born to be butchered.

There was no big picture.

But the salary was good. And Sara was still doing it for me. And two of the three libel cases slammed against us had already fallen by the wayside. Both politicians. It was a waste of time all around. Just one bureaucrat persisted. For the moment.

In contrast, the three idiots who had jiggled the asshole of the defence ministry with their fake cameras were still being put through the juicer. They popped up in the papers and on television screens now and then, raging, ranting, protesting their innocence. One of them—Jai's doppelganger—was a particularly bad case. The big picture type. He was most visible, most vocal.

Some fucks never learn.

Sub-inspector Hathi Ram felt the same.

'Once a scoundrel, always a scoundrel,' he'd said, banging the sides of a cream biscuit together and looking at me with steady expressionless eyes. It was January and the small study seemed tighter than ever with both of us swathed in extra layers. The policeman wore a cheap tweed coat and a brown muffler around his neck. His face looked leathery in the lamplight with the grey stubble pushing through. As always I would have to be patient to divine the true purpose of his visit. No Indian could ever talk straight or deal straight; presumably, it would bring disgrace to our complex heritage. 'There are exceptions,' he continued. 'Valmiki changed from brigand to poet and saint. But it's just as well that such things happen rarely. I am not sure we want too many saints. In this country, I often feel, better to have more scoundrels than saints.'

I was sitting with my feet tucked under me on the chair, a green monkey-cap on my head. Guruji always said the skull must be kept warm and the aura of brainwaves preserved close around the head. That's why the great rishis wore long hair, and eminent men tied turbans. I said, 'So what have my lot turned out to be—scoundrels or saints?'

Huthyam said, 'You know, I don't know anything about these things. This is the work of other, more important men. My duty is only to protect you. But I have heard things, not good things. I would have to be a saint to say that these men are not scoundrels. And you know policemen can never be saints. Scoundrels can be saints, crooks can be saints, murderers can be saints, but policemen can never be anything but policemen.'

I waited. He too was a master of his game. Like Kapoorsahib, like Guruji, like Sara, like Jai. In some ways he was more honourable. He had worked the gutter, not created it. He banged the cymbals one more time and then in slow sequence planted them deep in his mouth. All three buttons of his cheap tweed coat were stretched. He had put on weight in the three years I had known him.

'I am sure I am wrong, but my information is that it didn't matter at all whether they killed you or not. They were sent to get themselves caught, or shot. Of course they didn't know it. They thought they were on a mission.'

Fuck. Everyone spoke through frosted glass.

I said, 'But who sent them?'

He opened up a biscuit carefully and ran it lightly under his nose. 'I don't know. Someone powerful wanted to get rid of them or at least get rid of some of them. The contract on you was just an excuse.'

'So they were set up. They were trapped. They are, also, in a sense, victims.' Sara would have pinned a medal to my chest.

He banged the biscuit halves together and his face hardened. 'They are all scoundrels,' he hissed. 'Make no mistake about it. They are thieves, crooks, murderers. They are no more victims than any of us—trapped in the lives we've been given. One of them cuts men with a knife like ripe guavas. Two of them are dangerous drug dealers—one a Chinese—who have been killing since they were ten years old. From Kabul to Calcutta they control the narcotics route. The fourth one is a mastermind—a quiet Musalman from Bareilly who raped the daughter of the police chief and has a direct hotline to the Bombay underworld. He moves in and out of Uttar Pradesh's jails like a friendly pigeon and in every jail he is treated with fear and respect. And the last one, the last one is an asura. I would run away from the street on which his shadow fell. He is so strong he can turn an Ambassador car on its head. And they say, where other people have a heart, he has stone. Nothing can move him. And he wants nothing—not money, not women, not accolades. He just likes to kill. He smashes your head in so that even your mother doesn't recognize you. And he never fails. Once he takes a contract on you, you may as well just kill yourself. It's why everyone is whispering that this story does not add up.' He paused, sitting up stiffly in the chair, and looked directly at me, his mouth smiling, his eyes still. 'You are alive because you were not really meant to be killed.'

Through the closed door, melodramatic television sounds seeped in.

I said, 'But then, why were they sent?'

He said, 'That is the big question! Why were they sent, if not to kill you? I think they were sent to get caught. I think someone very powerful wanted to get rid of them. Maybe all of them; maybe some of them; maybe one of them. It's like a suspense thriller. All very complex. Till the last scene we won't know who the real killer is. It could even be the policeman. The very man who is giving you the information.' And he raised his eyebrows and held the pose.

I said, 'Do they always work together? Are they one gang?'

He let go of the pose and snorted. 'That only happens in the movies, my friend! Where gang members sing songs together, and buy sarees for each other's wives! These people know less about each other than I know, say, about your black rose.' He gestured with his chin towards the closed door. He meant Felicia. Her skin fascinated him. 'What is not clear is whether they were meant to get caught after killing you, or before. Whether someone wanted to just have them punished for a bit, or put away for good.'

Sara, the seer of our times.

I said, 'But why do it in this elaborate way, through a plot to kill me?'

The policeman had put the biscuit back together and was rotating it in his fingers like a coin. 'This is India, my friend. Why do anything simply if you can do it in a complicated way? Have you ever been to get a driving licence or a ration card? Have you ever filed a complaint at a police station? Have you ever got a child admitted to school? It's the brahminical brain, so wily, so twisted, it draws a straight line by making circles.'

I said, 'Sure. Then why the security cover? Why for so long? If I never was the target?'

He said, 'Because I may be wrong. This is only what I think. The men who decide these things, I don't know what they think. It's not my job to know what they think. My job is to do. If everyone thinks, there will be a mountain of thinking, and no policing. My job is only to protect you, and that's what I do. These doubts that I share with you, I share with you not as a policeman but as a friend. After all these years I am a friend, am I not? After some time even jailors and prisoners become friends—they realize one has no meaning without the other. And you and I are on the same side, are we not?'

He said all this with a soft mouth but hard eyes. I thought, what a peerless cop this man must have been. I knew he was six months away from retiring. He'd told me several times that his nights now were full of dreams of his village and his family farm. The mango trees, the sugarcane stalks, the ripening gold of wheat, the green tufts of cabbage, the odour of cattle dung, the woodsmoke in the dal, the milk warm from the udder, the haunting call of the koel, the rain falling on mud, and the skies full of stars. In typical Huthyam fashion he'd said, 'I want to decay and disintegrate where I was born and fashioned. I want my soul to wander in the fields of my childhood, not on the streets of Delhi, where it'll get run over every day by a new Maruti.'

I said, 'So which one of them do you think was the one that was being fixed?'

He said, 'Who can tell? They are all bloody maaderchods! They all deserve to be fixed. This country needs to hang a few thousand of them and the rest will fall into place. You know who I think it is—I think it's that quiet Musalman from Bareilly. They say he's very calm, never complains, says nothing, asks for nothing, except pieces of wood which he chisels all the time. No one has ever come to seek bail for him or to represent him in court. Such men carry worlds inside them. Such men can go anywhere, do anything. In this age of terrorism and Pakistan and the underworld and sinister politics, a man like him could have crossed many dangerous lines. They say he is resolute that he doesn't want bail. What kind of man says that? What kind of man fears freedom? Only one who fears the freedom of other men to kill him.'

I said, 'If you know all this, why doesn't the investigating agency?'

He pulled the biscuit apart—its soft pink belly holding fast—and said, 'They know what they are supposed to know. What they have been told to know. In the government it is never good to know more than you should. The government is a gigantic puzzle, and we are all tiny pieces of it. Our place is preordained, marked, defined. The best piece is the one that quietly fits into its place, that helps complete the puzzle. But you should not worry. They will definitely find what they are supposed to find. You must remember the government never fails and the government is never wrong. When stupid people think so, they don't realize that this is exactly what the government wanted! To fail; to be wrong. The government is always right.'

I looked at the spine of *The Naked Lunch* on the bookshelf. Huthyam had ignored it today. Burroughs would have loved him.

I said, 'So will they be let off soon?'

'Not if the government doesn't want them to be.'

'Will my security detail be finally removed?' A nondescript shadow lay sprawled outside, shapeless and unbuttoned, the 9mm iron cold in his crotch.

'Not if the government doesn't want it to be.'

I said, 'Can I get you another cup of tea?'

He said, 'One cup is friendship. Two is intimacy. And that is always reductive. As friends we talk about big things, philosophical things, national affairs. But in intimacy we will talk about wives and bosses and the price of milk and vegetables, and we will become small men obsessed with small things. So no more tea, my friend, no more.'

And with that he stuck the biscuit back together and gently placed it in his mouth.

Sara was, of course, from a different school. She believed in lightning intimacies. With her it did not lead to a sinking into mundanity but rang the bell to a higher order. For more than a year after we had handed over to Kapoorsahib and moved on, she remained resolute.

She dumped the sparrow and brought in two young lawyers, who shaved close, gelled their hair, and spoke in sharp accents. The few times I met them their colognes smelled so sweet I wanted to kiss them. They were hopelessly in love with her, and showed up at the Vasant Kunj flat whenever summoned.

One of them was the son of a very rich and famous lawyer, who, when he first met Sara, had the aura of someone who owned the world. He had worked for some years in New York but had obviously never encountered a force of nature like her. Since then he had undergone a full immersion into the socialist-revolutionary cauldron. Every privilege of his short life had been used to crucify him. Now he'd developed the sorry air of someone who had been caught mugging the world. Each time I met him in her flat he wore a look of grim, unblinking intensity as he stared at the diva, her thick legs folded under her long skirt, the light glancing off her photo shoulders and sharp clavicles. The world needed urgent saving. It was the Sara effect. It would wear off. But for some time he would be ready to slit his wrists if she only asked.

Sara knew the truth. Sara had found out the truth. Sara had worked to find out the truth. It had taken time and meetings and excavation.

At Gate No. 3, Central Jail Tihar, the guards all recognized her. She was issued her visitor's pass without a fuss. Even the other lawyers of the killers recognized this woman had an inalienable right to speak to their clients. Never before had she looked more fearsome. She had taken to wearing a big Naga shawl, in rich black, white and red stripes with several crossed spears woven into it. 'I am at war,' she told me.

When she strode out to do business, the warrior queen with two gelled boys in creased trousers, fragrant enough to be kissed, the commingling of all improbable things in the world was complete.

When I told her that Hathi Ram believed that Kabir M was the mastermind behind the conspiracy to kill me, she threw open her Naga shawl and snorted like she was going to charge. I almost ducked for cover as she jumped off the sofa and rushed into her bedroom. She came back with cupped hands and emptied them onto the green marble slab of her centre table. Six little wooden choozas. The sizes varied marginally. She righted each one and stood them in a line.

I said, 'Six little chicks went out to play, over the hills and far away...'

She looked up, burning me with contempt. 'Fucking bigot.'

I said, 'He's in love with you?'

She said, 'That Hathi Ram, who you think is a terrific guy, is finally just another idiot policeman. This is what the great mastermind does—chisel small chicks out of mango wood! How dangerous do you think that is, mr peashooter? The underworld! The poor man barely knew his grandmother! In fact, he doesn't even know his surname! He writes M. Yes, M—for motherfucked! By this country, day in and day out, from the day he was born! It's true the man prefers to stay in jail. Hathi Ram is right. He doesn't even want to apply for bail. But it's not because he's scared of someone outside. It's simply because he has no one out here. He finds prison a safer and nicer and warmer place. Can you understand that? That there are people out there who can't deal with your fucking horrible world! They need to hide in whatever dirty hole they can find.'

I said, 'I was only telling you what Hathi Ram said. I am sure he's innocent.'

'Not innocent,' she hissed. 'Wronged. Abused. Damaged. Victimized.' She was standing up now, pacing between the living space and the small dining-table, Naga shawl flapping along with her arms, like a predatory bird. 'When this man was a boy he was beaten to pulp by policemen for something his friends had done. Where you have a cock he has a small mash of chewed gum. They pulped it for him. The most it has ever done since then is pass water. This was a boy who went to a missionary school full of padres singing hark the herald angels sing! Try and imagine what the police did to him. In jail he learned wood carving, and that's what he does now. Tell me, how dangerous do you think these chicks are?'

I picked up one. It was quite sweet, actually. Light as a feather, the contours smooth, the beak sharp. I should have taken one and stuck it between Kapoorsahib's ass cheeks. Sweet bird of penitence: a token of love from the subaltern.

After a purple patch, when I'd been choreographing Sara like a maestro, I'd lost the touch again. These days I was not quite sure how to play her. I had no idea what would bring on real contempt, and what would ratchet up desire. Recently, several bold sorties had ended in crash-landings. I said, 'The police are out of control.'

She exploded, the red-black shawl billowing menacingly, 'Not just the police! Everyone! Everything! This whole country is out of control! You know what this great mastermind does? He simulates small car robberies, quickly gets himself arrested and heads back into jail. He is too gentle to even do something cataclysmic that will put him away forever. Stupidly, his father named him Kabir to honour the great fusion of Hindu-Muslim culture. The fool should have known it was the best way to ensure both sides would fuck him. Make the katua into the peessua! Well, the poor boy didn't take a contract to kill you. He merely agreed to drive a car to Delhi, with almost no knowledge of who was in the car or why the car was going to Delhi. And the one they call Chaaku? He was brutalized as a boy by high-caste zamindars and barely escaped with his life. And Hathoda Tyagi—do you know why they call him Hathoda Tyagi? Because he had to defend himself with a bloody hammer when his clansmen raped his sisters over a land dispute. As for those other two, Kaaliya and Chini, it's tragic. They don't even have the semblance of family. They grew up on the railway tracks and survived by scrounging offal. These are your deadly assassins!'

I said, my tone flat, trying to read where this was headed, 'The police distort everything.'

She flapped her red-and-black wings in such agitation I thought she would take off and land on me. 'Not the police! Not just the police! Tell me who creates the real distortion? Tell me what is it that you are supposed to do? Tell me who tells the police to do what it does? Tell me, mr peashooter, who is supposed to blow the whistle on those who tell the police to do what it does? And the men who tell the police what to do, who tells them what to do? Go on, tell me!'

I said, 'You are right.' I had no idea where she'd flown off to. She was in a long colourful skirt, some kind of Rajasthani mirror-work stuff. The shirt above was lime green, sleeveless and dainty on her frail torso. When she flapped her red-black wings, her tight caramel belly showed. I could have watched it all day.

She said, 'So go on, tell me. Who controls the men who tell the police what to do?'

Unsmiling, clueless, steepling my fingers under my chin, I said, 'What's the point?'

'The point, mr peashooter, is Kapoorsahib, and what he wants. What he wants is what finally the police will want, and the men who run the police will want. What he did to you and the three stooges is what he does to everyone. He is the beast of big money, and he can get anyone to suck his cock.'

For a moment I thought we were going to hit the groove. But Sara was in a different space—as she seemed to be more and more these days. Some of her ranting, it seemed, was beginning to run into her skin.

I said, 'I think it's far more complicated. It's a complex dance between political power, police and money. And yes, us guys too.' I sounded so good to myself. I could just bury my face in that caramel navel and never care to hear another word again.

She flapped her wings and snorted. 'It's not complex! And it's not a dance! Power pretends it's a dance, the police pretend it's a dance, and you guys pretend it's a dance! The beast of big money knows it's not. The beast of big money knows it's the beast running the rest as a chain-gang, getting them to do what he wants. He allows you all the illusion of the dance till it suits him. And when he wishes to, he slices your balls off. Remember Kapoorsahib, and all of you searching for your testicles!'

Messrs Kuchha King, Kuchha Singh and Frock Raja. The beasts of small money. And with them the two ignoble upholders of the public faith. All in search of their cojones, amid tinkling Clayderman in mast trees and naked weeping mermaids.

I said, 'That was different. An oddball situation.' And recklessly considered just picking her up and nailing her to the wall; ending this nonsense, this continual needling of the order of things. The world was what it was. Uneven, unequal, unjust, unfair. Didn't help to keep ranting about it. I did not move from the sofa because I could see an unwashed non-stick pan with the remnants of congealed egg in it lying on the dining-table and I knew in her current mood she'd hit me over the head with it.

'Not different, mr peashooter, and not oddball! That's precisely the situation in this country everywhere! The beast of big money has sliced everyone's testicles from Kanyakumari to Kashmir. Kabir is in jail because some Kapoorsahib wants him there. Or wants some of the others in there. He, poor sucker, was just the driver. Masterminding how to avoid ramming into the truck ahead!'

I said, 'But why?'

'But why what, you idiot?'

'But why this elaborate charade to get some guys in jail?'

'Because people are crooked and labyrinthine and elaborate! Tortuous routes are taken even for simple outcomes! What all do you do just to get laid? Because even if you are the beast of big money you can't just open the jail door and fling people in! Remember how Kapoorsahib walked you in circles for months? Because there may be factors at play here that we have no damn idea about! Simply, my dear, how the hell do I know? Do I look like the bloody Interpol to you?'

Not at all, my delicate one. Like a sweet bird of paradise flying on white lines of coke.

I said, 'So in a way, both Hathi Ram and you think the same thing. That there was no real contract to kill me. These guys have been basically fixed—for some reason that none of us know.'

The sweet bird of paradise emitted a heart-stopping screech. 'No! Hathi Ram and I do *not* think the same thing! He thinks they are hardcore criminals and it's just as well they are being punished! And you know very well what I think!'

No, I thought, you crazy banshee, I don't! I don't care any more what anyone thinks! I don't know who ordered up the killers. Some politician, or Pakistan, or the police, or some rich man, or they thought it up themselves in a moment of happy impulse! And I don't know why! I am just happy someone got to them before they got to me, and they have been firmly locked up behind bars for the last three years and no one wants to let them out! You may be right and they may be god's own angels with perfume for piss, but I don't want to test the thesis and have them wandering in the open again, trying to blow another hole in my buttocks!

I said, 'I hope you can manage to get them off.'

Her band of smooth caramel inspired dishonesty.

As if on cue the doorbell rang, and she flapped her way to the door. The two young crusaders walked in, faces grim, cheeks shaved to ceramic smoothness, files in their hands. They half hugged the sweet bird of paradise in warm solidarity, took off their black coats, loosened the knots at their throats, and sat down on the edge of the cane chairs, ready to best the state and its allies. I was accorded only a cursory nod. I was the moron who had created this human tragedy by almost getting murdered.

I got up to leave.

Sara said to them, 'Let's sit at the dining-table.'

I said to them, 'What's common between naked mermaids and innocent killers?'

They looked at me nonplussed. Sara turned to me with the eyes of an animal protecting her brood.

I said, 'I was just thinking of Uncle Kapoor.'

All the way home I thought I had to accept the fact that I had hit the law of diminishing returns with Sara. There was only so much of this chest-beating I could take. The last few months had been tedious, ending not in a rosy crucifixion on the wall, but in my fatigued flight. I had to figure a way of closing this chapter in my life. It had become a bad story. I no longer knew why I came to see her. And yet I could not keep away. Once, when I had managed to resolutely stay away for a week, she had messaged me two saucy words and I had rushed instantly to her flat. She had opened the door naked. It had transformed doorbell-ringing into a scrotum-tightening affair for me forever.

Over time I had become unsure whether I was playing her or she, me. When I saw her with her two clean-cut boys I felt I too was just being toyed with. But she did want to fix the world. There could be no doubt about that. To go to jails and lawyers and courts, week after week, month after month, year after year—you had to be imbued with lunacy, or a sense of purpose! In her case it was most likely both. I had slowly become convinced that I was just a prop in her scheme of the universe. The cardboard tree around which she played out her moves. The man who provided the assassins, who provided the meaning. Some days I felt even the passion was manufactured. Part of the theatre, the real purpose of which lay off-stage. What it was, apart from lunacy and idealism, I had no idea.

Now I felt this relationship would only be severed when the assassins had been accounted for—exonerated, sentenced, done away with.

Till then my best hope was I would ring the bell and she would open the door naked.

Guruji was naked but for his dhoti, though it was still only the end of February and slicingly cold. It was evening, minutes before the red of the sky fell to dark grey. From the terrace of the dera the fields all around were a sea of luminous green. In two weeks the wheat stalks would begin to ripen to burnt gold. Amid the waves of green could be seen splashes of sun, the delicate flowers of mustard. The lowing of cattle broke the air, and flurries of birds swept past calling out directions.

Guruji was on his charpoy, his long hair caressing his bony shoulders, his wiry legs tucked under him. All around me on the durrie on the floor sat village men, and a couple of women, cocooned in coarse shawls and blankets, spelling out their sorrows, taking home his benedictions.

I sat in a corner watching as one by one they edged right under him to whisper their woes. He listened with a cocked head, then spoke his wisdom aloud so everyone could collect it. Once the prescription was announced he put his palm forward to reclaim the coin he had handed out the last time they had visited. This he put in a slim tin cylinder lying by his side, and giving it a sustained shake, so that the rattle floated out across the fields, he opened the lid and pulled out a fresh coin, touched it to his forehead and placed it in the disciple's hand. Guruji's telecom service. The tin box was green, a Glenfiddich casing. Over the years all manner of containers had put in an appearance, including Dundee cake boxes. A spiritual master, transforming water to wine and paper to bread.

By the time the last devotee left, the fields were dark and the conversation of the baying dogs had begun. Behind the charpoy, Bhura knelt on the floor, pressing Guruji's stringy legs. A big brass tumbler of hot milk had been brought up for Guruji. This would be his dinner. I was handed a smaller one, of scalding steel. It had the heavy smell of a fresh milking.

Guruji said, taking a sip, 'You are still unhappy? Why?'

I said, 'What is there to be happy about?'

'Look around you. The wheat is ripening, the stars are shining, the cows are giving milk, the breeze is cool. Look at yourself. You are alive, your limbs are moving, your eyes can see, your ears can hear, there is a roof over you, a car under you, a wife in the kitchen, and money in the pocket. Is that not enough?'

I said, 'You know, Guruji, men do not live by all this alone. Men need much more.'

'Not need, my son, want. And there is nothing wrong in the fact that men should want. But men must not forget that there is always a price to be paid for want. When you go into a shop and buy three soaps instead of one, you pay for three, don't you? All the transactions of your life are similar. The more you want, the more you pay. Men go home from the market and complain they paid too much. But what they did in the first place was to want too much. That friend of yours—the one who gives you grief—you want her a great deal, don't you?'

I said, 'I am not really sure any more.'

Guruji said, 'Don't be held back by ghosts. Just as it is okay for men to want, it is okay for men to move on. Like desire, movement too is the essence of the world. Everything must continually be in a state of movement. Sun, moon, stars; air, water, earth; men, animals, germs. Everything must be in flux. And as you pay a price for want, you pay a price for movement too. The all-knowing one is also the shrewdest accountant in the universe—he maintains the perfect balance sheet of all our gains and losses. Nor should you be afraid of losses. At the end—at the very end—it will all be squared up. Till it is not, the journey will go on. Finally everyone will end up in the same place, everyone's balance sheet perfectly balanced. The only difference will be how each of us got there. We will be distinguished and separated not by the final destination, but the quality of the journey. The choices we made; the paths we took. That is the miracle of free will. That is the miracle of men. The opportunity is not moksha, the opportunity is life. Moksha is the same for everyone and we will all eventually get it. But life is discrete, several and separate; it is our indulgence and our gift. So, my son, do not be afraid to want, and do not be afraid to move on.'

Yes, I thought, looking around at the moonlight flowing through the wheat fields, this was the reason I kept coming back. A few sweet cosmic pills that made sense of all the crap around. A good glug of Vedanta. If only I could persuade ms terminator to try it once. She might discover there was a reckoning beyond the Constitution of India and the Criminal Procedure Code.

I said, 'Guruji, those men who were picked up and jailed—I still don't know the truth about them. Even now, three years after, the accounts vary wildly.'

Guruji was lying on his side. Now he sat up, his legs crossed under him, and Bhura began to knead his neck and back. The lines of his ribs looked beautiful, and with his open hair he could have been sitting on top of Mount Kailash. 'The men worry you only because they worry her, right? You would readily forget them if only she would stop obsessing about them, would you not? But let me tell you, son, she will not stop. That is her karma. Men make the great mistake of thinking that every woman's karma revolves around her man. The truth is, a woman's karma is far more varied and complex than a man's. Children, parents, servants, in-laws, the ceaseless war against the small injustices of the world, of small animals and small people, the quiet breaking down of walls, the quiet location of compassion. Being the sail that catches the wind of good fortune; being the cushion that breaks the fall of hard fate; being the poultice on injury, the pill against disease. In contrast, the karma of men is nothing but the pursuit of money and power, whose accumulations know no limit. It's the reason most men soon think their lives a failure, while women never cease to strive.'

I said, yes Guruji, and waited.

He put his hands on the wooden frame of the charpoy and slowly lifted himself up, sitting exactly as he was, legs still crossed under him. The veins of his stringy arms bulged. He let himself down slowly, and then went up again. Bhura's hand remained on his back as he performed the exercise half a dozen times. I could see the energy pulsing in him. The peasants and the locals were given wisdom in small quick pills; the full treatment was only for the men from the big city whose resistance to illumination had become dangerously high. He enjoyed us. We were a challenge.

'So understand, son, that she will not stop.' He was slightly breathless with the yogic demo. 'You must either travel to the end of the road she seeks, or you must move on. And remember, it is not you that she seeks but her own answers. The guru's job is to show you the many paths, not to tell you which one to embark on. That the seeker has to do; and to answer for. And one waiting path is: tighten your pajama strings and move on.'

How felicitously he put it. Zip up and run.

I said, 'And if I travel to the end of the road she seeks, what will I find?'

He said, his eyes closed now, 'You will find exactly what you did at the beginning of the road. Five men who were paid to kill you. And one woman who wants, for her own reasons, to make them seem what they are not.'

I said, 'So there can be no doubt all—they are all killers?'

Guruji opened his eyes and said, 'You speak as if the world has never seen killers before. What were the great kings? What are the great leaders of today? Covetous men have killed, as have saints. These men too are killers but they are not to be despised. Their reasons are neither wealth, nor sainthood, nor fame, nor fortune.

I said, 'You must then tell me what they are.'

Guruji smiled. 'Maybe you should take this journey to its end in order to find out. The goals of men may often be similar but the motives may not. My concern was only your safety. Well, you are safe and you will remain safe. Their moment has slipped them by. Their gunpowder will never be dry again.'

'So my guards? There is no need for them any more?'

'That is for the government to decide, not for a religious man. But yes, if anyone needs to feel fear, it is they, not you. They are only puppets on a string and their puppeteer may be losing interest.'

I was losing the thread. I tried one last time. 'But what of her? What should I do?'

He put his hand on the brick floor of the terrace and in one fluid movement went upside down, his ankles together, his toes pointing straight towards the stars. His hair fell on his splayed fingers and the white dhoti bunched small around his groin. It was a perfect asana, barely a tremble passing through his body. In that position, upside down, his face was nearly flush with mine. If Sara had seen us now she would have let loose a howl that would have made a hole in the skies. 'I always tell you, one must endeavour to be the mouth and not the mango. The mango is sweet, but it is the mouth that tastes the pleasure. No matter how perfect the mango, it is up to the mouth to eat it, slow or fast or not at all. I hope, my son, you have not made her the mouth. To me, upside down as I am, it seems a good idea to tighten the pajama strings and move on. Maybe it's also time for you to stand on your head and see how things look the other way around.'

Stand on your head.

And zip up and run.

At twilight, Kafka's castle lay inscrutable and brooding, exactly the way it had been on our last visit. The man on the stool by the front entrance was still playing with his mobile phone. Like the last time the lift crash-landed noisily and took off with a heart-stopping judder. Unlike the last time there was no Jai with me, but like the last time, I lost myself in the labyrinth of corridors and plywood doors and partitions, and was forced to phone Dubeyji who had to come looking for me. Like the last time the sub-inspector's moustache bristled like a squirrel's tail under his rodent nose and he wore a cream bush shirt, many frayed maulis on his wrist, a tin locket around his neck, and a happy expression. Like the last time we sat in his cupboard-sized office with the narrow window like a gun embrasure—through which one could not commit suicide—and allowed our knees to touch under the table.

The chargesheet was finally ready and about to be filed, and Dubeyji had said if I wished I could come and read it, and if I didn't that was perfectly fine too. When I called Hathi Ram to seek his opinion he had said, 'You must go and you must take it very seriously. Those men are real cops doing real investigations, not hundred-rupee rippers at traffic lights like the rest of us!' When I told Sara she snorted, 'Hah! Chargesheet! Should be fun to read the latest fiction from the government's creative writing workshop!' Guruji said, standing on his head or feet I could not tell, 'Of course you must go. Truth takes many forms. You must know the different truths so that you may know the one truth.'

Dubeyji patted his dented brown Rexine briefcase lying by his chair and said, 'Would you like to read it or would you like me to tell you what it says?' His moustache was moving and his eyes shone with information.

I said, 'Tell me.'

He said, 'It's true—you did not know anything.'

I said, 'I told you so.'

He bared his rodent teeth in a grin. 'We are not paid to believe what you tell us. We are paid to find out what is the truth.'

I smiled like a corpse and said, 'Always?'

He said, 'Always. To find out the truth, always. But not always to tell it. The telling or not telling of it belongs to the men above us. The nation is a vast and complex and glorious enterprise. Any truth that does not fit into it is dangerous and anti-national and has no right to exist.' He was no longer smiling, and his squirrel's bush was still.

I said, 'What you are going to tell me—is it the truth?'

He said, 'I believe it to be.'

I waited while he took out a brown file from his briefcase and opened it. Inside was a sheaf of papers threaded together. On the tiny ledge of the slit window sat a three-tier steel tiffin-box. Next to it, folded twice over, a printed pink-and-white hand towel. And next to it, in the only bit of space remaining, sat a fat Old Monk rum bottle, with two limp strands of moneyplant growing out of it. In his wallet I could bet there were a photograph of his mother and a picture of Goddess Lakshmi. When he went home to his rank-smelling government-issue concrete matchbox, his wife would rail at him about school fees and the price of vegetables, with no inkling that he helped hold up the nation.

Taking two loud sniffs of his moustache, looking down at his papers, he said, 'The mastermind and leader of the operation to kill you was the man they call Hathoda Tyagi. He is a hardened criminal and contract killer, originally from western UP, but mostly operating out of Chitrakoot.' He looked up and smiled. 'Many such men live in holy places, believing that a daily dip in Gangamaiyya will keep washing away their sins.'

I said, 'But why? Do you know that now?'

He said, 'First I am on the how. Later, we will try and understand the why. Shall I continue?'

'Sure.'

'This man—he is almost like a boy—does not work on his own. He works for powerful mafia leaders across UP and Bihar, and has a big reputation for never failing. Like Kake Da Dhaba, his speciality, it seems, is brain curry. When he first started out he used to make it with a hammer; now he makes it with sophisticated guns. Sometimes identifying the victims takes days and weeks. Our information is that this boy was sent to Nepal, to Kathmandu, to collect the contract by the man he mostly works for—a powerful dacoit leader with political contacts called Donullia Gujjar. On 16 February, four years ago, this boy travelled to Kathmandu by road—in a Maruti

800—and stayed there in the house of a man called Sher Singh Thapa, a local businessman dealing in imported cloth and electronics. A week later, he met two men called Sulaiman and Qayoom Ali, both from Pakistan, both agents of the ISI. For one week they all stayed together in the house. It was in this period that the operation was planned, and we have information that Sulaiman and Qayoom Ali handed over five lakh rupees and a consignment of four AK-47s, four AK-56s, and a dozen pistols to Hathoda Tyagi. Ten grenades were also given, along with two bulletproof jackets. Another seven lakh rupees was promised on completion of the job.'

A dour balding man appeared at the half-open door and handed over two glasses of tea without stepping in. Dubeyji slurped his down with noisy relish. Then he sniffed his moustache loudly and resumed: 'After Sulaiman and Qayoom Ali left, this Tyagi boy stayed on for another week. It's not clear why—but most probably it was to prepare the plan for bringing the weapons across. What we do know is that he did not step out of Sher Singh Thapa's house during his entire stay in Kathmandu. He did not go out sightseeing, he did not visit any temples, he did not go to any hotel, restaurant, or red-light area. A local man, known to us only as Naik—probably a former army man—did visit him a few times. We suspect he is the one who organized the delivery of arms across the border.'

He now stood up, placed his left foot on his right knee, clasped his hands above his head, closed his eyes, and stretched. He didn't look like Shiva. He just looked like a crackpot government officer. When he sat down again he said, 'If you take bribes at the traffic light all your limbs are exercised. But sitting in this hole you have to teach yourself simple asanas to keep the circulation going.' He needed to meet Guruji upside down and have his moustache stuffed up his nose.

'Soon after the deal was settled in Kathmandu the other four men were contacted. It's still not clear who contacted them—they all give typically vague accounts. Someone called Aloo or Gobhi or

Supari or Sandesh called them and asked them to report for an assignment. Of course they don't know the real names of any of the men who called! Does Chini expect anyone to know his real name? He doesn't know it himself. Interestingly, none of them named Hathoda Tyagi as the person who first contacted them. Each of them said when they found out that they would have to work with him on this job they felt both honoured and terrified.'

I said, 'Did they know the job they were being hired for?'

'Well, they all claim they did not know it was a killing. According to them, it was to assist in a jewellery shop heist. They are all lying. The men were picked with care and for specific tasks. Kabir, the Musalman, was to be the driver; he was to lift the vehicle they would use for the hit, and lift another for the escape. Chaaku was the man who knew Delhi and was going to navigate them in and out. And those two druggies, Kaaliya and Chini, were to be the back-up hitmen. Once the hit was made, they were to split up. The Musalman would lift a small Maruti, and Hathoda Tyagi and he would melt into the badlands of Meerut and Muzaffarnagar. The druggies would go to the railway station and catch a train to somewhere far away and stay away for some weeks or months. For Chaaku there was no real problem—he would smoothly retreat into the armpits of his political patrons. And you would go to the cremation ground and from there straight to Indralok, where apsaras would be waiting to dance the bharatanatyam for you.'

I looked at him grinning, and I thought maybe his moustache is false and I should pull it off and make him real. I said, 'What happened then?'

He said, 'What always does—man proposes, god disposes. But that comes later. First, we know for sure that in the beginning of April they all met at the outskirts of Gorakhpur in a house owned by a local trader-cum-smuggler-cum-politician called Panditji. The house is surrounded by fields and the rail tracks run through it—and they say many trains slow down in that stretch to allow men and material to be loaded and unloaded. We cannot arrest Panditji because the house is benami and the land is benami. If we start running down that road we won't be back for ten years, by which time your killers will have grown old and died anyway.'

I said, 'This Panditji was part of the plot?'

He twitched his rodent nose and grinned. 'No no, in this case we think he was only a hotelier, providing a place for them to have their conference. Like fine businessmen, criminals also need convention centres. Panditji's is one of the best in eastern UP. Many national and international summits on murder, smuggling and narcotics are held there. Impossible to get a booking unless you know the owner, or know someone who knows the owner. And we can't arrest him because it is all benami, and if we go down that road we won't be back for ten years.'

I said, 'The government provides you all dialogue writers?'

He said, 'Dialogue-writers?'

I said, 'Then what happened?'

He said, 'Soon after, the Musalman—Kabir—left with the two druggies for Patna and they came back some days later with a stolen Sumo. Over the next week Panditji's men from the city came and turned the white skin of the Sumo black, changed its numbers, and welded a five-inch deep and four-foot-long steel container under the rear seats. Only one AK-56, two AK-47s and four pistols were tucked in there. The rest of Sulaiman and Qayoom Ali's cache was left behind with Panditji. Chaaku—the political man—had come there with nice pictures of you—from some newspaper or magazine. He also had a map of your colony, with your house number circled nicely with a green sketch pen. We recovered all these things from them. The plan was first to stop on the outskirts of Delhi, in Ghaziabad, and leave the Sumo there. Then to undertake a survey of your colony. They did so. Only three of them came to your colony, in an auto-rickshaw, and walked past your house and around it. Chaaku, the Musalman and Hathoda Tyagi. Do you have a dog that limps?'

I felt my bowels turn to water and my legs lose all strength. 'Yes,' I said.

'Well, they played with it and fed it biscuits. Two days later, when they came for a second survey, Hathoda Tyagi brought your dog some meat and rotis. Then something, it seems, went wrong for a bit. There was some dispute. The strike was first planned for 6 May, then 9 May, and finally it was set for 14 May. We know this because the secret branch of Delhi Police had a tap on one of their mobile phones, on Chaaku's. He too, it seems, had three phones—but they had the number he was using for this hit job. By the way, the police was already covering you by then—from 4 May itself. Did you get to know at all?'

'No,' I said. 'Not at all.'

Without standing up he struck his mudra again, curving his hands above his head and clasping them and stretching his whole body. 'More than twenty men! More than twenty policemen were working around the clock to save you! Do you think anyone will give them credit? If you had banged into a pig on the Ring Road and hurt yourself and the pig, everyone would have accused the police of not doing its job, of taking bribes, of destroying the country. Tell me, what can the police possibly do if you and a pig collide? But when they risk their lives to save you from five killers, they get not a word of appreciation from anyone.'

I tried to look solemn. The armpits of his cream shirt had big sweat scallops.

He put his arms down and rotated his shoulders. 'On the morning of 14 May, at 7 a.m., a traffic policeman stationed at the traffic lights near Ghazipur stopped a white Sumo entering Delhi, to check the licence papers. He insisted that the Musalman step out and show him the papers. Twenty men, most of them from the secret branch, in five vehicles, were stationed all around. All of them were fully armed and none of them was in uniform. The moment the spotter confirmed it was Hathoda Tyagi and his men, two Gypsys banged themselves in front of and behind the Sumo and the traffic policeman grabbed the Musalman. Everything was over in ten minutes. The two druggies and Chaaku protested their innocence, insisting they had just hitched a ride from Ghaziabad. The other two, the Musalman and the killer, said nothing. And that's how it has remained. Those two never said a thing ever, and the other three have kept spinning out new accounts every day. In the prison, it seems, they have all gone back to type. The druggies, Chini and Kaaliya, are already a leading part of the prison drug mafia; they appear to be happy; they play carrom and table tennis and hang together all the time. Hathoda Tyagi is a complete loner but is feared by everyone; even the mafia does not provoke him; and it seems he sometimes protects some of the weaker prisoners. Chaaku's contacts ensure he lives well; money, food, cigarettes, even whisky, are made available to him; the warders treat him with care. The Musalman is the strangest. He knows some English and helps the prisoners in drafting their applications. But mostly he works quietly in the carpentry unit and chisels little wooden choozas all day—there are enough there now to open a full poultry farm.'

He paused for a moment, then said, 'But they are all third-rate bastards. Gutter insects.'

I said, 'But who wanted me killed? What does your chargesheet say?'

He said, 'Pakistan.'

I said, 'Pakistan.'

He said, 'The ISI. You know, their secret agency. More powerful than their politicians, more powerful than their prime minister, more powerful than their army. It looks after their national interest. It understands what is national interest. Not like us here—chained dogs that any minor government officer can kick! If we had the powers they have, we could clean up this miserable country. Get rid of every traitor, get rid of all the dogs, like the men who took a contract to kill you.'

And make every window a slim slit impossible to use for suicide, and put up a maze of plywood partitions everywhere so everyone can spend their lives opening and closing doors without arriving anywhere, and give everyone a bushy false moustache to wag at each other.

I said, 'But why?'

He said, 'To destabilize our government. Our country. Create chaos.'

I thought of Jai and the geopolitical oration he would have conjured out of this.

I said, 'No. Really. Why?'

He said, all trace of lightness gone from his voice, his moustache still and spiky, 'The enemy is cunning, motivated, relentless, and ruthless.' He was speaking mostly in Hindi now—anger had leached all English niceties out of him. 'He seizes every opportunity to strike. Because he cannot kill us with a single lunge, he wants to bleed us from a thousand wounds. Those other idiots, with their spy cameras, who messed around in the defence ministry, there is a contract out on them too. By whom? Yes, you guessed it right! And why? Yes, you guessed it right again! All of you—the people of my great country—live in a dream of innocence. And all the while, as you foolishly watch cinema and cricket, as you drink and smoke and eat and sleep, the enemy is hard at work, severing our arteries, slicing our muscles, injecting poison into our flesh, planting explosives under our feet, hollowing us for collapse. You all—I don't mean you specifically, but your breed—fill the newspapers with so much dung that no one can ever see the true picture. Even when a bomb goes off right under our buttocks we think it is the high note of a Hindi film song. I can tell you the enemy is thrilled with us. He can hardly believe how stupid we are. Hindustan, bada mahaan, mooh mein beedi, haath mein paan.'

Somebody needed to rush him to the nearest multiplex, sit him down in front of a manic multi-starrer and stick his rodent nose into a bucket of popcorn and a Pepsi with ice.

I said, 'Can I have a copy of the chargesheet?'

He closed the file, put his hand on it, and said, 'Not yet. It is still confidential.'

Behind the inspector's head was the lurid green poster on the wall, the handsome man in a peak-cap. Small minds: discuss people. Average minds: discuss events. Big minds: discuss ideas. Great minds: work in silence.

I said, 'I would like to know.'

He said, 'One day you will. Don't worry. We are taking care of everything.'

I said, 'It's about my murder.'

He said, 'That doesn't matter.'

As I sat in my study I thought, not bad, I've done it. Nearly a year had passed since I had seen Sara.

I had taken Guruji's upside-down advice: zip up and run. And I had taken the advice of the rodent in the castle, Dubeyji: that doesn't matter. It had proven easier than I had anticipated. The first few times the impulse to see her seized me, I laced up my keds and went for a run, jogging round and round the colony park like Forrest Gump till the children began to stop and point fingers at me, till all thought was thumped out of my head by my pounding feet, till there was nothing to do but go home and collapse.

We kept messaging each other but I erased all play from it, sticking to perfunctory information. I think she was for some time—typically—too self-obsessed to notice. Then, when I excused myself one more time from going over, she caught on. I received an envelope from her one day. In it was a foolscap sheet folded over like a card. On the cover were drawn two oval eggs, cracked open and spilling. Under it was written, A Tale of Leaking Testicles. The subtitle was: The Inspiring Story of Five Killers and a Peashooter. On the inside page she had pasted a colour picture of the goddess Kali, all her arms in motion, her eyes blazing, the garland of decapitated heads around her neck resplendent. The sign-off was: Your humble wall-hanging, Sara.

Kali, Mahakali, Inder ki Beti, Brahma ki Saali, Tera Vaar Na Jaaye Khali.

I was not sure if it was a provocation—as of old—or a real dismissal. I was tempted to retaliate, to set in motion the spiral that would end in a symphony of abuse against the wall. But I held myself in, and, slowly, her magnetic tug on me waned to the point that days would go by without any thought of her engaging me.

For a while, there was a writer on the features team of the paper I now worked for, an expatriate born and brought up in Birmingham, back on a roots trip. She was darker than Sara and talked incessantly of her pind in the Punjab—the village had emptied out in the fifties as the lower castes took flight to freedom and janitorship in England. We did a couple of lunches, then dinners. She had a nasal voice and a way of clucking that shot my nerves. When we finally got inside her bedroom in Defence Colony, her smell was rank. After that it was a struggle to be rid of her. Thankfully, expectedly, her discovery of India quickly floundered in the face of the heat, the traffic, the testosteronic north Indian male, and the third-rate journalism.

Someone then gave me the number of a massage parlour in Lajpat Nagar. It was in a building in the market, two floors up, with a shop selling steel utensils and bone-china crockery on the ground floor. The stairwell had posters of gods and goddesses and a bright blue print of Jesus on the cross. One of the six-odd parlour girls was the colour of bitter chocolate. She had hardly any takers. They all sat in a row on the plastic chairs, and the men would walk in and pick the fair ones and take them down the short corridor into the wooden cubicles, while bitter-chocolate worked a needle in a wooden frame, embroidering little birds and trees into existence. I picked only her, never asked her name, never spoke to her. Her hair was kinky, and her skin shiny and tight. And her hands—dipped in oil—were earning her great karma. She was sure to be born a princess in her next life.

The parlour was a true discovery. Once a week, twice, one could go there and square with the body. I was surprised I had not discovered such a relationship earlier—more honest, less neurotic, than any I had ever had. The body continually forces one to deceit. Here was a way to sidestep it. Along with the manic jogging, it also took care of the moments when Sara would suddenly invade my head.

I also absorbed the advice of the rodent and stopped thinking of the killers—with Sara's keening voice out of my ear, it was quite easy. In this time there was a last visit from Hathi Ram. His time in the police was done. He was going back to his village in Haryana, the childhood of koel calls, green fields, woodsmoke, and raindrops detonating the aroma in the soil. Sitting in my small study, he caressed *The Naked Lunch*, and said, 'For the rest of my life I am going to keep a fast on every Monday. I have to atone for thirty-two years of sinning as a policeman. Shiva is the easiest god to please, and Shiva knows all that I have done I had to. Shiva knows that the world has to be continually created and destroyed by the practice of right and wrong, and even those of us who do wrong are playing our designated part in the drama of the universe.'

Near the gate I nodded at the shadow—standing erect in the background—and said, 'How much longer?' He said, 'I don't know.' I said, 'Do I really need him?' He said, 'I don't think so.' I said, 'Then why?' He said, 'I don't know.' I said, 'Then who will?' He said, 'It's not even worth trying to find out. Do you think we ever know who is really issuing us an order?' From the gate he turned back and said, 'Don't feel guilty about it—just treat it as your rightful share of the great Indian government.'

Now as I sat in the study—all the lights off, my feet on the table—I felt empty. The din of television relationships floated through the closed door—Dolly/folly was drinking in her prime-time serials, chin in palms. Coal-black Elizabeth—coal-black Felicia had quit six months ago—had already brought me four cups of tea. In the big wide world only two decisions awaited my attention. One, on undertaking the thirty-day Kailash Mansarovar trek to the abode of the gods; two, about taking the television job Jai had put on the table for me. In favour of the trek was getting close to Shiva and fleeing Dolly/folly and the rest. Against it were all the paperwork and medical tests that needed to be done and the misery of being stuck for thirty days on Himalayan trails with shrill, eager, moronic devotees. In favour of the job was the mound of money on offer—clearly television was plugged into a pipeline that print had not yet found. Or it was some equation that said the dumber the medium, the more you were paid to abase yourself on it. That was what was against it, as also the neurosis of how you looked. The stiffness of collar, and the cut of shave. I knew, at the moment, money was winning and god losing. Jai had summed it up: 'You've seen it all by now. Decide. Do you want to be Chutiya-Nandan-Pandey or do you want to be run by Chutiya-Nandan-Pandeys!'

Suddenly in the dark there was an angry buzz and the glow of the phone opened up the room. I had her down in the directory as Kali. The message was one word: call. I hesitated for a moment, but it had been so long that I had lost my fear. She was business-like; a receptionist passing on information. I needed to see her. She had some important things to tell. When I asked where, she said, 'In front of the Taj Mahal, by moonlight, mr peashooter, where else!'

I told coal-black Elizabeth to tell her memsahib I might not be back for dinner, and I took the shadow along, sitting in the rear seat, his iron hard in his crotch. This one had come only six months ago and had no idea where we were going. She opened the door in a black sarong and a striated white vest, loops of coloured bangles on her photo arms. The memory of pleasure powered through me like adrenalin, and I wanted to immediately pick her up and hang her on the wall. But before I could say a word, a woman I had never seen appeared behind her. She was thickset, with short hair and wore a wide blue-and-red tennis band on her wrist. She could probably kill with a karate chop.

They were drinking rum with water, and they gave me a mug of tea. Big enough to bathe in. I tried to catch her eye, to create a synapse of intimacy—the sight of her had already undone my resolve—but her look gave nothing away. It seemed as if something fundamental had changed in her. Her nervous energy was low, her voice calm. When we were all seated—I on the cane armchair, she on the sofa, feet under her, and the karateka at the dining-table, chair angled towards us—Sara said, 'Do you want to know the entire story now?'

I said, 'Of what?'

She said, 'Of the building of the Taj Mahal, what else!'

I said, 'Are you saying you've been digging out more stuff on those guys?'

She said, 'Do you want to know?'

I said, 'Yes.'

I looked towards the dining-table. The woman was running her forefinger under the wristband and flexing it and looking directly at me. Surely she was accidental to the evening?

Sara said, her voice preternaturally flat and low, 'As I always thought, you were incidental to the whole plot. The plan to kill you had nothing to do with killing you.'

The rodent and she had been conspiring in the castle.

I said, 'Yes, I know. Pakistan. The ISI. They wanted to destabilize the Indian government.'

The geopolitical pawn explains his predicament.

She said, tonelessly, 'You hear nothing. You see nothing. You learn nothing. You are changed by nothing. Data, stimulus, experience, everything bounces off you like water off a rock. You obsess about your gods and gurus, you screw anything you can find, and you work only for money. That's it. That's all. Nothing ever changes you. Nothing ever affects you.'

I kept quiet. She was not angry. She was not baiting me.

'Everything those guys have been telling you is false. Often they don't even know it. Often they even believe it to be true. Most of the cops you talk to are themselves unwitting pawns in bigger games. Now listen carefully. The plan to kill you had nothing to do with your exposé or with the ISI. Yes, the boy Tyagi went to Kathmandu. Yes, he met men there who gave him a contract to kill you. Yes, they provided him a cache of weapons—including AK-47s. Yes, they gave him hard currency as an advance. Yes, the team of five men met in a farm outside Gorakhpur. Yes, they worked out the details of the operation there. But no, the primary purpose of the plan was not to kill you. And no, the men who gave out the contract were not from the ISI.'

She was speaking in a measured way, and now she took a break to drain her rum. A fly was buzzing in the room. The karateka rose, rolled a magazine, crouched for a moment, and then in a flash splattered it on the wooden table. Guruji would have said all life is potentially a black blotch.

'The real targets of the contract and the plan were the killers themselves. Not all of them. Just two of them. The rest were like you. Incidental fodder. Collateral damage. The two—yes, I am sure you guessed one right—were the Tyagi boy and the man they call Chaaku. Someone wanted to get rid of both of them. The real plan was to have them shot just as they were shooting you. You were all supposed to die in a dramatic shoot-out. The men who had sent the killers had also leaked the information of the hit to the police. The first two times they came to recce your house, they were being trailed by an army of plainclothesmen from the special cell. The orders were to shoot to kill. It was a sweet construct. The ISI would take the rap for your murder, and the police the credit for killing your killers. But something went wrong.'

She stopped and waved her empty glass like a flag. The karateka came over with two bottles and smoothly sloshed them into a perfect drink.

'It's still not quite clear what went wrong. But the agreed upon date for the hit came and went. Then, it seems, a new one was set. That too came and went. It's possible that there was some dispute between the killers and their patrons. Finally—and this even peashooters can confirm by just asking a few questions—the men were not picked up as claimed at the Delhi border on their way to the hit, nor were they picked up on the morning the news was broken to the media. They were picked up a whole day earlier, in the middle of the night, from the small hotel they were staying in, in Shahdara. There was no scuffle, no shoot-out. None of the men retaliated, or made a run for it. Not even the so-called beast, Hathoda Tyagi. For a day they were with the secret branch and did not exist in any paperwork of arrest. Then they were produced before the media and in court.'

I looked at her, the light glancing off her photo shoulders and sharp collarbones. She still needed an urgent inoculation of Vedanta, but she was mad enough to intuit the truths of this mad country. How could I have let her go? Had Guruji met her, he may never have advised me to zip up and run. For a moment I almost felt in love with her. Were it not for the karateka something pulpy might have slipped my mouth.

I said, 'But if the idea was to kill them, why didn't the police do it?'

She said, 'I don't think the police knew they had to kill them. Whoever was tipping them off on the hit was hoping they would kill them in the heat of the encounter. In the hotel in cold blood would have been impossible—too many cops involved, too many witnesses. Can be done in Bihar; tough in Delhi. Many wouldn't believe it, but we do have some kind of a free press and an independent judiciary.'

She said it flatly. Something had certainly settled inside her.

I said, 'So the main target of—whoever—was the Tyagi boy?'

She said, 'Yes. It clearly seems so. And to some extent, Chaaku. The other three were just journeymen, filling the numbers on an assignment. Those two platform boys, Kaaliya and Chini, are just happy-go-lucky fellows, content to make do with some money, some drugs, and some sex. Probably more decent than anyone you know. And Kabir—gentle Kabir!—he is a wronged angel. He should be wrapped up in someone's arms and protected. Even in prison he floats in an aura of peace, chiselling his choozas and giving them to everyone. Demands nothing, says little. Has no lawyer, doesn't want to file even a bail application. No one bothers him—not the inmates, not the warders. And slowly he is beginning to be called Baba. The Tyagi boy and Chaaku stay away from these three and have nothing to do with them. They stay away from each other too.'

I said, 'Will they get bail?'

She said, 'Yes, soon. But by then they will already have served most of their sentence. So it goes in this godforsaken country.'

I said, 'Where did you find out all this?'

She said, 'Mr peashooter, if you look you find.'

For the next fifteen minutes I tried hard to plug into the old socket that had electrified us, made our bodies sing and singe around each other. The delicate shoulders, the full black sarong, the caramel skin was filling me with an unexpected ache. I was hoping if I made the connection she would somehow get rid of the tank in the room. But she had thrown a switch and removed herself from my field. It could have been pretence, but she was not even looking at me any more, choosing to talk to the dining-table about some new law regulating inmates in the prisons of Haryana. She was like a bureaucrat who had finished with a petitioner and was, with polite exasperation, waiting for him to leave. For a moment I thought it was the old kind of provocation. But then I saw her eyes and there was nothing for me there. Besides, I knew if I essayed any move the karateka would pick the chair and break it over my head.

On a weird impulse—triggered by the meeting with Sara—a few days later, on a Sunday morning, I got into my car with my shadow and drove off to Muzaffarnagar. We left Delhi early because we were heading for serious badlands. My shadow—from the equally notorious area of Bulandshahar—said, 'We must leave that place well before the sun begins to go down. After dark, even armed policemen dare not venture there.'

Even early on a late winter morning—with the mist still hovering over the ditches—the roads were choked, and it seemed as if one would never exit Delhi's endless sprawl. Concrete finger on concrete finger, the ancient city seemed to extend itself relentlessly to swallow the countryside around. Where once seed of grain sprouted, now septic tanks bloomed. Out of every slain tree had grown a lamp post, and every dead nilgai had been replaced by two cars. The highway was full of sugarcane—on bullock-carts, tractor-trolleys, small trucks—on its way to the factories, and I drove with the windows up to avoid being speared by a swinging stalk.

The moment we were out of the hell of Muzaffarnagar we had to turn right off the highway, and then stop every ten minutes for directions. Gnarled trees with dust-coated leaves were all around and neat blocks of sugarcane ran to the horizon. I had taken the address from the files of the fat penguin, Sethiji. At some point the interior road we were chasing ran out of tar and we were rolling along on dust. A pool of stagnant black marked the entry into the village. The houses in it were a mix of mud and cut-rate brick. Television antennae sprouted like hair. As I drove around the outskirts asking for directions, I saw at least two small Maruti cars, the sun blinding on their skins.

Eventually we had to park by a field and walk a winding path through juicy green wheat fields and tall sugarcane. On the way was a grove of ageing mango trees, the leaves dull, the barks deathly. From that point the dogs picked us up and howled us all the way to the house.

The main section of the house was in plastered brick, while the rooms on the side were naked brick attachments with thatched roofs. In the front yard, by a long mud trough, five tethered buffaloes and two oxen masticated in tandem. I could see pipes and wires—running water and electricity.

Gyanendra Tyagi was leaning back on a charpoy, two grimy hard pillows under his elbow and an empty Bournvita tin by his side. He looked old. His eyes were rheumy. The white hair on his head, without its turban, showed sparse. His bad leg, clear of his pulled-up dhoti, was thin as a matchstick. Every few minutes he hawked and spat into the empty tin. Like every other Indian he was probably dying of tuberculosis.

When I told him I was a journalist, he spat a thick gob into the tin, and without preamble, mumbled that he knew nothing about his son, that he had not seen him in a few years. My shadow picked up a mooda lying close by, took it to the corner of the yard, and sat down, looking at me in contempt. It was his luck to be detailed to guard a low-life like me.

When I persisted, the old man said his son had been seduced by bad company and forced into the wrong life. There was a lower-caste man, a Gujjar, a sports master in his school, who had taken control of his son, debased him. Tyagis, such as he, kept no truck with that criminal caste—not of friendship, not of marriage. Did he know that before a Gujjar father married off his daughter, he checked whether his son-in-law could scale a tall wall quickly and as swiftly crack open a closed window? A man of such a wayward caste had snatched his boy away.

But the boy was his boy, still a good son. He had, over the years, taken care of their land disputes in the village, and regularly sent them money. When his sister was being tormented by her husband he had had the man's legs broken; then sent him money for the repair.

Just then a thin old woman came out of the black hole in the brick wall, her salwar-kameez frayed and colourless. The dogs rushed to her, circled her, tails wagging, and then settled back under the charpoy. She peered at me through her thin-rimmed glasses and asked, 'Guddu has sent you?' I told her who I was, and she said, 'Have you met him recently?' I said no, and she said, 'Well, when you meet him tell him that Lalli's husband has begun to thrash her again, and the doctor says his father needs to have his knees operated, and the buffalo we had bought from Ghomuru has died, and his mother moves closer to the cremation ground every day, and if he would just come by and show her his face once, she would feel bathed in the peace of eternity, and there is just no money at home.' She moved towards the cattle trough, and then turned back and added, 'And tell him I am still waiting to get him married so that Gyanendra Tyagi's blood-line does not die out!'

I was still framing a reply in my mind when the old man suddenly put down his Bournvita tin with a clatter and said in alarm, 'Is he okay? Have you come with bad news?'

The old woman said from the trough, 'The shastriji had said at his birth that no one can hurt him. His stars are like Hrinyakashyap's. He can only be harmed in a place that has both sunlight and shade; he can only be harmed when he is moving and not still; he can only be harmed when his belly is full; he can only be harmed when he is hidden from view; he can only be harmed by a slain enemy; and he can only be harmed when he is trapped between friends. For all these things to come together is a near impossibility. To kill the evil Hrinyakashyap, Lord Vishnu had to appear himself and bend the elements. And we know the gods don't descend into this country any more.'

I said he was fine. There was no bad news at all. As far as I knew he was in good health and high spirits. And Lord Vishnu had not yet descended.

Just then the shadow leaned back in his flatwood chair and took out the iron from his crotch and began to caress it. The old man instantly let out a bloodcurdling shout and began to wildly spew abuse, calling us sons of catamites, whores, eunuchs and sweepers. The woman turned around from the trough and charged on hobbling legs, screaming similarly. The dogs exploded like gunfire from under the charpoy, yapping and baying, and darting at our ankles. I tried to tell the old couple that he was a policeman, my guard, but they were beside themselves with drooling rage. The old man even managed to pick up and fling the Bournvita tin at me, and the crazy old crone charged as if she were an armoured carrier out to flatten us.

We beat a retreat with the dogs yowling us all the way to the car.

Inside the air-conditioned car, the shadow said, 'Arre sahib, why do you get familiar with such low-borns? One should always keep them at an arm's distance.'

That one foray cured me of all curiosity. I dropped my half-baked plans of visiting Bareilly, Chitrakoot and Keekarpur off the Grand Trunk Road and, in fact, failed to make it even to the nevernever-land platforms of the New Delhi railway station. Sergeant Sara and her bleeding hearts band could carry on with their show, egged on by cheering groupies. I had a life to live.

Guruji and Hathi Ram and Dubeyji were right—this country was crazy and out of control, and these men were killers and criminals and waywards, and had to square their sordid accounts. I was through with orphans, charmers, chisellers, knifemeisters, hammermen, penguins in courts and rodents in castles, and the labyrinth of all their travails. I did not make the world and I was not responsible for it. Bhallaji and Chutiya-Nandan-Pandey and silhouettes in castles were free to run it; and Jai and his media choir, to sing of it.

Vedanta had, millennia ago, declared it all an illusion. Maya. All of it. The suffering of the waif and the pomp of the emperor. To fret was naïve. In the scale of eternity we would all be perfectly balanced out. I forgot about my assassins, and after a few attempts at reconnecting—that were rudely snubbed—I forgot about Sara too.

I did not take the mound of money offered by Jai to squawk on TV, and I did not make the thirty-day pilgrimage to Kailash Mansarovar. The very thought of chanting alongside mindless traders trekking up to the icy abode of Shiva to ask for some more money exhausted me. Instead, I decided to learn Sanskrit.

It would have been as easy to learn American football. As I looked for a place to start, a bewildering array of schools and approaches hit me. I didn't want to sit in an open-university classroom, nor under a tree with my head tonsured. An old Tamilian at the newspaper's copy desk found me someone who would come home. This Dr Sarma was older than my father, wore a dhoti and sandals, and in his first few tutorials I struggled to understand a single word. It was not just his Telugu accent, it was also the numbing abstractions—of religion, language, and culture—that he piled up without drawing a breath. I understood why for centuries the language had been learnt by rote—there was no other way to hold on to anything. He sipped coal-black Elizabeth's tea and swayed to and fro, and intoned in a singsong drone, and I was mesmerized.

Some weeks later, I cornered my colleague and asked him for someone younger. The new man who came was from Kerala, wore jeans and white bush shirts, and cracked jokes in English. He was also a fan of Hindi films. Slowly I settled down to learn the mother of all languages, to acquire the words in which the cosmos was first explained, before colonial buccaneering vanquished it all, word and meaning.

At the newspaper I realized how far in the world a minor

reputation could carry you. On the basis of that one exposé which had brought on nothing but ruination and killers and shadows, I was treated as a savant. My specialization was presumed to be state policy and strategic affairs. For days I could coast around doing little, and then to register my presence, hammer out a few banalities about some national issue on one of the opinion pages. Sometimes, even simpler, there was an interview, a pointless ping-pong with some minor minister that could be conducted and banged out all in the space of an hour. Few things are less taxing than modern journalism.

For pleasure and peace there was the parlour on the second floor, above the crockery and the utensils, with Jesus Christ on the way up. The bitter-chocolate skin, the kinky hair, the hands dipped in oil, the fingers supple from needlework.

And I jogged every day at the Saket sports club, where the women got trendier and the men prettier. I would pound the bitumen track till I had sweat out all foolishness and sentimentality, and all illusion was dead and my mind was clear and still as a sheet of glass. It was meditation on pumping legs.

The shadows were still there, and I only noticed them if they were missing.

And then I had the encounter.

It was the month of March, and I was on my way to Abu Dhabi for a two-day conference on managing tensions in South Asia. At Muscat I had to change a flight and for the four-hour layover I had been seated in the first-class waiting lounge. It was cavernous and plush, and in bad taste. In India it could have housed twenty families. Apart from me, that vast space of sofas and settees and chairs and tables contained only two other women huddled in a far corner. They were draped in such comprehensive hijab that only their fingers were visible. After a few visits to the food counters and the toilets I slumped into a maroon satin sofa and fell asleep.

When I woke suddenly, chilled by the soundless air-conditioning, I found a man seated across from me, looking intently at my face. He had a neatly trimmed beard around a strong nose, and was clad in a cream-coloured salwar-kameez. His glasses were strung on a chain of black beads around his neck and there were traces of henna in his thick wavy hair. I gave him a tight smile, and he said, 'I know who you are and what you did.'

I said, 'What do you know?'

He said, 'I know you exposed corruption in the agriculture ministry, and I know there was an attempt to kill you. Do you still live under police protection?'

I said I did.

He said, 'But I hope you know that actually it was nothing to do with you. The plan to kill you was really aimed at getting rid of some others. It's true you could have been killed—but that wasn't really the purpose of the plan.'

I said, 'What *was* the purpose of the plan? To get rid of whom?'

He said, 'Did you ever meet your killers?'

I said, 'Yes. Once. In the courtroom.'

He said, 'Do you remember a young, very strong-looking boy?'

I said, 'Hathoda Tyagi.'

He laughed aloud and slapped his hands together. 'Hathoda Tyagi! Yes, Hathoda Tyagi! You know that name too! Do you know who he worked for?'

He was speaking in a flowing mix of Hindi and English, and now I noticed he had gold rings on most of his fingers, with different coloured stones in them.

I said, 'Some criminal don. In Chitrakoot?'

He said, 'Not just some criminal don, but Donullia Gujjar, one of the most dangerous and powerful dacoits ever seen in that part of the world. Do you know anything about him?'

I said, 'No.'

The air-conditioning had got to me and my bladder was bursting, but I didn't think this was the moment for me to break the conversation.

He said, 'The problem is, Donullia did not live his life in English. That is why you don't know about him. If he had been shooting beans instead of bullets, and cutting carrots instead of arteries, and speaking chutterputter English, everyone would have heard of him, from Delhi and Bombay to Madras and Muscat. And if he was a woman, like Phoolan Devi, you all would have made books and films on him and elected him to Parliament. But let me tell you, he is a far greater dacoit—far purer. He's always lived like one—on his feet, in the jungles and ravines. Do you drink Coca-Cola?'

For a moment I thought it was a trick question. Then I said, 'Yes.'

He got up and walked away to the end of the cavernous room and turned into the service area. The big face was not misleading. He was a large man, probably over six feet. Beneath his cream salwar-kameez he wore well-buffed leather sandals. I scampered to the toilets at the other end, and had to close my eyes to concentrate before my piss found its flow. The soap smelled like strawberry dessert, and I splashed palmfuls of water on my face.

When I returned, he said, 'I thought you had jumped on to the first plane and fled.' The two women in hijab in the corner were playing a hand-slapping game on the table, and tittering. It was impossible to tell how old they were, but from their frames they did not seem like girls. The man said, following my eyes, 'Beneath our skins we are all the same. All seeking a moment of joy.'

I said, 'And what's your name?'

He said, with a patronizing smile, 'Rashid Iqbal. They call me Iqbalmian. But how does my name matter? It could be Jalal-ud-din Akbar. What I know is what matters. What I have to tell you is what matters.' He took a sip of his glass and said, 'Coca-Cola from the tap is never as good as it is from the can.'

I said, 'What do you do, Iqbalsahib?'

He said, more Hindi less English with every exchange, 'Some business and some politics. But I could be a carpenter or a barber. How does that matter? What I can do for you is what matters. My main profession is the making of friends. In our village we say, profits are good but true wealth is friends. Now see, in the waiting room in Muscat, I have suddenly become richer. I have made you my friend. So you must call me Iqbalmian, and I must do whatever I can for you.'

I said, 'Iqbalmian, you are from Chitrakoot?'

'Thereabouts. Wherever the gods are, Iqbalmian is. I know UP is the size of three countries, but all of it is ours. You know this boy, Hathoda Tyagi, he was dreaded like few men I have heard of in my life. He had no weaknesses and he had no fears. He broke men's heads like you and I would break eggs, and he never failed. And he was loyal only to Donullia—he was like a son to him. They say when Donullia heard Hathoda had been arrested, he raged for days, slapping his men, demanding to know how it could have happened. Donullia may be a great dacoit, but he is only a Gujjar—a very cunning Gujjar, but nothing in the face of the cosmic wiliness of a Brahmin.'

I said, 'I don't understand.' I felt I needed to immediately put Guruji, Sara, Hathi Ram, and the rodent on the speakaphone to make sense of this one. And the king penguin, Sethiji, to read out my legal rights.

He said, no longer smiling, 'Bajpaisahib. The Chanakya of politics in our area is Bajpaisahib. For years Donullia and he were partners. Donullia ensured no one ever contemplated challenging Bajpaisahib's political hold in our area; he ensured the votes fell as Bajpaisahib wanted. And Bajpaisahib ensured no police officer could keep his chair if he dared to set his sights on Donullia. They were also business partners. Donullia's brother, Gwalabhai, was his frontman. Gwalabhai lives like a real seth while his brother sleeps under the stars and trees. For many years Bajpaisahib was aligned with the

Yadav supremo of our state; and as the Yadav came to power and prospered so did Bajpaisahib and Donullia. The dacoit often sent his men to the Yadav's aid in other parts of the state. Together, Bajpaisahib and Donullia were a lethal combination—political power, money, and the gun. But you know, while Allah gives men hope and paradise, he also gives them a chance to make a fool of themselves. Gwalabhai, sleeping on the soft beds made out of his brother's hardships, woke up one morning and decided good food and a good life were not enough, he too wanted political power. Cars with red lights, government bungalows, his picture in the newspapers giving speeches and cutting ribbons, and the superintendent of police and the district magistrate jumping to his instructions. Why should Bajpaisahib alone have it all—especially since it was obtained on their muscle? Do you want more Coca-Cola?'

I said no.

He said, 'I hate America but I love their Coca-Cola, and their movies. I have seen *Rocky* thirty times. Whenever I am depressed I slip the video in, and my depression lifts. When she wants something special from me, my wife calls me Rocky.'

The women in hijab had curled up in their chairs and gone to sleep. Two blobs of black ink, not a trace of skin or life visible. Even though I had said no, Rocky came back with two glasses of Coke. 'It's free,' he said, handing me a glass and hitching up his salwar as he sat down.

I said, 'So Gwalabhai got ambitious...'

He said, now talking almost exclusively in Hindi, 'Nothing wrong with that. Even an insect must harbour an ambition of becoming a bigger insect. But no insect must make so much noise that someone is forced to swat it. When Bajpaisahib began to move away from the Yadav chieftain and began to get close to the low-caste leader, Gwalabhai saw an opportunity. He forced his brother to give up his lifelong allegiance to Bajpaisahib, and began to directly pay court to the Yadav.'

I was still with him. I said, 'So Bajpaisahib moved away from the Yadav, but Gwalabhai and Donullia Gujjar did not. They established a direct link with the Yadav, and broke away from Bajpaisahib.'

He said, with relish, 'Not cut and dried like an examination result; nothing in business and politics is like that; but yes, more or less. The brothers thought they did not need Bajpaisahib any more. They were big enough to run their own political circus. Of course they were fools—at least Gwalabhai was. Never ever imagine that you can outwit a brahmin. Are you a brahmin? No. Good. A brahmin's brain is worse than a jalebi—impossible to know which thought leads where. Bajpaisahib had read the wind correctly. It was a bitterly contested election, as you know. And the low castes swept it. Now it was time for Bajpaisahib to neutralize Donullia and the foolish Gwalabhai. But as you know, a brahmin never attacks from the front. He poisons you slowly while warmly hosting you for dinners. Soon cases of income-tax and municipal violations began to be opened up against Gwalabhai. Then a tough superintendent of police arrived in the district. When the brothers petitioned Bajpaisahib for help, he promised to do whatever he could.'

I looked at my watch. I would have to board in less than five minutes. The ink blobs had woken, and gathering their black folds, had scurried off. I said, 'And what does all this have to do with my killing?'

He said, 'The man who was given the contract to kill you was the one man Bajpaisahib feared the most. He knew once the animus burst into the open, this man was capable of taking a shot at him. He knew Hathoda Tyagi was highly destructive and completely without fear, and that his loyalty to Donullia was complete. It was Bajpaisahib who arranged to have the contract for your killing given to Hathoda Tyagi—through Gwalabhai of course. Then he called his friends in Delhi who run the police, and waited for the action to unfurl.'

I said, 'So it really had nothing to do with me and our exposé?'

He said, 'Did it matter whether Saddam had nuclear weapons or not? Like Saddam, you were a pretext. Whether you were killed or not was of no consequence—the man for whom the entire operation was planned, the man to be killed, was Hathoda Tyagi.'

The decorously clad woman in charge of the lounge—her pretty face marred by layers of foundation, the stockings thick on her ankles—loudly informed me my flight was boarding. I stood up, my bladder bursting again with nerves and Coke. I said, 'Then what went wrong? Why didn't it happen?'

He said, 'You have a wife?'

I said, 'Yes.'

He said, 'A pretty one?'

I said nothing.

He stood up too, a big man, and said, 'You also have a dog? A lame one?'

I said, 'Yes, there is a mongrel that lives in our lane.'

He said, 'You are alive because of him.'

I said, 'I don't understand.'

He said, 'In your Mahabharata, I have heard, the only companion Yudhishthira had on his last journey was a stray dog. And it turned out to be god himself—dharma, there to protect him. Well, you too are alive because of your dog. The day Hathoda Tyagi came with his men to first survey your house, he found your wife at the gate feeding and petting the lame dog. When they returned to their room in Ghaziabad, he began to make inquiries about you. He wanted to know why you were to be killed. No one could give him a good explanation. Heated arguments ensued between him and Gwalabhai, who had been tricked into accepting this contract by Bajpaisahib. Some days later, reluctantly, he led his men to your house again, and once more he found your wife sitting by the gate playing with the lame animal. He had brought along some meat for it, and it seems he even exchanged a few words about the dog with your wife. By now he had found out you were a journalist and had nothing to do with ISI or Pakistan. This time when he went back he exploded on the phone to Gwalabhai. The special cell was already tapping his line, waiting for him to make the hit so that they could gun him down. But now Tyagi told Gwalabhai he was not going ahead: clearly this was not a hit sanctioned by Guruji, that is Donullia: and the contract money should be returned. At this point someone—obviously Bajpaisahib through someone, most probably the all-powerful PA of a top cabinet minister, a man known as Mr Healthy—told the police it was time for them to move in. It seems Mr Healthy—whose privates they say are bigger than his leg—also wanted to get rid of one of his inconvenient men in this operation. It's not true that Hathoda Tyagi and his men were picked up at the border. They were taken from a flat in Shahdara, in the middle of the night, two full days before they were shown as arrested. Not one of the five resisted, because they knew the cops were under orders to shoot. Of course the policemen who made the raid knew nothing. They thought they were busting a gang of genuine killers, with at least one of them a famous hitman.'

By now the lounge lady was grimacing as if her teeth were being pulled out. She was shuffling angrily and rubbing her hands. 'Please sir, the aircraft doors will close in a few minutes!' I had my bag on my shoulders, my visiting card extended in my right hand, and I had begun to move.

I said, walking backwards, 'Iqbalmian, will you call me when you are back in India? How do you know all this? Is there more?'

He said, looking at my visiting card, 'If you wish to know you can always get to know. And of course there is more. There is always more.' Then he smiled like a corpse. 'Till there is no more.'

Some hours later, from a posh, prosaically appointed hotel room in Abu Dhabi, I called the rodent, Dubeyji, on his mobile phone. It was nearly a year since I had last spoken to him, and he took a moment to place me. In a hushed voice—so unlike him—he asked me to call back in an hour. He was with senior officers. The DIG.

I watched the clock and stared out at the expensive emptiness of the city. It looked as uninteresting from the ninth floor as it did from ground zero. Two minutes over the hour, I redialled. The rodent said cheerfully, speaking in Hindi, 'It is an auspicious day. Rarely does anyone remember us once their work is done.'

I said, 'Dubeyji, do you know a man called Iqbalmian?'

He said, and I could see him smile and his moustache bristle, 'Which Iqbalmian? The world is full of Iqbalmians. UP and Bihar alone have enough Iqbalmians to create an army that could conquer Nepal.'

I said, 'A man from Chitrakoot—or thereabouts. A politician, or businessman.'

He said, 'All I know right now is about the case in front of me—a minister from Madhya Pradesh involved in an abduction and extortion case. There is no Iqbalmian involved here so far.'

I said, 'Do you remember—in my case—a man called Hathoda Tyagi?'

He said, 'Arre sahib, some characters you never forget. They are like Gabbar Singh in *Sholay.* Hathoda Tyagi—a killer of the highest order; north India's best brain-curry man. Steady hand, stitched tongue. We could get nothing out of him.'

Great minds: work in silence.

I said, 'Was he involved with a major dacoit called Donullia Gujjar, and a local politician called Bajpaisahib?'

He said, 'I don't remember the details of that case. I would have to check his file. But the file is pretty much closed now.'

I said, 'Why? Has the case been dropped?'

He said, 'Only his. The rest are in court. Surely you know what happened?'

Through the hotel window the sky was a dirty blue. Not one bird embroidered the air. Were there no birds in this world of oil and concrete?

I said, 'No, I don't. Tell me.'

He said, 'Of course, I forgot. You are a big English paper man. You don't read the Hindi newspapers. It's a weird world when people don't keep track of their lovers and killers.' I waited. He said, 'Everyone in our department knows about it; everyone in the state police knows about it. In our work we hear of strange things every day, but this one is the strangest of them all.'

I said, 'Yes, Dubeyji?'

He said, 'Two months ago Hathoda Tyagi had to be taken to Dehradun for a court appearance in another case of murder we had unearthed against him. Because of his reputation the guard had been enhanced. Three men of the Delhi Police, armed with rifles, were escorting him. All three were big men, known for their toughness. Tyagi had been roped to one of them. Their old Willys jeep broke down on the way and they were badly delayed. By the time they reached Saharanpur it was evening, and the sun was setting. Just outside the town the troop stopped at a dhaba for some tea and pakoras. They were sitting on charpoys out in the open and had just begun sipping their tea when two young men on a motorcycle stopped right beside them, pulled out pistols, and began to fire. All three policemen were instantly hit, and everybody else in the dhaba ran for cover. In a flash Hathoda Tyagi had yanked the rope off the fallen policeman, and jumped onto the motorcycle, between the two boys; and in a trice they were off, gunning the throttle. As they took off, one of the fallen policemen—a man called Pandey, Mangal Pandey—somehow managed to lift up his heavy 303 rifle and shoot off a round.'

The phone went silent. I thought the connection had snapped, but when I looked at the screen, he was still there. The rodent was telling too great a story to have no response from his audience. I said, 'Astonishing. And then?'

He said, 'It's called the Enfield. It's from the Second World War. It can kill an elephant from a mile. It stopped Hitler's armies. Mangal Pandey's single 303 bullet tore a hole through all the three men, going in through the back of one saviour and coming out the front of the other, passing through Hathoda Tyagi on its way. All three of them were killed instantly. By the time Mangal Pandey fell back with the rifle's recoil, dead, Hathoda Tyagi and his two rescuers were fully dead too.'

Before boarding my flight I called Guruji, and told him everything I had gathered from the stranger in Muscat and from the rodent in the castle. I told him my chief assassin was now dead. Guruji was silent for a long time. Then he said, in a soft voice, 'In the Bhagavad Gita, the great Lord Krishna tells Arjuna, the peerless scorcher of all foes: "Even when performed imperfectly, svadharma is superior to someone else's dharma, performed well. Sin does not result if one's natural action is undertaken. As nature ordained it. O son of Kunti! Natural action should not be discarded, even if it is tainted. Because all action is tainted, just as fire is shrouded by smoke."'

When I landed back in Delhi a late winter rain was falling. It was dark before the hour and the melee outside was worse than ever. My jacket was soaked by the time I corralled a cab. It was an old Ambassador with one door tied shut with a string. The old sardarji said, 'But three work.'

The car's engine was badly sick and it coughed and spat all the way, jerking through traffic snarls intensified by the unseasonal rain. The sardarji said, 'I hope it doesn't damage the wheat crop. As it is farmers have no future in this godforsaken country. Have you ever met anyone in your life who said they want their son to be a farmer? I tell you, today they work out of habit, not any commercial sense.'

I said, 'It'll all be okay. It's a shower. It will stop.'

The colony lanes were empty, the lines of rain sharp and straight in the light of the street lamps. The big trees were pouring rivulets.

I gave the sardarji an extra hundred rupees, and he said, 'May your words come true.'

My perennial shadow was missing from under the awning but just behind his empty chair, a small silhouette lay curled up. It started at my heavy tread and tried to limp off into the rain. I stood in its way, and rang the bell. When I put my hand on its head, it shrank in fear and tentatively shook its curling tail. Its pelt was damp and coarse and warm, and I was still stroking it when Elizabeth opened the door. I asked her to bring out some milk and bread.

Inside, in our room, Dolly was sitting in bed watching television. She jumped up uncertainly when I walked in, tall and slim in her blue jeans and white shirt. I took off my wet jacket and said, 'Do you want to go catch a film and get some dinner?'

Her eyes lit up as I had never seen them before.

Acknowledgements

Tehelka and its many public battles have ensured that my debts—of every kind—to a vast number of friends, colleagues, public warriors, lawyers and strangers, continually grow. Most of them have little to do with the writing of my books, but they have much to do with keeping me going.

Geetan, Tiya and Cara, my first readers, my first loves, the very coordinates of my life and peace.

Inderjit, Shakuntala and Minty, the original cocoon that I still turn to.

Shoma—among other things—for grace and courage in holding the line against crippling odds.

Sanjoy and Puneeta, fellow travellers without compare.

For love, friendship and support: Aditya; Nicku and Mike, Peali and Amit; Shammy; Priyanka and Raj; Manika, Gayatri, Yamini; Satya Sheel; Shobha and Govind, Sheela and Rajeev, Roma and Bilu, Bani and Niki, Nandini and Sumir, Preeti and Yuvi; Smita, Bindu, Varun; Mala and Tejbir; NJ; Renu and Pavan; Sunita Kohli; Sabeen and Zak, Dee and UD; Sunil Khilnani, Prasoon Joshi, Toliaji; Renu and Tibu; SM; Karan and Kabir; Gunjun, Chottu, Deepak; Adarsh; Nadira and Vidia Naipaul; Manish Tewari, Meet Malhotra, Doug Wilson; Tony and Ram Jethmalani; Rajeev C., Cyrus Guzder, Siddharth Kothari, MD, Jakes, Prashant Bhushan, Arundhati Roy; Prom and Kapil Sibal.

Susan, Ram, Ranbir and Ajay, for ironing out some of the crinkles in my day.

All my outstanding colleagues at Tehelka who consistently produce a journalism we can be proud of.

Ritu Sud who struggles to bring order to the chaos of my life.

Marc Parent for joyously embracing all my efforts.

Nandita for her excellent editing; and Karthika V.K. for her superb shepherding of the entire book.

Vera Michalski, Oliviero, Elisabetta, and David Godwin for gifting it their considerable skills and support.

My friend Vatsala, for her characteristic generosity in setting aside her many concerns to do a fine, final read.

Andy, as always, for intuiting the design.

And Bibek Debroy, for his translation of the Gita that I dipped into, among others.

Reading Group Guide for
THE STORY OF MY ASSASSINS

1. How is this storytelling style, with a multiplicity of narratives, different from the movie *Slumdog Millionaire*, the book *The White Tiger,* or other stories you've read or heard about contemporary India? Did any perspectives surprise you, or show you a side of India you hadn't seen before?

2. What were your first thoughts about the protagonist? Did your perception change as the story continued? The author has said he chose an "acidic, dyspeptic, carping, dislikable" narrator because that was the best way to open up the highly complex, polyphonic material of contemporary India. If the narrator had an earnest, sincere voice, do you think the story would be more banal? By not creating sympathy for the narrator, does the author make you feel more empathy for his story of India?

3. The question of fatherhood and responsibility arises several times in the text. On page 147, the sardar feels he didn't do enough to train his son for survival. What skills are necessary for survival in this story? How could the hit men, or the protagonist, have been better prepared for the events at hand?

4. You get a glimpse of each assassin early in his life. The author says he wanted to establish that "in the beginning, there is a kind of innocence in all things." How did the world shape each assassin into the kind of man who would kill another? How did it change your relationship with these characters?

5. What did you think of the narrator's relationship with Sara? Do you think she was misguided? What is the significance of the image of the goddess Kali on page 505, and Sara signing "Your humble wall-hanging"?

6. This story is deeply rooted in the *Bhagavad Gita.* What role does Hinduism play in Kabir's life? Chini's life? What about the life of a character like Ghulam, "who imagined god would take the larger view of the equality of supreme gods" (258)?

7. Did you believe Iqbalmian on page 524 when he told the protagonist that the latter had been saved by his dog? Why or why not? Do you see any similarities between the protagonist's journey and *The Odyssey*?

8. The author says the five killers represent five "fault lines" of India: caste, religion, class, language, and feudalism. With whom did you empathize? Why do you believe that character felt most resonant to you?

9. Why did you think Bajpaisahib was after the protagonist? Were you right, in the end?

10. How does knowing that *The Story of My Assassins* is based on true events change your understanding of the story? What emotions or scenes feel most "true" to you? The author says only one or two scenes were based on his own life. Were there parts you felt sure were made up? Why?